PRAISE

The Alone Time

"Twisted, cleverly red herring–littered plotting. Readers will gladly follow [Marr's] lead to the final page."

—*Booklist*

"A steady buildup that questions the origins of a tragedy and the motives of the survivors and pits survival, ambition, and perhaps the truth against each other, leading to a finale that will surprise even the most perceptive readers. Will appeal to fans of Jennifer Hillier, Jordan Harper, and Michelle Sacks."

—*Library Journal*

"A finely crafted work of psychological suspense thriller fiction from first page to last."

—*Midwest Book Review*

"Absolutely chilling, *The Alone Time* delves into the lives of sisters Fiona and Violet as they navigate life after surviving the plane crash that killed their parents. Each layer of the story is expertly revealed, leaving you in shock as you wonder what is the truth and what is only imagined."

—Lyn Liao Butler, Amazon bestselling author of *Someone Else's Life*

"Marr's *The Alone Time* is a captivating, thrilling, deeply haunting tale about familial bonds, family secrets, memory, and trauma. This book is so twisty that it will give you whiplash! Absorbing, beautifully written, and fraught with tension, *The Alone Time* will keep you in its grip until the very last page. Fantastic. It will leave you reeling!"

—Lisa Regan, *USA Today* and *Wall Street Journal* bestselling author

"In this story nothing is as it seems. Part mystery, part survival tale, and part family drama, this intricately woven tale had me flipping through the pages quickly. Told alternately between the present and the past, the pieces clicked into place one by one, each chapter adding another layer of mystery and suspense. There were several twists at the end, one that had me reeling. A beautifully written story with high-stakes suspense! You don't want to miss this one."

—Amber Garza, author of *In a Quiet Town*

The Family Bones

"Marr expertly builds tension by alternating between the two narratives, which eventually merge and build to an explosive conclusion. Readers will be captivated from the very first page."

—*Publishers Weekly* (starred review)

"With a fresh take on the locked-room mystery, Elle Marr weaves a perilous and pulse-pounding tale of nature versus nurture. *The Family Bones* is a clever, wild, riveting ride that amps up the tension until I couldn't flip the page fast enough. The interconnected threads, subtle clues, and jaw-dropping twists lead to a whopper of an ending."

—Samantha M. Bailey, *USA Today* and #1 national bestselling author of *Woman on the Edge* and *Watch Out for Her*

"'Dysfunctional' doesn't even begin to describe the Eriksen clan during this family reunion from hell. Elle Marr's twisty plot and even more twisted characters make *The Family Bones* a dark, delectable, and fascinating thriller that questions how well we know not only our relatives but also our own minds."

—Megan Collins, author of *The Family Plot*

"Smart, razor sharp, and shocking, *The Family Bones* will keep you up late with all the lights on. A family of psychopaths trapped by bad weather at an isolated retreat—what could possibly go wrong? With dual storylines racing toward a chilling climax, *The Family Bones* is a tense, must-read thriller."

—Kaira Rouda, *USA Today* and Amazon Charts bestselling author

Strangers We Know

"The increasingly tense plot takes turns the reader won't see coming. Marr is a writer to watch."

—*Publishers Weekly*

"Elle Marr is an author to know. Just when you think you understand the motives behind her characters and the way their storylines are being presented—bam!—Elle will hit you with twists you won't see coming. Told from multiple points of view, *Strangers We Know* is about more than Ivy learning of her past and, shockingly, the serial killer within her family; it's also about knowing who to trust and how to discern who's telling the complete story. Because if everyone has secrets, are they truly family or only strangers? Read *Strangers We Know* to find out."

—Georgina Cross, bestselling author of *The Stepdaughter*

"Elle Marr burst onto the suspense scene in 2020 with her bestselling debut, *The Missing Sister*, and followed up a year later with *Lies We Bury*, another trust-no-one murder mystery. With her third novel, *Strangers We Know*, Marr firmly establishes herself as a master of 'did that really just happen?' thrillers. *Strangers We Know* has plot twists so unexpected and characters so creepy you won't want to turn out the lights, and the ending is surprising in multiple ways. Who knew a deranged-serial-killer whodunit could leave you with all the feels?"

—A.H. Kim, author of *A Good Family*

"Dark family secrets, serial murder, and a cult? Yes, please. Twisty and a little twisted, the highly addictive and surprise-packed *Strangers We Know* will have you pulling an all-nighter."

—Heather Chavez, author of *No Bad Deed*

"From the first page I was gripped by *Strangers We Know* and read through the night till the end. The novel is thrilling beyond belief, with suspense and twists ratcheting up on each page. Elle Marr is brilliant at delving into the darkness of a seemingly normal family, and by the time she pulls back the curtains on each character, the terror has built so excruciatingly, you just have to keep going till you find out every single thing—you're afraid to know, but you have to know. This is the year's must read."

—Luanne Rice, bestselling author of *The Shadow Box*

Lies We Bury

"A deep, deep dive into unspeakable memories and their unimaginably shocking legacy."

—*Kirkus Reviews* (starred review)

"The suspenseful plot is matched by the convincing portrayal of the vulnerable Claire, who just wants to lead a normal life. Marr is a writer to watch."

—*Publishers Weekly*

"Marr's #OwnVoices, trust-no-one thriller unravels with horrifying 'THEN' interruptions, producing a jolting creepfest of twisted revenge."

—*Booklist*

"In *Lies We Bury*, Elle Marr (bestselling author of *The Missing Sister*) has brought a cleverly plotted and compelling new mystery with unique characters and truly surprising twists."

—The Nerd Daily

"A deep, thrilling dive into the painful memories that haunt us and the fight between moving on or digging in and seeking revenge."

—Medium

"Elle Marr's second novel tucks a mystery inside a mystery . . . The big twist near the end is a doozy."

—*The Oregonian*

"A twisted mash-up of *Room* and a murder mystery, Marr's *Lies We Bury* is a story that creeps into your bones, a sneaky tale about the danger of secrets and the power the past holds to lead us into a deliciously devious present. Say goodbye to sleep and read it like I did, in one breathless sitting."

—Kimberly Belle, international bestselling author of *Dear Wife* and *Stranger in the Lake*

"Dark and compelling, Elle Marr has written another atmospheric and twisted thriller that you don't want to miss. *Lies We Bury* delves into the darkest of pasts and explores the fascinating tension between moving on and revenge. This is a fly-through-the-pages thriller."

—Vanessa Lillie, *USA Today* bestselling author of *Little Voices* and *For the Best*

"This haunting and emotional thriller will keep you up at night looking for answers."

—Dea Poirier, international bestselling author of *Next Girl to Die*

"A clever, twisty murder mystery packed full of secrets and lies that will keep you turning the pages way past bedtime. *Lies We Bury* hooked me from page one and kept me guessing until its dramatic conclusion."

—Lisa Gray, bestselling author of *Thin Air*

The Missing Sister

"Marr's debut novel follows a San Diego medical student to, around, and ultimately beneath Paris in search of the twin sister she'd been drifting away from. Notable for its exploration of the uncanny bonds twins share and the killer's memorably macabre motive."

—*Kirkus Reviews*

"[A] gritty debut . . . The intriguing premise, along with a few twists, lend this psychological thriller some weight."

—*Publishers Weekly*

"Elle Marr's first novel has an intriguing premise . . . The characters are well drawn and complex, and Marr's prose offers some surprising twists."

—*New York Journal of Books*

"A promising plotline."

—*Library Journal*

"*The Missing Sister* is a very promising debut—atmospheric, gripping, and set in Paris. In other words, the perfect ingredients for a satisfying result."

—Criminal Element

"Brimming with eerie mystery and hair-raising details . . . A chilling read that shows the unique bond of twins."

—*Woman's World*

"This thrilling debut novel from Elle Marr is a look into the importance of identity and the strength of sisterhood."

—*Brooklyn Digest*

"An electrifying thriller. A must read—Karin Slaughter with a touch of international flair. Just when you think you have it all figured out, Marr throws you for another loop and the roller-coaster ride continues!"

—Matt Farrell, *Washington Post* bestselling author of *What Have You Done*

"A riveting, fast-paced thriller. Elle Marr hooks you from the start, taking you on a dark and twisted journey. Layered beneath the mystery of a twin's disappearance is a nuanced, and at times disturbing, exploration of the ties that bind sisters together. With crisp prose, a gripping investigation, and a compelling protagonist, *The Missing Sister* is not to be missed."

—Brianna Labuskes, *Washington Post* bestselling author of *Girls of Glass*

"A gripping thriller. *The Missing Sister* delivers twists and turns in an exciting, page-turning read that delves into the unique bond that makes—and breaks—siblings."

—Mike Chen, author of *Here and Now and Then*

THE
LIE
SHE
WEARS

OTHER TITLES BY ELLE MARR

Your Dark Secrets

The Alone Time

The Family Bones

Strangers We Know

Lies We Bury

The Missing Sister

THE LIE SHE WEARS

ELLE MARR

THOMAS & MERCER

This is a work of fiction. Names, characters, organizations, places, events, and incidents are either products of the author's imagination or are used fictitiously. Otherwise, any resemblance to actual persons, living or dead, is purely coincidental.

Text copyright © 2025 by Elle Marr
All rights reserved.

No part of this book may be reproduced, or stored in a retrieval system, or transmitted in any form or by any means, electronic, mechanical, photocopying, recording, or otherwise, without express written permission of the publisher.

Published by Thomas & Mercer, Seattle
www.apub.com

Amazon, the Amazon logo, and Thomas & Mercer are trademarks of Amazon.com, Inc., or its affiliates.

EU product safety contact:
Amazon Media EU S. à r.l.
38, avenue John F. Kennedy, L-1855 Luxembourg
amazonpublishing-gpsr@amazon.com

ISBN-13: 9781662528330 (paperback)
ISBN-13: 9781662528347 (digital)

Cover design by Shasti O'Leary Soudant
Cover image: © Yaorusheng / Getty; © Ben Heys, © Jade ThaiCatwalk / Shutterstock

Printed in the United States of America

For my youngest, who was a part of this book's ideation, drafting, and editing. You and me, baby.

PART ONE

Chapter One

Sally

Shadows stretch across my yard like tentacles reaching for the keys that slap my thigh. I have to get out of here.

"Hey! Sally! Where are you going?" Zelda pants from the doorframe, pausing from chasing me through my own home. A syringe is clutched tight in her fist. "Sally!"

I rip open the door to my SUV, then climb inside. Before I slam it shut, Zelda stumbles from the steps. She reaches out a hand, willing me to return.

"No worries, no problem," I call to her. "Stretching my head. I mean, just need to clear my head."

"Sally, don't do this. We can talk about the injection. Come back inside."

I hit the ignition button. "Will do. Be in a jiffy. Heading to the Wishing Tree."

Word salad spills from my mouth, and I know I need to tie up loose ends before my brain gets any worse.

I lift a hand, wave goodbye to Zelda and her looming scowl, then disappear down the dark road.

When I'm a mile away from home, from the windows that I always meant to cover with curtains or blinds but never did because I felt safe,

I inhale the deepest breath I can manage. Then another. When I begin to border on lightheaded, I relax.

Everything is fine. There's no one following me. Whoever has been watching me isn't right now.

Past the sprawling maple tree that marks the end of the residential neighborhood and the beginning of the wineries that dot the valley, a shadow steps from the dirt shoulder into my lane.

I slam on my brakes, swerve across the road to miss the figure, then lose control of the car. I crash into the ditch opposite my lane, the hood bucking against the uneven terrain.

A white bag bursts from my steering wheel, snapping my head backward, while my chest seizes.

No, my heart.

Sharp pain pinwheels out from my ribs, and I clutch at my skin. Crush my eyelids shut tight, then open them to see the figure approaching in the twilight darkness.

My lungs constrict as I gasp for air—stare, as the person's face becomes clear. The figure who has been following me. The monster from my nightmares finally catching me alone.

Tall yellow grass of the adjacent lot bends in the evening wind, illuminated by my headlights, as terror spirals across my body. Then my mind screams the words *I know you.*

Chapter Two

Pearl

One Month Later

Everyone harbors secret fears. A creature under the bed, a stranger following us home, an image burned into the mind's eye from a horror film viewed at a too-young age.

Not everyone chooses to specialize in their fear.

Plywood shipping boxes, plastic containers, and high-tech steel-reinforced cases overflow the storage docks of the windowless warehouse hall. Shoddy light bulbs flicker overhead, casting ominous shadows at nine in the morning. I usually avoid doing this task on my own, but I set my shoulders and clomp forward in my asexual flats anyway—essential footwear for any woman in historical studies. Gunmetal-gray scaffolding extends for rows from the doorway where I entered. The numerous aisles still fail to convey the extensive backlog of artifacts, waiting to be chosen for display in one of the museum's many exhibit halls.

As associate curator, I should be more comfortable searching through the wooden crates and plastic bins, perusing the white sticker labels slapped on top that often include notated shorthand and country abbreviations. But this is my first real museum job as a hired expert—no more seeking coffee orders as an intern—and, until now, most of my time has been spent researching my subject. Griffin, my boss and chief curator of the museum, has been dangling a promotion over my head since I was hired six months ago. I need to get this right, even if it means staring at the source of my childhood nightmares.

A Tibetan mask painted black with white spirals jeers at me through a plastic storage crate. I shudder, turning away.

"Pearl, right? What's your poison?"

A man emerges from the third row to my right, wearing blue coveralls and holding a box from this morning's delivery from Seattle. Xander, the director of collections, sports a too-chipper grin, considering the ghosts surrounding us.

I return his smile. "Twelfth-century China."

He clicks his tongue, bowing slightly as he flattens a hand across his chest. "Right this way."

We pass an endless series of tools, then turn right midway down the hall and along older rusted shelves. A laminated sign announces we're approaching Islamic art as our footsteps echo against Neolithic pottery shards, plaster casts of Greek busts, and other items from the epochs that museum curators deemed too disparate to form a collection worthy of display.

When I was first hired as associate curator of Asian art, I was elated. Thrilled that my PhD in Art History from Stanford wouldn't go to waste and that I'd be one of the youngest associate curators on record at the Portland Art Museum at twenty-seven. I was so excited to share the news with my mother, Sally, who first seeded my love of unrestored tapestries found in thrift stores across the greater Pacific Northwest. Then I learned my chief task would be to cobble together an exhibit with zero budget in time for the Halloween season—a massive undertaking. Sally wasn't impressed. When I shared the news, she spilled her tea across the counter, deliberately, then told me to clean it up.

But that's a bygone worry now. A bittersweet memory, I suppose.

A woven straw doll glares at me from a clear circular bin and an aisle dedicated to the Chinook. *What are you looking at?*

The Lie She Wears

After Sally died in a car crash four weeks ago, Griffin told me I could take as much time as I needed to process the loss. The offer lifted some of the depression cloud that had been following me. Had been trailing me since Sally's diagnosis of cognitive decline.

"Our cataloging process still needs work, but the next two rows should offer what you need." Xander gives me a thumbs-up. "You excited for the unveiling of the new floor?"

"If by 'excited' you mean terrified, yes." I offer a smile to soften the vulnerability of my joke, but Xander doesn't laugh.

"Sure. I was too for my first big project." He nods. "You'll do great."

I murmur my thanks as he goes, feeling as awkward as when I started back in April, when something scrapes in the aisle behind me. I turn toward the sound. But only shelves of dusty crates face me in response. The aisle extends another fifty feet, replete with half-empty receptacles that offer a view into their contents: deteriorating fabric swatches, thick plastic-wrapped tableaux, ancient paintbrushes, and ornate headdresses.

You never cared this much about anything, lazy.

I step forward. Closer to my quarry. A heavy metal door slams shut from the southmost corner of the room. Although the Portland Art Museum offers over 100,000 square feet of gallery real estate, the storage areas occupy another quarter of the property. So many discarded relics that will wait years to see a patron.

You care more about this than you do your own mother.

I clench my jaw, fighting the urge to argue. Force myself to focus on the labels instead of the haunting echo of my mother's voice. The first week after Sally's death was the hardest. I stayed in my apartment most days, sitting alone on the love seat in front of a Netflix marathon. Then, after the funeral, I started imagining her voice in some twisted form of masochistic grief, whenever I began a risky task or project that I knew I wasn't ready for, like cleaning out the gutters of the ranch house. The knee-jerk habit of conjuring up my mother's most disappointed comments has only grown more frequent, more poisonous, recalling her frustration with me. Though I know I'm in control of my thoughts, and even the ones that resemble Sally's oft-voiced opinions of me, the memory of her angry tone is a shock when I'm feeling exposed.

I follow the labels, now only haphazardly listening for the scraping noise. At the end of the aisle, where the shelves nearly touch the back wall, the years progress to reach the twelfth century and span the continent until "China" is legible in black ink against white adhesive.

"Gotcha," I whisper. "Now who's lazy?"

When I learned there were over four thousand items of Asian art gathered here, ranging from historical to contemporary, from South Asian to East Asian and everything in between, my chest tightened. As if spring cleaning had arrived yet again and my mother had banished me to the attic to organize the plastic rice bowls she'd saved across two decades. I was overwhelmed at the thought of how to highlight so many in an exhibit—how to prove myself to my employer in this make-or-break moment of my budding career.

Then I recalled the foundation for my interest in museum work. The catalyst to every random roadside antique store pit stop my parents made during family trips, and the motivator that made midnight visits to the bathroom a harrowing experience in our hallway: masks. Asian cultures, across countries and regions, have employed a decorative and practical range of facial coverings. My first exhibit could be no different.

Do you really think you can do this? You barely finish your dinner.

Ignoring the slight, I pause before stacked shelves of preserved jewelry and headpieces. Debate my next move. The only way to tell whether the boxes house the masks I need that relate to twelfth-century China—when opera and funerary masks were in common use—is to crack each one open.

"Good thing I had black tea boba for breakfast," I murmur.

The first three crates reveal early on that they're not what I need. The fourth—sourced years ago, judging from the black scuff marks around the opaque base—provides a half dozen Jing masks from the

The Lie She Wears

seventeenth century. A solid win, though not my target era. As Sally said when I got my doctorate in art history instead of finance: *Well, it's not nothing.*

Something scrapes again from the next aisle over. A box? I pause shuffling the crisp strips of paper that cushion the Jing masks. I thought I was alone.

Lifting my head, I make eye contact with a face, then startle backward. My throat constricts before I register the mask peering from the clear bin on the next shelf up. A Buddha with fat cheeks and a lolling tongue. Empty eyes return my stare without blinking.

You don't even know what you're doing.

Scrape. Scrape. Scrape. That noise again.

My pulse amped, I reach for my phone from my back pocket. Tap the flashlight option on the home screen, then slide my feet toward the end of the aisle, eyeing the floor for darting four-legged bodies. Rats and other rodents are common to museum storage spaces—hazards of cool, dimly lit environments meant to protect and preserve artwork and cultural objects.

"Hello?" I say. "Xander?"

A shrill chime erupts from my hand, and I jump. The name of my mother's estate attorney appears at the top of my screen. The attorney with whom I scheduled a meeting that started fifteen minutes ago. "Shit."

I hit the button to answer. "Hi, Mr. Singh. I'm so sorry—I know I'm late."

"Hey there. Just wanted to see if now still worked for you."

I nod to a bamboo scroll beside me, to its faded, curling calligraphy. "Yup. I'll be there in ten."

Construction rages on the concrete pavilion beside the main entrance outside. Workers in orange hard hats and bright reflective vests enter and exit through the museum's side door without pause. A broad canvas sign strung up across the building's brick facade announces an expansion of museum property to accommodate future specialty exhibits.

As I descend the flat steps onto the sidewalk of downtown Portland, I cross my fingers that my exhibits will be featured there soon. Dozens of them.

My optimism carries me three blocks north and one block east, and then I'm standing before the wooden portico of the boutique law firm. Although I grew up in Portland, I've never spent much time downtown; the last ten years in California pursuing undergrad and doctoral work made that hard. The lush green park that extends between the local university campus and the charming painted glass windows of the Alphabet District reminds me that I should go exploring.

Anticipation stirs in my chest as I reach for the tinted door. A canvas strip of reindeer bells wrapped around the doorknob jingles my arrival.

Sally would say that I abandoned her for California. But she would conveniently forget that she cajoled and pressured me to get a doctorate during the eighteen years prior. Although Sally was mad at me for leaving Oregon, I returned recently in order to spend more time with her—and with my dad, Liam, after he moved to a long-term care facility for his multiple sclerosis last year. Ever the dutiful daughter—though I bitched and moaned a good deal about it.

Still, maybe that act of sacrifice and loyalty meant something to her. Maybe she left me a surprise, one that would assuage the memory of the difficult years—the stretch of time where I ignored the half-hearted invitations to come home for Thanksgiving and Christmas and gleaned updates about Sally exclusively through my dad. He was the one who shared when Sally first began experiencing cognitive decline a little over a year ago.

"Pearl, there you are. Good to see you." Rohan Singh pushes up the sleeves of his blue pin-striped dress shirt, beside a reception desk and a young woman seated behind it. Aside from gray-streaked hair, he looks around my age.

Pointing two fingers down a hallway like a flight attendant, he grins. "Let's get to it."

I throw the receptionist a tight smile, then follow Rohan. Framed and redacted legal pleadings decorate the wall.

In his office, he offers a blue cushioned chair, then sits on the corner of a cherrywood desk covered in loose papers. "Have a seat."

"So, is this good news?" I ask. "I thought you were still waiting on confirmation from the courts about the estate stuff."

"Yes and no. I know you're busy, so I'll make this quick." He reaches to the corner of his desk to a brown expanding filing folder that's labeled "Wong, Sally" in typed capital letters. Opening wide the stiff cardstock mouth, he retrieves a standard letter envelope from one of the creased pockets. He hands it to me. Slanted handwriting occupies the dead center of the white surface: *Pearl*.

My mouth goes dry. I know that cramped cursive. "What is this?"

"Well, it's from your mother," Rohan says, his voice soft. "She wanted me to give it to you."

His words trail off as if someone dimmed the volume on an unseen remote. As if this is happening to someone else. When we met last week to discuss the will, he made no mention of a letter.

"How is that possible? Why didn't you tell me earlier?" Focusing on the envelope, I trace the capital *P*, the looping *L* that completes my name. "And why did she give this to you?"

Rohan clasps his hands, the blue pattern of his shirt contrasting with the black-framed diplomas behind him on the wall. "Occasionally, a client will include some instructions that they want delivered after they pass away. It's usually a declaration that the kids must equally divide a plot of land or share the priceless collection of Elvis records that a parent guarded all their lives. Something for which the parent doesn't want to see the fallout."

Rohan adopts a conspiratorial smile. "But you don't have to worry about that as an only child."

The envelope feels light, crisp, and preserved, as it was in the Redweld folder. It's thin. Part of me wants to hold it up to the ceiling lamp for more detail, like it's another featured museum item on loan.

"When did she give this to you?"

Rohan presses his lips together. "Two months ago. Dropped it off in person."

Things were okay between us toward the end, whether that was due to some mutually felt détente or her diminishing mental capacity. Could this actually be something positive? A note from beyond the grave to reconcile our harsh relationship?

Tentative excitement squeezes my belly. I pry the flap free from the glue, tearing it inch by inch and taking care to avoid any rips. I push out a breath. "Here goes."

Inside, a single sheet of computer paper is folded in three. The cramped cursive continues:

My Pearl. I never meant to tell you any of this. So please don't think differently of me.

"What?" I mumble.

"Good news?" Rohan asks, still perched on his desk. "The Elvis collection *and* Johnny Cash?"

Short, tense sentences roll over me in waves as I scan the paragraphs that follow.

I'm not sure how to say this. But I can't let this opportunity go by.

It was well into evening.

I did my best to talk him down.

His head cracked against the fireplace. Blood everywhere.

I'll never get the thick smell of blood out of my nose.

I read the words again in a fever, searching for the joke, the lie, the tell. But I don't see it. Instead, I memorize the crisp letter *t* that my mother crossed exactly in the middle—the even margins she created with a precise hand on either side of the page and the exactly spaced lines of text. Sweat breaks at my temples.

"Everything okay?" Rohan asks.

I drop the paper to my lap as if it has seared my skin. What the hell is this?

"Pearl, you look a little sick. Can I—"

"Um, I need to leave," I pant. "Right now. Thanks for your time."

"Oh, sure. Let me know if you have any questions—" Rohan stands, matching my movement.

His head cracked against the fireplace. Blood everywhere.

I fold the letter, then shove it back inside the narrow envelope. Nearly trip on the threshold as I speed past the secretary and rip open the office door to clanging bells.

When I reach the sidewalk, I break into a fast walk, despite knowing Rohan's eyes are on me—his secretary's too—through the one-way glass. I sprint across a two-lane street all the way back to the green parkway that I passed earlier, then collapse onto a bench. I was so stupid, so hopeful that Sally Wong left me a kind word in her will. Maybe another priceless mask. A reason to think better of her.

But no. Bile rises in my throat as the truth takes hold.

My mother killed someone. And she waited until death to tell me.

Chapter Three

The Redweld Folder

My Pearl—

I never meant to tell you any of this. So please don't think differently of me. I want you to know I love you. I know I don't say it that often, nor do I express it well when I do. But you have to know that everything I do, it's for you. Your well-being, your future, your sense of self and self-discipline. This intro might be enough to make you wary of what's to follow—but that's a good thing.

I'm not sure how to say this. But I can't let this opportunity go by.

It was supposed to be a good day. You had returned home from preschool with stains all over your brand-new white shoes with the shooting stars—why I thought it smart to dress a three-year-old in white, I have no clue, but there I am—and I was pretty upset with you. I didn't speak to you for a solid hour, even though you asked me to play horses with you. You wanted me to be your new pink-and-gold-chevron pony that pooped glitter, and I was always disgusted by that one.

Later, when there was a knock on the door, I wondered—had I been playing with you by the front door, would I have gotten there first? Would I have opened the barrier between us and the brutal, cruel world, or seen who was waiting there, turned the dead bolt, and called the police?

But it didn't happen that way. And you were at the door, sprawled on your stomach on the tile. You had just broken your little arm, and you were drawing on your cast with a Sharpie.

It was well into evening. And I did my best to talk him down. But his head cracked against the fireplace. The blood was everywhere. Bits of flesh and brain too. And now I'll never get the thick smell of blood out of my nose.

I wish I didn't have to confess these details to you—to anyone. But if you're reading this, things didn't go well for me. And you should watch out for anyone unfamiliar who takes an interest in you.

All a mother ever has for her children is fluttering wishes. Find mine.

If you're not careful, not on guard, the subject of them might come your way.

—Mom

Chapter Four

PEARL

The lobby of the museum echoes with conversation and boot-clad feet. Cloud coverage that blanketed the sky when I ran out to meet my mother's estate attorney—the man who cheerfully dropped a bomb into my lap—has abated. Streams of sunshine pierce the glass panels of the ceiling, illuminating the influx of patrons searching for the first stop on their visit, eager to escape the brisk September chill. A mother clips a harness onto a small child. She lifts a finger to her lips to signal for quiet.

I steady myself against the reception counter, where gold filament threads the surface. A red tile mosaic decorates the lobby floor—salmon launching themselves up a river, spinning in a whirlpool—and sucks my gaze down with it.

His head cracked against the fireplace. Bits of flesh and brain.

"Pearl? Are you okay?" A man seated behind the computer monitor clears his throat. From his shirtsleeve, a tattoo of bones covers his wrist. What is his name—Bryan? Brett?

Workers in hard hats enter and exit the side door leading to the pavilion under construction, while patrons flash their tickets on their phones as they cross the threshold of the main entrance.

The Lie She Wears

"Do you want some water?" he adds. "I have a little minifridge down here."

"No, no. Thanks. Sorry." I push off from the desk, wearing a strained smile. Will my feet to move normally. Halfway across the lobby, I cut right toward the Contemporary Art wing of the museum, recalling the tours my boss Griffin and a senior curator provided during my interviews. How in awe I felt to be this close to such historic tableaux. Monet's *Water Lilies*. Van Gogh's *The Ox Cart*. Jackson Pollock's *Number 12, 1950*. How ignorant I was to the heartache barreling toward me.

I continue past the photography halls, the loaner exhibits, and the visual art video displays, then turn left into the Authorized Personnel area. I key into a nondescript white hallway using the card that dangles from my belt loop. My stomach knots as I beeline toward the employee lounge on this floor and cheap, stale coffee. Anything to get my mind off Sally's perfect cursive.

I'll never get the thick smell of blood out of my nose.

"Oh, excuse me," a man says, turning when I enter the lounge. He smiles, standing beside a bulletin board of flyers and lifting a half-empty coffeepot. "Is this up for grabs?"

The new curator. "It is, yeah. I'm Pearl Davis, by the way. Asian art associate curator."

"Kai Weathers. Photography curator." Thick black hair extends past his ears. "Great to meet you. Could I ask your opinion on something?"

I hesitate, knowing my thoughts are as jumbled as a cubist painting right now. Pouring myself a cup of drip buys me a moment before I reply. "Uh, sure. What's it about?"

"If you could just follow me? It'll only take a minute."

Kai leads us down the hall to an open space with nearly empty black-painted walls. One of the staging rooms curators use before mounting an exhibit in the public areas. Plastic sheets are piled in one corner along the floor beside uncovered bins as Kai crosses to a polished bench and a notebook. The gray-and-white-checkered shirt he wears strains across his back, pleating across muscles that were understated in the weak lighting of the employee lounge.

Bits of flesh and brain.

I shake my head. Work to be present while Kai takes a sip from his mug. He flips through a notebook with a free finger.

Sally confessed to murder in the letter entrusted to her attorney. But it was a joke. It has to have been. Why else would she leave me a written account of killing someone? Why put pen to paper at all if it were true?

To add to the confusion, Sally mentioned that I broke my *little arm*. But the only body part I've ever broken was my foot when I was sprinting across our yard and tripped in a gopher hole.

"So, Pearl," Kai says. "Does associate curating Asian art include an awareness of spatial aesthetics? I've been trying to decide between linear and abstract presentation for my upcoming exhibit. What's your vote?"

He holds up two computer-generated images of what must be his artifacts displayed in different arrangements—mock-ups of the space. I drink deep from the cup, nearly draining it. "It depends on your subject, probably."

"Crime photography, mostly in Oregon. Part of the pop-up series the museum is doing for October."

"Oh, I'm doing that too. Only my exhibit explores fears through the ages in Asia. Using masks."

When Griffin asked that I contribute to the series, the first of its kind that the museum has announced, I was thrilled. A microexhibit like he described, and which has already gotten a lot of media attention, would allow me to launch my work with a bang.

Kai sips his coffee. Discerning brown eyes seem to memorize my face. "I like it. Very on brand for Halloween."

"Thanks. How did you settle on crime photography? Do you have a background in police work?" The words slip out of my mouth, followed by a nervous chuckle.

Chill, Pearl. No one knows about the damning letter from Sally.

"Not at all. Although I like the idea of helping people. Maybe one day." He smirks. "Normally, my passion is twentieth-century photography. Full stop. But interest in true crime has been a tsunami, so I'm rolling with it."

I scan the bins along the wall. "Looks like you have a lot to pull from."

He nods his chin toward a set of blown-up images on poster board. "Several midcentury crime scenes, but most are from the last thirty years. More than enough to fill this little room."

"The exhibit development team and project coordinators had a lot of great ideas for my exhibit, for presentation and subject cohesion. There's a sensory designer too. Have you met with them yet?"

"No, not yet. So many meetings are set up for next week." He smiles, surveying the fifteen-by-fifteen square feet. He's a few years older than me, judging from the lines around his mouth. Stubble marks his jaw, though it's not yet eleven. His gray dress shirt is buttoned all the way up to his throat.

"Do you have your schematic design? What's your centerpiece?" I ask.

"My what?"

"Your chief exhibit item. The one that you'll base the rest of your exhibit's story around. The idea you want to highlight to patrons as the takeaway."

Kai presses his lips together. "Maybe the teams can help me with that. My old museum in Chicago was more prescriptive, and I'm not used to having free rein at this stage. Or maybe you could?"

I glance at the clock hung above the doorway behind me. I haven't cataloged as many of my own exhibit's artifacts today as I should have. But I can't return to the storage hall now. Not when phrases from Sally's letter are still swirling in my head like the drying and decaying leaves outside.

"Sure. What do you got?"

He offers a rundown of the most famous and heinous crimes committed within state lines. False imprisonments, murder sprees, serial killers, trafficking rings, and heists whose descriptions cause me to shiver in this building's temperate seventy-two degrees.

Kai withdraws a clear plastic Ziploc bag enclosing a swatch of fabric. "I have a photo that might pair with this. It was knit by the Matron Murderer in the 1970s. The guy, a killer named Josiah Denton, was a huge yarn enthusiast, and he would target his victims during crochet circles along the coast. You think it could work as a centerpiece?"

"Visually, it's great. And the story is arresting. No pun intended." I grimace. I hate puns. "But I wonder if there's anything more recent. What about that stack of cards?"

Kai lifts a clear baggie containing three-by-five note cards bound together by a binder ring. "These? They're just the master list of items in these five containers. But there is a serial killer who was into writing."

I scan a pair of old-fashioned video cassettes nestled in the bin closest to me. "Like a novelist?"

"Fan fiction, mostly. Took the classics and made them gory."

"Even gorier than the Grimm brothers?"

"In this killer's version of *The Little Mermaid*, the mermaid ate her own tail, then ate the eyes of the prince."

"Yikes, next level. How does someone come up with that?" I wrinkle my nose. It's been an hour, and my stomach is beginning to turn the more I absorb these details. "Could those stories be your centerpiece?"

Kai shakes his head. Tosses the ring of note cards back on the pile. "Not likely. They're from the Turnpike Bloody Brontë in New Jersey, not Oregon. A serial killer who was known to be into writing because they sent threatening messages to their victims—to torment them a bit before stalking and killing them. They also sent out writing excerpts to the police, which is why we know about them."

I scan the boxes, the plastic bags, the knitted square of fabric, and the one item already affixed to the wall. "What about this? Is that an eye chart?"

"It looks like it." Kai steps closer. He points to the second line. "But it's a pretty basic example of ciphers—a system that encodes a message. Criminals have used them to taunt police."

I lean in for a better view, my arm grazing Kai's elbow. Heat climbs my neck, so close to a man, and I pull back.

"The alphabet is repeated over a dozen times here," he continues. "But with several letters in incorrect places. The oddly placed letters formed an ultimatum for the Salem police in 1987: 'Bring the ransom tonight, or she dies.'"

"Direct." I lift an eyebrow. "Was this author caught?"

Kai clucks his tongue. "Oh yeah. He was a necrophiliac. All hands were on deck for him."

"Ugh. Terrifying. Do all ciphers use letter or word patterns?"

"They can." He scratches his head. "But any kind of discreet sign enclosed within a larger message could be considered a code. Like a misquote of a famous text or the replacement of a key symbol with a modified version."

Cold air from the vent overhead twines around my neck. "Or mentioning a fact that everyone knows is incorrect."

"Sure." Kai downs the rest of his coffee. "Hey, it's almost lunch. Do you wanna grab a bite at the Thai place around the corner? I'm starved."

In her letter, Sally mentioned that I broke my arm and was drawing on my cast with a Sharpie when the intruder knocked on our door. Earlier, I wrote off the error as a strange mistake—or yet another indicator of Sally's diminishing memory. But what if she chose a false detail intentionally? What if she meant to send me a different message?

I shake my head. "Thanks for the invite. But I just remembered that I need to head home for a bit. I'll, uh—I'll see you later."

"Sure, okay. Nice to meet you, Pearl." He presses his lips into a line.

"You too," I reply over my shoulder.

The lobby teems with museum visitors, none of whom resembles my boss. I weave through the crowd until I reach the wide, flat steps of the front entrance, then jog to the employee parking lot the next block over.

During the drive to my parents' ranch house forty minutes south, I drum up the details that matter: Sally insisted on saving the cast of my broken foot, like some perverse relic of my childhood. She stored it in the attic, along with all the other mementos I was forced to dust during spring-cleaning. Sally could have misremembered which limb I injured when I was a toddler. Especially considering she wrote me a letter and then entrusted it to her attorney when she was already months into a diagnosis of mild cognitive impairment that could progress to dementia at any point.

Or my mother knew exactly what she was doing when she chose her words. Just as she maintained her carefully spaced lines and those exacting margins so straight that she could moonlight as a ruler.

Veering right onto the exit ramp that leads into the Willamette Valley, I wince. The closer I get to the ranch house and its attic, the tighter a pit of dread balls up inside my stomach.

Chapter Five

FANNY

New York City, 1992

The neighborhood playground hums with innocent activity, the picture of privilege. Eerie creaking that peals from the metal swing set pairs with the delighted shrieks of toddlers who beg to be pushed harder and faster by their mothers—nannies, more likely, here on the Upper West Side. Traffic continues to pulse around the leafy enclosure of the park, barely audible against the gossipy conversations among caregivers and the snot-nosed requests for yet another snack.

"Look at all these losers," I mutter, pushing my dark sunglasses higher onto the bridge of my petite nose. Damn things are always slipping, like I'm some dweeb on *The Cosby Show*—or, when they're halfway down my nose, like I'm haughtily examining whomever I'm looking at. The nose I was born with had a bump on the bridge that I always hated. But it held my glasses exactly where I wanted them. I sigh, knowing this is the price I pay for my vanity. Like Sisyphus.

A little girl in pink OshKosh B'gosh overalls shoots out from the metal slide, then lands on her sneakered feet. She takes off running, sprinting around the perimeter of the playground, just as a little boy in matching blue overalls drops his sand pail and tears after her.

"Galen, Tamara, come eat your ice cream," a woman calls from a bench on the opposite side of the park from mine. "It's melting."

The little girl's brother huffs and puffs after her, and she takes the lead she has on him to hide behind the seesaw. He doesn't see her. When he passes her hiding place, she sticks her foot out, tripping him in a cutthroat move more often seen in a WWF ring.

The little boy goes flying across the sand, then hits his head square on the metal ladder of the play structure. Deep, shuddering cries erupt from his mouth. Their mom screams profanity and threats to Tamara as she clutches her "precious baby" to her bosom.

I stand at my bench. Saunter along the perimeter of the sandbox, tracing with my sandals the tiny human footprints stamped in the concrete sidewalk.

The day is hot. Sweat dots my shoulders and under my bra, and I know the yellow cotton tank top I wear shows it. An old man with wrinkly skin leers at me from the next bench. I return his stare, then push my sunglasses back up onto my nose.

As I make my way to the opposite end of the playground, toward the exit that spits visitors onto Columbus Avenue, I take in the perfect scene of childhood. Games of tag among friends, parents shooing their kids toward the exit with promises of lunch or a snack, and the feral cry of a child who's burned their palm on the metal frame of the monkey bars in August. Juice boxes litter the ground beside discarded chewing gum, not too far from a trash basket with a hypodermic needle lying at its base. It's New York mixed with hope, mixed with nostalgia. It could be a scene from my own childhood—but after I ditched my abusive grandmother to reach the swings of my favorite park alone in the Bronx.

Boo-boos are kissed and reassurances uttered as I continue toward the street, past Galen and Tamara's cooing mother. Tamara glances at me as I approach.

I never had any of those extra hugs. And the ones I did receive from Ying Ying, after she spanked me with a wooden spoon so forcefully it broke on my backside, I didn't want.

The Lie She Wears

I felt the itch to explore. The impulse to flee into the unknown. To draw for hours on end or to get lost in the Met among its watercolors, my favorite place as a kid.

True, I've always done things my own way, and that's elicited some raised eyebrows along my path. Some broken hearts. Maybe some enemies. But don't I deserve the same things as everyone? Doesn't everyone deserve the love and reassurance on display here at the corner of Columbus and Eighty-Seventh? Don't I, too, have enough baggage to be considered broken yet beautiful by the right patient, good man?

The concrete path that encircles the playground turns right, through a thin copse of manicured baby elms recently planted by the city. I pause not ten feet from where Tamara pouts in the sand, having been verbally raked over by her mother. Galen sniffles on their mom's lap in the shade of the metal play structure, still milking a bruised elbow for all it's worth.

I clear my throat. Tamara turns big brown eyes on me, startled. Leaning over the bench and the cup of ice cream and two red spoons that rest on its lip, I place my hand on the diaper bag. On the Fruit Roll-Ups her mother so lovingly crammed inside.

"Tamara," I whisper. She darts her gaze back to her mom, who doesn't notice me—a young woman in her twenties on the Upper West Side, wearing sunglasses and a smile. I could be another nanny, just like most of the adults in this park. Someone with a cutesy name, like Fanny.

"Tamara," I say again. "Do you know what the key to life is? How to be successful in whatever you want, whenever you want?"

The girl shrinks backward. I smile wider, drinking her in. "Never let someone else change who you are."

With a flick of my wrist, I knock the cup of ice cream to the ground. The melting liquid splashes onto the concrete, the sunburned chewing gum, and the patches of grass growing at the edge of the playground. Bits of strawberry scatter across the soft, shallow dunes of sand like the artistic bleed of a Monet.

I drop my expression, allowing my smile to fade. The whisper of an urge floats to the surface of my mind. I could find out more about this girl. Follow her journey a bit, see how she turns out over the next week, year, or ten years. Watch what kind of woman she becomes, if her spunk simply makes her more likable in her career. Or if it grows into an asset to be wielded at all costs and sometimes to the detriment of others—like mine.

I could have Errol find out. Learn Tamara's home address. Her parents' names and bank accounts, her teacher's name and next of kin. As a Hound, he's one of the best.

Shaking my head, I resume my walk toward the main avenue, allowing the honks and swears of New Yorkers to drown out Tamara's plaintive wail. I haven't crossed that line with a child—not yet, and I don't intend to. Kids are boring.

As I reach the street, and the crosswalk that takes me to Park Avenue and my morning appointment, my sunglasses slip again. I catch the eye of a well-dressed businessman holding a cell phone to his ear across the way. Then I push my shield—I mean, my shades—back up where they belong.

Chapter Six

Pearl

The side door creaks as I enter the ranch house. The only sound across the sprawling layout that curves like a snake onto the field behind. Any lingering scent of the pulled pork we served at the wake has long since gone. My childhood home was warmed by the well-wishers who stopped by after Sally was buried, a few colleagues of my dad's from before he left the construction business, and friends of Sally's who were also antique hunters or collectors. Now, several weeks later, the columns of this house appear to me like the bones of a once-vibrant animal.

I step over a pile of mail by the front door, then glance to the kitchen. Immediately, my eyes land on the face that still haunts my nightmares—Sally's favorite mask.

Hung across from the fridge and the window that overlooks the front yard, the Venetian mask's smooth ceramic eye sockets peer at me. *A high-value item,* she always said. Judging me. Wondering just what the hell I'm doing cutting work to seek out a hunch, the first week after bereavement. Black stripes splash diagonally across the eyeline of the mask's two holes. Ocean waves undulate in white and sea-green froth across the nose and drum up the recalled scent of salt water on the Oregon Coast—usually my favorite place in the world. Garnet stones follow the pattern to contrast the stark-white base that resembles bone—a volto mask–style that was once worn by most people in Venice. A Giulio Venetta, the global brand based in Milan.

A pile of bills, postcards, and flyers litters the dark-brown tile by the mail slot. Beyond myself and Zelda, my mother's former live-in nurse who moved out recently, no one has been here since the wake. Zelda brought packages inside the house a few times to help out, but last week I finally asked her for her key.

Anxious and on edge, I step out of my shoes. Note the pepper shaker nearly hidden in a pair of slippers that Sally favored—strange—then continue on to the hallway. Passing the living room, I scan the collapsed cardboard boxes, not yet folded and taped together for use, piled in the corner next to my dad's faded armchair. I've got to start sorting and donating items soon.

When I reach the wrought-iron gate that encloses the sunken living room, a thought pulls me up short.

Postcards? Who sent Sally postcards?

I turn back to the pile beside the front door. My dad wouldn't have done anything so cute as to send posted correspondence to Sally, and definitely not recently, after she died. Sally's best friend Ursula told me at the funeral that she was available and in town if I needed anything. Could she have sent a physical note?

A flat rectangle of cardstock tops the mountain of paper. The heading reads "SPOKANE" in fat block letters, against an image of a bridge above the river that cuts alongside downtown. I flip the postcard over. In a scrawl I don't recognize, a note is written in large lettering: "Thinking of you"; then, underneath in smaller script: "Three weeks."

It's addressed to our house, and to my dad. The postmark is from last week.

Considering most family and friends would have learned by now that Sally died, a random well-wisher doesn't surprise me, or their reference to the wake being held three weeks ago. Neither is it odd that a note would have been sent here to the house and not my dad's care facility; we didn't widely publicize the move.

The medical bills underneath, the predatory flyers from local mortuaries and funeral homes, and the grief counseling adverts all addressed to me—my mother's next of kin—sadly don't surprise me either.

I turn on my heel, glad to leave the business of mourning behind.

Several masks appear like sentinels along the hallway as if guarding the path to the attic. Sally hung additional cherished versions in between family shots of us. A mask painted as a lion with a crow's beak—a scaramuccia—bears words in cursive: *Dance like no one is watching*.

Sally could be sentimental when it suited her. But rarely when it came to collecting antiques or thrifted items she thought were of value. Case in point: When she tracked down the final Giulio Venetta mask in a series of seaside designs, after the last decade of dedicated searching, she immediately called up a major auction house in Seattle. When the lot sold for seven figures, she chose her favorite photo of her and my dad to be published in all the news outlets that reported on rare antiquities. She wanted every person who ever doubted that her hobby was a useful pursuit to eat their words, despite my dad's protesting that they didn't need to boast.

As I reach the end of the hall, I pull the cord that releases the folding stairwell from the ceiling and take my last breath of well-circulated air. Try to temper my expectations. To buoy my stirring hope that my mom meant the horrifying letter as a joke. Whatever I find in the attic will, no doubt, confirm that fact.

A cloud of dust motes welcomes me into the cramped space. The outside adjacent noise of passing cars and coos of mourning doves heightens my sense of isolation here, while I stare at dozens of closed cardboard boxes and trash bags lying along the exposed joists of the floor. Without a better idea of where to start, I approach a box nearly hidden beneath puffy insulation that protrudes from the walls. Words cover the side of the box in black Sharpie: "Christmas '90s".

The apex of the house forces me to bend and duck my head as a memory returns to me of Christmas dinner in the early aughts. Of the scowl my mother lobbed at me when I was maybe eight or nine. She asked me to pass her a plate of steamed broccoli, but it slipped from my hand all over the soup she'd spent the entire day making. *I wish I had char siu instead of you—roast pork is at least useful,* she muttered. Though it was only the three of us at the table, Sally Wong never held her opinions in. She'd often blame her Chinese heritage, insisting the words weren't as harsh in Cantonese as they sounded in English. But then, I'll never know, as I only got yelled at in one language.

Sharp plastic edges graze my fingertips while I dig into the box. A thin container of cheap red and green ornaments that I'm pretty sure my mom bought from the Dollar Tree nearly covers a stack of frames. Lots of family photos, but no cast.

Drawings that I made as a kid are in the next box, along with birthday cards Sally thought to save. Ticket stubs and what appear to be love letters from my dad to my mom. One is dated from the early nineties.

I peer around the attic, at the corners where boxes and bags were piled against the wall at some point over the last twenty-four years. At the aluminum HVAC tubing that hugs a plastic bin whose label reads "Pearl, preschool."

Dust motes glide to the top of a box beside me as I reread the writing in Sharpie. I was in preschool when I broke my foot.

I lunge for the bin, and then my shoe catches on an exposed joist crisscrossing the pyramid-shaped space. Momentum throws me smack-straight into a pile of black trash bags that feel like they store LEGO bricks. Not pausing for the pain, I struggle to my feet and grasp the bin of memories. Pry off the lid to reveal a blue plastic bag whose shape resembles an *L*. Or a small child's calf and foot.

Anticipation courses through me. Sweat gathers under my arms as I lift the bag from the top of a stack of binders and what look like medical forms filled out in pen.

For a moment, I hesitate. Sally insisted that I never go digging through her stuff. That I should respect that she needed her own space, and allow her to have her secrets. Only, the letter I received from her attorney throws everything into question.

I scan the plastic, searching for a sign that a handwritten letter comes with it. Do I really want to know if Sally killed someone? Even if I uncover another note here and now, will that prove anything, or will it only confirm my mom's mind was slipping away faster than anyone knew?

My guts twist. Then my fingers are tugging on the bag's blue drawstring.

White plaster greets me, shrunken even further from its original size than I would have guessed. But it's here, exactly as I thought it would be. My foot was broken as a three-year-old—not my arm. A fact no one else alive but my dad might remember.

I reach inside the desiccated cast. Sharp pain rips through my fingertips, and I yank my hand back, further scratching my skin. Blood pearls across the top of my thumb.

"Screw this." I grab the outside of the cast, then turn it upside down and shake it until an object falls loose. A piece of white paper.

Red smears on the topmost side as I unfold the creased letter. The sound of the stiff material crackles in the small space of the attic. As I lay eyes on my mother's leaning cursive, her words register in my head:

Pearl, baby. I'm sorry to say that there's more.

Chapter Seven

The Attic

Pearl—

If you're reading this, you're in the attic right now and surrounded by memories of a different time—a different life for you, me, and your dad. I won't say I'm sorry for pulling back the veil here. Hell, I've been living with it the last twenty-four years, and you're an adult now. This is not simply your burden, too, but your armor. Pearl, baby. I'm sorry to say that there's more.

After it was clear that our guest was expired, I took him outside. It was a distasteful experience, but I knew it was necessary. I wanted it, even, because there was no turning back from what had happened. I'd known him for years, and part of me always knew it would end this way.

One long and horrifying night later, I laid him to rest in bed, in the place you knew as the most peaceful in your three-year-old's world, before it was the Museum. You were always a fan of high-flying balloons.

The Lie She Wears

Cleanup was atrocious. Chemical manufacturers should really include more specific details on their labels: "Begin dosing an inch-long stain on fabric with a tablespoon diluted with water; increase quantities as needed." I had to guess and check the amounts needed to scrub clean the mess that the friend left on the hardwood floor, after he burned through my hospitality.

But I have no regrets. He was always such a sloppy, violent person. He would throw plates at me—sometimes cutlery, to amuse himself—with no care for how I felt or looked the next morning. He was aggressive and often set his sights on you, Pearl, but I managed to divert his attention most times you were close by.

I don't know if that's any comfort to you now. I hope you'll forgive me for telling you in this way, after so many failed conversations and impasses between us. We've always been combative. And in the rare possibility that you find this letter sooner than I intended, you'll need to take precautions against me.

Why, you ask? Why would you need to be wary of your own mother? Because I can feel the memories shifting, dulling at their edges, to where sometimes I doubt what I've described above even happened. But you shouldn't.

Trust that, as your mother, I wouldn't involve you if something else wasn't forcing me. Something that scared me. And we all have to face our fears eventually. Otherwise, they catch up to us when we least expect it.

Like mine did, three years later. At that point, your swing set was my favorite way to fly.

—Mom

Chapter Eight

Pearl

"What is going on?" I whisper, my fingers at my lips. "What is this?"

The paper trembles in my hand. My voice is muted among the yellow insulation, as zapped of energy as my body feels. "What the fuck is going on?"

I reread the second letter, still not quite believing—definitely not understanding. I take note of the way Sally suggested the intruder was known to her and overstayed his welcome, versus the version in her first confession: He surprised Sally and me during the night and his head cracked against the fireplace.

I sink onto a joist, shifting my weight along the wooden grid of the attic. A car's muffler snaps and growls outside, passing the house in a roar.

Why make an effort to conceal a murder through euphemisms and storytelling here in this letter hidden in my old cast, yet lay it all out in the letter delivered by her attorney? Does she think someone else might have ventured into the attic looking for her words?

At the top and bottom of the paper folded in thirds, then folded again hamburger-style, the creases are neat. Precise. Deliberate, the way that Sally always aimed for in everything.

I scan the bins and plastic bags surrounding me, some stacked two or three high in the corners of the attic. My eyes begin to water as I take in my mother's insufferable pack rat habits. Although this letter doesn't suggest the conversation continues, there's no way Sally would end it on this cliff-hanger.

My pulse throbs at my temples as I grab the bin closest to me. The Christmas bin. I dig through heaps of cards and tinsel. A discarded pile of cotton balls that once adorned construction paper in a "Winter Wonderland" motif before the glue dried into crusted nothingness. A mountain of glitter and aggressive ornament hooks. I turn to the next bin.

And the next.

Each of the black plastic bags rips open easily. I find old knit blankets Sally made back when she attempted a traditional homemaking phase. Random toys from the nineties and early two thousands, newspaper-wrapped mugs from Starbucks, spiral-bound books from elementary school, magnets collected on travels around the Pacific Northwest, and some yellow knit baby sweater that she always said looked better on me than in the garbage. Another veiled insult. A frenzied search in some white trash bags and the solid IKEA storage containers turns up additional old clothing and toys.

But no more letters. Relief shoots through me with a jolt. Then I recall that Sally had several caches, and that according to Zelda, she began hiding things in earnest toward the end.

I descend the rickety steps from the attic and clatter into the house below. Panting, adrenaline surging in my chest, I veer into my parents' bedroom, rip open the empty nightstand drawers, then plunge into my mother's closet. A mixture of dust and camphor envelops me like a familiar second skin as I step into her space. Although I rarely came here while Sally was alive, now I uncover jewelry boxes, romance books with shirtless men on the covers, medical records from her doctor when she was first exhibiting signs of cognitive difficulty, and a Buddha mask that covers the wearer's entire head, with only holes for eyes, that I last saw at a cousin's wedding ten years ago.

I dump out shoeboxes, revealing unopened tea bags sourced from motels and continental breakfasts, and a host of other items but not shoes. Filing boxes beside them contain birth certificates and family social security records. A velvet box I haven't seen before protects her wedding rings, which she took off months ago for fear of losing them during a "brain fog." A large box with two wineglasses embossed on the side is wider than the shoeboxes, and I tear off the top. Seven silver handles are couched within a velvet fabric square with indented beds for eight—folding knives.

"Switchblades," I murmur. "Why keep seven of them? Where is the eighth?"

My phone trills, buried on the floor somewhere beneath dresses that I knocked off the garment bar during my search. *Griffin Dumont* scrolls across the square, visible through clear dry cleaning bags. My boss.

"Shit." I tear through the plastic, then smash my finger on the green button. "Hi, Griffin. How are you?"

"Good, good. Hey, Pearl. I dropped by the storage hall but didn't find you there. Any chance we can meet in twenty to discuss next week's plan?"

The dull murmur of a crowd hums in the background of Griffin's call. He's in the lobby of the museum, no doubt looking for me. He must be confused why I'm not hunched over a bin in my designated exhibit staging room, where I told him I would be most of the day. Building up the career I've dreamed of since I turned sixteen and realized I could essentially thrift for priceless objects indefinitely and get paid for it.

"Of course, sure," I say. "But I, uh, actually stepped out for a late lunch. Any chance we could meet in forty-five?" I wince, speaking the white lie.

"Sounds good. Just come by my office."

My eyes catch on one of the knives' silver handles. On the splash of red visible across a raised swirling design on the hilt. "Okay, see you soon."

The Lie She Wears

We hang up. I drop down to the winery box again, then shine my phone's flashlight across it. None of the other knives have any color across the silver handles. Is that . . . blood?

The closet spins. I lay a hand on the pile of plastic dry cleaning bags to steady myself. Lean back until my head connects with the wall, not caring if my hair lands in a swath of cobwebs. I inhale through my nose.

I need to go. Forty-five minutes is just enough time to park in the museum's employee parking lot, then walk through the building to reach Griffin's office.

Examining the winery box again, I pluck the red-splashed knife. Slip it into the pocket of my dress jacket, my work clothes. Sally never mentioned a collection of knives or any other weaponry. Just how many secrets did she take with her into death? And how many more am I going to discover while following her breadcrumbs?

With a shudder, I get to my feet, surrounded by my mom and dad's things. Although I turned over every possible hiding place in the attic and now here in their bedroom, I didn't find an additional letter. If Sally continued her scribblings beyond a first and second note, they're not here.

Put your back into it, Pearl. You might get somewhere.

I pause. I'm alone in the closet. Almost.

Steeling myself, I meet the hollow, empty eye sockets of the Buddha mask. The smile on its wide, oversize head, designed to resemble a giant laughing Buddha, appears to twist at the corners.

Another silent moment passes between us. Leaving the closet and my parents' bedroom, I turn on my heel, each step quicker than the last.

Construction crews jackhammer concrete beside the main entrance of the Portland Art Museum. I can barely hear my own thoughts, but I pause on the wide, flat steps of the brick archway leading into the lobby and text my mother's friend Ursula, asking for a phone call. Although Sally was always guarded with me about her past, I'm hoping she confided in a peer.

I want more than anything to go straight to my dad. But he and Sally were married for going on twenty-four years, and he would be the first to dismiss these letters as nonsense, despite being written by my mom herself. They were best friends. Closer than any of my friends' parents, growing up. Before approaching him, I need to learn more about Sally's recent state of mind. Whether I can trust her.

Sally also has a sister whom I've never met, whom I wouldn't begin to know how to contact. They've been estranged for as long as I can remember, although Shirley Wong lives up in Seattle. According to my mom, they were close as kids—their own team of two against the erratic schedules of their parents working multiple jobs during the 1970s in New York. But things changed when the sisters grew into teenagers. Shirley went the academic route, while Sally chose practical, vocational paths: internships for marketing firms uptown, assistant publicity jobs hounding competitors for tips on parties in the Chelsea scene, and odd jobs for anybody who would hire her at a decent wage in Brooklyn. It was a time in Sally's life that she only rarely talked about—and when she did, it was to impress upon me how lucky I had it. How grateful I should be that violence wasn't a part of my upbringing. Considering I know my grandparents were virtual pacifists, having left China during its civil war, I never understood what Sally meant by that. Hopefully, Ursula and my dad can fill in some of the gaps.

The lobby has thinned of visitors, so late in the day. I head past an easel advertising First Fridays, the monthly wine night at the museum, and straight for the elevator to Griffin's office on the third floor. I key past the opaque glass marked "Authorized Personnel Only," then arrive at a half dozen offices, all with doors open to the empty hallway.

"Pearl, there you are," Griffin says from behind his whiteboard desk. Black marker covers most of the surface save for the middle, where there's an open laptop; to-do checklists occupy the margins. "Have a seat. How was lunch?"

I brace myself for a reprimand as I slide into the straight-backed office chair opposite his, laying my brown leather tote bag across my lap. I took off for two hours this afternoon, during which I didn't get a single bite of anything—after I spent thirty minutes with Sally's attorney this morning. Employee of the month.

"Great. Just great," I reply, ready with my story. "There's this Thai place up in the Alphabet District. Best pad see ew of my life."

"Sounds delicious." Griffin smiles politely, which does little to put me at ease. Sally always delivered consequences with a tight-lipped smile. "And your exhibit?"

"Going well. I'll be starting work on my script next week. Though there's still a fair amount of inventory to sort through."

"Said every new hire to the Portland Art Museum. You'll find what you need." Griffin's eyes crinkle behind black-framed glasses, as if his words are a promise instead of a hopeful reply. Curly white hair contrasts the salt-and-peppered brown of his beard, and suddenly I wonder how many new curators like me he's supervised across his career and if my impostor syndrome is written stark on my face. I shift uncomfortably in the hard chair.

"Uh . . . thank you," I mumble.

We change gears to discussing a meeting on Monday that he'd like me to join. When he promises to send me an email with the basic notes of our meeting, I realize he's not going to yell at me for being absent—or absent minded—all day. As I rise to leave, I scan words scribbled on the corners of his desk and circled in felt pen: *theft* and *security policy*.

I take the stairwell down to the ground floor, relief making me light footed in my kitten heels. Their echo on the concrete steps announces that I at least tried to dress up for a Friday.

Near the second floor, someone else's footsteps ring out below. From the middle of the stairwell, a pair of tan shoes is visible at the base of the stairs; the rest of the person's body is obscured. The shoes pause abruptly before taking off, the heavy fire wall door slamming shut on the ground level.

Once I'm at the bottom of the stairs and walking the empty hall past an easel announcing an exhibit dedicated to ancient world maps, I drop the animated expression I wore for Griffin's benefit. My own mask, covering the terror that took root in my belly as soon as I unfolded the second letter in the attic.

Sally's words reverberate in my head, in the Ancient Wonders wing of the museum. *I can feel the memories shifting . . . Sometimes I doubt what I've described above even happened. But you shouldn't.*

My blood pulses in my temples, a pounding headache finally overtaking the adrenaline that's been fueling my steps all day. I pause at the entrance of the employees-only door leading to the warehouse to steady myself against the wall.

Can I trust Sally—that I should believe her despite all my doubts and the abrupt confessions she made in writing? Or can I trust that her mental state was beyond fragile at the time she wrote the letters?

If I'm being honest, my studies weren't the only reason that I stayed away from home as long as I did. I needed space from Sally's frustration, from her sporadic indifference toward me. I needed to reject her before she could reject me again. Can I really trust that she meant to protect me, as she suggests? Or is this only going to hurt me—Sally reaching out to exert one last heartbreak from the grave?

I key into the Authorized Personnel section with an electronic chirp of my card—but the lock doesn't release. I tap my card to the white keypad again, and the gears are silent. A light pull confirms the door is unlocked.

"Weird," I mumble aloud. "Construction must be happening back here too."

Scuffed hardwood beneath bright fluorescent lights leads past several empty exhibit rooms on my way to the storage hall. I need to finish cataloging the aisle I was in earlier, before I left to meet with Sally's attorney.

Just because Sally has dropped not one but two bombs onto my plate today doesn't mean I should neglect my duties here—my career.

Nothing in Sally's letters makes sense. And I need a break. I need to think about something other than my mom and homicide.

An easel I recognize from this morning remains in the hall next to Kai Weathers's exhibit room. I slow my pace to check in with him. See how his first day is going since mine tanked so spectacularly. Footsteps approach from the room.

"Hey, do you want to—" I swallow my words as a person darts into the hallway, narrowly missing me. Black pants and a wide-brimmed hat conceal their features—but not the tan pump boots they wear. Just like the person in the stairwell.

The boxes I watched Kai dig through this morning are all closed and covered now. His museum badge that marks him as an employee lies face up on top of one crate. Kai isn't here. He's not this person, either, judging from their average height and loose-fitting clothing.

"Excuse me?" I call out. "Have you seen Dr. Weathers?"

The figure pauses abruptly, scuffing the hardwood. But they don't turn.

My skin tingles beneath my hair. "Sorry, are you with the museum?"

More silence from the figure. With steady, controlled movements, they slip an object from their hand into their jacket pocket—a lanyard.

"You can't be here if you're a patron." My voice is weak, matching the muted volume of this employee hallway, wherein sound is muffled to enhance guests' viewing experience. Isolating me with a stranger.

My chest tightens. Some instinct in me searches for cameras overhead, and I find none—no need in a supposedly secure-access area. Why is this person here? Why aren't they replying?

Anxiety spikes my blood as I take a step backward, quietly, never taking my eyes from the figure in my path.

Bits of flesh and brain.

"Hello?" I try again. "I said, you can't be here without a badge." I look down, fumbling for my own. Sharp movement yanks my gaze, and

I catch the person sprinting away from me toward the warehouse exit. They turn left where the door is, and then a loud bang echoes seconds later, followed by quieter, slower thumps as the door settles.

My heart pounding, I approach the exit. Push against the bar in the center of the door until it swings forward with ease. This lock is busted too. Voices draw my attention toward the lobby. A security guard in a black uniform with a radio secured to his vest stands beside a marble statue of the Roman goddess Diana. He slips his hand into his pocket, then withdraws his phone, as if bored.

No sign of the museum patron.

"What just happened?" I murmur. Hiking my tote bag higher on my shoulder, I step into the hallway, scanning the individuals I pass. Suddenly, my apartment is sounding pretty good right now. Too much weird shit has emerged today, and I'm not in a great place to work through any of it. Briefly, I think of the friends I left in the Bay Area, the community of like-minded art lovers and overachievers that grounded me through grad school, and how nice it would be to unwind with someone—anyone—who I trusted right now. Then I remember I don't have any of their phone numbers since we only communicated weekend plans via Instagram or Facebook DMs. What kind of friends were they, when I can't even say what their area code is?

A heavy sigh shudders through my chest as I approach the security guard to tell him about the lock failure. I need about a gallon of ice cream and a six-pack of wine coolers.

Once Hank radios up to his boss, I set off toward the main exit, my shoes tapping their rhythm against the marble floor of the lobby. At the double doors, my back pocket vibrates. A text message—from Ursula:

Pearl, hey. If you're looking for info on your mom's childhood, we're going to need more than a phone call. Why don't you stop by my shop sometime next week? We can chat then.

Waiting more than a day or so to speak to Ursula is anything but ideal. But I'll take what I can get.

Glancing back through the lobby, at the aerial exhibit of ceramic balloons overhead, I scan the groups of patrons studying their phones. Examining maps of the museum and chatting casually about the highlights or what exhibit they'd like to view first. Then the crowds shift. The space between my shoulder blades tightens another notch as I spy a wide-brimmed hat visible from around the corner at the statue of Diana. Quiet conversations swell to a roar, bodies of the lobby moving—departing for their targeted artwork—and then the hat is gone.

Chapter Nine

Vicki

New York City, 1992

New money. New money. Inheritance. Old money. Wall Street.

    I set my sunglasses on the counter as I size up each pair of potential buyers, and their source of cash, that crosses the threshold of the eighth-floor apartment I need to sell. As a two-bed, two-bath in Manhattan, this place should have gone immediately, and well above asking price. But prospective buyers keep complaining the view of Central Park is obscured by the mature oaks. My client was already pissed that I insisted he should have it staged for this weekend's open house. If I don't close a deal, I'm going to get an earful.

    Shoppers ask me their questions, and I trot out the answers, like I'm that robot girl in *Small Wonder* but with a personality upgrade. The previous owners moved to Sarasota. Renovations were completed last June. The doorman downstairs is named Henry. All the while keeping an eye on the gentleman in the jean jacket who casually crosses the square footage. The guy is young, much younger than anyone else here, and could genuinely be apartment hunting. But when he doesn't emerge from the second bedroom for a solid five minutes, I have my suspicions.

A few minutes later, after my supply of complimentary cookies and champagne is depleted, I announce that the open house has concluded. If anyone would like more information on the property, I'd be happy to stay behind and chat. I hand out business cards with the name I use for official dealings already written on the back, then pack up my stuff to go.

Jean Jacket is the second-to-last person to skip out the door, and without so much as a goodbye. Naturally. Because he doesn't want to draw attention to himself—apart from the gelled hairstyle he sports.

"Amateur hour strikes again." I sigh, first locking the front door. A quick peek in the two bedrooms confirms that the young buck managed to jimmy open the rusted windows that access the fire escape. He intends to return here after dark and steal what he thinks is the high-end furniture and valuable artwork that I ensured were hung above the beds.

I wouldn't give it a second thought—I'll lock up and make sure the windows are secured, and that will be the end of that. But I also know that thieves have been stalking real estate agents in the city, seeking out ways to steal keys to luxury properties. It's a problem. And this man has piqued my interest.

Grabbing my purse, I head down the elevator and into the lobby just as his stonewash flits out of sight onto West End Avenue. I watch as he navigates the lunch rush that's especially robust on Saturday mornings. Take note as he bumps into a few well-dressed individuals on purpose, lifting small items of value, then pocketing whatever he finds using deft sleights of hand.

A half hour later, when he disappears down a set of stairs that lead to the 6, I follow him. My stomach growls, but I ignore the gnawing sensation in my belly. I don't pause at any of my favorite spots on this stretch of the city, but hop on the train within fifteen feet of this man. A part of me feels nourished simply by pursuing him. I feel drawn to him, unable to look away as he manipulates and confiscates items from additional strangers within the tight quarters of a packed car.

We go north for a while. Passengers enter, completely unaware they have just crossed into the realm of a master magpie, and exit lighter for it. After a few more stops and a quick switch to the 5 line, he gets out at 174th. The Bronx. My home. A light bulb flickers on the exposed electrical grid overhead.

I search the platform as a dozen other people exit with us—only I don't see his jean jacket. A sharp turn conceals the steps up to street level, but I'd swear he never got that far. I lost him. Shit.

"Oh, excuse me." Someone bumps into me, nearly jostling me off my feet. "Sorry about that."

I remove my sunglasses to brush the hair from my eyes, and then instinct tells me to look up. The train doors shut with a whoosh of compressed air, while a figure stares at me through the plexiglass window. Wearing a stonewashed jean jacket.

"Sneaky bastard."

My words are swallowed by the engine's roar, but he smiles, as if reading my lips. In his fingers, he lifts the delicate set of apartment keys that my client entrusted to me, dangling them with a devilish grin. Taunting me. Proving that he knew I was following him all along.

I glare at him as the train lurches forward and then enters the graffitied tunnel. We maintain eye contact until he is nearly engulfed by the tunnel's shadows, at which point I drop my expression of anger and defeat and instead allow this man and his show of besting me to disappear.

Then he does something else that grips my attention. He mirrors me exactly. His facial expression, which seconds earlier appeared bright and boasting, smooths into clean, unenthusiastic indifference as he slips forward out of sight.

For a moment, the light bulb above me flickers. Then its filament burns out in a flash of darkness.

Curiosity swirls inside me as I debate whether to catch the next train, to go farther uptown. To follow him now or to admit to the lead agent that I lost our client's keys.

No, I can't do that. To admit that I've been had by a random guy is not an option.

By the time the car arrives, I know my next steps: I'll bring in Errol and his network of Hounds. They'll know how to find him. And when they do, I will take back those keys if I have to rip them from Mr. Jean Jacket's talented, dead hands.

Chapter Ten

PEARL

Last night, while I was high on sugar and Netflix's algorithm, I sent an email to Security reporting that the locking mechanism was broken on the Authorized Personnel doors, and that someone suspicious was lurking in secure areas. Almost immediately, a brief reply hit my inbox confirming that "protective measures have been reinstated." I got the sense that I was being told to mind my business. And yet, here I am, back in the warehouse among priceless artifacts and wondering just how long the security system was compromised.

I glance around me at the empty aisles on a Saturday morning. Shouldn't someone be back here taking inventory, confirming nothing is out of place after yesterday's "protective" failure?

At my feet, in the crate on the concrete floor, specially wrapped items nearly overflow the steel-reinforced edges: Chinese sorcerers' masks, Tibetan masks, shaman masks, theatrical masks, New Year masks, and masks used to drive out evil spirits. I focus on the artifacts that I selected and Griffin approved, alongside a team of project managers, exhibit designers, and education programmers. I try to shut out other distractions. Although I'm aiming for twelfth-century China as my featured time range and location, next month's pop-up series is meant to cater to patrons who love Halloween and spooky fall vibes. If I happen to find a creepy doll used in Thailand and it helps me land a promotion, I'll gladly toss it in.

Alone as I am in the warehouse, I have my pick of the transport dollies at the end of this aisle. I choose one with an extrawide platform. The last thing I need after Sally's bombshell letters, and the havoc they've wreaked on my sleep patterns, is to damage priceless objects.

"All right, nightmares." I grunt, wrangling a crate onto the steel platform. "Time to relocate to your new home."

With a push, the dolly rolls forward, squeaking like a small rodent. I reach the hallway that connects to the empty staging rooms as voices rise from around the corner. A colleague who specializes in Indigenous art in the Pacific Northwest is speaking—Nettie? Natalie?

"Construction is taking forever outside," she says. "It's messing with the whole electrical grid of the building."

"Ugh, I know," someone else replies. "They fixed the special-access areas pretty quickly, though."

"Right. They did. They *better* have a team on standby. When I was working up in Seattle, the museum's backup generators shorted out during that blizzard in 2014. The craziest twenty-four hours of my career . . ."

The conversation peters out as I veer right, away from the main halls and toward the portion of the building that's under construction. In two weeks' time, the newly renovated, glass-encased fourth floor of the museum will be unveiled to the public, and I need my display locked and loaded by then. I arrive at the staging room assigned to me, then hit the lights, bringing them all the way up. I stop short. Something is missing.

The crates that I gathered and stored here are all accounted for—except the basic plywood crate that housed the Buddha mask historically used at Chinese weddings. It's the largest headpiece I chose, despite it being from the third century BCE, and it should stick out from any position in the room. It's not here.

You don't even know what you're doing.

Sally's critical voice echoes in my ears, louder than normal. This is bad.

Crisp fear shoots through my core. Did I see the Buddha head this morning, during the last two hours? I know I went back home yesterday and found Sally's own version that she kept in her closet. But I haven't reviewed all the museum's items that I gathered together until now.

"This is very bad," I whisper. A list that I keep on my phone confirms that everything I checked out from the storage hall is here—aside from the missing mask. Did someone take it?

It's invaluable. After an extensive archaeological dig in 1974, searching fruitlessly for Emperor Qin's buried fleet of solid gold horses from the third century BCE, this Buddha mask was discovered by accident. It was widely publicized as the find of the decade and splashed across all major history-based networks globally. No one had seen a mask like it, as well preserved as it was or as large as it was. Did someone know all that and steal it, with the intention of profiting from its priceless status?

Voices carry from the direction of Kai's exhibit. Though he's new to the Portland Art Museum, he's been in this world years longer than I have. Part of me wants to run to him for advice, considering I've got only six months of museum tenure under my belt and been largely isolated from other coworkers while researching my subject. But if I tell anyone, it should be Griffin. He can check security camera footage.

I run both hands down my face. For a moment, I'm tempted to scream into my moist palms. Hurl all the frustration from the last twenty-four hours into my cry. Instead, I stifle the urge, tuck in the back side of my blouse, then hurry to the next room.

Nettie Harbour—*Nettie*, I remember, *not Natalie*—the curator of Native American art and a juggernaut in the Portland art scene, bends across a carved wooden plank twice her size in the middle of the space.

"Hey, Nettie? Any chance you've seen an oversize Buddha mask?"

She straightens. "Huh?"

The Lie She Wears

"A mask. From Imperial China. It's used at weddings during a dragon dance to invite happiness and joy for the couple. I can't seem to find it," I mumble. Saying the words aloud adds a tenor of shame to my voice. "I just moved it from the storage hall to my staging room yesterday."

Nettie pushes up the sleeves of her green dress shirt. "Well, it sounds like it's hard to miss. Did you check with the new guy—Kai? He was working late the other day. Maybe he's seen it."

"I'll do that next," I reply, already moving down the hall.

But Kai's room is empty, apart from the crates of true crime artifacts he highlighted to me. He left all these priceless pieces of history—in some cases, of former evidence—unattended.

"At least I'm not the only one," I grumble.

After a quick scan of the room to confirm the mask isn't here, either, I head to the elevator and the administrative offices on the third floor. Griffin will have an idea of what to do next, and whether I need to notify some big-money donor that I'm to blame for the loss of a family heirloom on loan.

Could I grab my family's modern Buddha mask that's currently steeped in dry cleaning bags in Sally's closet? Pass it off as a nearly two-thousand-year-old edition?

"Great idea, Pearl," I say to myself. "If you want to be summarily fired."

The third floor is quiet, and I'm relieved to find Griffin alone in his office. I tell him everything. Alarm immediately tents his thick eyebrows, but he tells me not to worry, that it's probably been misplaced while everyone is readying for the microexhibit launch. He'll look into it and ask Security to search today's surveillance for signs of it.

The conversation goes better than I expect—better than I deserve—and I return to the first floor. My nerves are still strung tight as I reenter my staging room. If the Buddha mask isn't found, I'll have to rethink my exhibit's centerpiece and whole story—an undertaking entirely out of reach for me with the time I have left—two weeks. Not to mention, there will be some serious professional blowback.

Words from Sally's second letter reverberate in my thoughts, the way they did all night. *We all have to face our fears eventually.*

I stare at the pile of internationally sourced artifacts, preserved by teams of academics, diplomats, and archaeologists with far more diplomas and bigger paychecks than I'll ever have. I scan the faces worn by countless bodies across the centuries, the masks radiating judgment.

What did Sally mean by that? She knew I had nightmares about all the masks, but she kept them in the house despite my anxiety, despite my pleas to take them down. So, is she referencing her own fears in the letters? Not that she had any. The woman was unbothered by most things, citing her scrappy upbringing in Brooklyn.

Moreover, haven't I faced my fears by studying masks—by launching an exhibit on them? What does Sally know about me now and my life—what did she ever?

I pull up photos on my phone that I took of each note that Sally wrote. The first letter, divulging the death of someone, mentioned my broken arm—which was incorrect. The second letter offers more harrowing detail about the act and says where Sally buried the intruder.

"I laid him to rest in bed, in the place you knew as the most peaceful in your three-year-old's world," I read aloud. "Before it was the Museum. You were always a fan of high-flying balloons."

What peaceful place of mine is she referencing?

I tap my index finger to my screen. "Why not bury someone in a spot that Sally thought was peaceful?"

Sally had been in Oregon since her twenties, and always loved museums. Before she got into thrifting, she often spent her weekends at major art museums, science museums, and music museums in the region. She said more than once how tranquil she found them. The white noise of soft conversations analyzing an image, the sight of a watercolor that moved her,

The Lie She Wears

the sense that she was traversing continents and languages without having to make another three-thousand-mile drive.

And I have been working at the Portland Art Museum since April, a place Sally frequented in the past.

You were always a fan of high-flying balloons. Just like the ones in the lobby.

Striding out the door and into the main hallway, I barely break pace when I collide with a group of high schoolers. Dodging backpacks and selfies, I reach the polished tile mosaic of jumping salmon, then slow to a stop beside the information desk. I look up.

The ceramic balloons of the lobby's ceiling installation, mostly red in color, represent hardened dreams relating to climate change. I know this thanks to the plaque on the far wall that connects to the pavilion outside, which I've read a half dozen times. But I never understood how the artist intended balloons to be representative of the crisis currently plummeting us down the proverbial drain. Is it helium? Is the installation commenting that the helium that balloons use is destroying the earth? I figured that my liberal arts doctorate was to blame for my lack of understanding there. That if I had paid more attention in my environmental studies course, I'd know the link and find the installation to be poignant, or something.

My phone pings from my back pocket. I unlock the screen, and Griffin's name appears in my missed call log. "Shit," I whisper.

I need to get back. To check in with him. Hopefully his call is a good sign, that the mask was located, hidden at the bottom of some box meant for a museum loan program.

I cast another glance above. Tilt my head backward to take in the image one more time before switching course to the elevator and the third floor.

Over forty ceramic red balloons are suspended from thin cables extending from the ceiling. Whenever I entered the lobby and walked beneath them at a brisk pace, their arrangement always seemed arbitrary. Scattered, mostly, although a portion were gathered in a column for some reason. Yet now, I see them for what they are: a tree—which makes a lot more sense, as it relates to climate change.

The museum is the oldest in the Pacific Northwest, and one of the oldest in the country. Across from the pavilion under construction, a former Masonic temple built in 1926 is now an event rental space and features a collection of ancient texts. There are huge chunks of local history here. And this well-known installation was unveiled back in the sixties as a form of protest art born out of climate concerns that were already developing then. Sally was a fan of op art, illusion sculptures, and scavenger hunts, and she would have known what this was. What it meant. She would have seen the shape of the tree.

When viewed while facing the street, exiting to reenter the world, the balloons are in the shape of an oak tree, similar to the one planted on the ranch house's property. Near the location where I broke my foot.

Sweat breaks across my chest. While Sally's words echo in my thoughts like a siren.

I laid him to rest in bed, in the place you knew as the most peaceful in your three-year-old's world.

Chapter Eleven

Pearl

Outside the ranch house, a breeze hits the bushes planted directly beneath the roadside window. Leaves on the hydrangeas tremble, still clutching to their branches despite the autumn cold and recent slick rains. Lush grass sways; it's grown to mid-calf since I canceled the landscape service two weeks ago, reclaiming the yard.

"Me again," I mutter to the front door, pulling my blazer tight across my body. Beyond the house, the oak tree sits nearly at the edge of the property, shielding or wielding the truth about Sally's letters. I pivot to walk along the house and straight out to the field; then I pull up short. Pain spirals across my core, like some flicker of gastrointestinal self-preservation. Do I want to know the truth? Or is it better to live out my days as a slightly neurotic introvert surrounded by museum relics whose painful histories won't personally gut me?

When I returned to Griffin's office, he asked that I officially identify the missing mask in the museum's inventory database and write up a statement with Security. He assured me that these things happen every now and then, especially in a museum as large as ours.

When I asked him if he truly thought it was only lost, he stared at me, quizzically. "What else would it be?" he wondered, holding my eye contact. "Could someone have . . . stolen it?"

He stared at me then, innocent curiosity taking on the glint of suspicion in the course of five seconds.

"N-No. I would—that would be . . ." I stammered. "I would hate to think that were possible. The mask is priceless."

Griffin nodded, his glasses slipping forward to the bridge of his nose. "Quite right. Someone might try to take advantage of that fact."

Although he thanked me for doing everything I could to alert the museum, I left his office in a rush, eager to escape his gaze.

I spent the following hour in the office that I share with another associate curator, who's gone two years without a promotion—Peggy Vo—but I couldn't focus on the texts I need to create for each artifact in my exhibit. My mind was ping-ponging. Between the missing mask and thoughts of the ranch house, of Sally's cryptic letters, and the creeping possibility that she might be telling the truth, I skipped out as soon as Peggy took a bio break.

A breeze twirls the strands of hair that escaped my ponytail, where I stand fixed by the hydrangeas. I'm not ready for this—for whatever awaits me in the field. I need a minute.

The front door opens with a whine as I cross the threshold. A pile of leaflets, a letter from a real estate agent, and thin newspapery coupons litter the floor, same as when I was here yesterday—along with a new postcard. Unsteady handwriting on the back reads, "It's been too long" with "too" underlined. My dad's name and our home address are clearly written on the preprinted bars. In tiny script above the barcode, another phrase is written: "Twenty days."

I stoop to the tile. I scan the message again, and the overlapping postmark that shows this was processed sometime this week from Bend, a few hours south. *It's been too long.* Strange that this second postcard doesn't include a sender's identity either. Are these condolences? Or a secretive, romantic invitation to my dad?

What happens in twenty days? I thought the phrase on yesterday's postcard—"three weeks"—referenced the wake we held for Sally, but this second edition has me confused.

The Lie She Wears

On the other side of the postcard, a photo of a grazing cow is overlayed with the words "Greetings from Tillamook!"

I tap my finger along the edge. "Sent from Bend. Made in Tillamook. Because . . . that town is known for its romance."

My sarcasm lingers in the air as I rescue the second postcard, then toss the rest of the pile in the recycling bin by the garage door. I add the postcard to the items on the counter set aside for my dad, which I'll take to him soon: some advertisements for gutter cleaning and a few alumni newsletters from Dad's alma mater, Portland State University. Zelda gathered two more postcards for him in a Bankers box while she continued coming here the week after Sally's death. She offered to sort the mail on a regular basis, to dust, and to begin packing Sally's things, but I declined—snapped at her, *No*. I was still mad at her. *Am* still mad. As long as Zelda had the opportunity to stop Sally from getting behind the wheel, I always will be.

And, when I stop to acknowledge all the complex emotions I'm still processing, I can't deny the jealousy that colors my words each time I speak to Zelda. This professional, this nurse, seemed absolutely heartbroken when Sally died. An admirable trait, to demonstrate that much empathy for her patient. But all I could think while she blew her nose at the funeral was, *She wasn't your mother. She was mine.* Despite my and Sally's differences, I always wanted to please her, and never could. I wanted the mother who was showcased on prime-time TV shows while I was growing up, the kind who brushed hair and gave love and career advice to her daughter. Instead, mine leveled quiet insults my way, like comparing me to char siu pork.

I wasn't very nice to Zelda at the grave. When she went to throw a handful of dirt on Sally's casket, I elbowed past her to do it first. Zelda gasped, probably startled, but she took a step back and waited for me to have my time as Sally's only child. Zelda didn't speak to me at the reception after that.

I glance toward the sliding glass door that leads to the side of the house, then scan the kitchen, searching for something to do. The counters are spotless apart from the letters I've saved. No one has cooked here in over a month, since my mom died. Since her first letter came into play. Outside, the sun dips below the sloping hill beyond our field, its final rays clinging to the sky.

With a deep breath, I steel myself, then reach for the door handle. "Okay, Char Siu. Time for a walk."

Crisp September air envelops me, planting a chilled kiss to my throat as I step outside. The property unfurls across ten acres. A solid play area, growing up. A creek where I used to search for tadpoles with my dad lies just out of sight from where I stand beside the house. Fruit trees that we haphazardly planted years ago form a matrix of roots across the acreage, providing shelter for the family of squirrels that scavenge here and the errant coyotes known to visit.

At the very back of the property, with branches that stretch forward and mark the edge of our land, an oak tree holds court above the less imposing flower beds, bushes, trees, and grass that blanket the ground. Similar to the tree formed by the dozens of red ceramic balloons, which Sally's letter directed me toward.

It's possible that my mom had a cognitive lapse and imagined all the harrowing details she swears by in her letters. But I won't be able to focus on my exhibit or sleep a full night before I confirm the truth.

I grab a shovel and gloves from the adjacent shed, then set off across the gravel of the driveway. A horse whinnies from down the road when I reach the tufts of crabgrass that mark the end of the tiny pebbles; the neighborhood is otherwise quiet. Car horns honk from miles away, and the noise carries across the valley before it dips into the stretch of hillside wineries that put it on the map. I spot the oak tree from halfway across our lot. Sweat gathers beneath my ponytail and on my chest, the humidity signaling that a storm is coming. A satin blouse was a bad choice when I got dressed this morning.

The oak tree spreads along the early-evening sky. Stars are just visible in the pockets of light between leaves as I approach the thick, exposed roots of the tree's base, crooked and bent as if poised to escape. The heart that I carved into the trunk when I was eleven has smoothed into a cicatrix in the ensuing years, a marker that I allow to guide me.

Leaning onto the handle of the shovel, in front of the heart, I push into the grass until the metal head sinks like a hot knife. The ground gives with ease, moving under moderate pressure. Moisture from recent rains and today's overcast sky makes at least one thing about this wild-goose chase less frustrating.

The evening drags forward while I dig haphazardly among the tree's roots. At first, I attempt some kind of system. I visualize a grid, the way that archaeologists examine a site for remnants of the past, working my way across the surrounding area one square at a time. An hour passes, and then I begin poking the ground at will, desperate for anything from Sally—a sliver of a hint to confirm or disprove her words.

Our guest was expired. I'll never get the thick smell of blood out of my nose. Laid him to rest.

A donkey brays from the McCallister farmhouse, now a converted bed-and-breakfast a mile down the road. Night is falling fast and with it a chill that ignites the stale sweat covering my body. I chuck the shovel away from me. Take a seat on the grass. My fingers brush a cluster of dandelions that I suppose I should dig out while I'm wearing workman gloves, but I leave it be.

The half dozen mounds of dirt that surround me contradict any optimism I had when I parked my car in the driveway. The scene appears as if an overeager gopher attacked. Across the last two hours, I have guessed, shoveled, and dug by hand all the places that might hide a dead body: the hidden pockets between tree roots that lie beneath the earth and those that protrude like greedy tentacles from the tree's trunk. But each pile of dirt has equaled silence. There's nothing here. I misinterpreted the art installation.

Or, maybe, the lack of evidence is the confirmation I needed. Sally didn't kill anyone. Nobody is buried, dead beneath my feet. Sally's note pointed me here, to nothing, because she imagined the whole experience.

Weary and confused, I glance back at the house. The lights inside are off, creating an eerie contrast to the illuminated evening routines of the neighbors. In the Millers' house directly next door, Mrs. Miller spins about her kitchen, getting dinner ready. On the opposite side, in the Gooding house, the three teenage boys I still think of as toddlers watch something on TV. Shades of blue and green flash across the wall of their living room and emphasize the void of light from the Davis ranch house.

I don't want to go back in there. I never liked being alone with certain masks of Sally's, and especially not at night. But those are the only frightening elements about this place that are real. Sally wasn't part of a murder. The only thing that died here was a close relationship with my mother, which led me to usually refer to her as Sally instead of Mom.

I lie back, placing my hands behind my head. Pinpricks of distant stars twinkle within the never-ending black.

What a waste. I've expended enough mental energy to recreate a Van Gogh over the last thirty-six hours, and for what? To get outside and touch grass? To remind myself that I didn't trust much of what Sally told me while she was alive, so I shouldn't start now?

Behind my head, my fingers land on something sharp. Plastic. Still grumbling, I sit up and bring it to eye level—a weathered plant tag, nearly covered in crusted dirt. A label for sweet potatoes. From one of the many holes I dug, something white glows in the creeping darkness, something I didn't see in my frenzy to pockmark the grass. A tuber couched in dark dirt.

Sally had a vegetable garden here a long time ago. At least ten years ago. She probably missed harvesting this potato the last time she planted. And while only a portion of the tuber is visible, it's surprising that it didn't completely decompose, this long in the ground. I reach for it.

My fingers clutch on to the narrow, tapered end of the vegetable, and it feels wrong. Off, and without the ridges I would expect. A shock of cold slaps my hand, and I reel backward. It isn't—

What is it?

I get to my feet. Using the shovel, I move dirt around the object until all four sides are excavated, and reveal bone.

My mind empties. Horror crushes my throat as I stagger backward. *A bone.* Buried beneath Sally's former garden. Whose bone?

A long moment passes punctuated only by my labored breathing. The rush of a car swells, then dissipates as it continues down the road.

My thoughts race.

Measuring at least ten inches in length, the bone could be left over from a meal of one of the roaming coyotes. Then again, it's too large to belong to one of their usual kills of rabbits, rodents, and chickens in the neighborhood.

The clouds shift overhead as starlight illuminates the yard. Something else shines, still buried in the pit. I reach into the hole, my skin clammy. Fumbling fingers grasp the metal—a silver pendant with a thin chain that follows. I smooth away the moist dirt from the pendant's face with my thumb to uncover a figure of a man praying.

"What are you?" I whisper.

A breeze snakes through the thin fabric of my shirt, and then the wind picks up, tugging at my waist. Porch chimes crash nearby in dissonant clanging. I stare at the bounty from Sally's former vegetable bed. A bone and a necklace. If this necklace was buried with the bone on purpose, then I probably uncovered human remains—

My hand flies to my mouth. "Oh my God."

I dig higher and farther around it, then a shape of many bones takes form: a foot—though with only four appendages, missing a toe.

The ground tilts, shifts at an impossible angle. Vertigo punts me off-balance, and then I'm reeling backward, tripping on crabgrass. "Oh—"

I land hard on my tailbone as my stomach seizes, cramps in on itself, and I'm doubled over, vomiting onto the patch of dandelions.

PART TWO

Chapter Twelve

Emily

New York City, 1992

Well, shoot. The line for the deli and the sandwich that I've been craving since Wednesday winds around the corner of the block, all the way into the alleyway teeming with trash and discarded clothing. A woman ten places up sways to the beat of the new Michael Jackson jam—"Remember the Time"—blaring from the radio she carries by the handle, almost like she's trying to take out her own auditory function along with everyone else's within a mile radius. I am not waiting with these idiots.

After I lost sight of Mr. Jean Jacket, I took the next train back downtown to the offices to report on interested buyers and pass the sign-in sheet along to the senior agent, a polo-wearing narbo from Rhode Island named Tim. Famished, I booked it out of there as fast as I could and down the street to the present clusterfuck.

"Excuse me," I say, tapping the green-clad shoulder in front of me. I allow my sunglasses to fall down the bridge of my nose, then peer at the guy while batting my thick mascara. "Do you know what's going on up there?"

"Some new sitcom filming inside. They're still taking orders, though."

"Hence the line."

He smirks. "Right."

"Well, any chance you can save my spot for me? Nature calls."

He could be a taller version of Denzel, with soft brown eyes that glance at my cleavage, fully on display in my low V-neck.

"Sure, I can." He smiles, then tents his eyebrows. "If you give me your name."

"Oh, come on! You're not going to let her, are you?"

I turn to find six people have already lined up behind me, including this woman rolling her eyes at us, sticking halfway out just to comment on something not her business. Another idiot.

Ignoring her, I fix Denzel with a half smile. "Emily. You?"

"Gene."

"See you in a few, Gene."

"I look forward to it, Emily."

I strut down the street away from him, allowing him ample view of the tight seams of my trousers. The scowling woman glares as I pass while she strokes the raggedy fur of a small Toto dog in her thick arms.

"If you're not back in five minutes, Emily, you're losing your spot," she sneers.

Emily seemed like a nice enough name. Like the kind of girl Gene would want close to him and might defend against an angry mob of hungry morons.

It's a good thing that's not my name.

I drop my syrupy-sweet, wide-eyed expression, then pause beside Toto and his wicked witch. The woman shrinks backward an inch.

"Try me," I hiss. With a wink and a wave back to Gene, who's still watching—as I knew he would be—I continue toward a mimosa and a few chapters of the paperback I stuffed in my Liz Claiborne purse while I wait for the line to die down.

An hour ticks by as I savor the bubbles of diluted champagne and the antics of Richard III at a bar overlooking the park. An apartment on the fifth floor of the building across from where I sit is a pocket listing I've been trying for the last month to get one of my clients to buy. The money is too high for most, but the winds of change will come through soon. I know they will. It's rare to find a gem like this property for sale publicly at all, considering most apartments in New York pass from relative to distant family relative. My clients don't know how good they have it with me.

"Hey, you."

I turn to the familiar voice. Errol, wearing a Cheshire cat grin.

"Did the sanatorium let you out?" I ask.

He scoffs, then slides onto the barstool beside me. Palming his hair, he tucks back a choppy black curtain. "Nah, I called in sick to work today. I had other business."

He allows the flap of his Adidas puffer jacket to fall open, revealing a rubber-banded stack of bills.

I nod, appreciatively. Errol's lucrative side hustle of finding people has ratcheted up lately. He's not a private investigator—he has no ethical or legal restrictions that bind him, as he works under the table and largely for people who want to stay unknown. But thanks to his network of contacts and his smarts, he'll find anyone with a price on their head. Errol is a little like me in that respect. He doesn't have friends. He has a Rolodex of assets.

"Looks like it," I say. "Who was it this time?"

He pushes out his lips, scanning the sidewalk of passing bodies. "A missing coed from the Upper West Side. Her father is some television exec, and he offered twice my normal rate if I found her within a week. I found her in four days, hanging out in Miami." He shrugs in false modesty. "Thought I'd treat myself to a glass of Veuve at your favorite lookout spot, and lo and behold."

"My lucky day, then." I smile. "Though I've got to get back. A sandwich and a tall drink of water are waiting for me."

"A what?"

I roll my eyes at Errol's lack of imagination, then slide from the chair. "Lunch and dessert. Happy hour tomorrow?"

"Can't. I'm meeting with another Hound. Some guy who's got the beat on corrupt cops uptown."

"Friday, then. Oh, and I'm going to need your help finding a guy. I got pickpocketed earlier today, and he took my listing's keys."

"Really? I'm surprised you let someone get that close to you."

I shrug. "I kind of liked it."

After I pay my bill and wave goodbye to Errol, I head back onto the sidewalk. If I timed it just right, Gene should be approaching the front door of the deli soon—and I should be placing my order for the pastrami sandwich I've been dreaming about all week.

The image of Errol's stack of money lingers in my mind, though I make enough as a junior real estate agent and I like my work. Selling and buying properties allows me to observe people up close without appearing to overstep or making anyone uncomfortable. Not unless I feel like it.

I cross the street, zigzagging among cars in stop-and-go traffic. Take the next block over and sight the end of the line—shorter than it was, now at half past two. The tall fade of black hair and the dark-green shirt Gene was wearing earlier are only ten spots back from the front.

"Just like I thought he would be." I smile to myself. There's nothing like a slight buzz paired with fresh-cut deli meat.

"You gotta be kidding me." The scowling woman from earlier steps out of line to face me. Apparently, she's been watching for my reappearance ever since I left. The dog makes anxious circles at her feet. For a moment, we lock eyes, me and the animal.

Continuing forward, I adopt the wide-eyed look of an ingenue, ready with my story for Gene. *I had to search forever for a bathroom—you wouldn't believe it. Then, as I was leaving, a server spilled a drink on me and I had to air-dry using the hand blower in the kitchen. What a mess! So sorry it took me so long. I'll just slide in and you can tell me the plot of The Godfather.*

The Lie She Wears

A clawed hand grips the bare skin of my arm. "Oh no you don't." Triumph flashes across the woman's lined face, her heavy jowls lifting in smug victory. "You left over an hour ago, Emily. You're not cutting."

The New Yorkers around us mind their own business, eyes forward. "Get your hand off me, lady—" I raise my voice, hopeful that Gene will hear, intercede as my white knight, then give me *his* spot in line.

I struggle audibly, but the green shoulders up ahead don't turn toward my distress. "Let me go!"

"Get the hell out of here, girlie. You must be visiting the city for the day. You can't pull that bullshit with us locals." She twists my arm at the elbow, bending it backward and forcing me to take a step behind.

"I'm not—"

"Don't give me that. You've got *Connecticut* and *train ride* written all over you. Did you do your makeup on the long route in?" She mocks me with her tone, her fat lips pouting inches from my face. Her breath smells like cabbage.

"No, I was here—I'm not—" I sputter, waiting for Gene to turn. And if not him, for someone else to see that I'm just trying to get the sandwich I've been craving, just like all the rest of them, and to get this chick off me.

"The hell you were, Miss Priss. Get out of here!"

The woman raises her voice, and then all heads at the front of the line turn. The man wearing the green shirt has a beard. He's not Gene. I scan the window of the deli, past the figures of would-be customers, and spy Gene inside, seated at a table with an attractive blonde. A girl I recognize who was waiting farther back in line than I was.

Son of a bitch.

"Did you hear me?" Cabbage-breath woman digs her nails into my skin as she tries to toss me from the sidewalk into the gutter. "I said you can't pull that one on a native New Yorker—"

A city bus honks, barreling down the street next to me. The driver leans on his horn, warning me that I'm too close to the edge and am about to get sideswiped.

"—so go back to Connecticut!" The woman shoves me hard away from her, and I'm falling, leaning backward into the path of the diesel engine. My center of gravity gives, relegating me to roadkill status, when I cock my foot behind. Catch myself. I tighten my grip on the woman's arm and yank her forward, twisting to change places with her. Her heavy mass lurches into the road as the bus slams into her.

Horns blare and brakes screech in a metallic crescendo, while her bones crunch beneath the vehicle's wheels like breadsticks. A horrified otherworldly scream echoes against the maelstrom of noise before it abruptly ends.

I take stock of myself, six inches from the edge of the sidewalk, from the carnage in the street. I'm fine. I'm untouched. Adrenaline pumps through my body.

An arm protrudes from beneath a tire's burned rubber, fingers crooked toward the sky. Nausea roils my stomach as the smells of gas, exhaust, and gore mingle in an awful urban perfume. Someone in line beside me pukes, and then another person screams.

Shock glides along my chest—a pleasing feeling that I usually try to ignore. But I have the wherewithal to finish my final reply to the unyielding rage the woman spewed at me before the bus flattened her like a crepe.

"I'm a native New Yorker, lady. And I wouldn't set foot in Connecticut."

Chapter Thirteen

Pearl

Dishes crash in the kitchen of this café within view of the South Park Blocks.

I shake my head to the real estate agent across from me. "Sorry, can you say that again?"

He smiles and resumes talking about interest rates, property value, and the Portland market's viability. Key words for the real estate industry that I have little knowledge of and that I allow to glide right over my head.

After reading the solicitation letter he sent to the ranch house, I was curious about what he had to say, and also desperate for a distraction until Ursula can see me tomorrow. Meeting with this agent was supposed to get my mind off Sally's revelations. Off my decision not to contact the police yet, because I need to know more before my family home becomes the center of a crime scene investigation. But every time I close my eyes, I see the off-white, pale shade of bone beneath starlight. Lately, I find myself zoning in and out of conversations with coworkers, my boss, and via text message. Ursula sent me a text that I completely forgot about until hours later.

It's been three days since I last visited the ranch house. Seventy-two hours since confirming someone died on our property. Sally was telling the truth.

Or, no—not *died*. Was buried. Maybe they were killed and buried there?

"Miss Davis?" The real estate agent lifts both his eyebrows. "I was saying I have an interested buyer for your house."

"Sorry—what? It's not my house. My parents own it. My dad does, I mean."

Dane Ajamian narrows his eyes. "Then I'm confused."

When I called this agent after finding his typed message on glossy paper at the ranch house, expressing interest in the property, I knew I didn't have any authority to make decisions about selling it. But I was also curious. My dad's care facility isn't cheap, and I'm hoping he lives a good many years ahead. I want him to see dozens of my exhibits, if I ever finish this first one, to walk me down the aisle and play with my kids.

Right. As if the last two hopes are even plausible, considering my hermit lifestyle.

"I wish you would have shared that with me over the phone." Dane clears his throat. "What's his number?"

"He's in a residential care facility. I can tell him all of this later."

Dane nods. He drums long fingers across the chrome edge of the Formica tabletop. "Got it, got it."

He whips out a pen from the inner pocket of his tailored suit jacket, not to be deterred. Scribbling enough zeros and commas to elicit a stare from me, he punctuates the number with a stab.

"This is their *starting* offer, Pearl. What do you think?"

"I . . . I'm sorry, who did you say this buyer was? That amount is Mob money."

Dane leans back in his chair. He folds his hands across a large silver belt buckle that gleams beside the window. "I can't share their personal details. But they love the specs on the house and are intrigued by the area's portfolio."

"Meaning?"

"They're into wine. I don't know that they'd want to turn your property into a vineyard, but they want to live closer to all their current favorites."

Ah, one of those. Probably another California transplant from Napa looking to expand their grape empire, or their wine collection to impress friends back home.

I shake my head. "My dad—we'd really need some time to consider everything. To get the house and my mom's affairs in order. This is all happening so fast."

Dane nods. He knows all about Sally's passing, though I didn't tell him. Maybe he read the small obit I had published in *The Willamette Times*.

"Of course. No problem. Just know that the buyer is very motivated. And they'd like to move in sooner than later. If you decide to sell within the month, there could be additional money thrown in."

I let his offer hang between us—linger over the scratched table and our half-drunk coffee mugs. Part of me is tempted. As my dad's sole heir, I could use an impressive sum like that down the line. Make it last. Museum curating as an associate has been rewarding emotionally and academically, but not financially by a long shot. Sally left me some cash, but I won't see any of it until probate court has completed its processes.

"I'll let you know if anything changes. But a month still feels too fast."

Dane slides his pen back into his jacket pocket. "You have my number."

He walks outside onto the sidewalk without a backward glance, as if cushioned and content in the fact that another sale would be a net win for him. My family, on the other hand, now has everything to lose.

———

Dull sunlight pierces the glass windows of the fourth-floor museum penthouse and casts my boots in a puddle of warmth where I stand in my assigned cube. I survey the artifacts that I sourced from the warehouse, spread along the walls of my corner; I think I have everything. Low voices carry from the opposite end of this floor, where I know Nettie is arranging her exhibit on Native ghost stories for the pop-ups that launch next week.

"Knock knock." Griffin is stone faced as he leans into my cube. The track lighting here reflects against his large wire-rimmed glasses, making him hard to read.

"Hey, I wanted to talk to you." I stand, brushing imaginary lint from my loose slacks. "I couldn't find enough masks from the years and region that I wanted, but I think expanding the theme will be more inclusive anyway—interesting, I hope."

Griffin nods. "Pearl, do you have a minute?"

I pause. "Everything okay?"

"I'm afraid not. The board is pretty upset that one of our artifacts is missing."

"The Buddha head. I know, I'm sorry it hasn't been—"

Griffin steps toward me with open palms. "Pearl, I need you to be honest with me."

"Of—of course," I stammer.

"Did you take the mask?" Griffin asks, his voice gruff. "Did you decide it meant something to you? I know you said your mom had a modern version like it, but that doesn't mean you can borrow this—"

"I didn't take it. What? I didn't steal anything."

"If you took it, you can put it back. We can save ourselves the mess of . . . of . . ." Griffin drops his hands to his side.

"Of what? Of . . . firing me?" My words squeak up an octave. A sad, girlish sound. "I didn't steal anything," I repeat, pleading.

Griffin purses his lips. "Pearl, we've reviewed the security footage. You were the only person in your staging room the morning you reported the mask stolen."

Don't be weak, Pearl. "It could have been taken the previous night. Or during the day, when the electrical grid was out."

"The door locks were engaged manually within an hour. Our backup generator was up and running until the main generator was examined and fixed, and we had Security deployed on all floors."

"But—I don't—I'm sorry, this doesn't make any sense. I didn't take the mask," I say, punctuating each word. "Griffin. Come on, you don't believe me? I love this museum. I love my work. I would never compromise any bit of history that I come in contact with here."

"I want to believe you, Pearl. I do," he says, crossing his arms. "But the board has taken a strict stance on these matters. We all care so much about preserving the artifacts that are entrusted to the museum. You know this. I hope you can understand."

Pummeling fear drops into my stomach. "Understand what?"

"You're being placed on administrative leave. Immediately. I need to walk you out."

Griffin frowns, as if it hurts him to say it. I stare at this man, my boss of the last six months, with whom I've done company-sponsored karaoke and brewery tours. "When can I come back? My life is here."

He grimaces. "Museum policy is that any employee under investigation will be placed on administrative leave until the facts are confirmed and, if needed, a separation agreement is drafted and signed."

I blanch. "A separation agreement?"

"You're welcome to return, Pearl," he says slowly. "Whenever the mask comes back."

The walk out to the front lobby is a long one, with Griffin silently following me down four flights of stairs. Hank the security guard, a man I've seen stationed in the main hall every day since I started, leads my walk of shame. We pass the room that houses the new photography exhibit of sixties rock bands, the stairwell that leads to the American Art collection and its breathtaking portraits of Mount Hood, the Graphic Arts collection featuring my favorite etching on cream laid paper, and the hall housing the Native American Art collection that will move into the new pavilion once construction has finished. The mainstays of my professional world all slip behind me without the slightest goodbye. As if they, too, are already certain of my guilt.

Kai crosses into our path when we reach the front desk. I haven't seen him in days. He pushes back a shock of black hair from his forehead. "Hey, Pearl. Feel like grabbing lunch later? Griffin, you in?"

I shake my head, tears welling in the corners of my eyes.

"Pearl?"

But I don't reply.

At the brick entrance to the museum, Griffin reaches my side. "I'll be in touch. And if you decide to return the mask, you know where to find us."

The walk to the employee parking lot buzzes with construction drills and laughter from students of the nearby university. My phone pings, but I don't bother checking it. The text message, or whatever push notification, can wait.

I drive home on autopilot, braking when I must and accelerating when traffic does. Griffin may as well have fired me versus the drawn-out stifling of administrative leave. I don't know where that mask is. I haven't seen it since I first reported it missing. On top of the choking stress from my personal life, this professional setback is too much. Rage vibrates across my core like a jackhammer on the pavilion—I shouldn't have to deal with this, or Sally's bullshit letters—before the tears unleash, splashing onto the steering wheel. Sally's cryptic words, the human remains I found, and the questions she's force-fed me after death are more than any one person should have to process. Career implosion shouldn't be allowed as the shit topping of the day.

I park below my apartment. Peeling myself from the driver's seat feels impossible, too difficult a task to accomplish after the day's revelations—after the last week.

My phone pings again from my tote bag. "Not now," I growl, wiping my face.

The Lie She Wears

After trudging up the stairs, wishing for the umpteenth time that this complex had an elevator, I unlock my door, then slip inside.

Night falls quickly. Instead of choosing liquor or food, I collapse onto the couch. Scroll through options on the eight streaming platforms I subscribe to and will my brain to shut off.

Where did the mask go? Was it misplaced or stolen? Why in the world would someone want a third-century Buddha head covering? How could Griffin and the board even think I could steal it—throw away my career and all the schooling I suffered through to get here?

Maybe I do want a drink.

Two hours into three bottles of beer and a new dating show featuring ex-convicts, I glance at the love seat of my living room. My catchall location for items from my parents' house. Anything relating to the business of Sally's death.

When Zelda moved out, I asked her to gather up whatever she thought I needed to have or to see, since she was Sally's most recent roommate. Zelda passed me a Bankers box of things from Sally's room to sort through. "Family valuables," she said, that she didn't feel comfortable combing through herself. Sally wanted so desperately to unload her secrets onto me, posthumously. Let's see what she kept close to her in life.

I heave the box over to the main couch, where I've decided I'm going to live for the rest of my days. On top, a red silk pocket contains my grandmother's jade ring—something I've been obsessed with since I was a kid. Medical records, an address book, paperwork, postcards for my dad, and loose photos are underneath. And a gift-wrapped present, no bow.

"Now, what could you be?" Feeling the warmth of my liquid dinner, I peel back the taped corners. It's rectangular and could be a box of some kind. Maybe it's the knitting kit that Sally usually hid inside a tin of Danish cookies.

My phone pings again, beside me on the couch. A reminder about the push notifications I ignored earlier.

I unlock my phone while continuing to pull at the wrapping paper. A few news headlines pop up, a reminder to pay the utilities bill on the ranch house, and a security alert for my phone—a warning that an AirTag has been found moving with me.

I rub my eyes. Reread the text. The owner of this item can see its location.

"What?" Chills skitter across my neck. This alert first pinged when I left the museum. Someone has been watching me—following me—since downtown Portland?

For a moment I'm frozen, glued to the couch, staring at the phone. At the red dots that show the AirTag is basically on top of me. Then I hurry to the kitchen counter, where I left my bag. I dump out its contents. Feel inside the zippered pockets and press my hands against all surfaces of the inside and outside of the tote.

"Mia the Kia," I murmur. I run outside to my car, down the stairs to the ground level, and paw the interior of each tire enclosure beneath the yellow wash of a streetlamp. Palm each side of my Kia sedan until I grasp a small white disc taped to the bottom of the bumper.

I hold it up to eye level. An AirTag. Someone tracked me to the Northwest District and my apartment.

I glance around me, spinning in my panic. Scan the pristine white sidewalk that gets power washed monthly, and the old couple walking their shih tzu before bed beside the newly planted ferns.

I run back up the stairs. Step inside, then lock the dead bolt behind me. My heart thumps against my ribs—ticks up its rhythm—as I turn and peer through the peephole. No one steps into view. No one chased me from the parking lot.

I open my closed fist to stare at the disturbing white AirTag. My vision blurs for a moment, bleeding my flesh into the circle's outline. I flip it over, searching for any indication of its owner, but find none. I click into the notification on my phone and read the serial number of the AirTag but not the name of the person who planted it on my car.

The Lie She Wears

"What the hell is this?" I whisper. Sweat lines my collar and soaks the underarms of the black sweater I wear.

Someone wanted to know where I live. Probably to attack in the middle of the night.

The impulse to choose flight surges within me, and I dash to the kitchen counter where I dumped out my bag. Grab my wallet, double back to the couch and the gift, then retrace my steps to Mia.

Traffic is light this late on a Tuesday. I barrel into downtown, past the museum—adrenaline punting my buzz—and only slow my speed when I reach the Willamette River's edge. I park beneath one of the concrete overhangs. Turn off my lights before they blind one of the people sleeping huddled against the wall.

The rest of the wrapping paper on the gift tears with ease. If it is a Danish tin, I'll place the AirTag inside, then chuck it into the river to float upstream. With any luck, this AirTag—and the person who taped it to my car to track my whereabouts—will be in Washington state by tomorrow.

Light from a streetlamp reflects off the glass covering in my lap. Instead of an aluminum box of knitting needles and yarn, the gift is a framed photo of a sprawling tree.

A wave of new emotions floods my chest. Confusion and disappointment that I can't use this—can't make the AirTag travel somewhere else on it. Resting my head back, I consider my options. I still have the AirTag on me. I could throw it in the river directly and hope it travels a mile before it sinks. Either way, I'll be rid of it.

"Damn," I whimper in the near dark. "What is going on today? What is happening?"

Fresh irritation rises in me, and I toss the framed photo to my passenger seat, more violently than I intended. The image of the oak tree shifts, knocked loose against my passenger door. A lined piece of paper is suddenly exposed, behind the photo.

I inhale a sharp breath. With trembling fingers, I dismantle the backing board. Pluck the note, then unfold its creased paper, bracing myself for a new grenade from my mother.

Chapter Fourteen

The Photo Frame

Dear daughter—

You should know that I gave up my hopes for you, because the timing wasn't right. None of it felt right at the time, but I knew I wanted you to live and to have a life of your own. Now, I hope our relationship can outpace those doubts and fears. That it can finally be allowed to take root and thrive. It's a wish of mine, at least.

Wise old men plant trees whose shade they know they will never sit in.

Your father would agree. And if anything happens to me, remember this.

—Mom

Chapter Fifteen

Pearl

Wispy clouds stretch across the blue sky during my drive into downtown. Zelda was nice enough to offer to meet me near the museum during the week, since she had an interview in nearby Goose Hollow. I wanted to decline—didn't want anyone to catch me loitering after I was placed on leave. Instead, I readily agreed, and donned nice slacks and a goose-down vest. Business casual attire, in case Zelda assumed I'm taking a late lunch.

At this point, I have too many questions about Sally's letters, and about Sally herself. I need the eyewitness accounting of her former live-in nurse. I need answers.

After I read the new letter, and chucked the AirTag all by itself into the water, I sat at the river's edge for an hour, poring over each line and her choice of words. *I gave up my hopes for you. A life of your own. It's a wish of mine.* While it made sense regarding our strained relationship, she never spoke so candidly or kindly to me while she was alive. Each sentence was filled with compassion, with hope, and with ownership of her poor choices—everything I ever wanted from her. It was a balm to some of the hurt Sally inflicted across my life. I didn't trust it.

I parallel park on a street bookending Pioneer Courthouse Square, squeezing in between two electric vehicles. The plaza teems with shoppers, students, and harried white-collar workers grabbing a bite from one of the food trucks on location. I enter the urban park, scanning the crowds for a threat.

Since I discovered the AirTag last night, I've been on edge. No one has followed me that I can tell—no industrial vans with tinted windows or leering drivers staring at me while waiting for a light to turn green. Yet each time I leave my apartment, my insides twist, anticipating a stranger pursuing me, their footsteps quickening before I have a moment to scream.

If this is a stalker, it would be my first. And still, the AirTag doesn't feel isolated. It was taped to my car while I was parked at the museum—the same day that I was placed on administrative leave after the Buddha mask went missing. Are the two connected?

I stop short at a concrete fountain, my breathing rattling in time with my racing pulse. Who would know the value of the mask, if it was stolen, and why would they desire to track my whereabouts? I'm of no use to that person without my employee badge and its special authorizations. If I tell Griffin or the police about the AirTag, it could prove someone is targeting me—my career. But would it only heap more attention on me and the buried secrets at the ranch house?

"There you are." Zelda appears at my side. She smiles as she lifts a grease-soaked white paper bag. "Voodoo?"

I take in Zelda's innocent offer, the levity in her brown eyes. Short dark hair that curls in at her jaw reminds me of the haircut I gave myself when I was five years old.

"No doughnuts for me after noon," I reply. "Thanks."

"Suit yourself. Should we head over to the steps?"

Zelda leads the way through the crowd, against my better judgment. A pair of street musicians bangs out a melody on a keyboard and a cajón, drawing onlookers that stand shoulder to shoulder. My skin prickles, instincts rising to maintain my distance from strangers.

"Pearl?" Zelda glances behind to me, calling above the music. "You okay?"

People in front of me and beside me throw their hands from their pockets, bob along to the beat, and lean into my space. I freeze, unable to move. I focus on the ground, on the dozens of pairs of shoes stepping around me—now dancing back and forth—then the ground tilts up and away. I try to steady myself as a pair of tan pump boots crosses my eyeline. The same shoes of the person who was sneaking around the staff hallway of the museum.

I look up. A woman with dark hair is wearing the boots and is already five people ahead—now eight.

"Pearl? What's going on?" Zelda grabs my elbow, concern drawing her eyebrows together. Without waiting for an answer, she leads me away from the noise and the percussion, to a set of chrome tables and chairs. A man at the next table is taking a Zoom meeting on his laptop.

I sit opposite Zelda, still scanning the crowd. No way that could've been the same person from the museum—right? Was she following me?

Zelda tucks a fringe of hair behind her ear. "Are you okay? You look . . . unwell."

I purse my lips, searching for an answer. And although I don't owe my mother's former nurse an explanation—for several reasons—I need Zelda's recollections now. I need her to take me seriously.

"Too loud," I finally reply, lifting a hand to my flushed cheek. I lay my tote bag on the table. "I guess I'm a little sensory sensitive."

"No, I get it. The bass was hitting my chest too," she adds. "Made my ribs vibrate. Reminded me of back when I used to go to bars without earplugs."

I only nod, suddenly thinking about Zelda looking wounded, sitting five rows back from the front at my mother's funeral. As if she merited a spot next to the casket.

"Hey, Pearl." Zelda lifts an excited eyebrow. "What do you call a deaf dog?" She waits.

"I don't know. What?" I relent.

"It doesn't matter. It can't hear you anyway."

She breaks into a smile that gradually recedes, the longer I don't return it.

She pulls from the white paper bag a chocolate glazed doughnut with a set of vampire fangs. "You know, I don't think I've had Voodoo Doughnuts since I was ten years old. So many memories of summer trips to Portland, while growing up in Bend."

"Did you like it there?"

"Oh, it was all right. Definitely colder but not always hotter. Small but not too small. Friendly but people minded their business." Zelda smiles. She's not that much older than me, though some of her black hair is beginning to surrender to gray. A small mole sits above her upper lip.

"Was it nice growing up here?" she asks.

"Sort of. But I prefer the coast. What brought you to Portland?"

In the last almost year since Sally hired Zelda as her live-in nurse, I haven't asked this woman much in the way of personal questions. I didn't see her enough for that.

Zelda lifts both eyebrows. "Oh, work, I guess. More opportunity."

"I might have to do that—move, for a job." Wherever an art museum would be willing to hire me, after being accused of theft.

Surprise stretches Zelda's cat-eye eyeliner, and I hurry to backtrack. "Not that I would—soon. Just hypothetically. I mean, my current museum needs some upgrades, the electrical grid has been having trouble, shorting out."

I wince. Pause my babbling long enough to sneak a glance at Zelda's subdued expression and check whether she believes me. Although I know I didn't steal anything, I'm not ready to share that I got placed on leave.

A frenzied beat from the street musicians garners shouts from the crowd, while Zelda is quiet a moment. "Where would you move?"

I release a heavy breath. Push up the sleeves of my vest and the white cotton shirt underneath. "Sorry, I'm—I wouldn't. I'm not planning to. I'm still processing everything—" I wave a palm across the tabletop. "And I would never leave my dad. I'm going to need more time to . . . I guess find a new normal before I make any big decisions."

The Lie She Wears

The real estate agent's offer to buy the ranch house hovers behind my lips. Instead of blurting it, too, I find a crack in the table's sealant and run my fingers across the sharp edge.

Zelda retrieves a water bottle from her shoulder bag, then takes a sip. "Well, for what it's worth, I don't think your mom would mind you selling the property. She had become somewhat erratic recently. Not her usual self."

I stiffen. "What does that mean?"

"Your house is incredible. And you're the executor, right?"

"Our family lawyer is. Why does that matter?"

"I just mean, eventually, you'll hold all the cards as the sole heir to your parents. You'll be able to do whatever you want with the house. Must be freeing, I would think."

I peer at Zelda while she innocently takes another drink. This is a massive decision that I don't really feel like discussing with a near stranger.

"And what would my mom's erraticism have to do with her approving of a sale?" I ask, barely hiding my irritation.

Zelda shifts in her chair, the legs screeching on concrete. "I just mean Sally's memory was getting worse, and at an accelerated rate, toward the end. She'd probably be fine with whatever you chose."

"Worse, how?"

Zelda shrugs. "You know, she'd forget where her car keys were. She'd run around the house, looking for something, and then she'd forget what she initially wanted. She started leaving items in weird places, calling them her 'just-in-case stash.'"

"I saw there was a container of pepper left in a shoe by the front door."

"Then she called me the wrong name a few times. And her mood swings were getting rapidly intense. I tried to ensure she got the right nutrition and took her medication on schedule, but she wasn't the most, um, compliant patient."

I narrow my eyes. "No kidding."

The whole reason Zelda was hired to begin with was because my mom showed signs that her awareness was going. She would find herself outside with no idea why or how she got there. She left me a voice message where she couldn't remember who she called, and in the middle of a sentence, began leaving a message for the landscaping service. Sally, in particular, thought it would be easier to have a medical professional on-site.

Zelda sets her water bottle down. She sighs. "I do think that she never lost focus on what was most important to her: you. She always talked about you, wondered where you were and what exciting artifact you were examining at the moment."

I scoff. That's the kind of mother I would have liked—but that was rarely Sally. Her words were more terse, her expressions more critical than the engaged woman Zelda describes.

"That would surprise me," I say. "But I admit, the last few months left her . . . changed."

Retrieving my phone and the picture I took of the creased note that was hidden in the framed photo, I place it on the table between us. "Sally wrote this letter. And I found it in the box of stuff you gave me, her items from her nightstand. Does this make any sense to you?"

I scan Zelda's coiffed chin-length hairstyle, the clear nail polish coating on her manicured cuticles, and the stylish, oversize cream sweater that hugs her lean frame. Though she's ditched the nurse's scrubs she used to wear each time I came over to the house, she might still be willing to help. To gauge Sally's meaning. And I can't keep staring at these letters all by myself.

Zelda leans forward. She holds out her hand. "Can I . . . ?"

Although I have no clue who planted the AirTag on my car, and Zelda could be so much more than a slightly aloof nurse, I don't see another way. I slide the phone to her. "Sure."

She scans each line. "I think I know this. I mean, I know this quote. 'Wise old men plant trees whose shade they know they will never sit in.'"

"It wasn't Sally?"

The Lie She Wears

Zelda shakes her head. "No, I've seen it before."

A scream rips through the crowd of dancers and I startle, nearly leaping from my chair. Arms fly, pumping from the middle of the circle; then loud laughter rises, catching among the audience.

Zelda gathers our stuff while I work through my sudden panic. She motions for us to leave. We cross back through the plaza, taking the long way around the still-pulsing crowd of onlookers, walking south toward the Park Blocks.

"Down this way," she says, handing me my phone and my bag.

With each step closer to the museum, my stomach twists. I scan the people who pass us, men and women in suits and light jackets, men with handlebar mustaches, women with Mohawks and long braids in diverse Portland fashion. But no Griffin. No Kai. No Nettie.

As the brick entrance to the art museum looms into view, Zelda veers from the sidewalk. She marches across the grass of the park to the base of a large tree. Poorly carved initials and hearts cover the trunk, thanks to decades of teenagers wielding switchblades—or adults like me. My leather bag rests against my hip, reminding me that Sally's red-stained knife is zipped inside.

Zelda hugs the elbows of her sweater, peering at a bronze plaque laid in the ground. The words inscribed across the front read: "A society grows great when old men plant trees in whose shade they shall never sit."

"See?" she says with a smile. "The letter from Sally kind of paraphrases It, but It's nearly the same. I'm useful after all."

The hitch in her tone—was it playfulness or accusation?—catches my attention. She watches me with steady eye contact, while a breeze pushes a strand of black hair across her face.

This woman owes me after she let Sally get behind the wheel. And I'm done with vague statements. I inhale a sharp breath. "Why do you think Sally wrote this to me? What does her letter mean?"

The other notes I've found were all easy enough to understand, despite the coded words and phrases she chose. Each letter was clearly written to me, in the demanding and insistent tone she used with me in life—but also with more heart than I've ever heard from her face-to-face. To quote Sally, *That's not nothing.*

This message, though much shorter than the others, strikes me as the most confusing, the most veiled. Although she addresses me and mentions my dad, and the picture she chose is of the oak tree on our property that was hiding human remains, the text here is beyond cryptic.

Zelda turns to examine the tree's carvings. *Hollis + Lamar 4ever. PNW. PDX Life.* "I really don't know. I'm sorry."

I focus on her expression, primed to catch her in a lie. "Did she ever mention something about an intruder who came to the house? Or some event that scared Sally really badly?"

The sun shifts above the branches, and then Zelda's eyes seem to flash. "The month before she died, Sally was pretty anxious. She insisted that she was being followed."

"What made her think that?"

"Said she found something on her car. A tracking device, I guess. Sounds kind of silly now—"

"Was it an AirTag?"

"Maybe, I'm not—"

"Zelda, please." My chest constricts, and I work to keep the panic from my voice. "What was the tracking device?"

Zelda looks off to the side. "I really don't know, Pearl. She said that she found it while she was out running errands, then chucked it into a random trash bin. I never saw it."

Frustration battles with relief in my chest. There's no way of knowing, for sure, but the last thing I want is for Sally to have been harassed and stalked before she died. Almost as much as I want to believe the AirTag I found on my car was a random scammer looking to take advantage of me as a woman—not someone driven by more personal motives. Someone whom Sally knew.

"Did you believe her?" I ask.

Zelda twists her mouth to the side. "I want to say yes."

"... But?"

Zelda brings her gaze to mine. Her expression softens, and I know the words before she speaks them, my heart splintering a fraction further. "She was a woman with an early degenerative cognition. When I was first hired, I thought it a little silly, honestly, that she wanted a live-in nurse. I didn't think she needed one. Her condition was mild, in my opinion, and it was almost like she was lonely. Like she wanted the company."

I lift an eyebrow. "Or she was aware that someone was watching her and she wanted to feel safe, sleeping at night."

"Toward the end, I think her condition worsened quickly. Sometimes, she didn't know what she was saying, Pearl. She probably shouldn't have been driving those last few weeks."

I nod, working to contain the emotion that swells in my throat. Sally could have imagined the AirTag, it's true. But that wouldn't explain the bones I found in our field. How would that explain the messed-up scavenger hunt that Sally laid out for me before she died, and the real, physical AirTag that I found on my own car?

"Listen," Zelda says. "I have to get home. I have another interview scheduled tomorrow. Do you want to keep talking about this? I know it's helpful sometimes to review memories after a loved one dies with someone who knew them."

I open my mouth to speak when a lump lodges in my throat. "You didn't know Sally, though." I cough. "Neither of us did."

Chapter Sixteen

SARAH

New York City, 1992

The cleanup on Park Avenue was atrocious. I'm talking muscle matter, brain bits, and—I'm not kidding—teeth. Staying put as I was, waiting for every police officer on the island to take my statement, I had a front-row seat to the scene. Someone behind me, someone who was waiting in that godforsaken line to get a bite, wailed at one point, "She was someone's sister. Someone's friend. Someone's daughter."

I replied, "Someone's giant pain in the ass," but no one could hear me above the exhaust of the next bus that arrived within fifteen minutes. New York City Transit doesn't fuck around, even around crime scenes.

Not that any crime occurred. Almost every witness who was interviewed said that the woman slipped into the street while she was attacking *me*. According to the detective I spoke with, Sergeant Mills, only one person thought I might have deliberately pushed her. I asked him, pressed him for that person's name. Asked that they be pointed out in the crowd that was still onlooking, but the sergeant only scoffed. Said, *That won't be happening.*

I gave my name. My real name, as the cop made me break out my driver's license to confirm. He asked, "Someone else said your name was Emily," and I shrugged.

The Lie She Wears

"Everyone thinks they know me," I said, and he nodded, the detail explained away.

It was by luck that I made eye contact with her. A young woman with wispy blond hair and big brown eyes. She flinched when she saw me assessing the crowd, searching for my tattletale. She ducked behind a large man, then scurried off to the end of the street. When she reached the corner, she turned back. We locked eyes once more before she skittered away, and I knew. She reported that I pushed the dead woman, the native New Yorker, in front of the bus. Amy, I think I heard a cop say was the victim's name.

It was also by luck that the police finished with me a few minutes later. And a smidge of more good fortune that no one noticed me depart on the same route as the little busybody.

Heavy, hot air whooshes over me where I stand on the platform for the next 6 train, several feet away from the wispy blond woman. She clutches a handbag to her chest as she waits.

My fingers tingle as the train arrives and the doors part with a loud exhale of compressed air. I take the train car behind the one the woman chooses, and we ride together for ten stops. Each time the train pauses at a new location, she glances up at the passengers who enter her car before furtively casting her gaze down to her lap again.

"What are you running from?" I ask aloud.

The old man dressed in oversize trousers next to me sniffs but doesn't comment.

Though I have an appointment in thirty minutes to show that penthouse apartment to a prospective buyer, I stay seated. I watch and wait for this wisp to do something in the next car—I can't tear my eyes from her through the narrow glass window connecting us. A tingle begins in my fingers, then grows, moving into my chest. Usually, I manage to ignore the sensation—the itch that tells me I'm going to need to do something soon. Steal a pen from a convenience store. Call a suicide hotline and fuck with the counselors. Manipulate a man into giving me his credit card.

Yet, staring at the woman's wheat-colored, stringy hair, I feel a pull toward her. Like a magnet, propelling me forward yet forcing me to maintain my distance.

When we reach the next stop—Canal Street—my quarry gets to her feet. She sways unsteadily, but a nice gentleman in a graphic tee and backward cap offers her his hand. She recoils, ever the scared rabbit, and stumbles to the now-parting doors. I do likewise.

Excitement swells my chest as I continue following her, taking the stairs up and out to fresh air toward Bowery. A man whistles at me, a construction worker who appreciates my formfitting trousers. I ignore him, not wanting to draw attention, to elicit a glance behind from my new bestie.

She heads south down Bowery into Chinatown, and the perfume of ginger and soy washes over me. Instantly, I'm transported to Sundays when my grandmother would force me to constantly stir a giant pot of ching po leung soup as a child, while she made dumplings. Even when I was too tired to stand during the hour it cooked, and my arm dropped, burning my tender skin on the outer rim of the pot, she would insist I remain at the stove's edge or earn the stripes of her wooden spoon. She broke a lot of spoons on my backside. But eventually she upgraded to plastic when I was a teenager. And I got to return the abuse with a sturdier weapon the final time she came for me.

Outside a family restaurant called Golden Beak, the woman pauses. She rummages in her handbag, a worn black leather satchel, then withdraws a set of keys. A smile spreads across her heart-shaped face, and I'm close enough to spy the dangly earrings she wears—little hearts. She exhales, dropping her shoulders, as if she's been holding a breath since she left the so-called crime scene.

I clear my throat. The woman startles, nearly drops her keys, as she locks her gaze on my face. Recognition clatters across her small features. A man and a woman with matching braids exit the Golden Beak, laughing, stepping into her view of me. She twists around them, suddenly frantic to view me, to keep me in her sights.

The Lie She Wears

I lift my hand in a wave. Then I widen my eyes and smile as broadly as my lips will go until pain sears the corners of my mouth.

The woman gasps. She jams her keys into the street-level door, and then she disappears inside.

A grandfather type steps out of the restaurant, wearing a dirty apron and wiping his hands with a discolored towel. He glances back at where the wisp skittered up the steps to her apartment. He shoots me a wary glare.

"Everything okay here? Looks like you upset Mary."

"Oh, sure, all fine," I say, leaning onto my heels. "My sister's having stomach issues. You know, bad meat at lunch."

"You're her sister? I've heard a lot about you." The old man breaks into a toothy grin. "Nice to meet you, Sarah."

I return a warm smile of my own. "Likewise."

Later in the afternoon, a quick call to Errol confirms that he can find out sweet, vigilant Mary's place of employment. Rather, a Hound named Megan, who works at the post office, can. When Errol shares that he found Mr. Jean Jacket's address like I asked, I dismiss the info regarding the thief. That guy's old hat, and I already had the client change the locks on that apartment. I have a new object of interest.

"Leave it to you to track down anything and anyone," I say.

He scoffs into the phone. "Obviously."

As twins, Errol and I have always been close. But in moments like these, when he comes through in a way only a sibling can, part of me wants nothing less than to slice open his core and crawl inside for a warm snuggle. To take a happy nap together once again, like we did in the womb wherein the line between us was virtually nonexistent.

Normally, Errol is the only person I can tolerate being close with. But as my thoughts of Mary begin to come at all hours, the tingle in my palms says otherwise. I want to know her habits. Everything about her. Her routes for an afternoon walk. The hour she takes a dump and the time she falls into REM sleep at night, too deeply to hear the shift of her dead bolt, unlocking her apartment to the sick, sadistic world.

Click.

Chapter Seventeen

PEARL

My mother could be hard to read. Rather, she was perfectly accessible to my dad, to people she met while on the hunt for a rare find, to the PTA, which she chaired at one point while I was in elementary school. But never to me. I often wondered if there was something wrong with me, that she connected with everyone else to my exclusion.

Then, at one point, I began wondering if something was wrong with her.

Although she cycled through friendships and antiques circles throughout my childhood, a few years ago she crossed paths with someone new. An actual friend who seemed to stick, who offered Sally a firsthand look into wholesale. Ursula Romano.

Two notes ring out and announce my arrival to Ursula's antique shop when I pull open the glass door. Jon Bon Jovi belts out an eighties hit from the speakers overhead. On my way to the main counter, I pass a wooden shelf that displays specially designed pincushions—several resembling dolls of the voodoo variety—then a circular rack of vintage dresses.

As I approach the clear case, I get an abrasive reminder of why my mother loved this place—why she first met Ursula, and how they bonded over their eccentric interests. A trio of Venetian masks glares from the center of the wall behind the cash register. Each mask bears a different motif or theme: springtime, carnival, then bottle tops that an artist probably thought were akin to modern art. I swear under my breath. Avoid their eye contact as I hit the bellhop bell on the counter.

Someone clears their throat behind me. "Some people call it art. Like, art deco. You know, the world-revered style of artistic product design?"

I turn and lock eyes with an older woman. "Actually, yes. I'm an art museum curator."

She sniffs but doesn't reply. Blond and dyed-pink hair reminds me of Cyndi Lauper circa 1985. Heat flushes my cheeks as I resume waiting at the glass counter. On the wall, the mask's eyebrows now seem raised in judgment versus mere menace.

The door to a back room opens as a woman wearing a brown apron enters the shop. She passes an orderly display of license plates mounted on the wall, and a series of vintage postage stamps arranged on a corkboard. The shop's unique perfume of dust and hand sanitizer grows as Ursula approaches.

"Pearl, hey. You're early," she says, before she leans around me to address the nosy woman. "Hi, Connie."

"Hey. Did the mini gramophone come in yet?"

"Not yet. But I'll call you when it does."

Connie continues on her way, browsing through an aisle of secondhand books. Ursula greets me with a damp smile. She gestures toward a corner with an armchair, a rocking chair, and a child-size bookshelf placed on a worn rug. "Pearl, step into my office."

I follow Ursula, then take a seat in the rocking chair. After Zelda left to get ready for her next interview, I didn't want to hang around downtown and risk being caught out front of the museum. And although there's nothing about the third letter that suggests there are more hidden notes waiting for me to discover them, everything still feels unsettled. Imbalanced and teetering toward disaster.

"Thanks so much for meeting with me."

Ursula crosses a slender leg underneath her. Gray hair spirals from her ponytail. "Happy to. How are you holding up?"

"Good, I think."

Ursula stares at me. "Gosh, you look so much like her."

"Sally?"

"Well, yeah. I think it's your forehead. Or your cheeks. It's been ages since you and I have seen each other—before the funeral, I mean. We didn't really get to catch up there."

"Right." I nod. "When was the last time?"

Ursula turns her gaze up and to the left. She slides both hands into the pockets of her apron. A tattoo of three trees on the base of her index finger peeks out from the canvas material.

"Oh, I'll bet you were finishing grad school. So, a few years ago."

"That's right, you came to the dinner my mom held." Truthfully, Sally didn't want to host anything, but it was cheaper than inviting people to a restaurant and then footing the bill.

Ursula wears a sad, worn smile. "Your mom was pretty great. Even though she had her issues."

"Like, how secretive she was?"

Ursula smirks. "She liked her secrets. Sally was fairly open with me, though she was never into discussing her childhood in New York. Or the later years in New Jersey."

"New Jersey? When did she live there?"

"Ah, she didn't tell you? I wouldn't have even known but one time she shared that she moved there after meeting your dad in New York."

"Huh. I always thought they met in New York, then moved out to Oregon together."

"I think she came here from Jersey. Then he followed."

"Okay," I say, drawing out the word. "When did you last talk to my mom before she died? Did she seem worse than normal? Was she calling you different names?"

I remember, over the summer, Sally was wrapping a gift for the neighbor's grandchild. She told me to come look at a baby onesie she bought, but she called me Victoria. When I corrected her, she turned sheet white, as if she didn't recognize me.

Ursula's expression softens. Another hit from the eighties—a Michael Jackson song—hums from the store's overhead speakers. The front door chimes as the woman who was asking about a gramophone exits.

"Pearl, I can't begin to imagine how hard losing her was. She was your mother, despite any differences you had."

"But?"

"But Sally was as sharp as a tack the last time we spoke. She brought up a lunch we had three years ago, where a cucumber was"—she clears her throat—"oddly shaped."

I lift both eyebrows. "She remembered that?"

"The week before she died, yes." Ursula offers a knowing smile. "That salad, it . . . uh . . . it left quite an impression."

So, Sally's cognitive abilities weren't so shot when she died. Even though I myself witnessed some difficulty, and Zelda also confirmed Sally's memory was faulty, my mom had enough of her wits remaining to make a dick joke with her best friend.

"Why did you like her?" I ask in a quiet voice.

"God, I mean . . ." Ursula releases a heavy breath. "Sally was very thoughtful—always doing little acts of kindness and surprising me and others with them. A coffee that she picked up on her way here, or an extra bouquet of tulips that she got for half off at the farmers' market at Portland State. She was generous and selfless like that."

"Sure, I've witnessed that part of her. But when she wasn't putting on a show for everyone, when it was just the two of you, was she different?"

Sally's scribbles have haunted my thoughts, along with memories of her criticisms of my life choices, my career, my looks, and my clothing. She made it clear more than once how disappointed I made her. Just this last March, while Sally was in a daze, she said I could never be half the daughter she was meant to have.

Her words stung. And no amount of generous showboating could assuage that hurt.

Ursula shakes her head. "No, Pearl. I'm afraid not. She was the same way with me when we were alone—and I tried to return the favors to her. Whenever I had a new shipment of an item she wanted, or heard where a Giulio Venetta mask might be on sale in the Pacific Northwest, I'd pass along the info to her."

I purse my lips, unwilling to reveal my intense, conflicted feelings about this description of the terse woman who raised me. The fact that Sally was a kind and enthusiastic friend to her favorite antiques dealer—who regularly did her favors—actually tracks with her being covertly self-serving.

"Was there anyone who Sally didn't get along with? Someone who might have scared her?"

Ursula taps a white manicured nail filed to a point against the armrest. "I don't know that anyone scared her. Your mom had this way of reducing anyone that got in her way, of making people feel small who deserved it."

And others who didn't, but whatever.

"But Sally had an ongoing feud with a guy named Finn Hoskie. He was the head of client relations for the Gillian's in Seattle for twenty years. He frequently made fun of the items that Sally would suggest for auction. He never liked her, and she didn't like him."

"Any idea why?"

"I mean, it lasted so long, I'm honestly not sure anymore. Finn has been in the business for ages, and before then he hunted down antiques on his own, from what I hear." Ursula pauses, looking up to her left. "Gillian's is the big league for anyone like your mom—like me, and other amateur antique lovers. I know Sally felt looked down on because she wasn't a PhD. And Finn was probably annoyed at the seemingly random trinkets Sally would offer before she zeroed in on masks."

"But Sally brought in that series of Giulio Venetta masks. Altogether, the lot was a super-rare edition that Gillian's ended up selling for some insane amount of money."

Ursula nods. "My guess is that only annoyed Finn further, since he's been railing against her forever. A few years ago, he tried to get Sally banned from Gillian's. Later, when she ended up bringing that incredible find to the auction house, he was mortified. Sally threatened to sell each mask online herself if Finn wasn't demoted—Gillian's penance for the way they treated her in the past. And they agreed so they could take a percentage."

"Wow . . . Sally, vindictive? That tracks."

Ursula cocks her head to the side. "It was the beginning of the end of Sally's faculties, I think. She started behaving more inconsistently after that point, so I always wondered if her demand against Finn was a sign that something was off. That behavior was so unlike her."

"Sure. Um, do you know the last time Sally and Finn would have crossed paths? Would it have been for the auction in Seattle, back in February?"

The door's two-note melody chimes, and Ursula gets to her feet. Another customer.

"Finn has a second home here in Portland, so I'll bet they saw each other more recently than that. From what I hear, he goes to the Saturday Market for the community music every weekend."

I nod, then follow Ursula to the counter. "Did Sally ever tell you anything about someone who died—someone who may have threatened her?"

She shoots me a quizzical look, and I hurry to rephrase. "Do you think Sally was ever . . . violent?"

Ursula waves hello over my shoulder to the new shopper. Her smile is strained. "I think your mom had her demons. There were periods of time when she came off depressed, but she never told me what about. One time I asked if it was Liam that was frustrating her, and she said, 'What? Never.' Your parents respected and loved each other, I think, right up until Sally's death. If she had any big secrets, she kept them to herself."

"And Finn Hoskie? Do you think he would speak to me?"

If this Finn has been alive and antagonizing my mom for the last twenty years, he's definitely not buried in my backyard. But could he be the person Sally thought was following her? Did he plant an AirTag on Sally's car, then mine?

Ursula sighs. "Why are you so intent on digging up the past, Pearl? Can't a mother have her privacy, even in death?"

"Of course she can—I—I'm just tying up loose ends," I answer, chastened. "Plus, Sally was so organized. She would have wanted me to resolve them all, in her place."

I mumble my response, but Ursula is already striding behind the counter.

"Look, Pearl. If you just want to know more about her, I'd go home. She always said the ranch house was her happy place. Your answers are probably there."

I thank Ursula, then exit the antiques shop. Her advice is in line with Sally's behavior. Especially if Sally wanted to stick close to the evidence that she committed one of the worst crimes imaginable.

Gravel pings the underside of Mia the Kia as I pull into the driveway of the ranch house. Sunlight shifts during early afternoon, casting shadows across the chipped birdbath that Dad installed for Sally along the path to the front door when I was a child. I park just past it, still in view of the road.

The more I learn about Sally's mindset this year, her possible frame of thinking while writing the letters to me, the more I'm convinced I'm lacking vital details.

I skip entering the house, despite Ursula's advice to go home. I've been inside too often in the last week. Walking around the back to face the field, I pass the row of shrubs Dad sourced from a local nursery and that Sally planted beside the sliding glass door. One shrub has been nearly uprooted, as if trampled on.

"If Sally killed someone—or someone died on our property—how did Dad play into it?" I muse to the greenery. "Did he know about the death?"

During my next visit, I'll deliver the most recent batch of mail to him, currently sitting on the passenger seat of my car. Along with the two dozen outstanding questions I have.

If Sally experienced so much trauma that she refused to speak on it to anyone, maybe it started with her childhood in New York. Sally always said she left that place on a sprint, that it wasn't for her, and her life was made 1,000 percent better in Oregon with my dad—with me, she always added, I thought reluctantly.

If what Ursula says is true, that Sally was beloved by all except for Finn Hoskie, my priorities become twofold: I need to learn more about Finn and find out who else didn't love Sally—anyone who might have had reason to follow her using a tracking device before she died. Ticking that second box could lead me to the name of Sally's victim and help me understand who is watching me now.

Reviewing the third letter on my phone, I can see her hints pointing to the oak tree. To the burial location of the body and the necklace of a Catholic saint. The second letter I found in the attic is straightforward—except the final sentence. In writing about her fears coming for her, she wrote, *Your swing set was my favorite way to fly.* She wrote about flying with regard to balloons at the museum—which directed me to the oak tree on our land. Why mention the swing set?

I scan the stretch of yard directly ahead of me, to the small pond where my swing set used to stand, after it was moved from the shed's current location.

I turn to the small storage unit and lightly push its door open. Shelves that my dad installed here when I was six years old line the walls, above the compacted dirt of the floor. I remember my age because my swing set—a plastic structure gifted to us by a neighbor—occupied this spot, until one day it didn't. My dad relocated it closer to the pond about halfway down our property. When I asked him why he had moved it—swinging was my favorite activity at the time—from the very convenient ten paces from the side door, he replied that we all have to make sacrifices.

"As a six-year-old . . ." I muse to the rows of Craftsman hand tools. "I had to make a sacrifice in moving my swing set."

I touch the red rubber handle of a pair of pliers mounted on a tool board, reflecting on his words. *We all make sacrifices. Families do that for one another.*

I want to tell him everything so badly. But no detail of this should be uttered over the phone. And every time I've wanted to visit him this week, some new meeting or revelation has cropped up, freezing me in fear or indecision.

"We all make sacrifices." I trace the outline of a hammer, graze the business end of a pair of tree shears that could snap a branch the size of my arm, and pause at a clear tray containing nails of varying sizes. As a contractor, Dad was equipped for any client looking to reno their home.

"Is that why the toolshed is on the side of the house?" I ask, turning toward the garage. "Because he had to sacrifice?"

Built in the sixties, this house came equipped with a two-car garage. My parents shared only one car throughout their relationship, and Dad used the extra space for his power saw, for our extra freezer, for storage containers and dry goods. It would make sense to store all his tools in the garage, using the abundant space, instead of building a shed for them on the side of the house. Why sacrifice the convenience of storing his contractor tools in the garage and put them in an additional structure?

I toe the dirt with my boot inside the shed. The tip of my shoe sinks in an inch with little pressure at this time of year. I kick at the ground, and a chunk of earth dislodges. Using a shovel that rests in the corner of the shed, I start digging. Toss the dirt farther in, then return to the area until I hit something. Not rock. But something solid.

The light behind me shifts outside. Then a narrow beam highlights a black plastic bag poking through the loosened dirt.

My face blanches. The sweat that formed on my neck, across my chest, while I was digging freezes against my skin. I reach for the tip of the trash bag in a trance, unwilling and yet consumed with the need to see inside. My fingers shake as I tear a hole. Something pale appears, couched within the plastic, unmoving. Skin.

No. That can't be right. Sally hasn't mentioned a second body.

I lean closer, fighting the instinct that seizes my stomach and inwardly screams at me to run away—to slam the door to the shed closed and speed from here in a cloud of exhaust. Instead, I tear a larger hole in the plastic.

The something-pale takes further shape. A human hand covered in a waxy, soapy coating—and insects. Black bugs layer upon white larvae that freckle the skin, devouring their meal. I lurch backward before I count the digits; the thumb is missing. A dark-red stump is in its place, with insects steadily working the flesh in a never-ending feast.

My insides twist, and then my breakfast splatters onto the dirt floor. I crawl away, steeped in horror, knocking into a wooden drawer filled with washers—jostling the tool board above. Pliers crash onto the counter, my shoulders, down to the ground beside me as I scramble into the corner. Gasping, struggling to sit as far from the trash bag as possible, I scan the shed, frenzied. New paranoia chokes my sense of safety as I wipe my mouth and search for a new AirTag—evidence that I'm being watched as I digest the macabre truth: Sally killed a second person. A new John Doe on our property.

Eyes wild, feverish, I bend at an angle to suss out new hiding places. Anywhere a tracking device—a camera?—could fit, and see something that stops me short.

A letter. A piece of folded paper taped to the underside of the tool table.

As I reach for it with a shaking hand, a single word growls through my teeth: "Sally."

Chapter Eighteen

The Shed

Now, I can explain.
    I could tell you more about when the first man blindsided me and forced me to do the unthinkable, but I hate redundancy. And yet, you should know that it's context for why it all had to happen again.
    Your father and I were gone for the weekend, while you were at summer camp, thinking it was an opportunity to get out, just us. Do you remember? You were six years old and beyond excited to go to Canny Park with your friends.
    When we returned to the house, your father stayed outside to check on the vegetable garden, while I discovered a man hiding under our bed. He was lying in wait, the way that the bedtime stories always describe the monsters—crouched, curled, and eager to attack. Undetectable, save for the creaking floorboards that shifted with his weight when he tried to inch forward and take me by surprise.
    Most people think they don't have it in them to kill someone, let alone bury them on their property and

then walk past the site every day with their child. But when facing death incarnate, one unlearns all the social mores and ethics. Instead, one picks up a hammer and gets to work.

And even though I knew it was necessary—that there was no way around it—even then I feared what's recently come to pass. That, behind this man, there would be more.

Now, someone has been following me. I'm sure of it. And if I'm dead and gone, that could mean you're being watched too.

So, I guess I owe you an apology for looping you into my mess, and posthumously screwing up your life. Believe it or not, I've wanted you to thrive and done what I could to help you get there—even when that desire came out as more of a reprimand or a curse word. All I've ever wanted was to give you a fighting chance, Pearl.

To that end, my final wish will continue hanging, swaying in the breeze, waiting until you come for it. Or until someone else picks up a pen and damns you, too, to the next victim list.

—Mom

Chapter Nineteen

Pearl

My fingers tremble at my mouth, adrenaline flooding my veins. I scan the shed's interior, again, searching for a huddled black mass in the back of the ten-foot-long space, ready to attack.

Power tools and plastic bins of varying sizes of washers return my panic.

This, the clearest confession yet from Sally, confirming she killed not one but two victims. And she sounds confident it was the right decision.

The last paragraph makes no sense. What "final wish" is she talking about? How would I go to it?

"No, no, no," I whisper, pressing myself into the cobwebs of the corner. "This isn't happening."

The shed's door is slightly ajar, and then a breeze slips through the opening and rustles the black plastic. The sound unnerves me, as if the corpse is stirring—has only been waiting for its opportunity to break free the last two decades. I launch to my feet. Say goodbye to the fucked-up inheritance Sally left me, then slam the shed door shut.

I jump into my car. Compress the brake and throw the car into gear. Gravel kicks up as I reverse out of the driveway, but I manage to pull onto the road backward without falling into the ditch.

My engine roars as the countryside and the ranch house fade behind. I drive as far and as fast as I can away from the evidence of Sally's guilt, and the new target painted on my back.

A stoplight goes from yellow to red too fast, and I screech to a stop beside a massive high school that sprawls across a street corner.

There were no cameras in the shed, not that I saw. But that doesn't mean someone isn't watching me. Grabbing my phone from the center console, I check my notifications for any new AirTags nearby. None appears.

Ursula believed that Sally was in her right mind, far more than she wasn't, toward the end—a fact that checks out medically; depending on the situation or the conversation, people who have mild cognitive impairment can remember more details than might be expected. If Sally says she was being followed, she could have been.

Yet Zelda thinks Sally had completely lost it before she died. Something I only witnessed in spurts, after I moved home to Portland. So, which was it?

Would Zelda lie about how bad Sally's mental state was? Would Ursula gloss over the truth out of loyalty to an old friend?

My phone pings at the next light, nearly causing me to swerve across lanes. But it's only a text from the real estate agent, reiterating the offer from his clients to buy our family home. The hidden mess within.

Whenever I was this lost before, I always had my dad to go to. He didn't have all the answers—far from it. But he was an ear to my troubles when Sally wouldn't entertain me talking about boys or friends or anything that wasn't academic achievement.

I need to see him. And while I have debated whether I should contact the police out of a number of concerns—that my dad might be accused of involvement in these deaths, that I won't be allowed back to the ranch house to seek out more hidden letters—I can't spin my wheels any longer.

Sally has had enough benefit of the doubt.

Twin Pines Care Facility peeks out from a copse of lush conifers that secludes the quiet campus from the busy suburban boulevard. I park in a visitor parking spot—one of three—before the lobby's entrance. Street traffic hums behind me as I exit my car. The facility is a white stucco cube, one that I visited often when I first moved back home. When the stroke that we thought paralyzed the left side of my dad's body turned out to be the onset of multiple sclerosis, it took around six months before he volunteered to relocate. To take a *vacation to the resort of his dreams*, he said, not wanting us to fight him on it or to worry. Although the exterior of the building and the potted palm trees that flank the entrance could evoke Palm Springs, I'm too familiar with the interior at this point, with its faded and stained burgundy carpet, the plasma TVs that play morning talk shows without ceasing, and the food that, while prepared by a Michelin-trained chef, often ends up doused in olive oil to accommodate the majority of residents' dietary restrictions. Dad was only saying what he thought we wanted to hear.

The receptionist sets her phone down as I stride through the doorway, a manila envelope of mail for my dad under my arm. Air-conditioning swirls my hair, loose at the shoulders of my vest, as unmoored as I feel after yet another death discovery at the ranch house. The scents of cigarettes and something else—pine—mingle together in the lobby.

"Hello. Here to visit?" She taps the clipboard and its piece of paper. "Sign in, please."

I write down my name, my car's make and model, the time I've arrived, and my dad's name, Liam Davis.

The receptionist types on her computer's keyboard, large stone rings that she wears catching the light. "We've added some new off-campus excursions for residents who feel like a change of pace this fall. Have you heard? The Japanese Garden, the Portland Art Museum, and the Oregon Museum of Science and Industry. We encourage family members to join."

"The Portland Art Museum? When is that?" I startle from my daze. I didn't know my worlds would be colliding this season.

"Pretty soon. They have wine events on the first Friday of the month. We thought it might be fun for the night owls."

"Well, sign my dad up for that."

"And you too?"

"I—" I stop short before saying yes. I've been placed on administrative leave. I can't go to any event at the museum while I'm under investigation. Right?

Fresh disappointment drops my shoulders. "No, I can't. Not this time."

The receptionist makes a copy of my driver's license, then buzzes me in through double doors. On the path to the activities hall, where my dad should be, I pass a new room that's labeled "Spa and Sauna," stacks of fragrant white towels waiting on a wheeled cart beside the door. Another door that I pass is labeled "Calligraphy," beside a poster board detailing the off-campus activities the receptionist mentioned. Much has changed since I was last here—since before Sally died. A fact that has me on edge.

What will my dad say when he sees me? It's been five weeks since the crash, and I've only called him a few times. Each time I hear his voice, my throat locks up and I'm transported back to Sally's grave at Willamette Memorial Cemetery.

When my dad moved here, Sally visited several times a week. She didn't want him to feel forgotten just because he needed more consistent care than she could offer him, twenty-four seven. Considering she could barely return my phone calls some days, the duality that Sally presented stung.

Tears fill my eyes, unbidden, surprising me. I miss her, despite everything—or maybe the idea of her. She was my mother.

The glass-walled activity hall teems with sunshine when I reach its open doors. This, at least, looks largely the same as the last time I was here, but for a fresh coat of paint on the entrance to the enclosed garden outside. A new koi pond along the stone pathway shimmers.

Men and women sit in armchairs reading, laughing at round tables playing mah-jongg beside their wheeled oxygen tank carriers, or reclining on love seats in front of a plasma television where the movie *Die Hard* is playing. I scan the room, spotting my dad in his electric wheelchair in the corner, gazing through the glass.

Nerves zip along my skin as I approach him. My palms grip the envelope of mail too tightly, while guilt pinches below my jawline where the joint meets my ear. "Hey, Dad."

He turns, his eyes lighting up when he sees me. He lifts his left hand about six inches in a wave. Presses a button to turn the chair toward me.

"Pearl! You didn't say you were coming."

I lean down and give him a kiss on the cheek. Allow myself a moment to swallow the lump in my throat. "I thought I'd surprise you. VIP spot you have here."

When I pull back, his eyes are glistening, brown irises appearing golden in the sunlight. He pats my hand. Grips it tightly. We've always been so alike.

"I know," I whisper. "I missed you too."

He smiles. "It's good to see you, Pearlie. You've had a lot on your plate since the accident."

Although my dad's physical mobility is limited these days, his facial expressions and verbal communication are still pretty good. But during our phone calls, we've never brought ourselves to say the words *When Mom died*, or the more direct description: *Sally was killed in a car crash when she experienced heart failure*. It's always been *the accident*. Seeing him cling to those words, appearing to take comfort in them, reminds me that the love my parents shared is greater than anything I've ever experienced myself—or probably could ever hope to know. Another layer of sadness blankets my shoulders.

I smooth down the edge of the white cotton shirt beneath my vest. Tuck back the loose hair that clings to my wet eyelashes. Match Dad's

The Lie She Wears

smile with my own strained version. "Should we get some air? I'd like to talk to you about something."

He presses a few buttons, and then we're rolling out into the garden, still within view of the nurses and my dad's fellow residents. Some of them say hello as we pass, waving to me as if in gratitude that I'm visiting their friend. Another pang of guilt stabs my stomach, and I rub the spot at my waistline.

We pass lush, manicured bushes that run the length of the campus. Spruce trees decorate the perimeter and provide ample shade to the beds of black-eyed Susans that sway in the breeze underneath. Wooden benches with golden plaques memorializing former residents of this facility dot the enclosure, and I follow my dad, waiting for him to choose one to stop beside. Little beige stones—pea gravel—form the paths that intersect and weave between curated greenery.

To the brochure's point, and Dad's enthusiasm for this place when he first decided to move in: It's nice. But it's the vacation he can never come home from, and for that I mourn for him each time I visit.

Midway through the garden, Dad pauses his chair beside a bench dedicated to "Myrna Mensch, a Loving Grandmother and Artist."

"Here good?" he asks, slurring his words. "What do you got there?"

I hand him the envelope. "Mail that arrived at the house for you. And some odd postcards. They look like they were sent recently."

"Thanks for bringing them. Hey, you okay? You seem tense." Dad glances down at the envelope but doesn't open it. His eyes pinch the same way his mother's did in the only photo I've seen of her, right after she landed in New York by boat from Shanghai.

"Everything good at work?" he adds.

I sit on the wooden slats, then rub my palms against my jeans. A nervous habit. "Yeah, about that."

I tell him everything about the museum. How a mask went missing and I'm being blamed for its disappearance until it turns up, and that I was placed on leave. When I share with my dad about the real estate agent's offer, he lifts both eyebrows, attempting a low whistle. The sound is pitiful, with a fraction of the power he used to be able to achieve. Blue jays used to envy this man.

"Those are some serious updates," he says. "I'm sorry about the mask. It's gotta turn up soon, right?"

I nod. "I'm hoping."

He pats my hand again. "How did the real estate agent find you?"

"He sent a solicitation letter to the house, saying he wanted to speak, and I called him. It sounds legit, though almost too good to be true, right?" I laugh, my nerves showing. "You probably can't accept it because then we'd have to really clean the house. No one wants that."

Dad returns my darting eyes with his own subdued expression. "No, we don't. There are too many memories in that house, and it's too soon after the accident."

"Right. Okay, well, the other thing I need to tell you—"

"Pearl, just a second. I've been thinking about things too. I need to give you power of attorney. If anything happens to me, you'll be the one to—"

"Wait, what? How did we jump from real estate to power of attorney? You're alive and have all your faculties."

Dad maneuvers the joystick on his chair, then rotates the wheels to fully face me, kicking up pea gravel. "Do I? I just don't want us to be caught unprepared again. Your mom's accident—she didn't wrap up her affairs before she died, and it's become my job to sort through all the paperwork, which has been"—he waves a hand at his chair—"difficult. I don't want that for you. And if my health nose-dives, I want you to be able to make decisions for the house and our property, for my care if I can't decide on my own."

"Well, you can call up Rohan Singh and get an advance directive. I don't want power over you, over anything."

I hesitate as this beast of a man who raised me, my father, shakes his head. He was always doting with me, and yet his intensity sometimes scared me. Mostly when he drank alcohol and would say things I didn't understand. Rail against the government and its taxes, or "you-know-who" making a power grab for his bank accounts.

Dad doesn't reply, only returns my stare. A mourning dove coos from a nest in a nearby tree. "I might not have that time. Your mom should have already been granted power of attorney over me, since my nerves—this body—are a wild card. But she fought me on it. She didn't want it."

"I don't either."

"And I don't want to be in a wheelchair, but we all have to eat shit sometimes." He stops speaking abruptly. "I'm sorry."

"No, it's fine. You're allowed." I pause. Give each of us a moment to take a breath. "About Mom . . . What did you think of her memory, toward the end? Did she seem like she was still mostly herself—or was she getting confused in your conversations?"

Who is right about her: Zelda or Ursula? Sally was obviously telling the truth about the bodies in her letters. But was someone actually following her? Was she right to be scared—and how scared should I be now?

"She was herself. At least when she was with me. I think seeing me always jogged her memory better than when we were apart."

The perfect answer. The answer of a man still in love. I sigh, dragging a hand down my face. "Dad, isn't there another way, besides granting me power of attorney? I don't want to be in control of you. You're fine, you've been steady since you got in here."

"Pearl, you don't know when I won't be. I don't know."

"Let's revisit this when we need to, not when you're perfectly—"

"I'm not fine, Pearl! I'm—" He stops short, wincing in pain. The left side of his face squeezes tight. He struggles against some unseen jolt, his hands clenching the leather armrests of his chair.

Terror shoots through me as my father—my protector and ally—writhes in his seat.

When the moment passes, Dad drags his face up to meet my worried expression. Though he tries to resume our conversation, tries to speak, his jaw appears slack. As if those muscles have not yet reengaged. "I . . . I'm . . . I'm not fine, Pearlie. I think that's clear."

"Okay," I reply after a beat. "Okay, I'll ask Rohan to draw up the agreement. I don't want to cause you any more stress."

"Good." Half of his face tweaks into a smile, though he doesn't show any teeth. "So, tell me. What else has been happening in the great, wide world?"

When I parked my car outside, I made sure to grab the four letters that Sally wrote and hid, which I've been toting everywhere. I wanted him to see his wife's words for himself, to interpret them however he saw fit and then tell me how much of them I should believe. I wanted him to explain how there could possibly be human remains on our property. To either laugh off the awful suggestion with a mundane story about how the area used to be a pet cemetery decades ago before the house was built, or how a great-aunt on his mother's side demanded to be buried on the family land.

Facing him now, as his face spasms against the cruel neuropathic whims of his failing nervous system, I come up short. If arguing with my dad about granting me power of attorney over him caused him a small relapse, I can't begin to think what a confession of murder from Sally would do to him—even while I'm still unsure whether he was involved those fateful nights.

Besides, there's more than one way to get the answers I need. And while it's laughable to think my mother was a multimurderer, the bodies on our property don't lie.

When I look up from the pea gravel, Dad is searching my face intently, as if trying to read my thoughts.

"Did you . . . Did you ever know Mom to be violent?" The words trip over my lips in a gasp of unburdening. "Did she ever hurt someone at the house?"

His eyes narrow. As if he's looking for a twitch that says I'm angling for a laugh. "No, Pearl. Never. And I won't hear you disparaging your mom's memory. She could be challenging to some. But she loved you and me more than she could ever put into words. She just didn't have the vocabulary to always tell you."

His glare reminds me of moments from childhood just before I was punished—usually spanked harder than I ever thought necessary by my favorite parent. I gaze at the pea gravel a moment, trying to clear my head.

"Tell me more about the garden renovations, Dad. It's all so beautiful here."

His index finger flinches as he breaks into a smile. "Sure, Pearlie. New fountains were put in just past that alabaster bench. Let's check them out."

We make our way toward the sound of running water, while content from the letters continues to stab from behind my eyes.

Chapter Twenty

Sweetness

New York City, 1992

Mary Anker never met a stray she didn't like. She took in cats that were known to wander Chinatown, fed loose dogs that casually approached her for scraps, and attracted idiotic men who sensed her own gaping chasm for love and adoration, judging from the fishnet Madonna-inspired bra and biker shorts getup she dons every Friday night for hitting the clubs without fail.

The woman is a train wreck of standards. And I am ready to exploit them.

House music throbs from the speakers of this neon-lit room on the Lower East Side. The World is *the* spot for creatives and drug users alike to commingle and make some terrible decisions together. Mary stands by the bar alone, though beside other women who are also dressed up in the played imitation of the Queen of Pop's style. She sips a Diet Coke and rum, having already sucked the slice of lime to the rind fifteen minutes ago. Blond hair is teased out in a messy side ponytail. She blends into the sea of gyrating twentysomethings that surrounds us, though she's at least mid-thirties.

"Hey, sweetness. I'm on *The New York Times*' Most Eligible list. Can I buy you a drink?" A monster of a man, at least six feet, five inches tall, towers over me. He slides a hand onto my neck like he owns me, gazing down the plunging neckline of the formfitting spandex dress I wear. Strobe lights flash in random pops across my vision, but his maxed-out irises are clear. This guy is high. Loopy and looking for a bang.

"Hey, buddy, what'd you find?" Another idiot leans onto his shoulder with the same doped-out expression.

"Dibs, Rick. Find your own." Monster shrugs off the contact, never lifting his gaze from my face. "That drink, sweetness?"

My plan tonight is to get some pliable schmuck to find out more about Mary's likes and dislikes, on a personal level beyond what the Hounds have already accomplished. I want to know what her VHS collection is like. If she has a go-to comfort flick. If she prefers Jodeci or Michael Bolton while she's making love. I need an undercover agent who can get me that info without alerting Mary that I'm involved, take my money as payment, and ask few questions in the process. This beefcake has all the subtlety of chicken pox.

I shout to be heard above the music. "Not interested!"

He frowns, wobbly on his feet. "Well, I am."

Big, meaty hands grab me by the waist, and then his face is kissing my neck. His tongue slides down my skin, nipping at my jaw, while I push against his muscled chest. I scream, "Get off!"

He doesn't. I search around me for anyone watching, that guy Rick or someone else. No one is coming to rescue me, or—more likely—this crowd of people isn't high on just life. Glazed expressions pass over my struggling frame as this bear tries to suffocate me in the corner of a dimly lit nightclub.

Screw this. I retrieve the pen I always keep in my purse, then jam it straight into his kidney. The man rears backward, clutching his side. His howl is swallowed by the chorus of a new remixed U2 song, and I take my chance and escape.

As I pass the bar, Mary remains cocooned in the crowd. She's out of my reach tonight, and there's no way I'm waiting around for Sasquatch to regain his footing and come after me. I only gave him a warning jab, and he'll recover within seconds. I pivot toward the door, eager for the fresh air of this borough.

When I emerge onto the sidewalk out front, past the line of men and women dressed in their finest neon, I head for the subway stairs on the next block over.

Footsteps pound the pavement behind me. I turn over my shoulder, searching for the source of the sound when an arm snaps from the alleyway to my right, dragging me into the shadows.

"Sweetness, there you are." Black eyes drink me in, roving over my surprised expression. His smile leaves me chilled. "I saw you leaving so soon after you attacked me. I took the side exit and—boom!—ran into you here."

I did not expect that. For a moment, I think about screaming for help again as he pulls me farther from the sidewalk, away from witnesses. But crying out didn't work in the club. And it won't work out here now, not at this time of night.

He pushes me up against the wall behind a dumpster. Smashes my face against the brick, then yanks down the black tights under my spandex dress. He pants like a dog, frenzied and too excited at the first sight of a bone to know when danger is near.

He bends closer to me. The gin and tonic he must have downed saturates his breath. "Bet you're glad to see me again," he whispers huskily.

I clench my hand into a fist, then turn back to look him in the eye. "Oh, this is the first time you're meeting me."

Slicing the air between us, I stab my pen into his neck again and again, perforating his skin like a newspaper crossword. Blood that appears black spurts in the shadows of the alleyway as he reels backward. I grab him by the dress shirt that he wears unbuttoned to his chest, and he reaches for me—suddenly I'm in range. He clamps down on my shoulder, but I stab his arm—his chest—until he releases me, his frenzy contagious. As he slumps against the side of the dumpster, disgusting fast-food wrappers and a grease-stained cardboard square from a pizza cushion his plummet to the urine-soaked ground. His black eyes are completely dilated. Eerie blank spheres gape at me while blood floods his throat.

Adrenaline courses through my body—though not fear. Oddly enough, it's never fear. More like excitement, then relief from the pent-up energy that's been itching my fingers. Just like when that woman was hit by the bus three weeks ago.

I stare at this man as I did her. Curiosity tips my head to the side as I examine the wounds that such a mundane object as a pen was able to make. Scary, really.

A quick breath of satisfaction inflates my lungs. I didn't mean for this to happen, and I sure didn't invite my victim—attacker, rather—to drag me into this alleyway. But the universe must have sensed I needed this. That I was close to bursting with frustration after following Mary most of the last several weeks, in between real estate appointments, trying to make sense of her routine and failing to get close enough to her to have an impact. To decide what I want from her. To let her know that I am watching.

As I stroll out of the darkness, covered in someone else's blood, a man throws me a flirtatious grin. "Some early Halloween costume you have there."

I smile back at him, sure that my teeth are glowing white in the lamplight. "This old thing? It's only the one I wear all year."

Sauntering off toward the subway entrance, I can feel his eyes on my backside, undeterred and undisturbed by the layer of gore. Unaware that I was nearly assaulted by some Wall Street asshole who would otherwise have gotten away with it.

When I reach the stairs that lead down to the platform, I pause at the Clinton Street post office and its vending machine. I pop in some change that I find in my purse, then purchase a set of standard envelopes and a dozen stamps.

If Mary won't stand still long enough, alone, then I can contact her a different way. Tell her a story. Make her understand this truth: Whatever she thinks she knows about me is only what I want her to know.

Chiefly, that when people underestimate me, they always end up regretting it.

Chapter Twenty-One

Pearl

My dad's face, the saggy way the left side drooped, is burned into my retinas. The rest of the week and this morning, I've been replaying my conversation with him. Why was he so adamant about granting me power of attorney? If he were really so close to incapacitation, wouldn't his care facility doctors speak to me about it? Although I don't understand my dad's insistence, as fate would have it, Rohan Singh needs to chat.

The greasy smell of french fries hits my senses as soon as I enter the attorney's office. Tall and slender in a tailored blue suit jacket, Rohan appears from around the corner.

"Pearl, thanks for coming on short notice. I'll make this quick for you."

He waves me past the secretary's unmanned desk. A color-coordinated tray of legal pads and smaller sticky note pads sits in the top corner.

"Dakota is still on lunch. Otherwise, I'd pretend I'm important and make you wait five minutes." He turns over his shoulder to smile at me, but I'm too anxious to return a laugh.

After I left my dad's care facility, Rohan called me during my drive home. He suggested that we should meet as soon as possible, citing new

The Lie She Wears

information he wanted to share, and also confirmed that he'd draw up the power of attorney paperwork. Considering Sally's revelations and my possible stalker, I knew that delaying this meeting wasn't an option. Friday morning was his first available.

"Have a seat, Pearl." Rohan points at a thick-cushioned armchair with a dark lined pattern. He sits in the matching edition that faces it, instead of behind the impressive cherrywood desk, now tidy and free of paperwork.

"First off," he begins, "have you had a chance to become acquainted with Zelda Huang?"

"My mom's nurse? Uh, yeah. I guess so. I've seen her a fair amount over the last year."

"I imagine that you let her go after your mother passed. Is that right? Did she say anything to you then?"

I blink, twice. The air-conditioning is on blast in the middle of September's cooling weather pattern, and my eyes feel like decaying sponges in here. I've been staring at the letters too hard.

"About what? We've kept in touch. I know she's had interviews that haven't panned out. Not yet, at least."

Rohan maintains a professional, removed air—more so than what he presented me with before. My anxiety ticks up a notch.

"Why am I here, exactly?" I ask. "Did Zelda do something, like—did she contact you?"

Rohan inhales deeply, exhaling through his nostrils in a long, luxurious breath. "Zelda and your mother grew very close before she died, from what I gather. And . . . your mother did something, as a result."

My heart pounds against my long-sleeve. The strange letters I've been reviewing and accidentally memorizing leap forward in my mind's eye, snippets of aggression and violence I never recognized as a child.

Blood everywhere. I'll never get the thick smell of blood out of my nose.

"I don't understand," I begin. "Did she hurt her? Did Sally hurt Zelda?"

Rohan flinches. "Ah, no. Not—no, she didn't. It's—"

"Wait, did Zelda hurt my mother?" The hairs on my neck stand on end as I reflect on the strange attitude Zelda's adopted ever since the funeral. She nearly burst into tears when I had the director play a song by U2, my mother's favorite band, in Sally's memory.

"No, that's not it."

"Well, what—tell me what happened," I sputter.

Rohan tips his head to the side. He draws his full eyebrows together. "Your mother . . . Sally . . . She formally added Zelda into her will as a beneficiary. Zelda will eventually receive a portion of your mother's estate."

My mouth falls open. "Wh-why would my mom do that?"

"I'm sorry, Pearl. I don't have that answer. All I can tell you is that this change was made two months ago. I was waiting to tell you until I could confirm it was legally binding."

"Because she had already been diagnosed with mild cognitive impairment."

Rohan nods. "That's right. At the time I didn't think much of it, because she didn't share her diagnosis with me. After she died, and you shared her mental decline toward the end, I realized I had better cross my t's and dot my i's. The amendment is legitimate. Which means your mother's assets will be divided between your dad, yourself, and Zelda. I've already updated Liam, and I will be contacting Zelda soon."

I stare at him without speaking. I first met Rohan Singh nearly a month ago, within the week of Sally's death. All my interactions with him have been informative, compassionate, and geared toward executing Sally's will with maximum efficiency and clarity, against a sea of frustrating state laws and ambiguity relating to probate law that he's been largely managing with my dad. I've never had reason to doubt Rohan.

"Can I see a copy of that?" I ask. "The amendment or whatever."

He retrieves a piece of paper from his desk. "The last time we spoke, when Sally asked that I draft this, she seemed on edge. She

The Lie She Wears

mentioned that she wanted to change the beneficiaries of her will, in case anything happened to her."

I nod. Halfway down the page, the indented paragraph that shows the revision to a clause in the original will states that where there were two beneficiaries—me and my dad—now there are three: me, my dad, and Zelda.

"Did Sally say anything to you about her?" I ask. "Why Zelda Huang? She's known my mother for less than a year."

Rohan twists his mouth to the side. "Sometimes older people will choose to leave their assets to someone who shows them kindness at the end of their life. Like a nurse or therapist."

I shake my head. "That wasn't Sally. She didn't yearn for love that only Zelda gave her. I visited my mom every month, ever since I moved home, and always got the same indifference or criticism that I have nearly all my life."

I had hoped things might be different once I moved back from California. It was naive. Sanguine.

Rohan crosses his arms. "I'm sorry, Pearl. If you want answers, I would start with Miss Huang. It struck me as odd as well, but it's not my job to judge."

Sally just auctioned off those prized masks back in February with Gillian's. A cut of that would be pretty sizable, but I won't know the exact amount she left me until her individual bank accounts can be dissolved, until the paperwork that Rohan filed with the courts is processed. How much will Zelda receive?

I stare at the blinds of Rohan's office, drawn but semitransparent so that the parking lot of cars behind him is visible. "Hear me out. Could this be a trick? Could Zelda have put my mom up to this? Pressured her somehow?"

Rohan shifts in the armchair. He crosses his legs in loose-fitting slacks. "I couldn't tell you. All I can share is that Sally came here alone and of her own accord."

"But it's such an abrupt change," I say to his cherrywood desk. "Did she seem scared to you?"

"No, not that I saw. I hate to say it, Pearl, but this isn't going away. My best guess is you'll find more answers by discussing this with Zelda directly, or your dad."

With that he stands. "I'm sorry; I have another appointment in ten, and a burger to wolf down."

"Are you sorry?" Heat flushes my cheeks before I can think better of my retort. A heady mix of anger and then embarrassment travels down my neck.

Rohan frowns. "I'll see you out. And email you a draft of the POA soon."

"That's fine. Thanks."

Crossing back to the office's entrance and the rickety stairs of this building, I pause at the threshold. My shoulders tighten, just like when I discovered the AirTag on the underside of my car's bumper. I peer at the street through the glass, searching for the source of my unease.

I can't shake the sense that someone is out there—maybe it's Zelda. Is that why I've been tense in public places the last several weeks? She could have been pursuing me, waiting for me to learn the ugly truth, that Sally valued a near stranger's presence in her life as much (or as little) as she did mine.

What if it's not Zelda? Could Griffin be tracking my movements, on behalf of the museum, still suspecting me of stealing? Although I've stayed away the last week, I've tried my best not to think about him or to spiral at the thought of my tanking career. Now that Sally has levied a final rejection of me, my recent failures all rush my senses in a choking sob. I exit the building, anxiety twisting my chest, along with something like grief for the relationship that I always wanted with Sally but never achieved. And now I find out why: She tried to replace me with a more compliant stranger.

Two cars drive fast down this narrow street as I slide into the driver's seat of my sedan. Once they zip past, I start my car, then pull into traffic.

If Sally was losing her memory and her personality was undergoing certain changes, as is common in patients with cognitive impairment, how much did she confide in her nurse? As much as she shared in the hidden letters? More? Zelda could have coerced my frail mother into changing her will at the first sign of decline. This woman would have held a front-and-center seat to the earliest indicators that Sally was losing it; maybe Zelda took advantage.

Then again, none of that effort would benefit Zelda unless Sally died.

I slam on my brakes just before a woman walking a dog enters the crosswalk. A white minivan leans on its horn behind me, but I can't move. I scan my rearview mirror all the same, searching for her short black hair and the mole above her lip.

What if Zelda was somehow involved in Sally's death—or precipitated it?

Nausea punches my gut, and the cab of the car suddenly feels claustrophobic. If Zelda is the ghost that's been pursuing me—the prickle just beneath my ponytail—she knows more than what she's let on.

Zelda said that, at first, she didn't see why my mother needed a live-in nurse. But less than six months later, Sally is so completely indebted to Zelda due to cognitive deficits that she cuts her into the will, while Ursula and my dad maintain that Sally was still as sharp as a paring knife. Zelda has been awarded a chunk of my inheritance for simply leading physical therapy exercises and divvying out pills. What if it cost Zelda more effort than that? What if she had a more sinister, concerted agenda?

The white minivan honks, a series of angry, short bursts. I want to unhinge my jaw and roar a response out my window, to light a match and burn everything to the ground. Instead, slowly, I ease my foot onto the pedal, ever the presentable daughter, and roll forward.

As I reach the freeway and the split-direction on-ramp that leads either to my apartment in the Northwest District or east across the river, I recall Zelda's reaction when I first told her about the real estate agent. She said Sally wouldn't mind if I sold the house and all the memories my family shared in it. Zelda said Sally had become more erratic and indifferent toward certain things she used to care about. Her reply could have been rooted in her assessment as a nurse—or the selfish hope that we sell the house and she gets a solid cut of the profits.

Overanalyzing people and conversations has gotten me in trouble in the past. Not everyone wants to be examined and treated like an artifact for the general public to consume. But this time, I dropped the ball. The first real conversation I've had with Zelda since my mom died took place right after I found the nonsense letter and was placed on administrative leave from the museum. I accepted her words as truth too quickly; I was desperate for clarity. It's time I revisited the intuition that drove me to uncover the mangled bones buried on my family's property.

I hit my blinker, then turn onto the bridge for a new perspective. A bicyclist shouts at me, but I keep my gaze centered on the yellow dashes of the road, determined to maintain a steady course.

It's time I stopped accepting what people are telling me about my own mother. And instead listen to her words directly: Sally confessed to the murders of two individuals, no regrets. As I reach the middle of the bridge and note the white-tipped waves of the river, hundreds of feet below, a new thought swims into my brain, like a parasitic lamprey.

If Sally took the lives of two victims, however intended or not, what if there are more?

Chapter Twenty-Two

Pearl

The day I graduated from the doctoral program at Stanford, I was elated. My mom and dad had traveled down from Oregon for the occasion—a major undertaking for my dad, given his in-demand contractor work at the time. But the drive had been kind to them, and they held beaming smiles for me when I crossed the commencement stage. It was only when I found them after the ceremony, when my mom leaned in close to whisper something, that I knew it was all for show.

She had said in a biting tone, "Congratulations, my girl. You did it. I hope you made yourself proud, doing exactly what you wanted to do."

I pulled back, confused and hurt by her choice of words. Sally gave me a hard pat on the cheek, then turned to where my dad was admiring the Romanesque chapel that served as the centerpiece of campus. All afternoon and evening over dinner at some fancy restaurant I don't even recall, I considered her words. Had I chosen myself in pursuing museum studies—willfully ignoring my parents' wishes for me? Dismissing the effort and sacrifices they had made for me in the past?

Staring at the Portland Art Museum now, at the brick facade that marks its entrance, I feel nauseated. I chose this world and this institution, and it turned its back on me at the first hiccup.

Inside the lobby, patrons huddle over brochure maps, planning their stops. I weave through the weekend morning crowd, then head upstairs to the fourth-floor glass penthouse and the in-progress pop-up exhibits. Shades have been drawn across the clear wall facing the Willamette River, but unnecessarily, as it turns out. Cloud coverage forms a gray layer, as if in solidarity with my mood.

Kai stands just outside the partially enclosed exhibit that he has titled *True Crime: At Home in Our Backyard*.

"Pearl? Hey," he says as I approach. "I, uh, heard you were taking some time off."

I wave to Peggy and Nettie, who are both deep in discussion at the back of this floor. They make eye contact with me, then resume their conversation without even a smile.

Kai and the other curators will have learned everything by now. It's been almost a week since I was placed on administrative leave, but the things I've read, seen, and experienced all make it feel like a lifetime has passed since I was last here.

"Under duress, yeah." I search past Peggy and Nettie, scanning the few employees on this floor, and note that Griffin isn't one of them. Good. I'm usually an "ask permission" kind of person, but without knowing if I'd be allowed back on property without an escort, I'll ask forgiveness if I'm caught today.

"You've made progress." I nod toward Kai's wall of photos and the printed text script that he's still mounting to the right spots. Looks like he went with the afghan square for his centerpiece.

Will my story be up there one day—or Sally's?

"Your exhibit will be reinstated soon. I know it." Kai offers me a reassuring smile that I only barely return.

Griffin hasn't contacted me. I emailed him two days ago, wondering if there had been any news on locating the mask, begging him to let me return to work. His ensuing silence has been more depressing than if he had replied with a curt *No*.

"Not so sure about that," I answer. "My theme was in line with the spooky vibes of October. Somehow *Hidden Faces and Fears* as an exhibit title doesn't fit well with other seasons' themes of family togetherness and peace on earth."

Kai tents his eyebrows. "Hey, you never know. There is still a week before the first Friday of the month. Maybe you'll get approval to launch by then. I kind of thought our exhibits would be side by side. Literal masks and the faces that criminals wear."

I bite back a sigh at his kindness. "Yeah, that would have been nice. Listen, I'm only here because I—" I stop short, realizing what I was about to say before I did: I wanted to see *him*. My cheeks warm in the light heat of the building.

"Because?" Kai glances my way. A member of the maintenance staff pushes a mop across the tile, but hazel eyes focus on me with new curiosity. "Pearl?"

"Ah, yeah. I wanted to ask you something." I clear my throat.

Get a hold of yourself, Pearl. You barely know this guy, and you're barred from working with him at the moment. He's just . . . a friend?

"An artifact went missing from my exhibit's collection," I say. "And the day before the mask disappeared, I saw someone . . . I don't know, lurking in the special-authorization areas, and I've never seen them before. They weren't an employee."

Kai narrows his eyes. "That's weird. Did you tell anyone? Security?"

"I did, later that night. Was anyone loitering, or was someone that you didn't recognize around that day? I came to talk with you"—cue additional blushing—"but you were gone. This person was leaving at the moment that I walked up to your staging room."

My troubles at the museum started when the mask went missing. The same day that I was placed on leave, my phone registered that an AirTag was nearby and tracking my movements—the same as Sally insisted someone was tracking hers. If I could figure out one mystery in my life, the others might become clearer too.

Kai crinkles his forehead. "I'm sorry, Pearl. I'm still getting to know everyone, and I haven't yet put faces to names. I'm not sure I would have known who belonged and who didn't."

"I get it. No problem. I'll ask some of the other curators." Via email, since Nettie and Peggy seem glad to write me off already.

"Hey," Kai says, reaching a hand out but stopping short of touching my elbow. "Can we grab that Thai lunch? Just because you're not at the museum lately, doesn't mean we can't—you know, still get to know each other."

A tentative smile crosses his lips. Yearning tightens my core. I would love nothing more than to sit awkwardly across from this man—from his flop of long hair, his crunchy, unkempt Art History–nerd stubble, and his warm gaze. But today is the day that Ursula said she could meet again, after I called her on my drive home from Twin Pines. Instead of swinging by the shop as I did last time, she suggested I come to her house sometime after three.

"I'd like that—really, I would—but I've got a meeting this afternoon. Rain check?"

Kai looks down at the gleaming hardwood. "Sure, sure. Hey, it's Portland, right? Plenty of chances for those."

"Right, totally." As I return to the elevator, I wince. *Totally?*

Embarrassment battles with the excitement in my chest, when the elevator's chrome doors part to reveal an older woman dressed in custodial coveralls, clutching a walkie-talkie. A badge hangs from her pocket.

"Oh, shoot. Wrong floor," she says, stepping backward and making room for me. She hits a button, then smiles at me. "My first day. Still getting my sea legs. Lobby?"

"Yeah, thanks."

"Sure."

The elevator ferries us below. Steel cables groan as we come to a smooth stop.

"Do you work here?" the woman asks. Graying black hair is visible beneath a scarf. Dangly gold hoop earrings are the only jewelry she wears, reminding me of a pirate.

"I do—" *No, wait.* I purse my lips. "Uh, I'm Pearl. Associate curator of Asian art."

"Nice to meet you. Cherry, custodial staff."

The chrome doors part to reveal a small family waiting in line to board the elevator. I lift a hand in goodbye. "Well, have a good day."

"Be seeing you," she says.

As I head toward the brick exit, I don't have the heart to tell her that she probably won't.

The drive home zips by along the grid of downtown, delivering me to the Northwest District. I find myself zoning out, pausing at stop signs and crosswalks, not fully engaged with where I'm going. It's only when I parallel park on the street outside my apartment that I realize where I am.

A postal worker emerges from the covered mailboxes located on the first floor, wearing a scarf in the brisk temp today. I cross to mine, recalling that I haven't checked it in days. I've been consumed with the revelations from Sally and the ranch house.

Sally's letters suggest that she knew the first victim. That he was intimately involved in our lives, despite being unwelcome the night he came over. While I could ask my dad for names of acquaintances of theirs whose friendships date back to twenty-five years ago, I'd risk upsetting him further, and there's no need. I know everyone that Sally might have considered a friend, because she kept a physical address book with each person's name and phone number; Zelda gave it to me in the box filled with items from Sally's nightstand, the one in which I found the gift-wrapped photo of the oak tree.

I need to dig into each name. Find out if they were friends, or frenemies.

A small pile of letters greets me when I open my mailbox, covering a bulkier envelope. Instantly my curiosity wins out, and I pluck it from the bottom. Taking the stairs to my third-floor apartment, I pry the flap of the letter open, careful not to rip the paper.

As I reach my front door, I suck in a sharp breath staring down at the envelope's contents. A plastic baggie encases blood-soaked gauze wrapped around a small object.

A gust of air slices through my hair, circling my neck. "What the hell?"

I glance around me at the empty doorsteps of my three neighbors on this floor and their Ring cameras. Scan the top of the stairwell and hold my breath while listening for footsteps. The sound of someone following me, waiting for me to uncover this—whatever this is.

I unlock my door, then step inside to open the plastic sandwich bag. The sealed zipper cracks open, sending new jolts across my skin. The heady scent of iron emanates from the open mouth.

I stare at the bag and its bloody gauze. I have no business receiving anything like this. Who sent this?

Unwilling to dive into this mystery—not yet, not quite yet—I pace in front of the bag and the envelope on the kitchen counter.

It's clearly addressed to me, with no return address. Of course.

My lips are dry. Outside in the hallway, laughter rings up from the street level below. People going about their lives, enjoying time with friends, or finishing a business lunch.

Someone is trying to scare me. And haven't I already been scared enough by what Sally confided to me in her hidden letters? Haven't I already had what I worked so hard to achieve—my job at the museum—taken from me? What else do I have to lose by facing whatever stupid joke this could be? The AirTag hasn't even made a reappearance since I chucked it into the Willamette River.

Fuck it.

Donning one of the winter gloves that I just pulled out of storage and left by the front door, obliging the brisk weather that arrived this week, I reach for the object. My heart pounds, clangs against my ribs, as I grasp the gauze and carefully extract the folded bundle.

Once I place it on top of the plastic bag, to avoid contaminating my counter with whatever this is, I gently roll it forward. White unfurls into red. Red unfurls into purplish black.

The gauze releases a severed human finger.

I gasp, crashing backward into the kitchen cabinets. My hand flies to my mouth, while I struggle, staring at the mottled human flesh lying before me on the very spot where I normally chop vegetables. The stench of blood and something like rotten beef exhales from the plastic square. A decomposing body part.

A minute goes by. Sweat soaks my collar and under my bra. Before I gather the nerve to examine the finger up close.

Still and innocuous against the stained strip of fabric, the finger appears like any other—except for the small tattoo of three trees at the base of the digit.

I've seen that tattoo before. Bile rises from my belly, traveling up my throat in a bitter punch that flicks the back of my mouth. Ursula has one just like it.

I repackage the finger in the plastic baggie and envelope, grab my keys, and then race downstairs to my car. *Ursula.*

When I start the ignition, I pause long enough to dial the police. Ask for a welfare check to be done on Ursula Romano as I round the corner of the complex, then merge onto the boulevard.

I call Ursula over and over again, but she doesn't answer. Each hollow ring of the line ratchets my guts tighter as I enter the residential pocket of Goose Hollow. I park my car, then step onto the sidewalk before Ursula's idyllic cottage.

Whitewashed wooden steps creak beneath my weight as I pass a ceramic planter and a small pile of dirt spilled loose. I knock under a round fiberglass window in the door, then startle. The door is open. Slightly ajar, revealing a crack of darkness.

Alarm bells scream inside my head to turn around and run back to my car.

I give the door a nudge. "Ursula? It's Pearl. Can I come in?"

Slivers of the afternoon's fading sunshine cut through the shrouded front room. The sitting area is tidy, the throw pillows of the love seat arranged in the corners, then karate chopped in the center of each square. Undisturbed.

"Ursula?"

I barely know this woman. But I seriously doubt she would leave her door unlocked and ajar, knowing I would be here this afternoon. The back of my neck prickles, and I retreat to the front porch to wait for the police.

I call her phone again. A ringtone blaring Heart's "Barracuda" erupts from deep inside the house, before my call goes to voicemail.

"Shit," I whisper. I place one foot across the threshold.

"Ursula?" Then louder: "Ursula? It's Pearl."

I peer into the house. Blood covers the hardwood floor of the foyer leading into the kitchen, seeping into the cracks between boards. The ferrous stench reeks as my hand lands on the doorframe, sliding right off. Red coats my palm, bright and jarring.

"Oh—" I stagger backward. My fingers clutch on to the door's handle, searching for balance, when I remember: the finger. The blood-soaked digit in my pocket. *Ursula.* If she's hurt—dying—every second counts.

My knees tremble as I enter the house. I reach a stairwell that leads to the second floor, and then I lean against the wall, smearing handprints as I go. Pale skin flashes from the landing above. The bottoms of bare feet are unmoving, pointing straight up, as a car door slams shut outside.

Stomach acid lurches into my throat while I climb the steps. Police officers clatter up the porch, calling to me, mistaking me for Ursula.

I reach the second floor, a sharp cry blurting from my mouth. Ursula lies still and splayed on her back wearing a purple tracksuit, gray hair mussed in a ponytail. A postcard featuring rolling hills lies beside her. Her arms are raised to her shoulders, blood drenching one hand and stemming from the stump where her index finger should be.

"Ma'am? Portland Police. We're doing a wellness check. Can we come in?" a deep voice calls below.

My breath hitches. With a shaking foot, I touch my boot to the postcard. Flip it over where it's propped against Ursula's arm, not daring to use my bare hand. On the other side, a message written in cursive: "You can run . . ."

"Oh, shit. Maxwell, look," the police officer says. Footsteps canvass the floor below. "Portland Police! Whoever's upstairs, come out with your hands up!"

With a twist in my gut, I flinch as the blood-soaked package in my pocket presses to my side.

Chapter Twenty-Three

Leah

New York City, 1992

The first letter was a breeze to write. Whenever I had some free time between apartment appointments, I'd scribble down succinct little notes that I thought might get my message to Mary Anker across: *Keep your mouth shut. Watch your back. Make sure you stand three feet from the edge of the curb, or you might lose your balance too.* All pretty mundane stuff.

It was while I was bumming around Times Square, lamenting the difficulty in landing a listing in this neighborhood, that I began writing for myself on my notepad.

I started with the classics. Little Red Riding Hood. Mermaid tales. The Chinese monster that chases villagers into the new year every year. Warrior princesses. I was like a regular Leo Tolstoy. Leah Tolstoy, rather.

Instead of reiterating the same tired storyline, I made it interesting. I wrote, placing my own spin on the original story's details. More surprises. A few new twists. Perhaps a young blond woman who stuck her nose in other people's business, then found herself in a precarious position.

The Lie She Wears

I started sending these to Mary at the address that Megan the postal Hound found, hoping she would get the hint. Maybe she'd even find them amusing.

After a month of contenting myself with our one-sided correspondence, I watched her exit her apartment in Chinatown with a wary gaze on her face. Wide-set eyes darted every which way as she left the safety of her home above the family restaurant. She clutched her purse close to her body while scanning the sidewalk in front of her and behind, searching for someone.

For me.

Luckily, she didn't spy where I was crouched beside an abandoned construction site. These in-progress corners are like visual white noise in this city; no one bothers to truly look at them or see the people in them. I don't.

I followed her to the post office. Waited while she unlocked the small PO box she rented, and thumbed through her bills and adverts until her eyes landed on my handwriting. She stopped dead in her tracks, forcing other people to go around her. She read my words, my stories that always featured the little blond character getting her due. A shoe to the face. An axe to the brain.

She blanched, then scanned the morning crowds outside again, always searching unsuccessfully for my face.

After the third letter, she broke down and cried in public.

I smiled then.

Finally, we were getting somewhere.

Chapter Twenty-Four

Pearl

Officer Laurel taps her fingers against the tablet she holds. She's expectant, as if she asked me a question and I didn't answer her.

"Sorry, say that again?" I mumble. After the Forensic Evidence Unit swabbed my hands, covered as they were in someone else's blood, an officer gave me a washcloth and an antibacterial wipe to scrub my skin clean. I twist the small towel under my nails.

"Sure thing, Pearl. Did you touch anything when you entered the house? Notice anything unusual when you got inside?" Her voice is warm and reassuring.

"Anything unusual? Well, the door was open."

Officers in navy-blue uniforms walk up and down the stairs leading into Ursula's home, the steps creaking with each passage. A strange kind of melody, as their boots hit the wood. Creak. Scrape. Creak. Scrape.

"Anything else?" Officer Laurel asks. A voice speaks through the radio attached to her chest. A garbled string of sentences follows, citing a combination of numbers and letters that form police code.

"Just that. Oh, and the—there was dirt on the front porch. Next to her potted plant."

The police officer takes my rambling in stride, tapping in more notes on her tablet. "Okay. Walk me through your path in the house again."

I tell her everything, just as I did her colleague, a woman wearing a tight bun of auburn hair. How I had asked Ursula if I could drop by to talk more about my mom; about the blood that I smeared along the wall across from the stairwell that leads to the second floor of the cottage; about the position of the feet; about the severed finger I received in the mail today, which is now in an evidence bag held by a Forensic Evidence team member, and which spurred my request for a wellness check.

When Officer Laurel asks what I think the message on the postcard means, I answer honestly: *I don't know.* "You can run" could be a warning that Ursula received prior to her murder—maybe from a disgruntled and violent customer who made good on the implied threat that she could run but she couldn't hide. But a gut feeling coiling in my stomach worries the message is for me.

She finishes taking notes, then I raise a hand as if I'm school age. "What happened to her? Who did this to Ursula?"

Shortly after the police arrived, a fire truck came screaming in, followed by an ambulance and two paramedics. They went inside, but they came out fairly quickly. Ursula was dead. Had been dead for several days.

Officer Laurel is impassive as she taps the screen again. Not even a twitch or double blink. Wavy black hair is plaited at the base of her head, visibly pulling her skin. "What was your relationship to Ursula Romano?"

"I didn't really have one. She was my mother's best friend. My mom died about five weeks ago in a car accident."

More tapping, and then she looks up. "Sorry for your loss, Pearl. Detective Sims may want to speak with you later, but I think we're done here."

Released from the crime scene, I step in a daze from the curb to the street. Past the concerned noises of neighbors and several of their phones, which capture the horror unfolding on their peaceful block.

My car starts the way it always does. I merge into traffic, pretending to be a regular person—and not someone who just gazed on the mutilated dead body of someone I knew—then hit my blinker to merge into the right lane. I hold it together as far as the entrance to the I-405 freeway, where grief and terror burst from my mouth in a choked sob.

Who would hurt Ursula? She was a quiet and compassionate antique shop owner. According to the police, it appears as if she was getting ready for bed when someone broke into her house. The officer I initially spoke with threw around the phrase *home invasion gone horribly wrong*. But he changed course when I shared the bloodied human finger, still in its plastic bag.

Why the hell would anyone take Ursula's finger—then send it to me? The memory of the note left beside her body—*You can run*—initiates a new round of nausea that tickles my throat.

Sally was killed while driving at sunset, something that everyone considered a terrible accident. She veered off the road, crashed into a ditch out in the sticks of the Willamette Valley, where few cars ventured after the wineries closed, and suffered heart failure, according to the coroner. Years earlier, she apparently killed two individuals on her property. Now, her best friend was murdered and dismembered, potentially as a threat to me. Are Sally's and Ursula's deaths related? Is the AirTag that I found on my car connected to Ursula's severed finger?

Traffic is relentless on the freeway, and I exit as soon as I can into the grid of my neighborhood. My head aches. Within minutes and a few dazed left turns, I find myself at the South Park Blocks and passing directly in front of the museum.

A man walking in the opposite direction of the brick entrance zippers the black jacket he wears up to his chin. Kai.

I slow beside him along the sidewalk, then lower my window. "Still feel like a happy hour?"

He stops short, recognizing me. "Pearl. Are you okay?"

I wipe my eyes. "I don't want to be alone. Are you free?"

"Yeah, yeah. What happened?" The kindness in his voice almost undoes me.

"You won't believe me."

Kai slides into my passenger seat, and I drive the short distance to the block of breweries close to my apartment. As two wheats are delivered to the private table we chose in the corner of a circus-themed brewery, I take in the easygoing concern that knits his eyebrows as he waits for me to speak. The day we met, Kai had cataloged every detail of the artifacts he gathered for display. The main players involved in each crime, their motivations, the consequences of their actions, the mistakes that got the criminal caught.

I've been treading water ever since reading Sally's first letter, but lately it feels like I'm starting to bob beneath the waves. Kai, with his extensive knowledge about crime, ciphers, and law enforcement, might be the only person who can help me sort through everything without going to the police.

Kai said that my exhibit would be a good companion to his, and he's rooting for mine to be reinstated. Maybe he's being nice, or it's in his interest that we figure out who really stole the mask from the museum, just as it's in everyone's. I can trust him, I think.

With a deep breath, I tell him about finding Ursula and her finger. About the postcard I found beside her, and the letters that Sally left me, her confessions, and the hidden AirTag I discovered on my car.

"Holy shit, Pearl. That's—have you told the police all this?" Kai stares at me, slack jawed.

"About Ursula and her finger. Not about my mom's letters or the AirTag." I take a sip of my wheat, and the beer warms my stomach in a soothing layer before the chills return. I can't stop shaking.

"Do you believe your mom—about the bodies?"

Moonlight stretches across my memory, as I sat beneath the dark clouds in my yard, the Catholic necklace in my palm. The scent of earth and sterile plastic as I lurched against the interior of my family shed.

I shrug, not yet willing to divulge everything. "I don't know."

He reaches across the table to place his hand over mine. "And why are you telling me?"

I scan his eyes and the green that flecks one iris. I've gone through most of my life denying myself what I actually want for fear of Sally's disapproval and her constant criticisms. Aside from pursuing museum studies, I never stepped out of line with what she decided for me. Especially with men. *Go find a nice Chinese boy.* Now that she's gone, I feel . . . untethered.

I trace a sanded-down crack in the wood with my free hand. "Because I'm up to my neck in questions. And feeling insanely isolated, and . . . and I feel like I can trust you, Kai."

He takes a sip of his beer, never breaking eye contact. "You can. Definitely."

I wipe a bead of sweat from my pint glass. My feet wrap tightly around the leg of the barstool. "Are you the mild-mannered museum curator everyone says you are? Or are you a true crime–obsessed wolf in sheep's clothing?"

He chuckles, probably recalling our conversation the first day we met. "I promise you, I'm not. I only got into true crime photos—really, photography—because I liked being close to the action but not in it. Liked the distance that photography offers. It's helped me to, uh, deal with hard times in my life, being raised by my tūtū in Hawai'i."

I lean closer, relishing the moment. The normalcy of grabbing a beer with a good guy. "You're not the one sending weird semiromantic postcards to my parents' house?"

His eyebrows tent into his fringe of hair. "You'll have to explain that one."

I scroll on my phone to the photos I took of the first two that I found beside the front door to the ranch house. Along with two more that were in the box that Zelda packed from Sally's nightstand.

"No clue who sent them. The messages are all strangely intimate, though, like they're pining for my dad."

Kai clears his throat. "He wasn't, uh, having an affair?"

"'Fraid not. He's been in a long-term care facility for almost the last year."

Kai gestures for my phone, and I hand it over, pointing at the text. "See? The writing is pretty brief, but the postcards suggest a loving friendship of some kind with my dad. I gave them to him, but I don't even know if he read them. He had a setback in his health recently."

"Hmm. Well, if it walks like a duck and talks like a duck . . ."

I grimace. "You think it's an affair."

Kai zooms in on a photo by pinching two fingers across the screen. "That or the sender is also a true crime fanatic. These locations have all been the sites of famous murders."

"You're kidding. Spokane, Washington?"

"A babysitter went rogue and attacked the dad who was trying to seduce her in 1972."

"Okay. Seaside, Oregon?"

Kai turns his gaze up and to the right. "Uh, that would be a murder among altar boys."

"Lafayette, Indiana, and Clarion, Pennsylvania?"

"A homicidal cult started by high schoolers, and also a pregnant assassin who was finally caught after thirteen hits."

I lift both eyebrows. What kind of person can rattle off horrific stats like that and not be a cop—or a criminal? While he examines the photos on my phone, I scan his face, searching for a sign that trusting him was a mistake. "Wow. Okay, it's . . . scary how well you know your crime."

Kai taps his finger on the table. "If you view them with that knowledge, these messages come off a little threatening. Was there anyone who didn't like your mom or your dad?"

According to Ursula's anecdote back in her antique shop, Sally had a nemesis who worked at Gillian's. "Yeah. He apparently goes to the Saturday Market every week."

"I just went there last weekend. It goes until early evening, for the next hour."

"Feel like shopping?" I stand, leaving half my beer on the table, while Kai downs the rest of his.

Clusters of people dot the riverfront at the market. White tents form rows of artisanal goods, food vendors, and community businesses trying to amplify their visibility. A live band with a reggae drum occupies the raised stage just beside the impressive park fountain, still gurgling water at this late point in September.

I scan the crowd, searching for the patch of grass that an online neighborhood forum said would serve as the meeting point for music-curious attendees. Kai points toward the water's edge. "Over there."

He walks toward a row of naked cherry trees, their blooms long since gone, to the loose grouping of people beyond. Music from the community drum circle envelops us as we approach. Underneath the bare branches, a dozen adults and a few kids sit on woven blankets, patting, slapping, and methodically riffing on handheld drums to create the next off-the-cuff song. More kids dance in the middle, swaying their small bodies or swinging their arms wildly with instruments of their own in hand.

At the head of the circle, playing a wide drum tucked between his legs, Finn Hoskie is nearly unrecognizable from the archived headshot that I found on LinkedIn on my phone. Long black hair is worn loose and hits his shoulders, and the plaid green button-up he wears contrasts the image I held of him in my head, of a dark-blue suit jacket befitting the head of client relations. When compared to the photo from 2002, he could be someone completely different.

Finn looks up in my direction, the smile gone from his face. He gets to his feet, then strides toward us. His drum abandoned, a child in a tie-dye shirt picks it up and begins banging away.

"So, I assume you're looking for me." Finn teeters to a stop, his momentum swinging him forward. "Why are you here?"

"I-I'm sorry?" I stutter.

"You're Sally Wong's daughter. You look like Sally, at least. Except for your eyes."

I blush, hearing a stranger pinpoint the exact feature that I used to hate growing up. While my mother was beautiful and frequently complimented on the light caramel color of her irises, my dark gray was seen as a disappointment.

Finn narrows his gaze. He scans Kai, then resumes glaring at me. "So, what do you want?"

"I—well, I know you had some disagreements with my mother in the past."

Finn nods. "Right. I didn't like Sally. May she rest in peace. And I don't really like to gossip about someone who can't defend themselves now."

Direct and borderline cold. Got it.

Kai steps toward the drum circle, ducking his head. "Holler if you need me, Pearl."

I nod, then offer Finn a tight smile. "I'm just wondering why the two of you didn't get along, despite Sally bringing some significant pieces to Gillian's. I'm trying to learn more about my mother."

He narrows tawny brown eyes, and then he glances over his shoulder. "If you really want to know . . . ?"

"I do," I say, raising my voice to be heard above the din. "Ursula Romano said you worked for Gillian's Auction House. That you seemed to dislike Sally and she you."

"Ursula said that, huh? I remember her. Amateur antiquist, and pushy, the same as Sally. I was glad when I retired that I wouldn't have to deal with either of them anymore."

"When did you retire?"

He crosses his arms across his chest. "In February."

"Around the time of the auction. Of Sally's Giulio Venetta mask series."

"You're tracking. What else does Ursula say?"

"Not much, because now she's—" I pause, unsure of how much to share with this stranger. How bizarre it is to tell of her tragic end when she's still lying on some medical examiner's table. "She's dead."

Finn lifts both eyebrows. "How did she die?"

"Killed. Recently. The police haven't shared their theories yet."

I give him a moment, while he digests the news. I shouldn't add more detail to what I've said already. *I found her. She was waiting for me in her home.*

He runs a hand down his face, revealing white scars across his knuckles. Remnants from previous fistfights? "So, let me get this straight. Someone killed Ursula, and you've come to question me about my opinion of her? And what I thought of Sally?"

"I'm realizing you weren't that fond of either woman. I think the police might soon too." If Finn hated Sally as much as Ursula thought he did, he'd be one of the few to see past Sally's amicable outward displays. He might know the reason why someone was targeting her. I take in his long expression. His slow blink as he reflects on my statement.

"Pearl, right? What are you insinuating?"

We stare at each other, each bidding the other to crack against the soundtrack of laughter and shaking maracas. Kai glances at me every now and then, from the periphery. But he can't hear our conversation above the metallic rhythms.

"Look, I didn't hate your mother, or Ursula," Finn finally says, toeing the ground. "I just didn't trust Sally."

"Why?"

"Liam Davis." Finn watches a slender woman dance, flapping a long shawl that she wears like wings. He waves to her, then smiles without showing any teeth. "He's the reason."

"My dad?"

Finn nods. "Liam and Sally weren't good people."

"Can you explain? My mom—I understand why you might have had conflict with her, for your role at work—but my dad was never into artifact hunting," as Sally called her passion. "How would you even meet him?"

Finn stares at the grass, then the row of cherry trees behind me. He avoids my eye contact. "We met when Sally and Liam came to Seattle a few times, hoping to get whatever new item she thought was worthy of Gillian's attention into an auction collection. It was my duty to vet all invited guests to our offices. Gillian's works incredibly hard to secure its premises and to treat our clients with care."

"And you're saying Sally and Liam weren't trustworthy because you didn't like her offerings? She searched high and low for her finds. She had an appraiser on her favorites list on her phone."

"I'm saying, I looked into the background of everyone. And neither one of them was who they said they were."

A new song begins, raucous and upbeat. Matching my heightened pulse. I step closer to Finn, my skin vibrating. "And who were they?"

He purses his lips but doesn't reply.

I wait until he makes eye contact. "I need to know more about my mom. Reasons someone might have disliked her. I recently discovered she kept some secrets from me."

"Someone was targeting Sally?" A sly smile pulls up his cheeks. "She was such a lovely woman; I find that hard to believe. What about your dad's secrets? Do you know those?"

I scoff. "My dad? He was the balance to Sally's constant critiques and frustrations with me. He was and is an open book."

"Great. You should ask him for the truth that you're after. If he's so innocent, I'm sure he won't mind if you ask him about his work history."

"He was a contractor. He worked for himself."

"And for clients that he also personally vetted and chose."

Finn peers at me. A plane passes low overhead, during a lull in the musical action. The roar of the engine thrums my chest.

"I need to get back to my drums," he says. "It used to be my business to know everything about anyone related to Gillian's, but I'm retired now. And finally doing what I love, and I want to keep doing it." Finn steps past me, avoiding my eye contact. "Sally never knew when to quit. I hope you do, Pearl."

"Wait—"

He continues forward, and I blurt out my question before my confidence falters. "Did Sally ever—was she ever violent, to your knowledge?"

Finn pauses. "Well. Sally wasn't."

He serves me a knowing look, then stalks back to the drum circle. "What does that mean?" I call after him.

Instead of grabbing a cajón and taking a seat, he passes the party, continuing toward the street. By the time a different child seizes the maracas, Finn disappears into Chinatown, heading toward the Pearl District.

Kai approaches from my right. "Everything okay?"

As a woman with long curls takes a seat at the head of the drum circle, the bongos between her knees, I mull over the answer to Kai's question. Finn's implication that my dad is the villain I should be concerned by. That everything I know about his goodness and patience as a father and husband should be discarded.

I match Kai's tense expression with my own. "No, it's not. My dad may be more involved in this mess than I realized."

Chapter Twenty-Five

OPAL

New York City, 1992

The keys turn in the high-rise apartment's door with a slick metallic sound. I lock up. Today's showing was a good one. Twenty-three couples came through during the three-hour open house, and I'm pretty sure a member of Black Sabbath was among them. A few men nibbled on my baited line—a three-bedroom, two-bath penthouse with adjoining entertainment room and movie theater in one of the best neighborhoods in Manhattan—but no outright offers in person. I'll check back with the office this afternoon and see if I hooked any fish.

Silver doors part behind me as the elevator dings, announcing its arrival. An elderly woman wearing CHANEL tweed and carrying a well-groomed cat exits onto this floor, and I sweep into the elevator like I'm performing at Lincoln Center.

And in a way, I am, of course. Isn't everyone? Only a few people have ever truly seen the real me. Only one person has ever accepted me.

Outside the building and on the same block, an art gallery announces that its new collection will open to the public this weekend. Tonight. I'd love to attend, sincerely—who wouldn't love seeing the latest interpretation of this decade's bent toward Neo-Conceptualism? It's cutting edge—but I've got a prior engagement.

Catching a train downtown, I half doze in my empty car, lulled by the rocking motion. The late nights I've been having aren't good for my energy levels during the morning. It's been hard to wake up for early showings and even harder to maintain my focus during long open houses, like today's.

Still, I know my night owl tendency is for a good cause.

When I exit the subway station at Wall Street, I check my wristwatch and its 14-karat numbered face. It reads one thirty, the time for my twice-daily ritual this week. I step into the nearest telephone booth. Drop a quarter into the machine, then dial the number I learned by heart after locating it in the phone book.

Mary Anker's slight voice answers the phone. She nearly whimpers before speaking. "Hello?"

"Cousin, it's me. Opal. I just had to call you and tell you what excellent weather we're having in Fort Lauderdale."

A sob carries through the phone. "Please. Please stop calling me."

"Mary, darling, what do you mean? I'm just trying to update you on my life."

"Stop calling me that! My cousin never called me that."

"Darling, I'm your cousin. It's Opal. Today, Freddie and Timmy are going out on a boat to explore the Keys. You would love it."

Another strangled cry. "Fuck you! My cousin died in a boating accident with her husband and young son over a year ago. Quit fucking calling me! Not at night, not the afternoon, not ever!"

My lips turn up in a genuine smile. I wish poor Mary could see it. Especially after all the research I had to do to exploit Mary's family tree and learn what relatives were close by. I had to *earn* the context for this new phase of my plan.

The Lie She Wears

"The late-night calls have been hard on me to maintain, darling. Still, they are fun, aren't they?"

More whimpers. "Please . . . I've had a terrible year. I got dumped by my boyfriend after changing everything about my life for him. I can't handle anything else."

"We'll see about that."

"I swear to God, I've called the police on you, and I'll do it again. I know exactly who the fuck you are—"

I hang up with a sigh. Whenever Mary becomes so activated that she resorts to threats, I get bored. She dissolves into obscenities and crying, and the conversation inevitably stalls. I'm sure she's already called the police several times, but there's no way to prove I'm involved. I wish she would give us more time together. With each successive call this week, her temper has gotten shorter and shorter.

It's possible that the letters I keep sending are also wearing on her nerves. The information that the post office Hound, Megan, dug up for a small sum—Mary's previous addresses, her cousin's previous addresses and public membership in a Florida nautical society—has proven clutch in adding detail to my paragraphs. I love a good narrative.

I push back on the plexiglass door of the booth, then step out onto the bustling sidewalk. Almost immediately, I see the purpose for today's trip to the tip of the island. A blown-up photo of a good-looking man in a business suit and tie is perched on an easel in the lobby of the New York Stock Exchange. The guy from the nightclub who attacked me in the alley. His dark eyes appear warm and capable in the light of day, versus menacing and predatory in the oily darkness of a nightclub. A memorial for Geoffrey Winstead sponsored by the hedge fund firm where he was an analyst. He wasn't lying about being a wealthy Wall Street big shot.

As I approach the stone entrance, a doorman pushes against the brass handle for me. I scurry inside like I'm eager to get out of the brisk fall weather, shimmying deliberately in my tight pencil skirt.

In a conference room adjacent to the foyer, Geoffrey the Would-Be Rapist beams in another blown-up image, a different professional headshot.

"This guy loved his good lighting," I murmur, pausing beside the easel.

"Along with drinking and bothering beautiful women. But that was our Geoff." A man side-eyes me in a playful reprimand, and I deliberately startle.

I flutter my hand to the pearls around my neck. "Oh, gosh. I'm sorry, that was rude of me to speak about Geoff that way. God rest his soul."

The man tips his head. Hair plugs line his forehead, not yet flourishing. "Totally. How did you know him?"

A man and a woman in a black pencil skirt similar to mine slide past us to reach the conference room. The memorial is beginning.

"Oh, we dated for a while. It's strange that he's never going to call me again." I let my gaze fall to the polished tile, allowing my lips to pout seductively.

When I look up, the Wall Street tool is staring at my knit sweater, at the top button that I left unfastened. At the red bra I chose to wear underneath.

"Very strange," he says with a grin. "Listen, I'm Rick. Any chance you want to grab a drink? I can't stand cry-fests. What's your name?"

"Opal," I reply. "I'd love that."

Without another pause or the pretense of needing further time to mourn, Rick and I quickly find ourselves in a classic Financial District bar. All leather, dark lighting, and green-accented light fixtures.

I go to the bathroom to "powder my nose" and leave the white wine I ordered unattended on the counter.

When I return, Rick has a shit-eating grin on his face.

I make a show of dropping my napkin on the floor. "Whoops. Oh, drat."

"Don't worry, Opal, babe. I got it."

The Lie She Wears

As he dips down, I switch our twin glasses without spilling a drop. Rick returns to the counter's level, then raises his wine to mine for a toast. "To remembering the good times with old friends. And making new ones."

We drink, deeply. Within another five minutes, Rick has to steady himself with a hand on the bar. "Hey, I'm feeling kind of out of it. Can we hang later?"

He slaps some cash on the counter, and then he stands. I do likewise. "Oh, Rick, baby. You're not well. Let me help you."

Gently I guide him toward the bathroom, to the last stall on the left. A notorious location in a notorious bar known for its drug-induced antics, and its little regard for ethics—provided that its patrons have the money to buy silence. Rick is a regular here, as I found out after I followed him home last month from the nightclub where Geoff the man-monster tried to assault me. And he often leads women to this exact stall on the weekends.

When Rick is good and unconscious in the corner of the stall, I unbutton his pants. Tug them to his ankles. Then flip him over to a seated position next to the glory hole that I overheard him talking up to the bartender. Using my new Polaroid camera, I snap a dozen photos of him in questionable and compromising positions. The perfect image to place in Christmas cards to his boss and colleagues in the coming months.

Rick was Geoffrey Winstead's best friend and partner in crime. If Geoff got what was coming to him, it's only fair that Rick be served his own helping of karma too.

The bartender peers at me when I emerge from the bathroom, alone. "Hey, what's your name?" he asks.

"Opal."

"I'm Liam. Thanks for taking out the trash, Opal. Next one's on me."

Chapter Twenty-Six

Pearl

Shoppers at the market continue to peruse items beneath white tents, or they simply shelter from the storm clouds that burst in the sky. As soon as Finn Hoskie left, thick drops began to dot my zippered vest. It was a rough turn for my afternoon, after a devastating morning.

Ursula is dead. Finn thinks my father has more secrets than my mother. And I can't ask Dad anything because during our last visit, I nearly caused him another relapse when I initially refused power of attorney over him. I need my life back. I need to get back to the museum, to the career I worked so hard for. This is all too much.

"Hey, you okay?" Kai asks, gesturing for me to join him under a dishware tent. Woven straw trivets cover the wall behind him, while delicate ceramic plates are displayed on a serving tray.

The happy buzz I felt earlier after downing half my beer at the brewery now tastes like a stale blanket on my tongue. Still, I don't want to be alone. Not only are images of Ursula's blood-drenched body flickering across my vision every time I see a ponytail of gray hair in the crowd of shoppers, but I can't rationalize my receipt of her finger in my mailbox. Whoever killed Ursula knows where I live. They know

The Lie She Wears

what I look like, and they probably set the AirTag on my Kia. Being by myself right now is not a good idea emotionally, or physically safe. Kai's warmth, his genuine interest in me and my problems, and the extra thirty pounds he has on me seem like the right combination for a car pool buddy.

I shake my head. "Not really. I need a coffee somewhere. Come with me?"

My words come out pleading and desperate, and I hate myself a little.

Kai's expression falls, revealing his answer. "Ah, I'm sorry, Pearl. Griffin invited all the curators tonight for a dinner to celebrate our progress on the pop-up exhibits. Museum traffic has increased by twofold compared to what's normal this time of year, apparently due to the buzz alone."

"Gotcha. Yeah, of course. That will be nice."

"Okay. Well, if I can help otherwise, just let me know," he says. "I'm on your side about the missing mask business."

A fat drop of rain pelts me on the cheek. "You don't think I took it?"

Kai gives a tight-lipped smile. "I don't. It might come as a surprise to you, but I looked up everyone on the museum's website before I took the job. Like any good armchair detective, I tracked down your résumé, your background."

"What did you find?" My voice is suddenly small, as if he might know new details about Sally's murderous past.

"That you stuck out undergrad and grad studies at Stanford, although you could have gone anywhere. That you're dedicated to your work, as shown through the two papers you had published about Chinese pre-imperialist aesthetics. And that you're hardworking and loyal, as shown by the number of internships you completed with the de Young Museum. You didn't take whatever came your way. And you wouldn't jeopardize something you've worked so hard to uplift and preserve."

My eyes blur as I stand in the rain, staring into the white tent. At the only person who has made me feel seen since I moved back to Portland. "Thank you."

We say goodbye. Clear skies arrive by the time I reach the rooftop floor of a nearby luxury hotel, where crowds of people hover at the bar, most wearing lanyards. I walk through to the patio, to bumping pop music, and do my best to compartmentalize. The views of the cityscape, the number of bridges above the Willamette River, and the direct view into Pioneer Square, where I met Zelda, are all breathtaking at this level. A well-known mural that encourages passersby to "Keep Portland Weird" reminds me that art is not always encased behind four walls.

With only a few customers to contend with, I find a seat in the corner with a clear scope of the entrance. Order a coffee from the server who appears at my elbow, then wrap my vest tighter across my body. I stare from the patio to the interior of the restaurant for a solid minute, searching for anyone who might return my eye contact a little too long, a little too aggressively. When no one but a server and a busser step outside, I relax an inch.

Ursula was murdered. And her killer wants me to know that I'm accessible, that I'm within reach. Anyone is. But is Ursula's killer the person who was harassing Sally?

I take out my laptop from my cross-body bag. Glance up at the entrance to the patio again, and the crowded bar, where bodies shift beneath flat-screen TVs. A flash of white contrasts the black jackets of Portlanders, then two dark holes return my stare. The eyes of a mask worn by someone at the bar.

I gasp. Jerk to a stand, toppling my chair behind me.

The crowd moves, undulates like a wave, obscuring the mask—the bone-white contrast against colorful faces—then it's gone.

People at the edge of the restaurant cast me wary looks. Whispering. One person takes out their phone. At a loss, I glance behind me, at the metal chair that clattered to the ground, at the server who comes briskly walking toward me.

"Everything okay here?" She places a steaming mug of coffee on my table. "Can I get you some water?"

"No, I-I'm fine. Is there . . . is there a costume party inside? Is someone wearing a mask?"

Laughter rings out from the interior. I peer behind the server again. Do I know anyone here—recognize a suspicious face? Someone who might be taunting me with one of my longtime fears?

"No party. You sure you're okay?" the server asks, her eyes full of doubt. Her eyebrows are tented as if she's two seconds away from calling for help.

"Yes, fine," I answer gruffly.

She departs to the warmth of the restaurant and the chatty bar customers. I work to calm my nerves, as I right my chair. I'm too tense. This whole mess has me seeing things now.

An hour passes while I try to lose myself on my laptop. Read through emails, including one from the real estate agent with a revised offer from that prospective buyer: an extra $5,000 to buy the ranch house in the next month—which I ignore. While tempting, there's no way we can sell the house now, regardless of the money.

Following Finn Hoskie's tip to check my dad's work history, I search key words relating to his contracting business, until I'm certain he only ever had a few dozen positive reviews online. He never even kept a website to promote himself.

My phone must be listening to me, because several ads are pushed to my browser, suggesting that I'll find "just the right mask" at Michaels in time for Halloween. Earlier this week, when I asked Ursula if I could drop by today, I had intended to pose more follow-up questions about Sally and ask Ursula where I might find illicit objects and artifacts—like centuries-old masks that were stolen from naive yet well-meaning art museum curators. As it was, I'd searched all the major online platforms. Imperialist Chinese face coverings were nonexistent on eBay, Facebook Marketplace, Trocadero, and several Etsy shops.

A shudder twirls through my core as I recall the scent of blood that welcomed me into her home. The weight of the plastic baggie holding her finger as I gladly handed it to the police.

I shut my eyes tight. New laughter sounds from the bar, dragging me back to the present.

"Another coffee?" The server smiles with all her teeth, her long-sleeve black dress shirt crisp and stain-free.

Behind her, the group of red lanyards has dwindled to three older men at the bar, as the late afternoon turns to early evening. Sunset casts yellow and red beams across the glossy white patio tables.

"Is there a convention in town?" I ask, nodding to the men.

"Yeah, some kind of garage and vintage event." She shrugs. "People bring their stuff to get appraised. Old hairbrushes and creepy dolls."

A road show. The kind that features random trinkets, and sometimes priceless goods. "Is it in this hotel?"

"No, across the street, I think. If you're interested, all you have to do is follow the red tide."

I pay for my coffee, then pack up my stuff. As I take the elevator down to street level, I recall how much Sally loved these expos. How she used to drag me to them when I was a child, and knew everyone who was anyone within that circle.

The event itself is free, I learn as I enter the lobby and make my way toward a large conference hall. A few kids loiter along the walls or seated on cushioned benches. I pass through the double doors that lead inside and a rush of conversation and haggling swells. Hundreds of people mill about or gaze at objects presented on white tablecloths and hung from lattices. To my right, a large group gathers before a life-size Chewbacca doll while the seller entertains offers.

I search table after table. The usual knickknacks that crowd antique store shelves are present, including vintage clothing from nearly every decade. A few bonnets from the early twentieth century are encased in plastic and displayed in the center of the room. I find ancient LEGO sets, wooden trains, and rust-encrusted tools in the western corner of the hall, and it takes me another twenty minutes to peruse the tables that extend to the other side.

At one point, a thrill jolts through me when I lay eyes on a mask. As I hurriedly approach, I realize it's only a dirty luchador mask from the 1990s.

"Dang," I say to the empty eyeholes. "No dice."

The Lie She Wears

"Were you looking for something different?" A woman wearing a jean jacket nearly suffocating in flair—buttons, stickers, homemade pins—cocks an eyebrow.

"Yes, yeah. I was hoping to see some older masks here. From a hundred years earlier or more. Have you seen anything like that here today?" I don't bother specifying the fact that my mask is over five hundred years old. Oftentimes these sellers don't know what they have.

The woman purses her lips. "Sorry, I don't. But you might ask one of the organizers at the head table there. Or there are some appraisers that know everything on sale today, forward and backward."

My gaze follows her pointed finger to a large table blanketed in a white cloth, positioned on a small stage. A woman wearing a blue blazer and jeans speaks animatedly with her hands to an older man with a thick head of cotton ball–white hair wearing a necktie dotted with jack-o'-lanterns. The banner above them announces that famed appraiser Robert Pelham is the road show's guest of honor.

My tongue feels thick. I know that name. To the woman, I ask, "Have you seen that Pelham guy? Is he still here?"

"Right over there. The Halloween lover."

"Thanks." I dig into my bag, moving out of the way as more shoppers come to view the wrestling masks. Withdrawing Sally's address book, I flip to one of the last pages, which she titled, "Antique VIPs." Robert Pelham's name is written, the third one down, just beneath "Megan Stefanich" and someone else named "Tate Kozlov."

My heartbeat ticks up, its rhythm feeling erratic as adrenaline floods my body. I walk toward the table. Slow my pace while Robert Pelham and the animated woman finish their conversation.

He looks over at me, probably curious why I've approached him empty handed, without some childhood toy for him to examine.

"Hi. Can I help you?"

"I hope so. I'm Pearl. Sally Wong was my mother, and I was hoping you could tell me about her antiquing."

Pelham tilts his head. "I'm sorry. I don't know anyone by that name."

My stomach sinks. "Are you sure? She wrote down your—"

"I know Sally." The woman who was speaking to Pelham steps closer to us as another convention attendee approaches the stage. "What did you want to know?"

Pelham turns to the new arrival without even a backward glance at me. Dejected and disappointed, I purse my lips. "Yeah, uh, thanks. I was hoping to ask him about my mom. She died recently."

"Oh, I know. I heard, that is. I'm so sorry for your loss, by the way. You must be devastated. I'm Megan."

I take in this woman's thick blond hair, which she wears in waves, and the bright rouge that's reminiscent of 1980s fashion. "You're Megan Stefanich?"

The smile she wears dims. "Yes. How did you know?"

"My mom, she . . . she mentioned you as someone to speak with about antiques."

Megan folds her arms across her blue blazer. A beaded bracelet with unicorns is visible under her sleeve. "We did work together. I helped her find a few items over the years."

I nod, quickly trying to recalibrate my thoughts. Robert Pelham didn't know Sally—or doesn't desire to talk about her. Megan Stefanich does on both counts.

"Was Sally well liked in the antiquing community? Sometimes she spoke of drama at these events."

Actually, she never told me anything about the expos she went to, after she stopped dragging me with her. But that doesn't matter now.

"Everyone knew her and loved her." Megan lifts both eyebrows. "Did something happen before she—"

"No, I'm just curious because . . ." I search for a plausible reason instead of sharing the truth, or any version of it that might make Megan back away from me.

"I want to understand the world that my mom loved so dearly," I finish. "She sometimes spoke about people that were jealous of her successes."

I'm reaching here, but Megan brightens at the suggestion.

"That's right. When the series of Giulio Venetta masks were auctioned off, local antiquists were a bitter bunch. People talk to me, you know?" She gives a self-deprecating shrug. "They were all grumbling that they'd been antiquing just as long and it wasn't fair she happened to land on the Moby Dick of masks."

"Was that true? She just got really lucky?"

"Yes and no. She had a deep bullpen of contacts here. Knew most of the antique and secondhand shops in Oregon and Washington state, and they all knew she was into masks. But I actually found the final mask for her at a shop in Vancouver, BC."

"Oh, wow. Well, did anyone stand out for how angry they were about Sally's success?"

"None more so than the rest, like I said. But there was a man at Gillian's who looked almost offended while her masks were being auctioned off. I was watching the live stream, and he couldn't stop scowling."

"And who was that?" I ask, anticipation tingling in my stomach.

"Finn Hoskie. The head of client relations for Gillian's. I don't know what bee got in his bonnet, but the man held a grudge against Sally for years before, even. From what she shared with me, he seemed to, uh, disapprove of her thrifting."

"Too lowbrow? I know she collected vintage hair barrettes for a while."

"I guess." Megan nods, then peers around me. "Maybe he thought the items weren't becoming of the Gillian's brand. Then when she got him fired—"

"Hold on, I thought she got him demoted."

"No—pushed into early retirement. He was irate, from what I heard." Megan pauses, her gaze flitting over my head. "Sorry, were you looking for lucha libre masks? I saw you come from that table, and there are some collector editions there, over in the southwest corner."

No one that I've spoken with—Ursula, Zelda, or my dad—mentioned anything about Sally getting someone fired this year. If Sally was responsible for Finn Hoskie losing his job and being forced out of his industry, that gives him a significant reason to be angry with her, even more than the demotion that Ursula mentioned was enacted at Sally's request. It gives him motive. Either to harass her before her death, or maybe to continue harassing her family after the fact. Could that hatred of Sally extend to me—to involvement in my troubles at the museum? I saw him less than two hours ago, and he could be anywhere by now.

The woman with the jean jacket flair said Pelham might know about this show's offerings. *There are some appraisers that know everything on sale today, forward and backward.* Maybe Megan does.

"No wrestling masks for me." I shake my head. "But have you seen any masks from China? I'm looking for one that was used in weddings. It resembles a Buddha and covers the entire head. It would be very old."

And is priceless, and is the thin line between my employment and my termination from the museum.

Megan twists her mouth to the side. "I don't think so. No, I would definitely remember an item like that."

"Okay. Well." I pause, trying to get my bearings. "Well, I've been looking for that specific mask recently. Any advice for someone just starting out in antiquing and on the hunt?"

She shrugs. "Not really. You either have the passion for it or you don't. Me, for instance—I've always been good at finding things, since I used to work at the post office. Learned a ton about how to track down people and the packages or things they value."

I thank Megan for her time, then promise she can have first crack at Sally's antique collection once I finally sort through everything.

Outside on the street, rain begins to dot the sidewalk once more. Tension rolls across my shoulders as I recall Finn's own words of advice to seek out my dad's work history. Whereas before it felt like a helpful lead to follow up on, now Finn's suggestion strikes me as conveniently distracting from his grudge against my mother.

Chapter Twenty-Seven

Pearl

The night spins by in mental clips of the worst moments in my recent memory. Sally's funeral and her haunting favorite pop songs from the eighties. Griffin's puckered face as he escorted me from museum property. Ursula's dead body, the postcard beside her that displayed the rolling hills of some place in Oregon. *You can run.*

During the morning, Zelda shot me a message, checking in on me. She doesn't know anything about Ursula's death or how I discovered her, but she knows today marks six weeks since Sally's death. For a moment, I was touched that she remembered. Then I recalled that she's inheriting a portion of Sally's money. Nothing Zelda says can be viewed without that lens.

Oddly enough, when I read her words via text—I'm thinking about you—another conversation returned to mind: one I had with the new custodial employee at the museum, Cherry. She had said *Be seeing you* when I left the elevator. Something about her appearance, the dark hair and wide-set eyes, reminded me of Zelda, despite their age difference of at least twenty years. Maybe it was the way Cherry seemed to want to connect to me so quickly. Too eagerly, in Zelda's case. Suspiciously, in hindsight.

I haven't seen her since our meeting at Pioneer Square. But that hasn't stopped her from messaging me every few days, looking for updates on my headspace, how my dad is doing, and whether I need help cleaning out Sally's things from the ranch house. All this might strike me as thoughtful, coming from my mom's former live-in nurse. Except the questions she asks are too intimate. So personal and overreaching. As if she's snooping for information instead of contacting me as a friend.

Have you been sleeping well? Did you take that tea I told you about? What time of night do you wake up?

Is your dad doing well? How are his symptoms lately? He should really remember to call me if he needs anything, does he still have my number?

I hope you aren't overwhelmed by all the stuff at the house. Let me know if you need help. I can bring lots of boxes, maybe even ask some nurses I know to help. We could clear stuff while you're gone.

Zelda could be behind some portion of the last week's headache. Do I think she killed Ursula? No, not really. And yet, I can't help wondering what her last words were to Sally before my mom drove away that final time. Whether Zelda wanted her portion of the inheritance sooner than Sally intended.

Maybe that's just my mindset these days. Nothing feels easy or straightforward. Whenever I get close to learning who held the biggest grudge against Sally, something new throws me off-balance. Like the postcard that was next to Ursula's body, and that resembled others sent to the ranch house—but without any dates attached and with a harrowing message I think is for me. No *three weeks* written at the bottom, or *two weeks* to note the timing of some event. Just an implication that the killer has me in their sights, as if they knew I would find Ursula first.

The key to figuring out who is threatening me—who killed Ursula—is related to the dead bodies on my family's property. I'm as

The Lie She Wears

sure of it as I am that the mask was stolen, that it isn't gathering dust in some unmarked box in the museum's warehouse hall.

I've made zero headway on locating the mask. Although I've been allowing myself to take a passive stance since being placed on leave one week ago, I truly thought it would be found by security staff within a day or two, tops. The fact that Griffin hasn't contacted me and is treating the other curators to dinner without inviting me makes me feel like he's written me off.

Despite searching the internet forums all night and this morning, I've found nothing relating to the missing imperialist Chinese artifact. I checked whether other antique road shows might be coming to the Pacific Northwest, in case the mask is already making the rounds between online marketplaces and in-person venues. But the usual show schedule begins and ends in the fall. The convention of sellers and buyers I stumbled into was the last of the season.

I sigh, rolling my shoulders back. Try to coax some of the tension from my muscles while seated at my kitchen table, waiting for Kai to arrive. He agreed to use his powers of online research to assist in locating the Buddha mask. I hope we don't find it on eBay. But I also simply hope we find it.

Voices from the sidewalk below carry up to my third-floor window. A couple arguing over whose turn it is to cover utilities. Footsteps clamor up my complex's stairwell, and then a firm knock raps my door.

"Okay, Pearl. Relax," I say to my reflection in my laptop's screen. "He's just a boy. And you're just a girl looking to find a mask and solve some murders."

Wearing a wry smile, I approach my door. Prepare to invite a guy inside for the first time since I moved back home. With a quick eye at the peephole, I catch Kai sliding his hands into his jacket pockets.

"Hi," I say, stepping back for him to enter. "You found me."

"I did. Great spot you have here. Is that a McMenamins brewery on the corner?"

"Which one?" I smile. "They're everywhere in Portland."

I lead Kai into my kitchen and to the round table set against the window. He lowers a red Nike backpack, then withdraws his laptop as I serve us both fresh coffee from Stumptown Roasters.

"I always forget to come up to Northwest," he says. "But you've got so many cool bars and eateries."

"We do—or so I hear. Since moving in, I haven't really visited many."

He tilts his head to the side. "You okay? You seem . . . tense."

I push out a breath. Recall that he handled my confessions well yesterday at the brewery. "Yeah, I was just thinking about that postcard that was found on Ursula's body."

And those that I found mailed to the ranch house and addressed to Liam. They all had a criminal connection, according to Kai. It's strange that Ursula would have received one, too, and around the same time.

I still don't know if the dates mean anything, written at the bottoms of the postcards. I tried using a calendar and mathing out when those dates could be referencing, but unless I know the postcards were written the day of the postmark, it's hard to say. They could be a countdown—but to what?

"Did something else seem off?" Kai asks, opening his laptop.

I shrug. "Maybe. I wonder if it could be related to the others I told you about."

Kai narrows his eyes. "What was the image on the postcard?"

"Oregon, but I'm not sure where. The heading read 'Natural Beauty in Oregon,' and green hillsides were pictured, with a cityscape in the background that looked like Portland. Plus, a snaking river cutting through vineyards."

He nods. "A big murder-suicide occurred in the Willamette Valley a long time ago. There was a family back in the 1940s that was launching their own wine, when a son went off the rails and shot and killed everyone. I came across a wine bottle from the vineyard while I was researching my exhibit. Apparently, the son didn't want to carry on the family business."

The hair beneath my ponytail rises along my neck. Another connection to a crime.

"Strange choice to send to someone," I reply.

Kai logs on to his screen. "Strange choice to send to someone who was murdered shortly after receiving it."

My breath quickens as I recall that someone sent flirtatious postcards to my dad. Is each postcard actually a threat, like the one that Ursula possessed must be?

Should I worry about Dad's safety? I called him a few days ago to see how he was doing, and he hasn't gotten back to me.

"Listen, not to overstep—I know I came over here to help you search for the missing mask, but I think we should be looking into these postcards. The whole thing just feels off to me, Pearl. Would that be okay?" Kai sips the coffee I brewed.

"Yeah. Yeah, you're probably right." I settle in next to him, the weight of the week feeling heavier with each hour.

"But I don't know where to start," I add. "How do we research crimes that happened in the postcards' locations, beyond what Google will show us? I mean, that would cover decades upon decades of events for each city."

Kai begins typing. "Back in Chicago, I did a Citizen's Police Academy, where I got to spend the day with local law enforcement officers. I was researching the history of crime scene photography, and one of the forensic analysts shared links to online forums that delve into old CSI protocols. Eventually, I discovered the forums each have a dedicated bulletin board for true crime enthusiasts. There are web rooms where people search for missing objects related to cases, but also message boards to trade information. We can dig into them together."

He shoots me a smile that thaws some of the icy stress encasing my heart, even while new worry for my dad rears its head.

Together. "I'd like that."

We set up side by side. The Discord page he shares with me displays all the most popular forums in the left-hand margin, then breakout rooms underneath for more nuanced subject material. The true crime forum, predictably, has a dozen breakout rooms pinned, with additional sub-breakout rooms fanning below. Brief headings for each one describe the room's content by region, then state, then crime: false imprisonment, torture, assault, harassment, murder. Plenty of rooms seem to overlap.

"Wow, this is wild," I say, clicking into yet another tree of subheadings. "This one talks about three women who were kidnapped and imprisoned for years close to here in Portland, who then had three little girls by their captor. And this one talks about the Turnpike Bloody Brontë. The gory fan fiction writer, right? You told me about them the first day we met. The forum says they like to take a finger from their victims."

My nose scrunches.

"That's the one, over in Jersey." Kai taps his keyboard. "Hey, check this forum out. It's got photos and descriptions of archaeological finds from the world over. Sometimes, you can find items that were stolen from tombs or other museums, but you have to sift pretty hard through the clutter."

"Challenge accepted. You're describing my daily routine lately."

Over our coffees, we stalk the rooms. Count how many times an "armchair detective" wishes for a book deal like the most famous among them, Michelle McNamara. When we find mention of any of the four cities featured in the postcards, we cross-reference the details with online articles from major newspapers of the region.

An hour goes by, then two, before my phone rings. The default ringtone breaks my tunnel vision, and I scan my phone's screen. It's my dad's care facility.

"Hello?" I answer, then mouth, *Sorry*, to Kai. He stretches his arms behind his head, nonplussed.

"Hi, Pearl. This is Paloma Burgess, the director of Twin Pines." Someone coughs in the background. "I have an update for you on your dad, Liam. Is now a good time?"

"Yeah. Is everything okay?" I stand, then walk over to my kitchen sink. Kai lifts his head from his screen.

"Ah, yes and no." The woman pushes out a noisy breath. "Your dad has experienced a setback. He's . . . His speech has been significantly restricted."

I steady myself with a hand against the wall. "How bad? When?"

"We've been running tests, and our doctors are still evaluating him. This happened on Tuesday. At his best, he's slurring. At worst, he can still write with his left hand and is able to type text into a tablet we have for communication assistance as well."

"Did something happen? Did he say anything before the relapse occurred? Like, was he feeling sick or not himself?"

"I've asked the staff several times. The only thing I can think of is that he appeared bothered after your visit last week. Shaken by something."

After I thank the director, I hang up. Worry a dry piece of skin on my index finger with my thumb. Rotate it back and forth until a sting travels across the digit.

It's my fault. I stressed him out too much during our conversation about me being granted power of attorney over him. I should have been more open to it, less anxious. He's still processing the loss of Sally, and the complicated tragedy of losing control over his own body. He needs me, and I've been so depressed about being placed on leave from the museum, and too focused on deciphering Sally's letters, on the dead bodies on our property, and now on the murder of Sally's closest friend. All are horrible. And yet, none as terrifying to me as potentially losing my dad.

My heart squeezes again.

Especially when my carelessness is the reason he's in so much pain.

Chapter Twenty-Eight

Opal

New York City, 1992

Downtown is breezy in mid-October, especially at the edge of civilization outside the police precinct. After the last hour, answering the asinine questions of an Officer Stimpleton, the fresh air feels good on my face. The Hudson River smells less like sewage in the fall.

I follow the sidewalk farther south, taking care to avoid a taxi's sideview mirror that nearly clips the curb. Normally, I wouldn't mind a morning off from listing appointments, provided they came with a nice drink or a handsome face willing to buy that nice drink. However, revisiting the details of that dead woman's bus death and denying that I've ever been in contact with Mary Anker—striking just the right balance of confusion and indifference—is tedious. Unproductive.

Also, interesting that the police haven't contacted me about Rick—surname Shit for Brains—and the obscenely compromising photos of him that I sent to his boss. Although Rick didn't know my real name, I imagine he would have asked that cute bartender, Liam, about me. If, that

The Lie She Wears

is, Rick was willing to continue speaking about his humiliation. And my guess is, he wasn't. Not with that arrogant stink on him.

Stupid Mary Anker, letting her paranoia get the best of her. I was scheduled to show an apartment on Fifth Avenue today, and now another junior agent will get a cut of the commission if it sells.

"Crybaby," I grumble.

With my schedule cleared, I continue ambling toward the tip of the island, and that cute bartender. Over the years, people like Mary, who have piqued my interest and the unusual need that I have to fixate on them, have often wondered, *Why? Why me?*

The answer is always that I don't know. I don't know why a man or woman elicits my attention more than anyone else, beyond the obvious reasons—a woman tries to throw me in the street, or a man attempts to sexually assault me, et cetera. I don't know why someone like Mary Anker has held me rapt, unbeknownst to her, aside from that she tattled on me. I guess the moral of the story, if there is one, is to stay on my good side. Catch my flies with honey.

As I approach the bar where Rick Shit for Brains—*of the New Hampshire Shit for Brains*—led me, believing I would be an easy victim for the taking, I think of the honey waiting for me inside. I think of his long wavy black hair and the light-brown eyes that saw me right away for what I am: a woman with just enough apparent baggage to be considered broken yet beautiful by the right patient, good man.

Or, at least, that's what he'll think. Heaven forbid he actually understand what goes on inside my head.

"Hey, Opal, right?" Liam says, wiping the counter with a white dish towel. Two patrons sit at the far end of the bar top, near the Restrooms of Despair.

"That's right. Nice to see you again, Liam."

I strike up a chat, discussing the new construction going on at the World Trade Center.

"Hey, I get off in five. Do you want to go do something?" he asks, a shy smile on his face.

I shrug. Bat my eyelashes and voice a coquettish murmur. "Oh. Yes, that'd be fun."

Liam cashes out as the evening bartender rolls in to take over. He holds the door open for me as we step out onto the street.

The conversation continues as the sun slips behind tall buildings, hitting all the highs of a first date—where'd you grow up; have you always wanted to be a bartender / real estate agent; which is grosser: Times Square pizza or street vendor hot dogs?

Lights glow from an art gallery on Park Row. Jazz music *bum-bum-bums* as the door opens and someone steps outside with a plastic cup of clear liquid.

I turn to Liam. "Feel like a little culture?"

"M'lady," he answers, offering me his elbow.

We step inside. Head straight to the refreshments table and pluck two cups of chardonnay from the black tablecloth. As we tour the gallery, remarking on the tableaux that feel unique or funny in whatever way, Liam suddenly stops short.

I follow his gaze to the Kabuki face covering mounted on the wall. Spirals of bright-pink paint splash along the cheeks in a Lee Krasner–y way. Thick circles of red highlight the eye sockets.

"Not a fan?" I ask.

"Well, I used to hate masks," he says, slowly. "It started when my uncle donned a ghost mask and jumped out at me at Halloween when I was six. Scared the shit out of me; I thought I might puke."

I lift both eyebrows. "He sounds like an asshole."

A smile returns to Liam's face. "Very astute. I think he was actually going through something, though. Like, he checked into rehab for alcohol the week after. So now, whenever I see a mask, they just remind me that you never know what face a person is presenting to the world. You know?"

I brush a hand across his chest. "Are you always this deep? Should I call a lifeguard?"

Liam's gaze roams over my mouth, then my neck, and my chest. "Only if you're scared."

"And what if I like it?" I purr.

He wraps an arm around my waist, then pulls me in for a kiss. The buttery wine complements the mint from an ALTOID he popped earlier, and I find myself leaning deeper into him, his space. Wanting more than what he's offering.

When we break apart, flustered and flushed, I glance to the wall again. "We have an audience. Is he going to bother you?"

Liam chuckles. "The fearsome item of my youth, getting a free show? Very kinky."

After another passionate embrace, we walk out of the gallery, hand in hand. Liam catches me watching him, and I throw him a winning smile while I make a mental note of his little Halloween anecdote.

He's cute. Disarming and smart. And retaining personal information about someone I like—for leverage or otherwise—is always in vogue.

Chapter Twenty-Nine

PEARL

To his credit, Kai asked all the right questions after I shared the details of my call with the care facility director. *What makes you think you're responsible for your dad's relapse? Isn't multiple sclerosis unpredictable?* Hot shame washed over me as I explained that I got into an argument with him during my last visit. I upset him. I did this. And no reassurances from Kai would convince me otherwise until I saw my dad face-to-face.

As Kai was packing up to leave, the shame I felt was quickly replaced by regret. That each time I think I'm making progress in one area of my life, a giant roadblock pops up in another.

The next day, lemon cleaning solution strikes my senses when I step into the lobby of Twin Pines Care Facility. The director I spoke with on the phone—Paloma something—is apologetic as she escorts me to the garden. Dad hasn't improved since our call, and the only way the doctors think that he might is with time. Alternatively, she warns me, he might not.

A new wave of grief swarms at my edges, ready to flood my chest. I step forward into the garden enclosure, leaving the director behind.

"It's not anything that he did or didn't do," she says to my back. "These things just sometimes take a turn."

Without replying, I continue toward the center fountain, where the director told me to find him. The wheel of his chair is visible from behind a tall hedge.

"Dad," I say, reaching his side.

He looks at me, though he doesn't turn his head. His lips flinch as he tries to say something. The tablet he uses for basic communication with the staff is in his lap.

"No, don't. I'm just—I needed to tell you something. I'm sorry," I begin. I lay my hand on his, still expecting him to move, to clutch my fingers in a show of recognition and love; he doesn't.

"I'm sorry I was so stubborn during my visit last week. I stressed you out. I brought this—this—"

Tears prick my eyes. I struggle to get a hold of myself as Dad only blinks at me. A prisoner in his own body.

"I'm sorry," I say again. I take a seat on the bench beside him, leaning against the memorial plaque installed across the backrest. Wondering if one day too soon, I'll be creating a special bench for him.

I stare at his profile, willing him to move, to speak and reassure me that he's going to be okay. Instead, I turn toward the fountain and the soothing rhythm of water splashing from a cherub's mouth into the pool below.

Rather than bring up Ursula's death or the postcards that I dropped off last week, or question him about Sally again, I choose safer topics. I ask him about the food here, then share a review of the pad kee mao that I ate last week and the beer from the brewery that I visited with Kai. I even dig into the happenings at the museum, despite the pang of hurt that grips my chest, in order to fill the space between my breaths. After an hour of talking to my dad, though he can't reply, I say my goodbyes. Clutch his hand once more and tell him I'll be back soon.

His fingers move. Spasm? I glance down at his hand, then back to his face. "Dad?"

He blinks. Twice. Three times, faster than I think is subconscious effort. Is he trying to say something?

When he doesn't tap the tablet—the sign Paloma told me would indicate he wants to write a message—I get up to leave.

The parking lot is nearly empty as I reach my car, feeling worse than when I arrived. Then my phone pings from my jacket pocket. I yank it out, fearing that another AirTag has found its way under my bumper again—but it's only a text from Kai.

> Hey, Pearl. I spent some time this morning trying to figure out what winery that murder-suicide happened at, but it's been torn down. This one is closest to the original site:

I scan the link that follows. Some place called Pour Water Vineyard.

"Never heard of it," I mumble. I slide into the driver's seat of my car, only half glancing at my phone while the website loads. A carousel of photos rotates across the landing page: a close-up of thriving grapes; a view of the Willamette Valley in all its lush green; a photo of an older man and woman.

My mouth gapes open at the couple. I know that guy.

The photo spins away, replaced by the thriving grapes again, and I stab at the screen to scroll through to the end.

Finn Hoskie's beaming smile is unmistakable, his long hair pulled back in a ponytail, though not hidden beneath the broad-rimmed cowboy hat he wears. He hugs a woman tightly—his wife? The subheading on the image lauds Pour Water as the first Native-owned vineyard in Oregon.

Finn Hoskie owns this winery. A quote farther beneath says how deeply he believes in regenerative farming, how his Indigenous ancestors have done it for centuries.

I sit frozen, my seat belt forgotten. Finn Hoskie owns a winery not three miles from my family's ranch house. What did he say at the Saturday Market? *It used to be my business to know everything about anyone related to Gillian's, but I'm retired now. And finally doing what I love.*

Standing next to the drum circle, I thought he was talking about making music. Spending time with his community. Playing crosswords, or something else totally banal. Not helming a winery.

Clutching my phone, I open my inbox and search for the recent email from the real estate agent. Dane Ajamian mentioned how motivated the buyer was who wanted to close on my family's property. If Finn is that buyer, it would make sense that he wanted to expand his own wine empire, which is nearby.

A message scrawled on one of the postcards rises in my memory. *It's been too long.* Finn said that Sally and Liam went to Gillian's headquarters in Seattle a few times, but he didn't specify the dates. Could that message be referencing Sally's trip earlier this year for the auction? Could Finn have written it?

But the other postcards all suggested some kind of friendship; whereas Finn said that Sally and Liam weren't good people. Why would Finn write them vaguely romantic messages, if that's the case?

I shake my head. Shift my car into gear. Despite my lingering confusion, I need to see this winery for myself. If Finn wants my family's property, maybe as revenge against Sally, I wonder if he would also place a tracking device on my car. Some form of insurance to know when the youngest Davis would be at the house—and when he could otherwise come inspect the property himself.

"Twelve. Thirteen." I count the number of signs for wineries that dot the shoulder of the highway leading into the Willamette Valley. Vineyards are scattered across the landscape in the region, although there is only one still within the Portland metropolitan area: Pour Water.

Rain taps my head when I step from my Kia sedan onto the gravel parking lot. I climb the steep hillside, annoyed that I chose blue flats with no socks this morning.

A central rotunda on the top of the hill, the clubhouse is nearly empty but for a bachelorette party clinking glasses. Big silver balloons that spell out *Bride* decorate the corner of the tasting room. An added reassurance that my innocuous questions should be the least interesting sound bite today.

"Morning," I say to the back of a winery employee.

A man with shaggy-cut hair and chunky blond highlights lifts his head. He turns, holding a stemless wineglass. "Welcome. Here for a tasting?"

"Actually, I was wondering if you had any art on display on property. Or antiques?"

I doubt Finn Hoskie would be so vengeful as to use his connections to steal the Buddha mask from the museum, but I might as well keep an eye out. The fact that he keeps cropping up in my search for answers means this is where I should be—even if I'm not clear on what questions need asking.

The man scrunches a pointed nose. "Not that I know of," he says slowly. "The owners mostly focus on wine. Go figure."

I ignore the sarcasm. "Sure. Okay. Well, I'm . . ." Brochures for related wine tours of the area are scattered on the countertop, next to a stack of flyers that describe the benefits of membership at Pour Water. "I'm interested in becoming a member. Are there areas dedicated to members of your wine club here, or—"

The bachelorette party erupts in laughter. "Maybe a more exclusive clubhouse?"

The man gestures down the hall to the left, past a potted palm frond. "Down that way. It's open for visitors now, but we hold private events there for the holidays that are members only."

"Great. I'll take a look."

Along a narrow, dark hallway, I shuffle past framed photos of the property over the years. The images progress chronologically until a final photo presents the same hillside and gravel parking lot I climbed minutes earlier. In the photo, a balloon arch crests the roof of this building against a banner that reads "New Ownership May 2018."

Brushed glass obscures the view of the members-only conference room until I step inside. Forest-green armchairs cluster in pairs around short tables that could double as footstools. An ornate ivory chess set is displayed before an imposing fireplace with majestic horse heads carved into the mantel. It's a good-old-boys smoking lounge from the 1960s, complete with images hung on the walls of men hunting and of Marilyn Monroe laughing in various positions at a party, holding a martini in hand beside Dean Martin. Other framed photos include a black and white of a Native man, a member of the Confederated Tribes of Grand Ronde, digging into the soil.

A thud occurs from the corner of the room. Past the fireplace and beside the broad windows bookended by brocade floral curtains. Behind a door marked "Personnel Only."

Music that wasn't audible beside the bachelorette party trails from speakers in the corners of the ceiling. "Fly Me to the Moon," but in Italian. I creep forward to the office. If I see Finn, I'll have plenty of new questions for him, but if I happen to land on a missing imperialist Chinese mask, all the better.

My feet carry me to the opaque panel. "Hello?"

A light is on inside, evident from behind the brushed glass of this door and its etched lettering.

"Excuse me?" I knock with my knuckles. Try the handle to find it unlocked, then push inward to reveal a broad oak desk, deep bookshelves built into the wall behind it, and a series of black-and-white photographs of a wine bottle mid-pour.

A box of flyers sits in the middle of the desk, similar to the ones that decorate the bar counter of the main clubhouse. A spiral-bound ledger and laptop are side by side, handwritten numbers visible from where I inch farther into the office. A neon-pink sticky note on the ledger reads "New shipment Chab 10/30" in big block letters.

The office is empty. I'm going for the laptop when I notice a drawer in the desk, partially ajar. Filing folders are organized within, neatly labeled in pen. The first dozen appear to be months of the year, then people's names follow.

Across one file's protruding edge, Sally's name is written clearly. Directly behind it on the next file is my dad's. Finn kept records on both my parents.

Shouting occurs back in the clubhouse, and the sound of glass breaking. Exaggerated groans mingle with laughter, reminding me that I have minutes before someone comes looking for me. Maybe less.

I reach for the files, then sift through the assorted papers within. Documentation of Finn's interactions with Sally: emails she sent to Gillian's, phone calls with details written on loose computer paper and the back of a Starbucks receipt, printed images of items that Sally wanted Gillian's to include in their auction collection. A page from a Gillian's brochure of the season's offerings includes the rare seaside series of Giulio Venetta masks from the 1970s that eventually landed Sally the massive sum of money and media attention back in February. A half dozen addresses are included on a report of Sally's known residential history, most of them in New York, one in New Jersey, and the rest here in Oregon.

Dad's folder is thinner, less robust. Finn did background checks on both my parents, which would be standard practice for Gillian's, if Liam and Sally said they jointly owned the artifact. Dad's report contains certain new-to-me details—namely, that he was married before my mom. His first wife, Madeleine, apparently shared a residence in New York with him. Judging from the xeroxed legal pleading, it looks like she filed a battery complaint against him twenty-nine years ago. Dad was accused of violence by his then-spouse.

"What?" I whisper. "That can't be right."

There's also a list of clients that my dad must have worked with as a contractor. One client's name is provided only as Bert; next to it, the address for my family's ranch house is included.

The Lie She Wears

"Weird. Why would this Bert be living with Sally and Liam?"

Although strange, this detail might explain why Finn told me to look into Dad's work history. Or maybe Finn wanted me to find the legal pleading. It looks like the accusation against my dad was ultimately dropped by his wife, but it gave him a record of abuse charges.

A new thought stops my reading. What if "Bert" is actually Robert—Robert Pelham, the appraiser who said he didn't know Sally? But why would he claim our address for his own, and why would Dad have named him a client?

A moan rips through the silence of the office, jarring me from my thoughts. I peer over the side of the desk, then a loud thud shakes the cabinets beneath the bookshelves. I whirl, terror shooting through me, when the cabinet door swings open. A bloodied hand surges from the dark. Wide brown eyes reel as Finn Hoskie struggles to lift himself from under the bookshelf, then spills forward onto the floor. A gash cuts clear across his forehead. He's been attacked.

"You . . ." he whimpers.

I stumble backward. "No. I'm just here to—"

Red oozes from somewhere else on his body, soaking the white dress shirt he wears. "Go . . . Get . . ."

Words fail him. He winces against some pain that vibrates across his skin in a shudder.

"I'll get help. I'll be—" I spin on my heel to reach for the door.

"No!"

His plaintive tone stops me from running away from this scene, the gore, the horror of seeing someone in agony—and giving in to the fear that whoever did this could be close by and watching now. Anxiety trips along my nerves, setting my teeth to chatter. I return his stare, unable to move.

"No," he says again. I step around the desk to meet him on the rug. A postcard featuring an image of a pedestrian bridge in downtown Portland fell with him to the floor, with a message written across the preprinted lines: "I'm sorry I killed him. —Pearl"

A rush of cold floods my limbs, then I snatch the postcard up from the rug. Shove it into my pants pocket, choking back a sob.

Finn crashes, his eyes closed, as if mustering every ounce of strength that remains to him. "You did this." He pushes the words between clenched teeth. "You, when you got her . . ."

"Got who?"

"Get . . . Liam—" Coughing racks his frame, and then blood is spurting, gushing from his neck.

I get to my feet and sprint into the tasting room, shouting for help. The man behind the counter runs into the hallway, in the direction of the office where I told him Finn is dying, but I stay in the rotunda. My fingers smash the emergency call button on my phone, and I answer questions from the operator with stilted answers: *Yes. No. I don't know. I don't know. I don't know.*

When sirens finally reach the parking lot, I submit to the shock that seeps across my core.

An hour blurs by while I'm questioned by police officers. Detective Sims and Officer Laurel each take a turn asking me to recount what I witnessed, their skepticism of my story growing more pronounced with each raised eyebrow.

I came to question him.

About what? You don't exactly run in the same circles.

He held a grudge against my mother.

So you came to avenge her.

No, no, no. I think he's been following me. I think he tried to buy my family's property.

And now he's dead, conveniently killed right before you arrive. Just like Ursula Romano.

"Don't leave town, Pearl. We'll be in touch," Detective Sims says to me, in ominous goodbye.

The drive home unspools in a daze. I listen for directions from my GPS because I don't trust myself to get there safely on my own.

The Lie She Wears

Finn directed me to look at my dad's business records. I found several online, but none looked unusual or out of the ordinary in any way—none of the search results contained a history as detailed as that which I found in Finn's files. Now Finn is dead, as proven by the black zipped bag that the paramedics wheeled forward from his office.

Finn owned the Pour Water winery and vineyard, the next chapter of his retirement that he mentioned at the Saturday Market. Why did someone kill him? Why do people I contact in Sally's circle keep ending up dead? The folded postcard in my back pocket that seems written to me—no, *by* me—only confirms that my understanding is lagging behind. I'm not neck and neck with this killer; I'm losing ground.

Tears well in my eyes as I pull onto the smooth asphalt of my apartment complex. Staccato breaths hitch my shoulders as I unleash the stress and fear of the afternoon onto my steering wheel in strangled sobs. Another mistake from a daughter who can't seem to untwine the tangled ball of her parents' secrets.

The failure in her chosen career.

The prey that keeps turning in circles as a nameless, faceless pursuer follows.

Chapter Thirty

PEARL

As a child, I never left my room after dark. The masks that hung in the hallway were like guards that ensured my compliance with Sally's rule: *Stay in bed; you can come out when you smell coffee brewing from the kitchen.* One such mask, a Giulio Venetta that was so common it wasn't worth anything, hung directly opposite my door. Its mouth was open in a half smile that, at night, resembled a sneer. A waiting nightmare, primed to gobble me up if I risked disobedience.

In contrast, Sally's letters have held little clear instruction, except to watch my back. Don't go looking for the details of the past she describes, but also don't be caught unaware.

"So, which is it?" I ask my breakfast table, the stack of loose papers across its surface. Sunrays peek through my open blinds, illuminating the tops of commercial and residential buildings around me. "Why tell me so much but nothing concrete? Why not give me a name or a description to watch out for?"

Sally knew someone was following her. Was Sally's subsequent death, after writing these letters, truly an accident? Or did this stalker attack her when she least expected it?

I shake my head. I'm getting turned around now, confusing myself. Sally died in a car crash—fact. No one attacked her with a knife the way someone did Ursula and Finn.

I scribble my thoughts onto the back page of Sally's address book. Everything I know thus far, including that Ursula had her finger removed postmortem, according to Detective Sims. I search my jumbled scrawl again for a pattern. A name. A reason why the killer would pretend to be me in a written confession that I've now kept from the police.

Panic claws at my edges as I recall the snap judgment I made to protect myself, which has earned me my first crime committed. I couldn't have left the postcard there, could I? Leaving it would have meant the police suspecting me, no matter what I said in my defense. No matter the signs pointing to Sally's enemies.

"Think, Pearl, think." I push out a hard breath.

I review the letters that Sally hid, but none of them tells the whole story. It's only by processing them together—as the forest, instead of simply the trees—that I spy hints of the woman so many believed her to be: funny, caring, intelligent, and strategic. Whereas my stunted, antagonistic relationship with her always struck me as negative and borderline offensive. Heartbreaking that it took Sally dying for her to reveal more of herself to me.

Or, maybe, it's the other way around. I could never see her for who she truly was, apart from the mother I disappointed.

I sketch out a cluster of trees with my pen, thinking back on my conversation with Ursula. She must have known something about Sally that set a target on Ursula's back. While Finn would have uncovered the same details during his time as head of client relations for Gillian's Auction House—the last ten years, according to the LinkedIn profile I found.

I touch the edge of a folded letter, whose page was originally ripped from a spiral-bound notebook. "Sally wrote me letters. Sally killed two people. Dad was also violent, as uncovered by Finn."

My inbox pings with a new email on my open laptop. The real estate agent. Dane Ajamian shares that the offer to buy my parents' property is off the table. That the prospective buyer was killed, and that I may have seen it on the news? He owned a winery nearby. *A real tragedy. A loss for the community*, Dane writes.

My throat closes, recalling the scene yesterday. The velvet decor of the winery's offices. The black-and-white images framed on the walls.

I shake my head. Bite back the emotion that wets my eyes, just like it did all last night. At least I now have confirmation that it was Finn behind the offer.

"Concentrate, Pearl. Who is killing people connected to Sally?"

Finn wanted to own something of Sally's when, in his mind, she had cost him his job and taken so much from him. Tit for tat. The first victim who came to the house at night, whom Sally killed, had it out for her, too, according to Sally's letter.

I stare at the papers before me. Zero in on elements that summarize this whole debacle. "Letters. Murder. Secret life. AirTag."

Ursula was found with a postcard beside her, the same as those that were sent to our house. I would have thought that Finn was behind these, knowing what I do about his intention to buy up our home, and the fact that he knew both Ursula and Sally from his work at Gillian's—but Finn was murdered too.

"Letters. Murder. Secret life. AirTag. Postcards. True crime."

I suck in a sharp breath. Realization tightens my chest as the key words slot into place, like a spatially designed exhibit.

"If it walks like a duck and talks like a duck . . ." I say, borrowing Kai's words. Letters, murder, violence, and a secret life are all details consistent with—

"The Turnpike Bloody Brontë," I whisper. My pen slips from my fingers, clattering on the table.

Kai's explanation of the famed killer's highlights comes back to me, along with the smell of the stale coffee we drank together the first day we met. They're a serial killer who's never been caught, who first tormented their victims with haunting letters, who would eventually kill the victim, then remove a finger.

The first dead body on my family's property was missing a toe; the second, a finger. In her letters to me, Sally was insistent that these people surprised her in her home, that she was only defending herself. But what if they knew her as the Brontë? What if they meant to strong-arm her—blackmail her—because they knew her secrets?

I don't know that Sally sent letters to her victims in advance, but Ursula learned by chance that Sally lived in New Jersey for a time. Ursula and Finn each received a postcard, same as Liam, who suffered a massive relapse after I came for a visit—during which I delivered to him four postcards. Whoever is killing people now could know about Sally's murders back then.

A Google search on the Turnpike Bloody Brontë on my laptop returns hundreds of websites, forums, and op-eds. Apparently, the police debated endlessly whether the killer was working with someone else.

I flip to the middle of Sally's address book, to the page that includes Robert Pelham's name. The file that Finn had on my dad noted one of his clients was named Bert, who also listed our home address as his. Was that Robert Pelham, going by a nickname—Bert? He could have been lying to me at the convention when he said he didn't know Sally. Could he be attacking people now who knew Sally's history of violence—tying up loose ends on behalf of his former partner in crime?

There's also a Robert Truman in the address book. But a browser search offers little in the way of details on him. And nothing that overlaps with Sally's world like Pelham's career in antiques.

The room sways as I write notes in Sally's address book linking my mother to multiple murders. None of this seems completely right. And I can't go to the police with my theories, or base a murder accusation on the fact that Robert Pelham may have lied to me.

I set down my pen. It's nearly nine o'clock in the morning, and Kai should be at the museum by now. What I have to ask shouldn't be sent via text or spoken over the phone.

My heeled boots echo on the gleaming tile mosaic of the museum's empty lobby. The receptionist at the welcome counter speaks into the desk phone, and my labored breathing is the only other noise as I turn the corner into Contemporary Art.

I take the elevator to the administrative offices on the third floor, knowing most museum employees start the day at their desks. Without my badge, I pause beside the locked door that leads to the administrative wing. I cup my hands to the opaque glass, trying to catch any movement on the other side, when it opens. Griffin begins to apologize, and then he starts, recognizing me.

"Pearl, what are you doing here?"

I hesitate, knowing the truth is too outlandish to share, especially if I want to resume working here at some point.

But he continues, "Never mind. Come with me."

He leads me past shadow boxes mounted beneath plexiglass and into his office, where he shuts the door behind me.

"Did you find it?" I ask, taking a seat in one of the hard-backed chairs. "Did you find the mask?"

Griffin frowns. He crosses his arms, leaning against the door. My exit.

"Yes, I'm afraid. In your office. Museum security located it, the second time they searched. It was discovered in an empty filing cabinet."

"You—you're kidding."

"I'm not. We also found two other masks that you said you didn't need for your exhibit. You tried to steal three priceless masks, Pearl."

"No, I swear I didn't. I don't know how they got there, but I never took them away from the staging room. I mean, I share office space with Peggy Vo. Are you sure it wasn't her?"

Griffin sighs. "Peggy wasn't in the building during the time you said the mask went missing. And she's been out recently due to the flu. Security footage is being downloaded from the main server to confirm the exact day and time you took them, but the writing is on the wall, Pearl. You're fired. I wish it didn't have to come to this."

The Lie She Wears

The building quiets as my world plummets around me. I struggle to fill my lungs with air. "Please . . . Please, I can't lose this job. I would never, ever harm an artifact that was entrusted to me, I swear."

Griffin nearly rolls his eyes, peering up at the ceiling. "You think I make this accusation lightly? I don't. Believe me."

"Then why—"

"Pearl, you and Kai Weathers were the only employees badged into the Authorized Personnel areas at the time that you said the mask was likely taken—sometime between Friday afternoon and Saturday morning. It's either you or Kai who took it. The computer entrance records don't lie."

I stare at him, unspeaking. Shake my head, still unable to process what he's saying. "But it wasn't me."

"Right. I figured you'd say that, Pearl. I don't blame you for holding to your story. But Kai had no reason to sabotage you during the first week of his employment. And you have a personal interest in a priceless version of a mask that you said yourself resembles one you have in your family. You were the one to check this mask out of the warehouse. I'm sorry, Pearl. You'll be receiving an official notice of termination via email from HR shortly."

Griffin purses his lips, appearing as sorry as he might if the sun broke through today's cloud coverage. He's made up his mind.

"Okay, I understand. I, uh, just need to hit the bathroom. Then I'll leave."

"Why are you here, anyway?"

I think back on the frenzied thoughts that were pinging through my head on the drive here. My instinct that I was close to solving at least some of the riddles that have plagued me since Sally died. That Kai would have the answer as to whether my mother could've been the Bloody Brontë. Instead, I'm even more confused—devastated—than when I entered the lobby.

Kai, who stole the mask, then pretended to help me search for it. Kai, who befriended me, made me feel seen, and with whom I dropped my guard when the world was breathing down my neck. Kai, to whom I told everything. Kai lied to me, but I still don't know why. Unless—

"There was someone else in the employee wing," I blurt out. "During the security glitch when the locks weren't working. I emailed about seeing them—"

"Right, I remember. The strange person who only you saw." A scoff quirks Griffin's mouth.

"But it could be Kai. He could have been wearing different—"

"It's no use, Pearl. Give it up."

Panic hums against my ribs. Either it's Kai or it's an unknown thief whose name and appearance I don't have. No. To borrow Kai's own words, if it walks like a duck and talks like a duck . . . Kai's badge doesn't lie.

I meet Griffin's self-satisfied expression. He seems more at ease now that I've quieted.

"I . . . uh . . . Well, to answer your original question, I came to check on Kai, actually. To ask him some questions about his exhibit."

Griffin nods. "I'm sure he'll be relieved to know the mask has been found. He's been spending more time in the storage area lately, trying to help locate it and not knowing that you had it hidden in your desk all along." He opens the door to allow me to leave. "I'll be right here when you're done."

Without replying, I reenter the hallway. Walk toward the employee restroom. Turn back at its entrance to confirm that Griffin is watching, then I disappear behind the door. After I count to ten, I poke my head out and find him gone—returned to his office. I break into a sprint that carries me all the way to the stairwell at the end of this floor.

Down three flights of stairs, I enter the ground level, then continue straight. I pass the push bar exit that leads into the Contemporary Art wing, still moving within the employee-only area, and slide inside the warehouse.

My footsteps tap the concrete in dull echoes as I jog past the first few rows. The aisles that were once mystical and mythical to me, holding artifacts from decades and centuries past, all seem foreboding and sinister now. Reflective of the lives lost in warfare, the cultures destroyed

The Lie She Wears

but for tiny remnants that we protect and preserve, and the hopes of a once-naive associate curator who thought she could thrive in this field.

I didn't steal the mask. Kai stole it.

Kai bends over a circular container in the East Asian art section. Japanese scrolls that I passed over months ago curl in a crate at his feet.

"Pearl. What are you doing here?" He stands, dusting his hands on his slacks.

"What are *you* doing here? Are you getting ready to steal something else?" Rage boils beneath my skin, from behind my teeth—this man has been pretending to help me for over a week, when he is the only other person who could have taken the mask, according to Griffin.

"What do you mean?"

He takes a step toward me, and I mirror him, only backward. "Don't come any closer. I know you took the Buddha mask. Then you planted it in my desk, along with two others."

Kai breaks into an incredulous smile. "You're joking, right?"

"I wish. You lied to me. To everyone. Only I'm the one who's getting fired for it."

My burgeoning professional reputation is destroyed. I'll never get another job curating. I'll have to start over. Move to Canada, and even then I'll probably be rejected by any museum with ties to the Pacific Northwest. Not to mention the impending lawsuit and criminal charges Griffin is sure to tack on.

"You ruined my career, Kai. My life. How could you do this?"

He steps toward me again. "Pearl, I promise you, I didn't—"

"Stop," I say, my voice bordering on shrill. "Stay where you are. You've been following me. Maybe it's you who's been sending the postcards, imitating the Turnpike Bloody Brontë. Your true crime crush."

Something Kai said to me at the Saturday Market boomerangs in my mind. *I looked up your résumé, your background.*

"Is that why you researched me? You admire her?" I scan the shelves closest to me and spy a samurai sword encased in a swath of Bubble Wrap. I grab it, wondering if it can still stab despite its protective layering.

"Who? Pearl, just hold on! What the hell are you talking about?" Kai shouts. He plays the victim, lifting his arms and widening his eyes. He's almost convincing, but for the smirk that plays on his lips. Laughing at me. Enjoying my spectacle. Just like the mask hung across from my childhood bedroom.

"It all makes sense," I murmur, trembling. Stepping one foot behind the other, holding the sword in front. "Your obsession with crime. You badging in to steal the mask and make it look like I'm responsible. You must have known Sally was the Bloody Brontë and that she told me her secrets. You wanted the fame and attention for yourself, after you out her as a killer, just like the armchair detectives in the forums."

"You—you're not thinking clearly, Pearl. Put the sword down."

He's right. These jumbled facts, the dim lighting for artifact preservation, the lack of sleep—all of it is giving me a headache.

"Kai, you have been playing me since we met. Not the appraiser. It's you, out of some twisted desire to imitate one of your favorite killers. A form of flattery. You killed Ursula and Finn."

My vision blurs, causing me to lose my balance. I grab on to the shelf beside me to steady myself and nearly pull down another crate of scrolls. When I look up, Kai has moved closer.

"I said, stay away from me!"

"Pearl, you're unwell. I know you've been under a lot of stress. Just, give me the sword."

He lunges, and I fall backward, landing hard on my tailbone and losing my weapon. I scramble to my feet, then limp, loping into a run farther, harder into the darkest part of the warehouse.

"Pearl, come back!" he shouts. "I won't leave you like this!"

My phone rings, a blast of high-pitched notes alerting him to my exact location. I silence it, then see Zelda's name scroll across the screen.

"Zelda," I answer. "Zelda, listen to me. I'm in the warehouse part of the museum. Kai Weathers is chasing me. He killed Ursula and Finn. He's coming after me. Get help."

My heavy breathing almost obscures the sound.

"What?" Zelda asks on the line. "Where are you?"

A scratching noise. Coming from the next aisle over, shrouded in darkness.

"Who's there?" I whisper. "Zelda?"

A figure steps out from around the corner, their black rain slicker swishing with the movement. Tall, yet slim, and wearing one of the masks that I chose for my exhibit and left in the staging room. A Chinese opera mask whose bright-red painted eyes slice through the dark. The figure takes another step toward me without speaking.

Terror ripples down my back. Instinct rises in me and bellows from outside of myself to *run*.

"Who are you? What do you want?" I whimper.

The figure doesn't reply. Instead, they raise their fist until the lighting overhead gleams against a shining kitchen knife.

Sharp fear catapults me, launches me toward the emergency exit and its glowing green sign as footsteps give chase behind me. I reach for the push bar of the door. Strain to move my limbs, to hitch my knees higher and burst into the light of the loading dock outside, when a haunting voice whispers, "Got you."

Pain sears across my back as the blade sinks into my skin. A kaleidoscope of hurt spirals as I writhe, twist, stretch, scream to get away.

I collapse to the ground. Turn to the side at the approaching steps, then spy the tan boots I noticed weeks ago in the same stairwell I just took from Griffin's office.

A woman.

"You . . ." I manage. "You're . . ."

Fireworks explode across my skin in a burning wave, new agony pulsing from my wound.

White static fills my ears, but her voice carries over the noise: "Yes. Me."

PART THREE

Chapter Thirty-One

OPAL

New York City, 1992

Liam the bartender wraps his arms around my waist, then lifts me into the sky. I kick my feet out, allowing my skirt to catch the wind, and giggle maniacally. A bit of it is actually sincere. I'm having fun, goofing off in Central Park, with a cute guy I met while giving an asshole his due.

Lowering me to the ground, Liam presses me against his chest. He curves his hand around my neck beneath my hair, then brings me in for a soft, sensual kiss that sends my stomach twirling. I climb my fingers up his chest, then give his nipple a gentle squeeze.

He breaks off, laughing. "Really? You had to ruin the moment, huh?"

"You know I do. My brother is going to be here any minute." I shoot him a playful look so he knows I'm torn between wanting to bed him in the bushes and sending him on his way.

Liam runs a hand through wavy black hair that he keeps long. In the bar's deliberately poor lighting, I thought he resembled an Asian Jim Morrison except for his goofy grin. Liam's two incisors are slightly crooked and make me like him and his imperfections more. He comes from an immigrant family, like I do, so he's always trying a little too hard. He's just the right balance of broken and desperate for connection that I'm looking for.

"I could stay, you know. Meet this famous brother and tell him how hot I think his sister is."

"Oh, right, because that sounds like a party."

Liam encircles my waist with his arms again. "It does to me. When can I see you again?"

I meet his earnest light-brown eyes and find myself wondering the same thing. I like this guy. I haven't liked anyone in . . . ever? Not this way, at least. In the past, I've chosen all my boyfriends for their utility and what they brought to my life.

Chuck Webster let me copy his homework in middle school. Toby Harrison had a roaring Mustang that I drove everywhere in high school. Benson Tran was an up-and-coming politician in the Bronx who had connections into the best restaurants and clubs all over the city.

Liam rubs his thumbs in circles across my lower back. He's got the same night owl tendencies that I do, appreciates a good art gallery, and can talk for hours about building codes thanks to his stint with his uncle's demolition company, something I do find interesting as it relates to real estate. Plus, all that desperation for connection on his part translates to serious enthusiasm in bed. I love an eager man.

"Baby, you'll see me when you see me," I purr. "Now, off with you, before my big brother comes round."

Liam smirks. "I mean it, though. I'd like to meet him soon. I want the world to know I've found my match. That I've been looking for you, for some time."

"Oh yeah?" I lean in close, offering up the emotional intimacy he's obviously craving.

"Yeah," he says in a low tone. "I actually just had a really bad breakup a few months ago. It's almost like . . . I don't know. You and I were meant to be."

The Lie She Wears

He leans in, and then another gentle kiss turns into a passionate embrace, and I'm thinking again about dragging him into the roundleaf bush in broad daylight. Central Park has seen worse.

"Okay, okay," I murmur between kisses. "I'll introduce you soon. But not yet. Call you later."

"I'm counting on it." Liam leaves, a shit-eating grin on his face, then narrowly avoids getting run over by a bicyclist.

The sound of that woman getting hit by the city bus surges in my memory in a metallic crunch. I grimace but lift a hand to wave as Liam turns the corner. What a mess that was. And what a gift that it brought me Mary Anker.

"Is that your latest plaything?" My brother follows my gaze to where Liam disappeared. "Looks a bit meatier than you usually like."

I shrug. All affect that I usually demonstrate for others gone. "I don't usually like anyone."

"Touché."

"Where should we eat?" I ask, gesturing for us to walk.

Errol frowns at a hot dog cart that's stationed by a large water fountain. We sidestep a pair of little girls jumping rope and wearing thin jackets. "Chinatown?"

"Let's."

The train ride downtown passes while Errol and I ride in silence. Our preferred way to spend time together. As twins, we're usually in tune with one another's emotions, and always have been. When Errol used to ask our grandmother for ice cream, his favorite food, I would echo his feelings—anger, fatigue, sadness, longing, whatever it was—until she relented, preferring a pair of kids on sugar highs to the angry little pixies we could be.

Errol already knows about my recent harried weeks. The uptick in real estate activity, the rude woman who made her bed with the bus, the man who almost assaulted me and subsequently died alone in puddles of piss not his own, and the wisp of a woman who thought it a good idea to bring up my name to the police, multiple times now. What Errol doesn't know is what I plan to do about her.

We exit the train and climb up to the fresh air of Bowery. On the opposite street corner, the line for Mei Lai Wah is nearly around the block, and the smell of freshly made dumplings reaches my nose.

Errol sniffs. "Can we talk shop over a bolo bao?"

"Always."

Fifteen minutes go by quickly at this cozy, no-frills eatery. Every customer knows exactly what they want, and the restaurant preps and serves it with ease. Errol and I post up beside a bike rack and behind a sign for a bus stop, then dig in.

The textured bao is sweet and fluffy, the perfect snack. Steam snakes from the bread as I rip into the crumbling yellow, buttery crust, keeping an eye on the southwest corner of this block.

My Swatch watch ticks to ten after ten. A door with bars across the window opens beside Golden Beak restaurant, and then a slight woman emerges, her long blond hair twisted up in a scrunchie. The loose-fitting T-shirt and jeans she wears are what she dons every day that she works uptown in a basic café across from the deli where she waited in line with the rest of the idiots.

Mary Anker walks briskly to her metro stop, as if she's forgotten that I am always nearby, as well as nowhere. She only spots me when I want her to, and now is not that time.

Errol watches her path, wolfing down the last of his bao, then wipes his hands on his pants. "Shall we?"

I drop my napkin into a trash bin, while maintaining Mary in my sights. For the last week, the girl has been hauling ass from the café to tutoring some kids in French on the Upper West Side, to her job at a bar starting at seven at night. Poor thing. She won't have to worry about such a helter-skelter lifestyle for much longer.

My hands flex at my sides, fingertips itching for release. Angry little pixie that I am, that I've always been.

I give Errol a nod. "Yes. Let's."

Chapter Thirty-Two

Zelda

Silence is the first thing I register when I step into the warehouse from the museum's loading dock, slipping beneath a retractable garage door. No voices. No hushed convos. No museum visitors lollygagging around this back entrance. Where the hell is Pearl?

Footsteps march in my direction, and I duck behind a stack of empty wooden pallets as a man in blue coveralls walks by. Security footage will alert the museum soon that I've snuck in, but I'm good with that. Better to have anyone with a gun be on the move to help Pearl. I just need to find her first.

I hurry down the length of this hall, passing a rat trap, doing my best to tread quietly past signs that list regions and time periods. "North America, 17th c.—" "18th c. Europe, Pre-Industrial." "Industrial Revolution." "South Asia." "South Asian Colonial." I don't know what aisle Pearl was in when she answered my call, or who this Kai person is, but he sounds like bad news—like Pearl was terrified of him.

A lighting panel overhead flickers in an off-beat cadence, and I try to ignore the slasher vibes. I pick up my pace, jogging past white crates and clear bins. I focus on my phone. On the little green circle of dots that tells me I'm getting closer.

"Pearl?" I call, louder than feels safe. Anxiety blooms in my body the longer I don't hear anything from anyone. Didn't Pearl say she was here? Is there another warehouse section of the museum?

There might be an exit at the far end of this hall.

Where are the dots leading me?

I keep an eye on the blank wall as I pass. If Pearl was attacked, I need to know where any and all resources close by might be—like a defibrillator and a first aid kit. Lots of private businesses keep them in view, though they're only mandated in public places. Otherwise, I've got an EpiPen and Narcan nasal spray in my handbag. Neither one feels appropriate for Pearl, but I've been surprised before in my work as a nurse.

"How was the patient cured from lying?" I whisper my nervous habit as I scan the aisles. Wary of someone jumping out at me. "A de*fib*rillator was used."

When I was first completing nursing school ten years ago, I took a self-defense class that was offered alongside others, like Anatomy and Clinical Psychology. The ten-week course stressed to me how to block a punch, and also how unpredictable a career in service of others could be, the kind of conflicts a nurse can encounter when treating the general public.

I never imagined my work as a home-health nurse would lead to this.

The green dots on my phone coalesce into a larger, almost solid dot ahead. I'm getting closer. As I approach the end point where my AirTag is directing me, I strain my hearing for sounds of a struggle—or worse. Grunting, whispering, pleading, crying. My mind flies off into dark corners that I don't visit anymore—not since I spent those four years in therapy—and I do my best to focus on the here and now, to ground myself in reality.

I reach out, then graze the shelf closest to me with my fingertips. A labeled plastic bin at eye level contains woven baskets apparently earmarked for an Indigenous art collection. The bin is smooth and cold to the touch, reminding me to stay present.

A door slams somewhere nearby, and I set off again at a brisk pace. The fact that I was able to slip an AirTag first on Pearl's car, then in her tote bag is a damned miracle. I don't know that Pearl has ever trusted me—my close relationship with Sally and the obvious acrimony between them made that difficult—but when we met at Pioneer Square a few weeks ago and she handed me her phone to show me a photo of a weird letter, I was able to disable Item Safety Alerts notifications in her settings. Otherwise, I don't know how I could have followed her as closely as I have.

I slow my jog to a walk as I reach the end of the aisles. There's no one here. Bins of colorful tapestries occupy the shelves, but I can't imagine why Pearl would have come this direction. There is literally nowhere to hide.

I check my phone for the location of my AirTag. The arrow points toward the end of the shelf from where I stand, where a puddle of water covers the floor, but no Pearl and no Pearl's bag, in which I stashed my tracking device.

"So much for technology doing its thing." I sigh. The dark liquid gleams, reflecting the wobbly cadence of the lighting panels. I step toward it, and then a punch of tangy iron hits my nose. My stomach clenches. I know that smell: blood. Not water.

Instantly, I search behind me, in the shadowy corners in front of me, and toward the emergency exit sign that glows green ten paces ahead. No footsteps come barreling forward, but my muscles tense anyway. What is blood doing here—a lot of it?

Where the hell is Pearl?

"Pearl?" I whisper, chills zigzagging down my back. "Hello?"

On my phone, I switch to my call log, then hit Pearl's name. The outgoing ringing sound hums through my speaker—then I hear it. The default ringtone melody. Pearl's phone is ringing.

Terror unfolds across my body as I locate the sound. It's coming from one of the bins.

Not daring to breathe, I inch closer to the end of the aisle, toward the plastic containers. A black mass is visible through the bin, what resembles a small square. I bend down, then tug the bin from the shelf with shaking hands. The container clatters to the floor, but still no footsteps come for me.

Prying the top off is easy, and then I'm face-to-face with the brown tote bag that Pearl wore when I last saw her up close in Pioneer Square. With shaking hands, I unzip it and reveal Pearl's phone screen lit up with my name scrolling across.

Something from the corner of my eye draws my gaze. I look over to the bottom shelf from which I just tugged the large bin and find Pearl folded behind, doused in blood. Her eyes are half closed as if in a daze, while blood gathers at her collar and soaks her white shirt.

I gasp. Struggling to my feet, I lurch toward her. Grab Pearl's arms. Ignore the blood that stains her torso, unstanched and pulsing from some wound on her body. Drag her from the shelf, then push up her sweater sleeve and press my fingers to her wrist to check for a pulse. It's faint. I draw in another breath, whimper at the carnage on this woman's frame. At the rip in her clothing down her back.

"Pearl?" I whisper, pushing the matted hair from her cheek. "Pearl, wake up. Pearl?"

I draw in a sharp breath, then turn back to the walkway. "Help! Somebody, help!"

Footsteps clamor at the opposite end of the warehouse, and then I remember how I'm here and how badly this all could go in a heartbeat.

Tearing open the brown tote again, I unzip the inner pocket and snatch the AirTag that I hid during my meeting with her at Pioneer Square, knocking out a book and some loose papers as collateral damage. I shove the AirTag in my pocket, then grab the book to place it back in her bag when I see my name scrawled across one of the last pages. *Zelda, motivation to lie?*

The Lie She Wears

"What the hell?" I say.

Heavy footsteps grow louder, with the audible jostling of equipment. I grab the papers, throw them in the book, then slam them into the deep pockets of my coat.

"Security! Pearl Davis, you need to leave the property, now—" A man wearing a walkie-talkie strapped to his belt loop and a black utility vest stumbles as he realizes I'm not Pearl. That Pearl is badly injured on the floor.

Another man wearing a blazer nearly crashes into him. "Who are you? What happened to—Pearl!"

"She's been attacked." I roll Pearl onto her stomach, find the wound, then apply pressure to it on her back. Blood squelches through my fingers.

"Your jacket. Give me your jacket!" I shout to the younger man when he doesn't move fast enough. He rips off his blazer, gives it to me to press to Pearl's body.

The security guard swears, and then he's clutching his radio and speaking code into the box. Orders and demands for details are swapped back and forth on the radio, in tandem with the younger man's retching that carries from the next aisle.

More people arrive, police officers in uniform and some in plain clothes, and I'm pulled away from Pearl. The talking and questions and my own sobbing all become white noise to me as they load her onto a stretcher, then slam open the emergency exit door into the alleyway.

Flashes of the first time Pearl and I met and other moments surge in my mind, of the way she rolled her eyes at me when I said something silly, and the warm smile she held for me when I made a joke that landed. The way her black hair swished below her shoulders, the same color as mine, and the gray eyes that were always so analytical.

A police officer leads me out to the museum hallway as patrons are escorted from the property by other uniformed officers. A voice over the loudspeaker announces that business hours are cut short today, starting immediately.

The officer looks me in the eye—Officer Laurie . . . Laurel?—beside a blurry oil painting of a trio of kids. "Ms. Huang, start at the beginning. Tell me how you found Pearl."

The details spill out of me with clarity and precision—I'm in shock. I also realize, as I'm explaining to her that I happened to call Pearl while she was being chased by someone named Kai Weathers, that I'm directly casting suspicion on Kai. Still, I give this officer everything I can—including how I placed a 911 call immediately after the line with Pearl dropped—up to when I discovered the contents of Pearl's bag.

The officer pauses taking notes on a tablet. "Is there anything else you'd like to add, Ms. Huang?"

I hold her eye contact as the truth flashes behind my teeth. *Yes.*

"No. If I think of anything, I'll reach out."

She nods, tapping out of a screen. "You do that."

Once a different officer escorts me to the edge of the building, I descend the stone steps in a daze. Images of the last two hours fight for stage time in my head, like frames from a movie. What just happened? Did that all just happen?

As if in answer, my thoughts go to the book and its loose papers still hidden inside my jacket pocket.

Chapter Thirty-Three

Zelda

Live out loud. Live by faith. Live, laugh, love. All the hokey kitchen knickknacks that decorate my apartment counters seem trite this morning. But I suppose anything bought on clearance from Kohl's would, the morning after I discovered someone at death's door.

"Live," I say, slowly. "Still got that box checked, at least."

When Sally died, I found a spot to rent and moved out of their house as quickly as I could. Pearl made it more than clear she wanted me gone. And now Pearl is in the hospital, unconscious and alone.

Pearl was attacked. Sally is dead. How did everything change so drastically?

Traffic hums from outside the window of my townhouse. The suburbs are not my favorite place to be, but most clients who need intensive nursing care prefer them to downtown. I close my eyes. Listen to the acceleration of passing engines, and music from a stereo as it rises and falls like an ambulance siren.

Late last night, I tried seeing Pearl. After her emergency surgery to repair the knife wound in her back, and the blood transfusion she needed. The only time the medical staff spoke to me, aside from when they asked me to leave finally at ten o'clock, was to ask if I was family.

Tears fill my eyes, and then my vision goes blurry for the hundredth time since I drove home yesterday. I had an interview this morning for a new job—a patient with dementia—but I told them I couldn't. After everything that transpired, I needed to stay home. And I probably would have, bingeing Miyazaki films all day, had the police not called directly afterward, requesting that I come into the precinct for "a few more questions."

I scan the narrow coffee table in my sitting room overlooking this complex's courtyard. Sally's address book appears innocent enough, surrounded by mismatched drink coasters.

After opening the book at home for a better look, I realized almost instantly two things: Pearl had been filling in the last few pages with notes—her suspicions. And some of her own misdeeds, too, when she incorrectly circled Finn Hoskie's name, suggesting he was her pick for a killer—a man I learned was recently murdered, when I searched online for the names she added.

All of Pearl's notes were easy enough to decipher, including the words and phrases she wrote down about me: "Zelda's motive to kill." "Inside knowledge of Sally's past." "Deep medical knowledge could lend itself to murder." "Involved in Sally's death?"

Although it shocked me to read the last question Pearl had written, it gave me solace in a weird way. Pearl didn't lose consciousness convinced that I had murdered her mother. She only suspected me of it.

The letters, however. Reading those had me decimating my supply of ginger ales and chocolate kisses. Back at Pioneer Courthouse Square, when Pearl asked me to read the one note, she didn't mention there were three others like it—explosive in their hints and suggestions.

Sally's confession to not one but two murders just about undid me. I looked around my apartment, searching for the blinking red light. The *gotcha* indicator that proved this was all an elaborate hoax to swindle me out of another year's subscription to Hulu for access to its *Snapped* docuseries.

"Sally, the murderer," I said to my coffee table. "The twice murderer."

Pearl's notes on her mother as someone called the Turnpike Bloody Brontë sent me down a deep rabbit hole—first on the internet, and then I searched for any mention of the serial killer on Netflix, my go-to source of relaxation and research. There were plenty. In dramatized shows and documentaries, interviews abounded from true crime buffs who had studied this "Brontë's" habits of writing harassing letters before killing victims in inconsistent yet gruesome ways. In one, little-known details were supplied by a former sergeant who received handwritten stories from the Brontë, a Detective Mills. When he looks at the camera dead on and says that the killer often took fingers from their victims as trophies, I shivered, then turned off my TV.

The rest of Pearl's notes were less clear to me. Some mention of an antique appraiser, Robert Pelham; an antique "finder" named Megan; a mask that I guess went missing from Pearl's care at the museum during the electrical grid fails; and random names like Bert and Gillian's didn't overtly slot into the puzzle she had outlined. Neither did she mention how she had created or obtained what look like background checks on her family members, then folded them into the pages of the address book.

Her final questions were double underlined, emphasizing just how screwed up things are.

Who killed Ursula? Whoever killed Ursula likely knows about Sally's history, 2 dead bodies.

1st dead body: Name?
2nd dead body: Name?
Who killed Finn?
See the forest through the trees

"Okay, Pearl . . . See the forest through the trees?" I mouth the end of my pen. Prioritizing the bigger picture of a problem—the forest—has never been my strong suit. That's why I'm so good at live-in nursing; I identify the emergent symptoms and treat them accordingly, before a specialist is consulted. Triaging one problem at a time has been my default for every problem in my life, which has made overall planning tricky.

I inhale through my nose. "Yikes. If that's the final riddle of this mess, Pearl and I will need to move away from any greenery. Maybe the beach."

It's tragic that Pearl was attacked, after everything. Tragic, also, that I'll probably be in therapy for the rest of my adult life after discovering her. A day later, I can close my eyes and instantly smell the stink of the blood that covered the floor beside her abused frame. My throat closes as I recall the way her hair fanned out around her neck. How her eyes were half closed as if dozing.

The grief of nearly losing another life bubbles into my throat, and a deep sob racks my shoulders. My stomach muscles clench with each shuddering breath until I'm sore all over from sleeplessness and crying.

Pearl doesn't deserve this. She just moved back home this year. Liam doesn't deserve this either—to possibly lose his daughter, after burying his wife.

Another minute passes, and then I pack up the address book with Pearl's notes and Sally's letters. I'll stash them in the trunk of my hatchback, beneath the spare tire, and I'll return to the hospital today after going to the precinct. See if Pearl's state has improved enough for me to ask her about these notes, if she's awake. Find out if she knows who attacked her.

As I pull onto the highway next to my townhouse complex, a hint of selfish relief comes over me. While it's a shame that Pearl didn't get the answers she was seeking, whoever attacked her probably thought she was getting too close to the truth. If Pearl had only asked me her questions directly, instead of avoiding my calls and hiding away out of—probably—some asinine jealousy of my relationship with Sally, I could have helped her. I could have given her some closure beforehand, at least, about the identity of one of the dead bodies.

The precinct lobby is barking loud when I arrive, and Detective Sims is already waiting for me. Several women in spandex shout about fentanyl and where else should they sleep during trips if not doorways while Detective Sims ushers me into the back. We pass an open desk setting, where police officers make phone calls and flip through file folders, and then we step into a small office cluttered with paperwork. The walls are nearly empty of decor, but for a diploma declaring that Fabrice Sims graduated in 2012 from the Portland Police academy. Beside it, a framed stick figure drawing in crayon.

"Take a seat, Ms. Huang. Can I call you Zelda?" He points to one of the two folding chairs. "I have a few questions for you, as the last person to speak to Pearl before she was attacked."

I smile. I'd rather he doesn't call me at all, but this visit is about more than any follow-up he's doing regarding my discovering Pearl. Judging from the way he studies my hesitation to reply, he knows it too.

"Sure. That's fine," I answer.

"Good, good. Well, we've been busy, as you can imagine. We've been working for most of the night. It's not often that a museum curator is targeted, let alone one so young."

I don't reply. In my line of work as a nurse, I find the best way forward with an uncomfortable conversation is often to let the other person talk.

"Especially after Pearl herself found the bodies of two other victims."

I wait. Try to quell a muscle spasm beneath my eye.

"So, Zelda. When is the last time that you saw Pearl? Were you close? You shared that she was on the phone with you while she was being chased by Kai Weathers, and that's how you knew where she was."

"Right. I guess I last saw her a week ago."

"And did Pearl tell you anything about why she was meeting with Ursula Romano and Finn Hoskie?"

"She didn't. I didn't know she was meeting with them at all, until you just told me."

Don't blink. Don't blink.

Detective Sims nods. "See, to me, it looks like Pearl was questioning these people about her mother for some reason. They're associates of Sally Wong, after all—not Pearl. And each time she went back to question someone for a second round, they were found dead. Or dying. Except for you."

"Oh?"

"Witnesses say you met with Pearl at Pioneer Courthouse Square last week, and Pearl's neighbor saw you deliver a Bankers box of items to her apartment a few weeks back. Before we go any further," Detective Sims continues, "is there anything I should know, Zelda? Because now would be a good time to get it off your chest."

My heart slams against my ribs. *Yes.*

"No. I can't think of anything. I think I might still be in shock, honestly."

"Oh yeah? Why's that?" Sims leans against his desk, forcing me to look up at him from the folding chair.

"Finding her. It was . . . traumatizing on several levels."

His eyes pinch, and I know I've mis-stepped. "I'll bet it was. Do you know who Rohan Singh is?"

I purse my lips, unwilling to incriminate myself.

Sims bobs his head. "Oh, you do. We're both aware. After we got a warrant, we checked Pearl's call log and saw he was a repeat number in her phone. Mr. Singh is Sally's estate attorney. He was in touch with Pearl a lot recently, and he shared some very interesting information with us."

Sweat beads across the nape of my neck beneath my short hair. "What would that be?"

"When we asked him if he had any idea who would want to harm Pearl, he didn't hesitate. He said you, Zelda."

"What?" I blanch. "No way; he has no reason to think that."

This has taken a turn. I didn't expect the accusations to come flying so quickly, but there I go again being an optimist.

The Lie She Wears

Sims levels me with the same kind of bullshit-detecting glare that my first foster mom used to wield on me. "Mr. Singh said that you were very close with Sally, beyond being her nurse. Could you elaborate?"

My vision blurs at the edges. The room spins, twisting at the corners. The truth of my relationship with Sally has never been spoken aloud before, not since Sally figured it out herself about six months ago. But the police will figure it out. And then I'll look even more suspicious.

"She . . . Sally was my mother. My biological mother."

Sims takes his time, weighing my confession. "Really? Who else knows? Did Sally?"

"Yes, she knew. No one else, though. I don't think." Tension eases in my chest, though less than I would have thought at telling someone. Instead, the act feels dangerous.

"Interesting," he murmurs. He eyes me a moment longer. "We're still waiting on the warrant for Mr. Singh's files on Sally, but I have a feeling we'll find something related to you in there. Maybe in the will. Considering you were the hidden half sister—maybe I'll find a motive to want to attack Pearl Davis."

I shake my head. "I swear I would never hurt Pearl. Sally left me some money, but Rohan is still determining the final amount. That's all I know."

"When did you know about Sally being your biological mom?"

I hesitate again, knowing this could sound weird. "I found her myself, after searching for her online. I'm thirty-one, and I wanted to learn more about fertility and whether there might be some genetic anomalies rolling around in my DNA. I discovered who she was and where she lived a little while before she began shopping for a live-in nurse. She hired me without knowing who I was. She figured out the truth about six months ago."

"What was her reaction? Happy? Sad? Angry?"

"A little bit of everything, yes. She never meant to meet me, but she was also overjoyed to be spending so much time together now. Her words, not mine."

"Why didn't you tell Pearl?"

Examining Pearl's face that day in Pioneer Courthouse Square, I wanted so badly to confess our relationship. We were half sisters. I was mourning the death of my biological mother in a similar way that she was mourning the mom she'd spent all of her twenty-seven years loving and fighting against. Earlier, I had placed the AirTag on her car in the employee parking lot of the museum because she didn't seem emotionally well after the funeral, and I wanted to keep track of her. Selfishly, I also wanted to know when Pearl would be at the ranch house and when she wasn't. There was something Sally had promised me, and I didn't trust Pearl to hand it over.

"I don't know. I wanted to tell her. But the moment never felt right."

Detective Sims leans toward me. "So, let me get this straight. You found your secret half sister attacked, only a month and a half after her—your—mother died."

"Well . . . yes."

He nods. Crosses his arms across his broad chest. "If there's anything in Sally's will, anything you're required to split with Pearl, that won't look good."

I purse my lips.

"If it's a lot of money—maybe you had something to do with Sally's death too."

"No, no, no. Hold on. My whole job was to help Sally."

"Was there any bad blood between you and Pearl? From what I've gathered from her colleagues, she didn't mention you much."

"Why would she have? I was just her mother's nurse, for all she knew."

"The help. Did that bother you—that you were considered an employee versus an equal to Pearl?"

"No, I—"

"Did it make you feel less than you already felt? The juvenile department in Bend said that you had some trouble down there. A few misdemeanors for stealing and damage to public property."

The Lie She Wears

"My parents—my adoptive parents—called the police on me after I took my dad's wallet for a run to the candy store because he was too drunk to accompany me. I was twelve. After that, I was in and out of foster homes. My adoptive parents were good to me at first. But when my dad died in Iraq, my mom realized she never wanted a child. She always told me it was my fault he died, and seeing me every day was too hard."

"So, you didn't have a nice homelife or upbringing. You come to Portland to seek out the mother you never had, then discover a younger version of yourself already at home. Pearl."

"No, that's not how I—"

"Let me tell you something, Zelda." Sims lowers his voice, as if he's going to confide in me. He clasps his hands together across his lap. "I've been doing this job a long time. And my gut is usually correct when it comes to homicides. Right now, my gut is saying you aren't telling me the whole truth."

He pauses. Waits for me to self-incriminate, but I manage to keep the urge to defend myself in check.

"Zelda," he starts again, softly. "Is there anything you think I should know about Pearl? She was the first on-site at two different murders, and now she's been attacked. What am I missing here? Who doesn't want Pearl nosing into their business?"

I shake my head. "I couldn't tell you."

Another dubious stare. "That's too bad. If there is a pattern, as the first person to discover Pearl, you just fell next in line to be targeted."

He stands, and I mimic him, too stunned to say anything while I follow him to the door.

"Oh, and Zelda." Detective Sims turns back. "Do you know where Pearl's keys are? Her car keys weren't found at the scene, despite her Kia sedan being parked on the street out front."

"No, I don't."

He nods, jutting out his lower lip. "It must be exhausting, maintaining this show of ignorance, Zelda. Let me know when you get too tired and feel like talking."

As I exit the police precinct, adrenaline courses through my body, making each step faster than the last. I need to get away from here. From Detective Sims's accusing eye contact and the terrible possibility that I might slip up in a Freudian gaffe and do the police work for him.

The police think I attacked Pearl—maybe Sally too.

I have to find out who went after Pearl, before Detective Sims hits the easy button and formally accuses me. And, maybe, in discovering who her attacker was, I might learn who killed Finn Hoskie and Ursula Romano. The deaths seem to be connected, if Pearl's theories are correct, and it all comes back to Sally. Just like my Clinical Psychology class in nursing school suggested, it always comes back to the mother.

Chapter Thirty-Four

Zelda

The freeway is nearly clear at midmorning, and I zip down to the ranch house in the Willamette Valley. I haven't been here in weeks, not since Pearl suggested that I return my house key to her, after Sally died. I did—that copy, anyway.

It's a shame that Pearl stole from the museum—and also, so bizarre. I never would have pegged her as capable of such career suicide. Not after being raised by Sally, with her expectations of academic and professional success. Plus, yesterday at the police station, I overheard a man named Griffin talking about the theft while Detective Sims walked me out. Theoretically, why would Pearl risk so much in order to own an ancient version of an item that Sally already had?

I pull into the gravel driveway, hopeful that no nosy neighbors are watching. Though I'm sure they don't yet know about Pearl's attack. No one but the police, the museum, and probably Liam has been made aware. Entering through the front door, using my spare key, I step over the pile of mail that papers the threshold.

Although I don't know her well, the more I learn about Pearl, the more I can see the similarities between us. We both keep mostly to ourselves, we both found introverted careers that we were passionate about, and we both wanted to be loved by Sally in our own ways. We each felt the sting of her rejection, though at different times.

However, Pearl grew up resenting Sally's mercurial parenting, feeling unfairly judged, based on what Sally told me. In contrast, I know the judgment I felt during my childhood was deserved, in a way. I had a hand in my dad ultimately dying in Iraq, thanks to the stress I caused his marriage and his decision to escape it by enlisting. Fair or not, I've worked every day as an adult to make people's lives better, to counterbalance that fact. I've worked to accept myself, in spite of the pain I've caused.

Pearl was indoctrinated at a young age to always respect Sally's wishes and her rules, whereas I don't feel the same obligation. She was my biological mother. And what am I, as her oldest child, if not entitled to a little late-stage rebellion?

First things first. Check the attic.

Past the folding ladder steps and inside this stuffy level of the house, I find a dozen plastic trash bags. In the third that I open, a small pink fabric bag is zipped shut. White thread stitches present a capital letter *V*, suggestive of the name Sally told me she wanted to give me at first—Victoria.

I unzip the bag, then breathe a sigh of relief. I found it, the handmade yellow baby sweater that Sally said she knit for me. It's soft, and perfectly preserved up here in its protective layers. I doubt Pearl would have ever gotten around to going through all this stuff—she was vehement that nothing be touched after Sally's death—and I'm glad to get closure on this item now. This is a tangible link to Sally as my mother.

A wave of sadness billows across my shoulders as I perch in the family home of people I could have called kin. Inside the open plastic bag, stiff macaroni pasta decorates some sheet of construction paper, a craft Pearl must have made in grade school. Tears well in my eyes while I imagine what having a younger sister would have been like while growing up.

The Lie She Wears

When Sally realized our connection, she was coming out of one of her hazes—the kind during which she sometimes called me her mother's name, Estelle, and asked when the milkman was dropping off fresh bottles. Her eyes focused on my face as I was helping her up from where she'd fallen in the living room. Her hand reached up and touched my chin.

She said, "Do I know you?"

I replied, "Yes, I'm your nurse, Zelda."

She shook her head. "No, I think you're called something else. We're related, aren't we?"

I stared at her for several seconds, unsure how to reply, shocked at the nonchalance with which she had sussed out my true relationship with her: family, instead of hired employee. Then I told her everything.

I shared how I found her online first, after discovering notes that my adoptive mom wrote in the back of my baby book. How I moved up to Portland to be closer to her. It became my habit to sit outside Sally's house in my car, hiding around the corner of the next street, just to get a feel for who she was as a person. Whether I even wanted to meet her at closer range. Strange and off-putting to admit everything out loud, but I also didn't know if she would retain any of the conversation.

When a job alert hit my inbox, mirroring Sally's details—"In-home care needed for female patient suffering from cognitive decline; Location: Newberg"—I submitted my résumé and crossed my fingers. When the hiring firm specializing in medical care contacted me for an interview, I gave silent thanks to my foster mom, Karen, with whom I stayed for a year before my mom decided she wanted me back. An oncology nurse who pushed me into medicine, Karen steered me to this moment.

After several interviews, I got the call that I was hired. Sally chose me. And I felt some of the hurt that I'd carried with me since childhood ease in the slightest way.

Underneath the folded yellow baby sweater, loose items line the bottom of the bag. A hospital bracelet that bears my birth date—June 7—discharge paperwork, and a creased photograph of a baby wearing this exact yellow knit sweater, cradled in the hairy arms of a shirtless man who has a tattoo of a murder of crows on his neck. A silver necklace grazes the baby's cheek, the pendant of which looks like some kind of Catholic saint.

I trace the baby's little head and the man's shoulder. This is me. I'm sure of it. And if this photo is in the only bag related to my infancy here with Sally, before she gave me up for adoption at eight days old, this is probably my dad.

Balancing on the exposed wooden joists of the attic, I sit down cross-legged, careful not to rest too much weight on the tufts of insulation. The baby's eyes—my own—are a dark color, while a tuft of black hair protrudes from a tiny knit cap that matches the sweater.

When Sally realized I was the baby she adopted out, she apologized. I won't say that she begged my forgiveness, but she made it clear she regretted the decision. Said that she made it in a fit of passion and anger against the father. I wasn't looking for an apology, honestly. I told her I only wanted to know more about my genetics, my background, and maybe my biological father's identity.

At that point, Sally closed up shop. She refused to discuss that time in her life further. She rose from the living room couch and stalked into the kitchen. Said that she angered a lot of people close to her and couldn't—wouldn't—revisit those memories. The only bit of information she would share about my dad was that he was dead. Died a long time ago. And there was no use in inviting ghosts to our present.

The next time she slipped into one of her "brain fogs," as she called them, she told me he died here on her property. I knew then that, if she was telling the truth, her mild cognitive impairment had gone from basic to severe. She said she had never told a soul before now, aside from "him—"

Then she cut herself off. Shook her head like she had water in her ears. A smile spread across her face, and she laughed. Said that she really had me going, didn't she?

The Lie She Wears

I suspected she needed to see her doctor to get a new diagnosis—possible Alzheimer's or dementia—but she refused to make an appointment. The next month, she slid behind the wheel of her SUV for the last time.

The confusing conversation ran across my thoughts every time I stared into the acres of field behind the house. While I was cleaning up after Sally, during the wake, after the funeral as I packed my things to move out. *He died here.* Turns out, the letters she wrote to Pearl were clear enough. And Pearl's notes confirmed the presence of not one but two bodies.

Grabbing the pink fabric bag and my own backpack that contains Sally's address book, I climb down the attic steps, then head for the nearest exit to the back field. I open Sally and Liam's bedroom door, then startle when a face greets me from the bedspread. The mask that resembles the one Pearl stole from the museum. The Buddha head.

Catching my breath, I cross to the quilt. "What are you doing out of the closet?"

I glance from the bed and the mask to the open closet door. The closet being open isn't out of the ordinary. But the light inside being left on is.

A flash of Pearl bloodied and attacked crosses my vision. I stagger backward, leaning into the doorframe.

Detective Sims's voice fills my ears. *Do you know where Pearl's keys are?* Did her attacker snatch up her car keys for her house key?

Tension spirals down my back as I approach the closet. Inside, the clothing and boxes are as I last saw them several weeks ago. Nothing is amiss aside from the illuminated light bulb overhead and the Buddha mask on the bedspread, scaring anyone who dares enter Liam and Sally's space.

Without a clear reason to run, I take a breath. Reach for the sliding glass door adjacent to the bed and step outside as I lean into my nervous habit. "What do you call a pianist on life support?"

A bird's melody peals across the field and the neighboring yards of the valley below. A crisp breeze twirls the tall yellow grass as dark clouds begin to mass overhead. I tuck back a strand of black hair that flies across my eyes.

"An organ donor."

Thanks to Pearl's notes, I know where to start. Toward the back end of the lot, a freshly upturned pile of dirt lies exactly as she said, beneath the oak tree. I nudge the ground with my boot, clear some of the dirt away. The bones of a human foot appear, missing the second toe.

"Oh, shit." I gasp, lurching backward. Reading about Pearl's discoveries in advance doesn't dull the shock of seeing them up close myself. Instantly, I search the neighbor's field for spying eyes, and find none. Nausea rocks my belly, but as a nurse I've seen more than I'd care to, and I tamp down the urge to heave my breakfast.

Disturbing. And so is the silver necklace beside it. My dad's necklace, apparently. The same one from the photo I just found in the attic. Sally was telling the truth that day. He died here on the property.

Grief mushrooms in my chest as I sit with my new reality. My birth father is dead, and I'll never know him. Never have the moment of clarity that I had with Sally, never achieve a relationship with the first man who was supposed to love me. Though Sally's letters suggested he wasn't a great person, the little girl inside me wanted to see for herself.

Reluctantly, I leave him to his earthy bed. A quick walk over to the shed, to the location of the second body, additionally confirms Pearl's findings. As I exit the small structure, taking care to close it firmly, my nervous habit of making puns during the most inappropriate times fails me. It used to be a coping mechanism for stress that started back when my dad died, but my mind is on overdrive lately. I can't find the punch line in this mess.

Eager for warmth, I head into the house through the kitchen's sliding glass door—only, it opens with ease. The door is unlocked. Something that Pearl and Sally never allowed. Sally, in particular, was militant about locking all doors and windows.

The Lie She Wears

The hairs on my neck stand on end, and I turn to the road out of instinct. Search for a person waiting and watching me traipse across the property.

Whoever came for Pearl was playing the long game. As I stare out over the yard, at the locations of the two buried bodies, and the empty driveway that might always stand bereft of Davis cars now, I wonder just how long.

Chapter Thirty-Five

Opal

New York City, 1992

Footsteps come pounding the sidewalk behind us where we stand on the corner, uptown. "Hey, babe! Opal, wait up!"

Liam, the attractive bartender who gives excellent head, bounds up the concrete like a golden retriever. He slows to a walk when he reaches me and Errol. Gives me a kiss on the cheek, then pulls back and offers my twin his hand.

"Hey, man. You must be the famous brother I've been hearing so much about. Nice to meet you. I'm Liam."

Errol breaks into a broad smile, slapping palms with him. He balls up the paper wrapper that came with the bolo bao he wolfed down earlier. "Hey, likewise. Opal has been raving about you."

We exchange a look, though Liam doesn't notice. Errol is always good for a round of improv.

Liam pants, still out of breath. "What are you two doing up here? I thought you were going downtown for brunch together?"

Errol doesn't miss a beat. "Oh, we did. But then I realized I forgot my wallet at my place. Idiot, right?"

"Nah, happens to everyone." Liam slips his arm around my shoulders, then focuses on my face. Tentative hope brightens his eyes. "Any chance I can tag along?"

Behind him, Mary Anker scurries farther up the street toward the café job she works in the mornings. In another two blocks, she'll be gone, and so will our chance to pounce.

"Ah, sorry, babe. We really need sibling time this morning. Call you later, cool?" I give him a peck on the cheek, then pause to graze my hand across his groin. Liam jerks backward like I burned him.

"Oh. Uh, okay. No, that's fine. Yeah, call me."

As he retreats down the sidewalk in the direction of his favorite doughnut shop, which he usually hits before his shift at the bar, Errol cocks an eyebrow. "He's an eager one."

"He's exactly what I need." I shrug. "Someone to play with who can offer me alibis at just the right time."

"Are you sure? It almost seemed like you liked him."

"It seems like you're reaching." I continue walking at a brisk pace, determined not to let this morning go to complete waste.

"You do," Errol insists. "Or you're even starting to fool me."

"Don't be dumb."

Mary Anker skips across the street in the face of a flashing red crosswalk hand. As if she senses that we're close. A big rig barrels through the intersection, effectively blocking our path, followed by a trio of cargo trucks that sandwich in behind. By the time traffic lets up enough for us to dart between cars, Mary has reached the café and disappeared inside. Probably she's already running into the kitchen, grabbing her waitress apron and black book for taking orders. When I went in for a latte last week, on a day I knew she wasn't scheduled to work, I popped into the employee-only areas for a quick peek around and was pleased with what I found.

"Fuck," I say above the din. "Well, now there's no fun in harassing her as a pair. Not around her coworkers and people who can ID you later on."

"Right. Want to go to a movie? You don't have to work today. We could sit behind some teenagers in the dark and whisper lines from *Friday the Thirteenth*."

I tilt my head to the side. "Go there, buy two tickets, and then tell everyone that we did."

A grin spreads across my brother's face. The grin we share when we are genuinely excited. When we're about to scratch the itch that needles us both, but which I accept more blithely.

"I'll pick a good one," he says.

"Nothing horror."

"Obviously."

Without a hug or kiss goodbye, per our practice, Errol trots down the street toward the nearest metro line.

I turn left at the next block, then cut right into the alleyway behind an apartment building, a Laundromat, and the café where Mary works. The shadows that engulf the back exit slant across the square of dumpsters and garbage bins shared by neighboring businesses. Errant newspaper trash and a romantic pairing of rats line the perimeter.

From my large purse, I withdraw a wig whose platinum-blond color should instantly draw recognition from Mary, and pull on the latex gloves I brought. I scan the corners of the building, searching for those new pesky security cameras that are starting to pop up everywhere. There are none. Good.

The back door to the café bangs open. A tall man with ruddy skin drags a large black trash bag from the kitchen to the dumpster beside me. He pauses when he sees me—a blond, petite woman wearing big sunglasses and a light-blue sundress during October. The carbon copy image of Mary's dead cousin, judging from the photograph she keeps on her employee locker at work, beside a sticker with writing in fat bubble letters that reads, "It's the Journey."

The Lie She Wears

"Can I help you?" he asks in a deep baritone.

"Shit. This isn't the entrance to the café, is it? Mary told me to come pay her a visit when I got in from Fort Lauderdale."

The guy shakes his head. "No, you have to walk around."

I gesture at my tan boots. "Ugh. You're kidding. I already walked eighteen blocks, no joke, in these things. Couldn't get a cab in traffic and I hate the subway."

He scoffs. "A real out-of-towner. Okay, I'll tell Mary you're out back."

I watch as he lumbers inside the building. Then I hide behind the dumpster.

A few minutes pass, and then her soft footsteps in those Keds sneakers pique my hearing. She pauses, and I hold my breath, almost giddy with anticipation.

"You can come out now," she says.

I ignore the invite, though I am impressed by her new backbone. Over the last three weeks, each time I've called her, sent a letter describing all the ways she can suffer by my hand, or shared a new page with her of my version of classic stories, she's cringed or cried or screamed for me to leave her alone. All the things you want to avoid with my kind: predators who get off on the chase. Who enjoy playing with their dinner before consuming it.

"I said, come out!"

I rise from where I stashed myself.

"Why are you here—dressed like that?" New fear tightens her words. She takes a step back, her pale-blond pigtails trembling. The clear plastic gloves she wears while she's preparing garnishes in the kitchen appear freshly applied.

"You're dead," she adds.

"Who, me? Because I took a week off from our correspondence? I just had my day job to attend to." I twirl a strand of bright-blond hair around my finger.

"No, no, no. You're dead. You're dressed up like my dead cousin, you sicko!"

Anger twists her face, despite the tears wetting her cheeks. "Get out of here. Leave me alone! Stay dead!"

I step toward her, gesturing with the black gloves I wear. "Poor Mary Anker. Just when you think I'm done, I come crawling out from the shadows."

"Why are you doing this?" she whimpers.

"Because, Mary. Even when I'm dead, I'm never really gone."

She turns to dart back inside, but I whip out a knife from my bag, then plunge it into my thigh. I scream in agony as the blade slices through muscle.

"Get off me, Mary! Stop, please!" My cries dissolve into sobs and true horror as I feel every inch of the sharp metal underneath my skin.

Mary stops in the doorway, staring at me with wide eyes as I wince, peeling off my gloves, then tossing them into the dumpster.

The thin man I spoke with earlier emerges from the building. "Oh, fuck! Ambulance—call an ambulance!"

As he rushes to me, I collapse to the disgusting chewing gum–covered ground, though I sneak another glance at Mary.

Sweet, terrified Mary raises her hand to her mouth as fresh tears trip down her chin. "No. No . . ." she mumbles. "I didn't do it. I didn't touch her!"

Paramedics arrive in white uniforms just as blood begins gushing from my wound. With each beat of my pulse, the stream throbs around the knife. White spots dot my vision, while a halo of blackness dances at the edges. Using my last ounce of energy before I pass out, I lock my gaze on Mary's. Dig deep for the effort, then stretch my lips into a smile.

Chapter Thirty-Six

Zelda

Inside the house, I pause at the sliding door's threshold, rain now pummeling the glass behind me. I check in with each of my senses, as if I might be able to tell whether some aggressor has been hiding in the pantry for the last hour. As if the same instinct that zinged down my spine at finding the door unlocked could intuit danger inside the house.

I should leave. Accept that I'll be soaking wet in the thin jacket I wear by the time I reach my hatchback, and just go. Instead, I step farther onto the Spanish tile of the dining nook, still straining to hear sounds of a threat. Although this property is now the last place I want to be, I'm not done with it. Sally left more for me to uncover here, beyond a yellow knit baby sweater.

I survey each corner with new awareness. Was the pile of mail by the front door the same size as it is now? Has Pearl been retrieving the mail regularly here while on leave from the museum, and all these letters, advertisements, and postcards are new additions from yesterday and today? Two postcards look like they were sent just this week, judging from the postmarks. At the bottom of the older one, someone wrote, "Three days." At the bottom of the newest postcard: "One day."

I shake my head at this situation, at the enormity of my being here alone at all.

Heavy rain continues, and I make sure each door and window is shut and locked, confirming no one is hiding in the dark corners of the house. Using my laptop, which I brought in from my car, I spend the next hour researching what I can based on Pearl's outstanding questions. Who was this Bert who Liam worked for as a contractor, and why did he use this address as his own? Was he a partner in crime to Sally, if she really was the Turnpike Bloody Brontë, and is he behind the murders of Ursula and Finn, and Pearl's attack?

News of Finn's death has spread across the internet, and tributes to his winery are flooding the hashtags #pnw and #pnwwine. Strange to think he wanted to buy the ranch house and its acreage out of some long-held grudge against Sally. Pearl notes that a real estate agent shared that the offer was, obviously, off the table after Finn died.

I press my fingers to my temples. Outside, the evening unfolds, rain drumming against the windows. An animal howls from a distance, while the sound of passing cars becomes more infrequent.

My blinks come slowly as I reread the letters that Pearl discovered. Are there any more hidden? Am I going to find them while I'm here?

Exhaustion creeps across my body, and I know I need to drive home, but instead I sit on the couch to review the letters one more time. If there's another obvious hint that Pearl or I missed, I want to discover it before I leave. As I lift the letters to eye level, against the living room window, sunshine slices through the rainclouds for a moment, and casts a glow around the paper edges, lulling me into a long blink.

I open my eyes.

My vision adjusts to the semidarkness. Unease tightens my throat, clenching my muscles as it goes, for a reason I don't quite grasp. Outside, slanting sunshine has given way to a twilight sky, soft colors blending into a gradient that bows to black. How long was I asleep? What woke me up?

I get to my feet. Wipe the trail of drool that formed in the corner of my mouth. Gather the papers, the address book, and my laptop from beside me on the couch, then shove everything into my backpack, beside the Taser I always have on hand. Near the kitchen, where I left my shoes at the side door, I pause. A beam of light rebounds from Liam and Sally's bedroom into the hallway.

Hairs on the back of my neck stand on end where my short lob grazes the skin. I suck in a sharp breath. I didn't leave any lights on. And I should go out the front door now, before the person in the bedroom hears me.

Someone is in the house with me. Someone is rummaging around in Sally's drawers.

My fingers flex, my muscles taut and ready to launch myself from the property.

And yet. What if I could find out who attacked Pearl, without them noticing? I could avoid being interrogated by the police again. I could get justice for my remaining living biological family member.

"What do you call a farm animal who flunks out of kindergarten?" I whisper to the front door. "A dumbass."

I creep down the worn carpeted hallway, the way I did for months, carefully placing my feet around the creaking floorboards that might wake Sally too early in the morning. I grip my Taser in my left hand, car keys jutting from my right fist.

A figure searches in a nightstand drawer beside the bed, their phone casting a glow. Their hood shifts, revealing a white painted face with black ovals around narrowed eyes and a sneer across the mouth. Gold glitter diamonds pattern one cheek. They're wearing a Giulio Venetta mask. The one that hung across from Pearl's bedroom.

I gasp. The intruder startles, turning sharply to stare at me.

"Who are you—" I say, but they lunge at me, knocking me into the hallway.

Strong hands grab my throat, and I scratch, claw, and twist away from them before they grip my shoulders and I cry out. I point my fingers and jab them into their side, nailing the kidneys like my self-defense class taught. They yelp—a man's voice?—and I push them away. Grabbing the Taser I dropped, I shoot as they tear across the bedroom, toward the sliding glass door. The darts hit the comforter, and then the intruder yanks the door open and disappears beneath starlight.

I launch myself to the door. Lock it. Load a new Taser cartridge. Quickly, sprinting through the house, I check all the doors and window locks again, then realize that none of them are broken. The intruder had a key to enter the house. Pearl's keys, if Detective Sims still hasn't found them at the crime scene yet.

My face draws long in horror, and then I'm hyperventilating, slouching onto the burnt-red tile, Fat tears wet the thighs of my jeans while I take stock. I could have been killed. I could have been knifed and left for dead, since no one is returning to the ranch house anytime soon.

Knowing this person can come back and use the house key, I realize I should go. Quickly, while holding my car keys pointed like a weapon. But the intruder was searching for something in Sally's bedroom, and I interrupted them. Whatever they wanted, it's still hiding somewhere within, something that might finally give us leverage over this monster.

I can't leave yet.

Five minutes pass before I can stand without my knees buckling, without flinching whenever a gust of wind rustles the trees. My hand shakes as I raise my Taser aloft, then limp, padding down the hallway, returning to the bedroom. This is a stupid fucking idea. When I reach the far end of the house, my heart thumps against my skin. Just in case Sally left me her whole damn estate and the police learn that I tracked Pearl for two weeks, all the way to the site of her attack, I need a plan. The way to secure proof that I'm innocent and get justice for Pearl isn't something I'll randomly discover in Portland by myself; it's here.

I enter the bedroom to stare at the nightstand. Circular stains ring one corner of the flat surface, likely from coffee mugs over the years.

The Lie She Wears

Scratches bite into another corner in light-brown lines. The nightstand comprises a single drawer and a large space underneath for slippers, books—whatever someone wanted to stash beside the bed that didn't fit on top.

Sally kept all her most useful items here, and certain valuables. Plastic bottles of prescription and OTC medicine, her address book, pages of medical printouts from doctors' appointments, financial statements that showed her worth skyrocketed after the auction, and a list of passwords to all the apps on her phone. I gave all of this to Pearl in the Bankers box that I delivered to her apartment.

What if Pearl and I both missed something?

Dropping to my feet, I peer underneath the bed. A handful of dust bunnies returns my stare, accumulating during the last month and a half that Sally has been gone. In the closet, plenty of shoeboxes conceal old cards, magnets from past travels, and—oddly—a box of six switchblades, but no additional letters. No fireproof safe. No sealed envelopes. Checking underneath the counters and inside the cabinets of Sally's bathroom returns the same result.

"Come on, Zelda. Think." I huff the hair that begins to stick to my cheeks.

I scan the room, surveying the corners and caches I just poked into. Then my gaze reverts to the nightstand—the original hiding place that Sally chose. A place where she could keep items close to her in case of any crisis.

Dropping to my hands and knees, I change my viewpoint. Twisting my body to see beneath the nightstand, I spot multiple lines of blue painter's tape—along with layers of postcards that the tape secures. Whenever Sally received a new postcard, she must have added it to this hidden upside-down pile.

"There you are," I breathe.

I pry the postcards loose, then spread them on the quilted comforter. The ranch house's address is clearly penned on each, though none is addressed directly to either Sally or Liam. Eighteen postcards were sent from various locations around the country. Picturesque images showcase various cities and towns. If I line them up according to the most recent postmark date, they begin in August in Nebraska, then move back east through Illinois, Indiana, Ohio, Pennsylvania, New Jersey, and New York. The oldest postcard begins in New Jersey, in February—right before I started working for Sally.

I open the web browser on my phone. Sally sold the ultrarare Italian masks through Gillian's Auction House and made national news for it in February. A picture of her and Liam was featured on all the antique, archaeology, and collector community platforms.

The date of the sale appears in the first search result: February 2.

The postmark on the postcard mailed from New Jersey shows it was sent a few days after the auction. In tiny script at the bottom are the words "Eight months."

My neck tingles where my jacket's collar brushes my skin. One by one, I flip over each of the postcards to read the sender's written messages.

Miss me?
I found you.
I'll always find you.
Congratulations on your new life.
Hi, again.
I think it's time for a reunion.
Did you think I would forget?

Unease curls across my stomach. A countdown is included on each card at the bottom, just like those that Pearl noted in the address book. Using my phone, I add and subtract dates until I'm almost certain the sender was looking forward to October 3. Two days ago, the day that Pearl was attacked.

Foreboding ripples across my skin. Whoever wrote these began sending them right after I was hired. Instead of finding the detail here that vindicates me of Pearl's attack—and worse—I've stumbled on another link that suggests I'm the cause of the last *year* of pain. I suck in a sharp breath. I'm screwed.

Suddenly the house feels claustrophobic, every shadow taking on a human shape. Staying here was a mistake. My fingerprints now cover these postcards. I grab the stack, then speed walk back to the front door and out to my car. Though I'm on high alert as I reach my hatchback, no one jumps out from the darkness.

Each mile I put between me and the ranch house helps to ease the tension stitching my chest, but not erase it. Far from it. Once I am safely parked at the Fred Meyer down the street and feel confident that no headlights followed me out of the valley, I catch my own reflection in the rearview mirror. Dark half-moons ring my eyes from underneath while my face crumples. Deep cries shake my shoulders, trapping my mouth in an anguished smile.

I struggle to catch a solid inhale. A pounding headache attacks my temples, and I feel like a puddle strapped to the driver's seat. It's been two days since I've eaten a full meal. For so many reasons, I'm still reeling from discovering Pearl on the warehouse floor. From learning that many of Pearl's theories in the address book are true.

Moonlight bleeds into the neon haze of the grocery chain's front signage. Shoppers still bustle in and out of the main entrance, grabbing essentials for tomorrow morning, while my heartbeat slows to a normal rhythm.

Was the intruder searching for the stack of postcards in Sally's nightstand? I cleaned it out two weeks ago and delivered to Pearl the address book I found, along with loose papers lying within. Who was that person? Pearl's assailant?

I take the address book from where I chucked it on the passenger's seat. Withdraw the letters that Sally wrote. Each of them is disturbing, except for one—the letter that Pearl showed me while we were seated at Pioneer Courthouse Square, and which I knew off the bat was meant for me. Lighter in tone and almost meandering in its language, the letter held a quote that I also recognized as being similar to a plaque at a downtown oak tree. But what if the letter held something more?

Dear daughter.

I hope our relationship can outpace those doubts and fears . . . It's a wish of mine.

Your father would agree.

My face blanches as I think back on the packaging of this letter—placed within a wrapped, gifted photo of the oak tree at the edge of the property. I found it stashed in her nightstand, with no other note or explanation attached. No sense of to whom the gift belonged or when Sally had wrapped it. Why would Sally write me this note, and the rest to Pearl?

"It's a wish of mine." I repeat Sally's words to my steering wheel as a man in an oversize coat pushes an empty shopping cart away from the entrance to the grocery store. When he reaches the street, he pauses at the quiet intersection.

"It's a wish of mine . . ."

Sally deliberately included a quote about plants that was found beneath an oak tree across from the museum. I pull out the letters again and note three other instances of Sally wishing.

In the first letter: *All a mother ever has for her children is fluttering wishes. Find mine.*

The second letter, which Pearl found in the cast: *It's a wish of mine.*

The fourth letter, which she taped to the underside of a counter in the shed: *To that end, my final wish will continue hanging, swaying in the breeze, waiting until you come for it.*

Sally included some form of the word *wish* in each of her letters. A fact that can't be a coincidence, knowing Sally.

"Wishes. Wishing. Portland is full of trees. City of trees. Wishing trees."

Neon tentacles stretch forward from the entrance, reaching for the man and the empty shopping cart as they enter the crosswalk, shuffling out of range.

The Lie She Wears

Realization floods my fingertips, making the pages tremble. "The Wishing Tree."

Sally knew she wasn't the only one to write and leave cryptic letters in Portland. In fact, hundreds of people have done the exact same thing on one particular street corner that she mentioned to me the same day she died. On her way out the door, nearly stumbling for some reason, to the driver's side of her car, she mentioned the Wishing Tree.

The drive across the river takes a half hour, and I steep in phrases from the gifted letter the whole way. Her choice of words, the mention of my dad, the fact that Sally and I never had a relationship until just recently. Yellow streetlamps wash the road in stretched ovals that remind me of a video game. Fatigue and stress mingle together, amplifying the headache that started at the ranch house, until I slow to a stop beside a residential curb. Across from the famous Portland icon.

It's my first time visiting, but I know enough about local lore to be aware it exists. Now, during fall, the leaves of this tree layer the sidewalk, exposing the hundreds of paper wishes festooning the branches with string. It's the one place Sally could expect to have her confession completely blend in.

Using my phone's flashlight, I scan the papers swaying in the breeze. I tuck my peacoat tighter around my body. There are literally hundreds, maybe thousands, of small squares of paper dangling before me.

"Where did you put it, Sally?" I wonder aloud.

She often teased me about being tall—just the right size for a live-in nurse to assist her—before she discovered our true relationship. She was average height for a woman but found it frustrating to never be able to reach the highest cabinets on her own.

I circle the thick tree trunk, reading the squares of paper as I go. The bulk of them are amassed at the average eye level, while only a few brave souls bothered to climb higher and affix their notes.

The tallest square is easily a full six feet up, several inches above me. And encased in a sandwich baggie gouged into the tree by a tack.

Looping cursive marks the plain square within as raindrops begin to paint the shifting plastic. I find a foothold in the trunk, smooth and lighter in color than the rest of the tree's bark. My hair mats against my head as the rain falls harder, but I step up, then reach for the protected page—one that Sally would have had to stretch to place.

I blink away water. Writing at the top begins, "My girls."

With a lurch, I snatch the square, then slip. Shock rushes my senses as I fall from the foothold to the ground, to the small rocks layering the tree bed below. My foot twists sharply, and then pain sears my ankle, ripping across my leg.

I lie panting, rain mixing with my tears as my coat absorbs some of the moisture beneath me.

Several minutes pass. A man walking a dog on the sidewalk opposite me hurries past without stopping.

As I struggle to a seated position, I clutch the paper tightly, not willing to risk letting this final message escape. The mouth of the baggie opens with a sharp snap, and I remove the page from its sealed bed. Instantly, the writing—the ink—begins to bleed.

Chapter Thirty-Seven

THE WISHING TREE

My girls,

By now, you must know the truth about your relationship—about my relationship with you two: I'm your mother, Pearl's and Zelda's. I'm sorry I didn't tell you together, or sooner, but I didn't want you asking too many questions. Not when I wasn't sure how much I needed you to know. How much was safe to tell you.

Someone has been watching me. Following me—now, I'm sure of it—and waiting for me to lead her straight to what she wants most: revenge. And despite what you may believe at this point, I love you both. And a good mother always protects her children.

If you're reading this, things have taken an unexpected turn. I wasn't able to avoid her in the end. And that means she's set her sights on you. You must be wary of anyone new in your life taking an interest in you or your activities. She hides in plain sight and can be charming to people who don't know who she is. Hell, I don't know her, but I know of her, plenty. Her name is Elsie.

Bottom line: You must rely on each other. Don't let her catch you off guard.

Zelda and Pearl, you're each other's best hope out of this now.

Chapter Thirty-Eight

Zelda

I stare at the square of paper until the ink trickles down my palm and my hands tremble from the cold.

"What the fuck," I breathe out, stretching the swear word into three—four—syllables.

Pearl is in the hospital. Pearl is my best hope out of this?

A woman runs past me with a slicker pulled over her head, and I remember that I don't even have a hood on this jacket, and it's nearly ten o'clock at night. I cross the street, then slide into the dry safety of my car, my wet hair sticking to my neck.

Pearl thought that Sally might have been a serial killer. She guessed that someone who knew about the original murders could be tying up loose ends now—going after anyone who had knowledge of Sally's buried bodies. But this letter confirms there's someone after us whom Sally didn't know—not a longtime partner.

Some real flesh-and-blood killer took the lives of two people, recently. And, as difficult as Sally and Pearl's relationship was, Sally wouldn't have worked with anyone who would attack her child.

A new killer is out there. One Sally thought Pearl and I could escape from before we were attacked—this Elsie. That we could overcome if we only worked together, as sisters.

This letter from Sally, and her instruction that Pearl and I should lean on each other, is the clearest one yet. But without needed information to identify this threat.

I shake my head. Focus on the heavy raindrops splashing against the glass, and the square of paper still clutched in my palm.

"What would Pearl know better than anyone?" I ask my windowpane. "Why would she be my best hope out of this?"

As the rainfall picks up in intensity and speed, I start my car. Pull forward into the puddles of the street, toward the one person who can answer my question.

Chapter Thirty-Nine

Pearl

Beep, beep, beep. Incessant noise breaks through my thoughts. No—my dreams. I open my eyes with effort, then take in the whiteboard across from where I lie in my bed. "10 mg oxycodone. 600 mg ibuprofen."

No, not my bed. My hospital bed.

I lift a hand to trace the rail that hugs both sides of this stiff mattress. An oxygen sensor clamped to my index finger limits my range. An IV is attached to a port in my arm with clear tape.

"What?" My voice comes out hoarse, like I haven't spoken in hours.

Several buttons line the railing—some arrows pointing up or down, a keypad that indicates volume, and a square with a glowing outline of the word "Call."

The door opens, pausing my impulse to reach the nurses' station—anyone who can tell me what is going on.

A nurse enters wearing green scrubs beneath an oversize black zip-up. The hood is drawn over their head, mirroring how I feel. This room is cold—arctic in its temperature and sterility. Aside from my bed and the machines beeping beside me and monitoring my heart rate, there's nothing in the space but the two chairs facing me from across the room.

"Hi," I begin, speaking in my frog's voice. I struggle to sit up as pain clenches my shoulders. Then I remember the buttons on the railing. A few stabs at the up and down buttons do nothing, though, and I prop myself up with my elbows instead. Pain screams through my body in response, and I gasp before I lie back down.

The nurse—a woman—pauses at the door, her figure visible in the dim glow of the machines. It must be two or three o'clock in the morning. No noise reaches my ears from the hallway or from anywhere on this floor of the hospital. We might be the only two awake.

She doesn't reply. Instead, her gaze searches the tile. Is it a spill? Would I have hurt myself further if I had gotten up and stumbled to the bathroom?

"Hello?" I ask. New cold—fear—sweeps across my body as I take in this silent form. Am I dreaming?

I remember driving to the museum to confront Kai. I remember speaking to Griffin and him firing me. Then running through the warehouse, certain Kai would catch me any second. Then someone did.

"Are you the night nurse? Why am I here?" I ask again, my voice louder this time, clearer.

The person moves. She lifts her head. White skin appears with black voids where the eyes should be. Red, glittery lips part in a cackle or a threat as she raises a scalpel that catches the light from the beeping machines.

I scream, a noise that tears my chest and ripples across my skin beneath the paper gown. My toes arch against the scratchy fabric of a tan blanket, and I count down from ten with my eyes shut tight, determined to wake up from this nightmare—from all of it.

Beeping continues its relentless rhythm all the way to one. I open my eyes. The room is empty. Footsteps tap in the hallway leading to my door, and I brace myself to come face-to-face with the hospital ghost once again.

A man and a woman burst into the room, both wearing green scrubs.

"Pearl? I'm Emma, your critical care nurse. Are you okay? We heard screaming," the woman adds.

"You didn't—Was there a—" I point to the hallway, breathless, toward the direction they just came. "Did you see anyone leave my room?"

The man shakes his head. He turns over his shoulder to scan the notes on the whiteboard, then exchanges a look with his colleague. "Pearl, it's almost eleven. No one was out there."

"But . . . there was a woman . . . in green scrubs and a . . . she was wearing a black hoodie. You didn't see her? She just stood in my room without speaking. It was . . ."

Frightening. Ominous. Menacing.

"I don't know what happened," I finish.

Emma purses her lips. She pops off a cap from one of the whiteboard markers, then notes the time beneath the medications list. "You've been in and out for the last two days. Sometimes, patients experience vivid dreams during intense periods of sleep. Especially with the fever you had thanks to infection."

"What?" I blanch, the warmth retreating even further from my body.

"You might be seeing things. Feeling colder than you normally would thanks to the saline drip you have there to maintain your fluid levels. The police brought you in. You were attacked."

Emma strides to the computer next to the monitor. She types on the keyboard. She reaches for my wrist with a kind of handheld scanner that makes a chirp as it lands on a plastic bracelet I wear.

"The rest of the staff will be excited to learn you're up and talking." Emma smiles at me with warm brown eyes as she asks me questions about the year, my full name, my date of birth, and other broader questions, like what country we're in.

Images from my sprint through the museum warehouse—of the agony when someone took a knife to my body—flood my mind. Fresh tears fill my eyes, and then my chin crumples into a quivering mess.

"Why did this happen?" I whisper.

Emma turns to the nurse behind her. "We don't really know yet. The police will want to speak to you. Probably in the morning. Get some rest now, okay? You're safe here."

As both nurses leave, I scan the room, not at all certain that's true.

Voices in the hall interrupt my nurses' departure, and then the door opens again. Zelda steps into my room, wearing a gray cardigan and a tentative smile.

"Pearl? You're awake."

Instantly, my body tenses as I try to place my feelings for Zelda. Fear, relief, suspicion all course through my veins faster than any shot of oxycodone. Did I imagine the masked figure that just entered my room, not twenty minutes ago? Or is it a little too convenient that Zelda just happened to be nearby, waiting to surprise visit me within the hour?

"How are you feeling?" She approaches my bed, concern etched across her forehead. "Hospital security has been making the rounds. Apparently they check on you every so often to make sure you're still . . ."

I lift an eyebrow. Gesture to the tubes taped to my arm, to the blood pressure cuff I'm wearing. "Do I look okay to you?"

Fatigue draws across my chest as an electric blanket might. My eyelids droop.

"Pearl," Zelda whispers. "I know you're tired. It's late, but I had to come see if you were awake yet. What happened to you in the warehouse? Who attacked you?"

"You did," I mumble. "No, Kai. No . . . I—I don't know."

Zelda draws in a sharp breath. "I promise you, Pearl. I didn't have anything to do with this. But I need to find out who did. I think you were close to the truth about Sally and that's why you were attacked. Will you help me?"

My mind empties as I take in Zelda's words. The fact that she knows—about everything. "What are you . . . You didn't come for me? That wasn't you?"

Her shoulders slump, blurring in my vision, melting into the dark corners of the hospital's pale-yellow wallpaper. "No, Pearl. I could never. I dedicated myself to helping people, not hurting them."

I clutch the scratchy blanket beneath my fingers. Twist the fabric in my fists until the echo of footsteps and an eerie whisper recede from my thoughts. *Yes. Me.*

"I want to believe you."

"Great. That's great," she says. "So, I need you to tell me about Elsie. Who is she? Your mom—" Zelda pauses abruptly. She darts her eyes to mine. "She . . . Sally mentioned Elsie to me as someone to watch out for."

"When? Like, before she died?"

Zelda licks her lips. "Yes. Have you heard of Elsie? Sally thought she could want to hurt us, maybe attack Sally herself."

I take in Zelda's stitched expression, like she's choosing her words carefully—should I? "I have no clue. What's her last name?"

"I don't know." Zelda shakes her head. "Who would know about the buried bodies? About the two people Sally killed."

I lift both eyebrows. "You've been in my notes."

"Yes. Which of Sally's friends would know about the bodies? Maybe there's a connection to an Elsie."

I shake my head an inch. Not quite grasping Zelda's line of thinking. Bone-deep fatigue makes it hard to concentrate. "Sally didn't have friends. She had tools to accomplish a task."

"Ursula wasn't her best friend?"

"The exception. Like my dad. Sally used most of the people in that address book for a specific reason."

"Does your dad know about the bodies? About—all of it?" Zelda waves her hand in a circle.

"I don't know. Part of me thinks, there's no way. He wouldn't stand for Sally hurting anyone. But he also placed a shed directly on top of the second victim."

"Right. So, if the killer knows about the dead bodies on your property—if they knew Sally's secrets when no one else knew—they must have been close to her at one point, closer than Ursula. Maybe provided a service to her—something that Ursula couldn't."

A yawn surprises me, stretching my jaw to its limit. "The only scenario in which Sally would deliberately hide something from Ursula . . . would be if they wanted the same antique."

"Would the appraisers in her address book help find items? Could Elsie be one of those?" Zelda chews on her thumbnail.

"I already googled or reached out to everyone whose name was written down. Some of them, one appraiser named Bert Pelham, didn't even remember Sally. A finder named Megan Stefanich said Sally earned some enemies after the big auction for that series of masks. But no one else aside from Megan and Bert seemed to overlap between antiquing and the address book."

Zelda peers at me. The beeping of my heart rate monitor fills the room.

"What if Megan was one of the new enemies?"

I pause. A shiver steals across my body beneath the papery gown. "Megan said that she helped Sally find the mask."

"What if Sally didn't pay her what Megan thought she was due?"

"Sally was rarely generous. She could have stiffed Megan—"

"Would she be angry enough to do something about it?"

Zelda's question hangs between us as I try to recall my conversation with Megan. "I took a picture of her business card when I met her last week. Hand me my phone?"

Zelda plucks it from the chair next to me. I find Megan's phone number, then send it to Zelda via text.

"I don't know about any Elsie. But if Megan really is holding some massive grudge against Sally," I begin. "If she's capable of killing Ursula and Finn and attacking me . . . then you should be very, very careful."

Zelda nods between my heavy blinks. "I will. Have you told the police any of this?"

"Only the stuff I thought was relevant."

"Okay. That's good. But remember: They don't need to know everything, right?"

She leaves my room, while I'm still puzzling over her final words. The door creaks shut as I close my eyes tight, ready to pass out.

Two black holes set against white-painted skin flash across my thoughts. Then I surrender to the sharp pain pulling me down.

Morning comes quicker than I would like, despite Nurse Emma returning in the middle of the night with new pain medication. I reach for my phone where I left it, on top of the plastic bag of my personal items on the chair beside me. Although Zelda warned me against being too transparent with the police, I send Detective Sims every single letter that I discovered written in Sally's hand. I can't protect my dad, my family home, or myself while I'm shut away in the hospital. I need help.

I'm not sure what is actually happening anymore, or whether I'm imagining—dreaming—certain events. But I am aware that the threat of someone wanting me dead is very real. And the terror of it all may be starting to alter my reality. Just like Sally's.

Chapter Forty

Zelda

The next day, charred hillsides pockmark the green forests that unfurl alongside the freeway heading south. The remnants of recent wildfires, alarming and tragic.

"Another metaphor for this week," I murmur. A giant roadside sign overhead announces my exit is next up, and I hit my blinker.

Despite Pearl meeting Megan Stefanich at an antique convention in town, Megan doesn't live in Portland. She lives in Eugene, *an enthusiastic college town*, according to Megan, when I called her using the number on the business card. Although she has a busy day ahead as a vet tech for a local veterinary hospital, she agreed to see me during a twenty-minute time slot.

Last night after leaving the hospital, I was exhausted when I made it back to my apartment. I still am. And, dragging myself from bed this morning, and the safety of my locked apartment door, I considered staying home. To sleep. To grieve. But I have to keep moving, rather than risk the police showing up with handcuffs. I wouldn't hurt a hair on Pearl's head. And I'm also enough of a realist to accept that my role in this horrible mess looks bad.

As I zipped up my ankle boots, I thought of Pearl. Of the sad bruising that covered her arm where her attacker must have gripped her, dragging her to the shelf where I found her. Of Pearl's gaunt

The Lie She Wears

appearance after devoting most of her days and nights recently to uncovering the killer's identity. And of the knowledge that I may have already come face-to-face with the killer while they were rifling through Sally's nightstand. I could be square and center on their radar now, and that means I have several reasons to haul ass to Eugene.

At first, Megan was hesitant when I mentioned that Pearl had been attacked—*I don't want anything to do with it*. But then I shared that the police are looking for more information on Pearl's attacker and I could always have them reach out to her directly. She got more accommodating after that and agreed to discuss her side hustle and true passion. Finding and obtaining rare objects.

My car coasts to the curb of the one-story building on the corner of University and Thirteenth Avenue. The sidewalks throng with students still fresh and excited for the first semester of the school year. Out of the handful of people who make eye contact with me, no one appears aggressive or wears rumpled clothing that says they, too, sat in a car for two hours, following me from Portland. Then again, it's hard to tell what anyone looks like behind a Giulio Venetta.

My shoulders hitch as I limp to the cement walkway of the veterinary hospital. After I fell from the Wishing Tree and landed wrong on my ankle, I didn't get a chance to ice it or elevate it when I got home from the hospital; instead, I flipped my dead bolt, then passed out in bed. Shards of pain stab my swollen ankle from all directions by the time I reach this beige one-story building.

Inside the lobby, the scent of pine hits my nose along with the more subtle perfume of dried dog treats. A young woman wearing Greek letters and carrying a tiny, fluffy shih tzu nearly collides with me before she exits, apologizing under her breath.

I tell the receptionist my name, and then a side door opens and a woman in blue scrubs and an open knit sweater peeks out. She pushes back long blond hair behind her shoulder. Purses her mouth into a strained smile.

"Zelda. I'm Megan. Come on back."

I follow her to a room at the end of the hallway, passing scales and small metal exam tables. When the door is safely shut behind us, the woman whose image I tried to find online—and couldn't—strikes me as old Hollywood beautiful. Large brown eyes and an olive complexion contrast wavy blond hair that she secured with two butterfly barrettes on either side of her face. Not exactly the image I'd expect of either a middle-aged vet tech or an antique-finding enthusiast.

She turns to me, tucking a pen into her shirt pocket. "You have ten minutes."

"I . . . You said twenty over the phone."

"I did. But I'm running behind today." She gives me a steely look, not bothering to consult a watch or the wall clock for the time.

"Okay. Well, someone attacked Pearl, and we're wondering who would have been upset that Pearl was questioning Sally's contacts. Who might have been bitter about Sally's successful auction at Gillian's. She found a very valuable mask that—"

"—that I found."

". . .You did?"

Megan narrows her eyes. "I found it for Sally earlier this year. I located it in Vancouver after searching all over North America. Then she routed the sale through Gillian's."

"And that bothered you?" The angry way Megan's jaw works back and forth seems in contrast to her innocent appearance.

Pearl's warning returns. *If she's capable of killing Ursula and Finn and attacking me . . . then you should be very, very careful.*

"Of course it did. She paid me the usual finder's fee, but I should have gotten a lot more after the amount that the mask ultimately went for. Not many people can hunt down an item across six months of work, working transnationally with Canada to figure out its location in an old farming shed in Vancouver." Megan grimaces. "I had to call deep into my network for tips and tricks."

The Lie She Wears

"That would frustrate me too," I reply, choosing empathy. "How long did you know Sally?"

"A few years. I've been doing finding work for decades."

A dog howls from the room next door. "How did you become a finder? Was it tough work to break into?"

Megan relaxes, as most people do when you show an interest in their hobbies. "I started back in New York, where I'm from. I was working at the post office and found there was a lot of overlap with finding, in tracking packages and their recipients."

I pause, taking in the scowl she continues to wear. I'll bet, judging from the way she speaks in a near whisper, she hasn't told her employer that she does finding work on the side.

"Why didn't you want me to tell the police about you?" I ask, raising my voice. "Have you been holding a grudge against Sally, and now her daughter, all this time?"

Megan starts, as if she might grab me. "I—Look, I only have another five minutes on this time slot. Keep it down and I might make it six."

"Sure. But you want to stay off the police radar because finding hasn't just been about old antiques and masks, has it?"

Megan purses her mouth again. "No. It can deal in legal and illegal items. But Sally knew that. Anyone who is on the hunt for antiques knows that."

"Did Sally employ anyone else as a finder?"

"I couldn't tell you. But there's a woman up in Astoria and another Hound in Bellingham who are well known for finding. That's it for the Pacific Northwest. It's a pretty exclusive circle nationally, for the best of the best. Us."

"Hound?"

"Ah, yeah. Yeah, it's an old term for finders. Anyone who uses it probably worked on the other coast, and goes all around the country, depending on the job."

"Anyone make it out this way, besides you, who might know Sally from New York? She was born there."

Megan turns her gaze up and to the side. She drums her fingertips against the metal exam table behind her. "Errol Peng. That guy could find anyone. Last I heard, ages ago, he was zigzagging across the country looking for something."

"Someone?" I ask, my heart creeping into my throat. The masked figure in Sally's bedroom could have been a man.

"A girl in Portland. A kid."

"When was this?"

"At least twenty-five years ago. But I didn't help him myself, then. I directed him to a guy who could."

"And who was that?"

"His name was Finn Hoskie."

My stomach drops. "As in the former director of client relations at Gillian's Auction House? The guy who hated Sally Wong? You were friends with him?"

"I wouldn't say that. I knew him. Knew he was a Hound and good at what we do. I met him a few times, years ago." She nods, pinching her eyebrows together. "He was killed recently."

Finn had a grudge against Sally, and Pearl thought he knew about the dead and buried bodies. Maybe Errol Peng knew, and Errol told Finn about them.

Megan checks her watch. "That's our time. You're gonna have to go. Now."

"I have one more question." The rain-streaked letter's words remain clear in my mind. "Does the name Elsie mean anything to you?"

Megan narrows her expression. "What does it mean to you?"

"Nothing. That's the problem. But I think Sally was scared of her, whoever she is."

Megan looks past my shoulder. "Zelda, a bit of advice: When you encounter a rabid animal, you get as far away from it as possible. And if I were you, I'd stop asking so many questions."

New barking erupts in the hallway, snarling and snapping reaching a crescendo. Human voices yell commands, and then hushed whimpering leaches into this room.

"You know who attacked Pearl. Don't you?" I whisper.

After a long pause, Megan wraps her arms across her chest. "I've got to get back to work. And remember to leave me out of any conversations with police."

Back in my car, I hit the locks on the doors. Reflect on my conversation with Megan and take note of the anxious way she ushered me out of the exam room. She didn't want her boss—or anyone else, for that matter—knowing I was there.

I open the search browser on my phone. Finn Hoskie's wife is all over articles about his death, imploring people to support the winery he so loved and to honor Native efforts to reclaim local viticulture. A search on her, the only family he has left, doesn't return much.

When I google Errol Peng, several obituaries populate in the results, for Arnold E. Peng, Errol Seng, and Errol Paine. No matches for the finder that Megan named.

Students pass my parked car, chanting a school fight song.

"E. Peng" returns nothing useful either. Too many results get tripped up by the use of a single initial. I do a search for "Megan Stefanich" with the keywords "Elsie" and "Post Office," but all I get is disparate nonsense.

Next, I input "E. Peng New York," then watch as a full page of websites, articles, and links appears. My heart racing, I click on the first link that details an attempted murder back in the 1990s—still, no Errol Peng is mentioned.

Finn Hoskie knew Sally and Ursula, yet there's no way to connect the finder Errol Peng to any recent violence. Especially without anyone knowing his location. It's only too ironic that a finder wants to stay hidden.

I look up from scrolling on my phone. Catch the eye of a dog walker who quickly crosses the street.

What if Pearl was so organized and orderly that she already compiled everything we need?

Safely nestled in the passenger footwell of my car, the address book is nearly covered by my backpack. I grab it, then flip the book open to the pile of loose papers I stashed within. The letters that Sally wrote—the five of them—appear like harbingers of all the horrible things that have happened since she put pen to paper.

Beneath the letters are several loose sheets—the reports detailing each individual's life: Sally's, Liam's, and Pearl's. Sally's and Liam's each contain dates of birth, old addresses, full legal names, professional histories, associates' names, along with their respective areas of interest. Art, art galleries, and thrift stores for Sally. Construction, building law, and privacy law for Liam. Incomplete sentences line the bottom of each page, as if they continued onto a second page.

Pearl's page is similar, though the details are briefer. Hers contains her education history, noting that her projected graduation date from Stanford at the time of the report was in one year's time.

"Who made these?" I wonder aloud, rifling through them again. "Why did Pearl have them?"

Halfway down Liam's page, a name stops me from scanning further. Madeleine Davis. Liam's wife whom he married in 1994, who filed a battery complaint against him that was later dropped. Although Liam has never struck me as the violent type, I've only met him a handful of times.

"Yikes. Poor Madeleine."

I flip back to Sally's page, to the family section that shows Sally had a sister named Shirley, whom I've never heard of, and to the section beneath family—marriage records. The space is blank.

"Well, well," I murmur. "Sally and Liam never married."

People shout outside, huddled and walking quickly as a burst of wind shakes one of the manicured sidewalk trees. A bicycle zips by.

The closest I find to a Madeleine in the address book is an entry for a Misty Fairley. I flip back to the first page. Cross-referencing the names listed on Liam's and Sally's respective reports, I search for any overlap between them and the address book that Pearl wrote her theories in, which my attacker may have tried to steal from the nightstand at the ranch house. By the final pages, it's clear that Ursula Romano is the only one of the two dozen names included in Liam's and Sally's reports that also appears in the address book.

I tap the bottom of my steering wheel. "If Pearl thought Madeleine was important, she would have written so in the back pages."

Pearl circled only one name on Liam's report: someone listed simply as Bert.

Robert Pelham didn't remember Sally, but I google his name anyway and the other similar name from her address book, Robert Truman. Nothing useful for my purposes returns on Pelham. But my search of Truman's name lands an image of a man running the Portland Marathon in 1995 at the top of the results. A thirtysomething man wearing a white T-shirt and a runner's bib across short shorts. A tattoo of a flock of birds nearly covers his neck, visible despite the photo's long frame.

"Robert 'Bert' Truman climbs the St. Johns Bridge during Portland's annual marathon," I read aloud.

I trace the tattoo, which is clear to my eyes in black-and-white contrast. The same tattoo as in the photo of the man holding me as a baby that I found in the attic. Emotion closes my throat, and my eyes well with tears. Is this my dad? The person for whom I've been searching since I came to Portland?

My lips part in quick shudders as I examine his face. The curve of his chin and the straight line of his forehead could both be my own features. His hair flops in the wind, the same dark color as mine. Relief threatens to overwhelm me. Joy at seeing him alive and healthy in this photo, when I so recently found him dead and buried on the ranch house property.

I rub my chin, my thinking habit. Bert Truman was missing a toe, based on what I saw amid the overturned dirt—similar to how the

Brontë's victims were missing a finger. Is it a coincidence? Or another indication that Sally really was . . . a serial killer?

Confusion washes over me. The excitement I felt moments before now feels inappropriate and empty while I stare at my biological father's picture. I push a breath past my teeth, then unlock my car. Stepping outside to stretch, feeling my muscles protest after sitting for so long, reminds me again how little I slept last night. A walk would do me good.

I set off on my tender ankle toward the town square park, slowly weaving through a group of runners wearing University of Oregon jerseys. Postcards that were sent to the house and addressed to Liam struck Pearl as both sinister and benign. I agree based on the text she transcribed in the back of the address book, and the ones that I found by the door and added to the Bankers box. *I miss you. Can't wait until we meet again.*

The locations of the images on the backs of the postcards, however, were strictly creepy. She noted that they were each the scenes of gruesome crimes, and they also all had a countdown of some kind—maybe to Pearl's attack, in hindsight.

A mother runs past, pushing a jogging stroller with three wheels, listening to blaring music through her headphones.

As a drop of rain hits my cheek, I stop short. It slides down my face like a bead of sweat, while the volume of conversations among passing students seems to dim. If the postcards' countdown was always about Pearl, why did the postcards begin arriving before she moved back to Portland?

My phone rings, vibrating in my back pocket and startling me. Detective Sims is calling.

"Hi, Detective," I say, stepping out of the walkway for a husky and its owner to pass.

"Zelda. I thought you were going to send me to voicemail."

My heartbeat pulses in my fingertips, while I grip my phone. "No, of course not. Has Kai Weathers confessed to Pearl's attack?"

A garbled voice spurts through a radio close to Detective Sims. *Officers en route.*

"Could you come downtown, Zelda? We have some updates that we need to share with you."

I still. "Can't you tell me the updates over the phone?"

"Afraid not, Zelda. You can come in by yourself . . . or we can escort you."

New tension cinches my gut as the unspoken meaning between his words sinks in. The police are going to arrest me. They must have gotten a warrant for Sally's attorney's files, and whatever cash she left me has heaped even more suspicion. If I go to the police precinct, I won't walk out.

"Oh, sure. Of course. I'll be right there." *Shit. Shit, shit.* "An hour, more or less, depending on traffic."

"I'll keep an eye on the clock," the detective says.

I hang up without replying. Fight the panic that pinches my chest, coursing down to my coat pocket where I stashed my Taser. The police think I'm involved in Pearl's attack. Are they even looking at Kai Weathers now?

A siren wails from a distance, its sound carrying across the grid of this town.

Someone has been sending threatening postcards to the ranch house all year. And Pearl wrote in the address book that she dropped new postcards for Liam at his care facility, recently. Although she transcribed the messages, if I want to prove my innocence and figure out who has been playing the long game with the Davises—I need to see the final two for myself.

Chapter Forty-One

Zelda

The lobby is empty when I limp onto the tan hardwood of the Twin Pines Care Facility. The tissue around the bone of my ankle remains inflamed, and I do my best to ignore it. To push through before Detective Sims realizes I'm not coming to the precinct.

Easy listening jazz slips through the overhead speakers, countering my frantic energy with an eerie ambience. I've never been here before, since Sally always insisted that she go alone. Double doors that might lead back into the facility open, and a woman in a bright-pink blazer emerges. She plucks a plastic novelty clock bearing the phrase "Back in Five" off the counter.

"Hi there. Visiting today?"

"Yes. Liam Davis."

I hand over my driver's license, and she takes a photo of it with a tablet. She gives me a paper badge with my name, my face, and Liam's room number. Although I texted Pearl about my visit to Megan, my new theories relating to Finn and Errol Peng, the useless Google search results, my biological father being buried beneath the oak tree, and

The Lie She Wears

everything else I thought might be relevant, she hasn't replied. I had hoped she might before I arrived here, to give me some insight into how to approach her dad, but it's too late now.

"You can key in over there. Your dad's room is all the way at the end of the first hallway on the right."

I blush, though I don't correct this woman. "Thank you."

I press the badge to a black keypad beside the polished door handles, and then a beep announces I'm in. The woman's instructions lead me directly to Liam's room, where I pause. My Taser is tucked inside my jacket pocket, where it's been since yesterday, though I don't intend to use it. There's no way that Liam had anything to do with the mess of Pearl's attack three days ago—which the police must have notified him of by now. Still, I'm not close with this man. I've seen him only a handful of times since Sally hired me back in March, including at her funeral. I don't know what to expect behind this door.

Inhaling a sharp breath, I tap my knuckles on the metal. When no one answers, I try the handle. It's unlocked.

"Hello?" I press the door, and it cracks open, revealing an empty bedroom. I step inside quickly, before any of the staff notices.

The room is trashed. Sheets lie rumpled on a twin bed pushed into the corner, as if freshly slept in. Loose papers cover a narrow desk tucked against the opposite wall—articles on Sally, search results on Pearl—while a plate of untouched smashed meat loaf is nearly hidden beneath a newspaper. On a mounted corkboard above, four postcards are tacked on display, message side out.

My skin vibrates as I approach the desk. The words scrawled at a slant are clear.

Can't wait until we meet again.
I miss you.
Thinking of you.
It's been too long.

The handwriting is a match for the other postcards sent to the house that Sally cached underneath her nightstand. Based on the postmark dates, the sender only started addressing these cards to Liam directly after Sally died. They knew about the car crash.

The words on the first two postcards are familiar to me since I added those to the Bankers box. At the bottom of each, a countdown is written—same as the others, but which I failed to notice over a month ago. *5 weeks*. Then *4 weeks*. Referencing my calendar against the postmark dates, the countdown doesn't match the night of Pearl's attack. If I assume that the postcards were each written the day they were processed, the countdown leads to—

"Today," I whisper.

Cold air cuts through the fabric of my sweater as I scan the room—glance at the unlocked door. Rack my memory for any suspicious cars in my rearview following me from Eugene.

Where the hell is Liam?

My hands tremble as I remove the tacks from the postcards and examine them up close. The phrases are almost intimate, as if the sender is a friend. Maybe a lover. But Liam moved to this facility over a year ago, at great cost to Sally. I doubt he started up an online entanglement from within the care facility. Thinking back on the financial records that Sally squirreled away in her nightstand, Liam and Sally were almost broke until the auction sale. Would the sender think that Liam must be flush with cash, assuming that Sally left him something? Who would stand to gain from scaring Sally, and now Liam?

Sometimes, my role as a live-in nurse is to identify abuse that may be contributing to a patient's diminishing health or finances. Who would stand to gain from everyone in Liam's life dying or getting injured?

A framed photo is all that decorates a short set of drawers, wheelchair height. Liam and Sally at their wedding, with both of them dressed in white. Green eucalyptus leaves adorn Sally's dark hair in a crown.

The Lie She Wears

But Liam and Sally were never legally married. And the background check that ex-Gillian's employee and former Hound Finn ran showed he was never divorced.

Voices echo in the hallway. I yank out the address book from my backpack. Find the report on Liam and scan the page until my eyes land on the marriages section. On Madeleine Davis's name. His first wife. His only wife.

"Madeleine Davis" doesn't have a large internet footprint, according to the search browser on my phone. Aside from a few pings related to real estate back in the day, nothing turns up.

Shirley Wong, on the other hand—Sally's sister, who lives about three hours away in Seattle—has page after page of social media posts, ranting about the government. The high cost of eggs. The inefficiency of food stamps. And how family is "never there for you when you need them."

I pause, consuming the long caption Shirley posted to Instagram beneath a photo of herself at seven years old. Against a backdrop of brick buildings, on a dirty stoop, a toddler sits beside her wearing ripped overalls, their matching black hair pulled tight in twin pigtails. Sally.

"Despite being told that family is always there for you, that you should always be there for them, it was all bullshit," I read the caption aloud. "The only person you can depend on is yourself. The only things you can rely on are what you can grab."

My stomach churns in a slow, sickening shift. Shirley, Pearl's aunt, could have been tracking and attacking everyone. Seattle is in only the next state over. And a quick drive to Spokane, one of the locations featured on these postcards. But would the anger behind Shirley's Instagram post translate to the ability to attack her niece with a knife? How does the name "Elsie" tie into anything? Megan's sudden unease when I asked about it tells me that Sally didn't make it up; this Elsie person is dangerous. But how are they related to Shirley—or Madeleine?

The image of Pearl's contorted body, folded beside the storage bin of the warehouse, flashes to my eyes. A surge of horror licks between my shoulder blades, and I shudder, reliving the scene. Whoever attacked Pearl didn't hesitate, didn't feel any momentary concern before they tried to kill her.

"Excuse me?" The receptionist stands in the doorway. She smiles, her eyebrows forming a tent. "I'm sorry to interrupt. I just realized that Mr. Davis isn't here."

"Right. I was just coming to ask. Is he okay?"

"Oh, yes. He's doing much better, actually, since his relapse last week. He's with Twin Pines on a special off-campus excursion. You can come back and see him tomorrow if you'd like."

I shake my head. Tomorrow might be too late. "What excursion?"

Chapter Forty-Two

Pearl

Beep, beep, beep. A moan escapes my lips as I try to block out the noise, pressing my hands to my ears.

It's endless, the sound from my monitors—torturous. Beep, beep, beep. Nonstop. Invading my mind. Agonizing when I remember that I didn't choose this. Didn't elect to take a hospital stay. Every single monotonous note is a reminder that I was attacked and forced to near death. That a murderer came for me, who has already targeted and killed others. I tried to get a nurse to turn down the volume, but she insisted it remain at the normal level.

"Why? What's the point?" I asked, grumbling.

"You are," Frances, the new-to-me nurse, answered. "Your stability. Your health. Don't want you hemorrhaging alone now, after your second surgery in two days."

I only nodded, my head already flat on the pillow.

Beep, beep, beep. The wall clock says it's nearly ten o'clock at night. Footsteps in the hallway have become less frequent, conversations hushed. And yet I can't shake the feeling that something bad is barreling toward me across the scuffed tile.

True, I've remained heavily medicated since arriving here. So much so that I'm having trouble telling the difference between my dreams and reality. A painting on the wall across from my bed—a framed print of Mount Hood by Ray Atkeson—sometimes blurs into my dreams, mentally leading me to believe I'm in the Columbia River Gorge taking in the sights, before I wake up to the scent of cleaning solution. The black-and-white peaks, so artfully captured by a celebrated Oregon photographer, remind me of my former life. The routine I maintained before everything went to shit. Wake up, museum, lunch downtown, museum, home. Occasionally work-sponsored karaoke. Rinse, repeat.

While I haven't seen any other full-on masks worn by the hospital personnel since Zelda's visit, I know something is out there. Waiting for me.

Zelda has been keeping me in the loop via text. I can't seem to connect with her when I'm awake—the pain meds have me dozing at most hours of the day—but she sends me updates that I read when I can. More than once, the nurses have caught me trying to draft a response and struggling to stay awake. After the last time I dropped my phone to the floor, cracking the screen, and almost fell out of bed trying to reach it, they took it from me. Placed it at the opposite end of the room while assuring me that anytime I needed it, they would retrieve it for me—*Just ask.*

I stare at my phone where it sits underneath the Ray Atkeson print. At the brown-and-dark-red cubic pattern of the love seat on which my phone rests.

Beep, beep, beep, the monitors taunt me, resembling Sally's critical voice. *You can't go anywhere. You made your own bed here.*

Reflecting back on Zelda's conversation with Megan Stefanich, I'm not sure anything was gained from the road trip. Although I appreciate Zelda's sudden commitment to finding out the truth, Megan's revelation that Finn knew Errol Peng doesn't help us.

And yet. If Errol and Finn were both Hounds, maybe Finn helped Errol find the girl he was searching for out west. It's possible that antique-lover Finn crossed paths with my mother twenty-four years ago, when she was first getting into antiquing as a bored stay-at-home mom. I had just started going to preschool as a three-year-old, freeing up some hours in her day, and she said that was when she began itching for something that was hers alone.

Was Errol searching for "some girl," when he actually meant a grown woman—Sally? Did Finn direct Errol to our address—after which Errol was never seen again?

New dread tightens my belly, sending streaks of pain down my ribs, in time with the machines' relentless beep, beep, beeps. Finn didn't hate Sally. He was scared of her—of what she was capable of.

Chapter Forty-Three

Zelda

Pop music bumps across the glass-walled penthouse of the museum's fourth floor. Visitors shout to be heard above the noise as I limp into the gallery space. Pop-up exhibits are spread across this level, separated by walls of short lengths that cause the layout to resemble a maze.

It's nearly the end of the first Friday of October—some special wine tasting event—and festive costumes span the room. Crowds of people filter toward the exit, some pausing to examine a true crime photography exhibit, while other visitors in matching witch hats chat beside the Native American pop-up that explores ghost stories. A man wearing a devil mask leers at me beside an artistic display of empty soda cans. Face paint and face coverings begin to outnumber the patrons who forgot to dress up, like myself, the farther I walk into this floor.

As I make my way through the crowd, I search the backs of T-shirts for the Twin Pines Care Facility logo. Scan groups of people for wheelchairs and Liam's face. Exhibit after exhibit fails to produce either by the time I reach the end of the hall near another elevator, disappointed and on edge. A

The Lie She Wears

patron in costume as a police officer nearly knocks into me, drinking from a fake, plastic gun barrel.

Not Detective Sims. Not the Portland Police coming to arrest me.

Pale white catches my eye from the final pop-up exhibit in the corner of this floor. A mask hanging on the wall, next to a dozen others. Colorful designs, tassels, and gold-painted Chinese characters are splashed across these face coverings in diverse images and themes. A blown-up poster board reveals the exhibit's title: *Hidden Faces and Fears: An Exploration of Asian Masks Throughout the Centuries*, by Pearl Davis.

Several patrons finish their viewing, then exit the space, leaving only myself and a man staring at a black-and-white professional photograph of Pearl that I recognize from the museum's website. Liam, seated in a wheelchair, reading a foreword written by the museum in tribute to Pearl's work, given her current hospitalization. Anticipation surges in my chest, followed by fear. I found him, Pearl's dad. And now I have to tell him.

Reaching out to tap him on the shoulder, I pant, "Hi, Liam? Do you remember me? I just came to check—"

I stop short. From the corner of this alcove, someone steps forward wearing a mask. Black ovals rim the eyes above the gold diamonds that decorate the left cheek, while glittering ruby red–painted lips are wordless. Hairs ignite across my skin in recognition.

The Giulio Venetta that hung across from Pearl's bedroom. The same mask this person wore when they attacked me in the hallway.

Nausea churns my gut, and I step back. Place a hand on Liam's chair to pull him with me, when the person moves from beside a catering cart draped in a black cloth. They withdraw a gun—a real one—from the folds of the dark cape they wear, freezing me in place.

"Please don't do this," I choke out. "We don't have any of Sally's money, I swear. It's still in probate."

Adrenaline shoots through my body, dousing my limbs. No one has heard from Sally's estranged sister in years. If she decided to attack people who facilitated an influx of cash that she felt entitled to—it would make sense. Ursula was a resource for Sally in the antique world; Finn played a role in the auction that netted Sally her big payday.

"Shirley, you don't have to do this. Put the gun down."

Music continues to pulse from the museum's speakers. I could scream, though I doubt anyone would hear me. Voices carry from along the glass walls overlooking the city, half the length of this floor, but the patrons have all but left. Shirley must have been watching Liam's care facility, seizing the only moment he would be unprotected, away from the campus walls.

"Do what? Get exactly what I'm owed?" Her high-pitched voice sounds like a deranged doll's, daring me to protest. My skin trembles in response.

The gun's barrel points squarely at my chest as a strobe light pulsates across the penthouse floor in time with a new song. My heart stutters this close to a murderer. The four feet to safety outside this pop-up is too far.

"Why do this? Why attack Liam? Your brother-in-law?" I grip Liam's chair, inching him closer to me.

She laughs behind the mask. "Is that what he is?" The blood drains from my face as she places both hands on the gun. "If you believe that, then you had this coming."

Pain explodes in my stomach as the gun fires—spirals, flooding my limbs. I drop to the floor, my hands clutching at the wound, trying to stanch the blood as all my nursing training flees my brain. "No, no, no—" Before the pain lessens. Subsides. Warmth replaces the bright agony stemming from my core as the lights dim overhead. The sound of visitors and blaring music fades.

The event is over. The museum must be closing. Locking us inside together with the monster behind the glittery mouth serving poison. Shirley's mouth.

Liam says something—shouts—but I can't make out the words.

A figure looms over me, black surrounding them. "Oh, look. Another idiot."

My mind slows. Images of nothing and everything leach into my consciousness. Blend into the emptiness of my vision. A door slams close by. Cold water trickles down my arms.

Then silence.

Sharp pain taps my head. Tap. Tap tap tap. A stab of fire shoots from my stomach, rousing me awake.

I open my eyes. Shirley stands several feet away, still masked, observing me as I come to. Liam is seated in his wheelchair opposite from me in the living room of the ranch house. We're back.

"You can't keep us," Liam grunts. "Twin Pines will be on high alert, looking for me. You think they won't come here?"

I lift a hand to my head. Cringe against new pain. Shut my eyes tight. "What happened?"

The mask scoffs. "Tomorrow morning they'll check in. Now it's much too late. The police won't be able to track the digital key in your wheelchair until the manufacturer opens for business in nine hours. I'll be done with you by then."

"Why are we here?" I ask the room, still disoriented.

I was drugged. No, shot with a tranquilizer, judging from my memory of the sharp pain that burst in my side.

"A long-awaited reunion," the mask says. "I did miss you, Liam."

My tongue feels thick, like the tranquilizer that hit me was calibrated for a large man. "Shirley . . ."

She lifts a silver pistol from underneath the cape she still wears—different from the dart gun wielded in the museum. A gloved hand disengages the safety. Click click.

My heart flinches with each crash of the metal gears. "Listen, Liam isn't to blame for Sally's shortcomings . . . He's disabled. Leave him alone."

A shudder passes through my body as I recognize how close Pearl was to the truth when she was attacked. The postcards, the reports from Finn, and the hints that directed to the Wishing Tree with the most explicit instructions that Sally had written. Pearl had all the information in front of her but didn't see the forest through the trees.

Liam takes in this exchange while barely moving. I don't know how recovered he is from his recent relapse, but he's probably exhausted. Shirley must have wheeled him out of one of the emergency exits, like the one beside where Pearl was knifed. Taking me with them.

Shirley is impassive behind the mask as the gun moves between my chest and Liam's head. It shifts into an easy rhythm, passing from one mark to the next, and I close my eyes a moment, unable to withstand the terror that seizes my chest each time it moves.

"He's the most capable man I've ever met," Shirley says. The voice is throaty, deep, and androgynous across the few words that spell violence.

Liam flinches. Our captor pushes the mask over her head, revealing pale skin, a pert nose, and dark-rimmed eyes that peered at me from above while she tightened her grip on my neck in the hallway. Black straight hair frames narrow, lined features that settle into a smile.

"You attacked Pearl," I say. "You attacked me. You're behind all of the killings. Why hurt so many people?"

The familiar weights of my Taser and my phone are missing from my jacket pocket. I visually search the shag carpet beneath me, then the coffee table three feet away, for something heavy to swing. Sally must have stashed one of her just-in-case items nearby.

This woman locks her eyes on my face. "Oh, you dumb girl. You don't know who I am, do you?"

Sweat beads my neck. The name from the Wishing Tree. "You're . . . you're not Shirley. You're—"

A blur of movement surges from across the room—Liam rising, lunging out of his chair. He wields a switchblade like one of the six that Sally kept in her closet. Moonlight flashes on its steel as he brings it down toward the woman's head.

But she doesn't flinch. She fires the gun at his leg, then he crumples to the floor. A strangled cry howls from his mouth.

I reach for Liam—muscle memory kicking in to rush to him and apply pressure on the wound—but this woman clears her throat, stopping me.

"I'm not Shirley, dum-dum." She lowers the gun with eerie calm. "My name is Elsie."

Chapter Forty-Four

Elsie

New York City, 1992

Seated outside at a pizzeria across from the Bronx post office, I moisten the glue of the envelope with a wet paper napkin.

Errol takes in my precaution with a skeptical cocked eyebrow. "What are you doing?"

With gloved hands, I press the flap shut, sealing my letter taunting the police within. "What does it look like? I'm going to mail correspondence."

"You addressed it to Sergeant Mills. A guy that works in homicides. What the hell are you after, Els?"

Errol folds his slice in half, then wolfs down a third. The tooth that he chipped on the skating rink when we were twelve peeks out from the side of his mouth. I always admired that about my twin. Although our grandmother scolded him for skating backward before he could even glide forward, Errol made it a pastime to fuck around, then suffer the stitches that inevitably came. He learned what the inside of a Bronx emergency room

The Lie She Wears

looked like, which initiated a world of interest in pain. In cause and effect. In what actions are likely to elicit serious consequences or slaps on the wrist.

My brother limited himself to mostly socially acceptable forms of deviance. Sleeping around. Spitting in the food of customers who were rude at a chain restaurant where he was a waiter. Stealing from the paper supply company where he currently works as a purchasing director.

Although I entered real estate for all kinds of reasons, my favorite was how little oversight there is when I'm out and about showing properties. The bottom line is what counts in that industry; did I land the sale or didn't I? Just like when my fingers start to itch and I feel compelled to snatch a blanket from a baby in a stroller, pinch a perfect stranger in a crowded subway car, or—yes—terrorize certain individuals who had it coming, the bottom line is all that matters: Was I caught? Or wasn't I?

Errol wipes his mouth with a paper napkin. "How's Mary doing?"

"Not sure. She won't answer my letters." I pout, pushing my pizza around my plate with a plastic fork.

"Rikers isn't supposed to be great." Errol shoots me a look, which I ignore.

"I'm sure she's fine. She did attack me, after all."

"She told the police on you about pushing that woman in front of the bus."

A man in a business suit glances our way, but he continues hurrying down the sidewalk.

"Who cares?" I roll my eyes. "She was a tattletale. I hope she's learned her lesson not to talk. Rikers is no place for bitches—I mean, snitches. Since when are you so high and mighty?"

Errol shrugs, then folds his hands across his flat stomach. Wipes his fingertips on the Metallica logo on the graphic tee he wears. "Please. I just worry about you. I wouldn't want my little sister going away anytime soon."

We've talked about the possibility that my antics might get me arrested, or imprisoned, at some point. We've talked about the necessity of blending in, because most people don't think the way that I do—feel the way that I feel.

I have emotions and see other people having them too. Mine just happen to be driven by my own interests and needs. I don't understand this idea of putting myself in anyone else's shoes, when mine fit right and earn me yearning looks from high-powered individuals on Fifth Ave.

"Might be time to start lying low again, Elsie." Errol purses his lips. "You know, just for a bit."

I pause, weighing his words. Debating when this fit of conscience might have overtaken my brother. "Was it the kitchen knife? A little much?"

Errol leans sharply over his paper plate. "Elsie, you put yourself in the hospital. And for what? To frame a nuisance of a woman and send her to prison for assault with a deadly weapon."

I wave off his concern. "It was one night. Three stitches. And I won't be doing that again; it hurt more than I expected."

Actually, it hurt exactly the amount I wanted it to, but I don't tell Errol that. No sense in revealing how much I enjoyed the abrupt shock to this mundane, gray-filtered life. Truly, the only time I feel like I see color lately is when I'm preparing one of these letters to send out.

Rick the Wall Street Predator started looking shaky after I sent a few to his loft. He would exit the subway and arrive at his office in the World Trade Center while looking over his shoulder nonstop—for good reason, it turns out. It took some time for the right moment to occur, but after one debaucherous night of him pressing his girth up against women in yet another nightclub—the idiot didn't learn any lesson from his friend Geoff—I finally found myself alone with him in the alleyway beside the building. A quick shank of my utility knife earned him an easy death and me my first trophy: his index finger. For all the times I watched him stick his hand up the dresses of women who were not receptive to his advances. And because I think there could be a certain poetry to taking fingers of my victims from now on. Especially from their dominant writing hand. I do so love drafting letters and writing stories.

The Lie She Wears

I'm not yet sure how the sergeant I keep sending little missives to is enjoying the stories—classic tales interspersed with details from real crimes I've committed, and which he must be picking up on by now—but that's not important. It's the journey, after all, to borrow Mary's favorite platitude.

"Fine," Errol concedes. "Okay, you got me. I want you to lay off. Find some other shiny object to focus on that won't attract the attention of the NYPD. Like that guy you're seeing. The too-eager puppy dog you had me meet at Central Park."

"The bartender? I haven't called him in weeks. He was fun for a bit. But then all he wanted to do was play bocce ball and talk about construction projects he has planned for his own bar one day. Beyond boring."

Errol lays a hand on mine. Something he knows I hate—physical touch unless I initiate it. "That's exactly why you should be with him. If you have to, keep doing whatever you want on the side, but you need a safer cover. Mundanity, if anyone were to take a closer look."

A bicyclist speeds past, darting between braking taxicabs on the street. A trash truck rolls forward from behind, the force of its engine vibrating our table.

"Elsie, come on. You know I'd do anything for you. Go anywhere, do anything, really. You're my sister, and the only person I actually care about in the world." Errol tilts his head. Gives me a half smile the way that he's done since we were kids, about to do something else foolhardy and hilarious at the playground.

My twin brother's words remind me that he, too, feels the itch in his fingertips. He just feels it less strongly than I do, less often. He really would do anything for me.

"I know," I say. "And you're probably right. I'll call Liam up later today and see how he's doing. I'll have to tell him my real name at some point, though."

"Sure. Just say Opal was a nickname."

"For what?"

Errol shrugs. "For being a gem."

"Hardy-har."

We throw our plates and napkins in the trash, then start off in the direction of the next subway stop.

As we approach the steps that lead to the platform below, I side-eye Errol. "What would I ever do without my big brother by two minutes, my protector and Jiminy Cricket? What hot water would I get myself into if you weren't around to nag?"

Errol throws me a devilish grin, then pushes his long dark hair off his forehead. "Let's hope the world never has to find out."

Chapter Forty-Five

Pearl

The sharp plastic railing of my hospital bed cuts into my palm as I grip the bar. I slam my thumb against the built-in call button that connects directly to the nurses' station.

"Yes?" a voice answers through the speaker by my head.

"Could someone come in here and help me? I need my cell phone and it's on the couch." I wince, sounding like a teenager, but I need the damn thing now more than ever.

"Be right there." A click confirms the call ended.

Adrenaline washes down my body as I stare at the door, willing it to open. "Come on, come on. Let's go, Nurse Frances."

Errol Peng must have gone to Sally after asking Finn for directions to the girl he was pursuing. But why does Peng sound familiar?

Zelda has the address book with all my notes, she said. I was too out of it to ask for it back last night, but I've stared long enough at my own writing to recall basic facts. Peng wasn't in there.

No, it was in the text Zelda sent me two hours ago. It was the name of some assault victim she read about from the nineties. Madeleine E. Peng.

Madeleine. I've heard that somewhere else.

"Yes . . . but no." I drum my fingers on the beige blanket across my lap. I've seen the word Madeleine, the text visible behind my eyelids. It was on a printed piece of paper. On the reports that I found in Finn's desk drawer.

"Oh no," I whisper. I hit the call button again.

"Yes?"

"Can someone please hurry?" I ask, breathless. "I . . . I need my phone. Like, right now, please."

"Sorry about that, Pearl. We're coming. Just got a little backed up, but we'll be there. Give us five minutes." A flurry of voices hums through the phone.

"No, please—" But the call clicks dead before I finish speaking.

A moment passes with me staring at my phone all the way across the room. Zelda texted me hours ago. She could be anywhere by now and with anyone watching her every move. She may not have five minutes.

Jamming my thumb across the incline button, I raise my hospital bed. Inch is gained by inch, against the loud, shuddering motor, until I am nearly seated upright. Pulling my legs to the side of the bed, I wince as pain shoots from my upper-right shoulder, where the knife sliced into my muscle.

I set my jaw, planting my feet onto the gray-flecked white tile, then push to standing. Leaning into the stainless-steel IV pole, I take a step. White stars explode across my vision, but I take another. Then another, toward the love seat, cursing the nursing staff in between raggedy breaths. My hospital gown flutters open at every angle, so that I alternately hope a nurse comes to help me and that this ward empties of all life.

A burning sensation begins at my side, but I keep going—scraping my feet forward the bed length that still separates me from the couch.

Blood begins to dot the tile, seeping from my wound's dressing. I block it out. Focus on the burgundy upholstery ahead, and my phone. Panic that I might fall and crack my head on the tile drives me the final two feet, and then I collapse onto the couch, still clutching the IV pole for balance.

I grip my phone, searching through my photos as pain screams along my sutures. My head feels heavy. My eyelids like velvet curtains.

I pause to read. Enlarge the background check that was generated for Liam.

"Madeleine Davis," I whisper, reading the name of my dad's first wife. "Another Madeleine."

It doesn't make sense that I never knew about Dad's first marriage. Was Finn so sure it was real—that it wasn't some AI error during the background check?

I open a new search browser tab. Input my dad's full name—Liam Fu Davis—alongside Madeleine's name. Include the keywords "New York," "Marriage record," and "1990"—any marriage would have taken place before I was born in 1996.

An archived newspaper article for the *New York Daily News* turns up on the second page of results, stealing my breath. New pain stabs my ribs as I read the first line: *The marriage of Liam Fu Davis and Madeleine Elspeth Peng took place October 6, 1994 in St. Charles Church, Brooklyn Heights.*

"Madeleine Peng. Just like Errol Peng." I gasp. "Oh fuck."

Zelda said she didn't find anything on "Madeleine Davis," and Google provided only a page of results on this woman, a real estate agent in New York. But after learning from Megan that Errol Peng came looking for some girl out West, Zelda searched the phrase "E. Peng New York" trying to understand how he might fit. She found an article about an attack in the 1990s. She didn't see anything useful about it, but it gives me what I need now. A link.

I find the article, then scan the details in a fever. Madeleine E. Peng was attacked by a woman named Mary Anker. At the bottom of the page, in an update published after she was released from prison in 1999, Anker reiterates that she's innocent and vehemently denies hurting anyone, calling

Peng unhinged. Anker says she would be relocating to Illinois to "get as far away from that woman" as she could.

"Madeleine Peng will stop at nothing and for no one once she gets obsessed with someone," I read Anker's words aloud. Cold air slices down my open gown, setting my skin prickling with fear.

Madeleine Elspeth Davis is the married name of Madeleine E. Peng. I'm as sure of it as I am that I just fucked up the surgeon's work on my back. Errol Peng and Madeleine Peng are related. And the Elsie that Sally mentioned in her letter tied to the Wishing Tree is likely a nickname for Elspeth.

If that's all correct, then Zelda is in more danger than we ever guessed.

She doesn't have five minutes. I doubt she has two.

Jolts of pain shoot down my torso, then nausea buckles my body. Vomit spills onto my lap. My muscles scream at me to lie down, close my eyes, but I struggle to write out a text message to the only person who can help now.

I hit send as the door to my room smashes open. Then someone calls for a cart.

Chapter Forty-Six

Zelda

Elsie lifts her chin. A smile as grotesque and haunting as that of the mask she pushed onto her head twists her mouth at the corners. Liam cries on the carpet, swearing and clutching his wounded leg. He drags himself to a seated position against the armchair he vacated in a flash—contradicting the "severe" relapse he supposedly had.

None of this feels right. Nothing is making sense.

"What the hell, Elsie? You shot me!" He moans. "My leg, my . . ."

Blood gushes from his calf as if the bullet went straight through. Liam presses firmly against his wound, sobbing.

"I'm not here for you, darling," Elsie replies, matter of fact. "But I can be. You broke your marriage vow to me. You remember? It was twenty-nine years ago as of today."

"Madeleine. You're Madeleine, his first wife. That's what the countdown on the postcards was for—your wedding anniversary." My heartbeat stutters as the details align.

"Slow clap, Zelda. Keep it up. I thought it would be fun to celebrate with a body—I mean, a bang."

"Well, he was married to someone else for the last twenty-four years." I get to my feet, though I'm wary of them both. Terror tightens my throat as more cries trickle from the man Pearl thought was brutally trapped in his own body.

"And yet I have all the legal rights. I'd be careful, Zelda, if I were you. I didn't tie you up because I need you, but that could easily change." Elsie turns her attention to Liam, spreading her feet in tan heeled boots. "Originally, I dreamed about bringing your remains home to New Jersey. To the house that is still in our names, to the first place we decided we wanted to try for a family."

Her voice trails off, as if wistful, before her gaze sharpens. "Then I realized you were alive."

Elsie takes a menacing step toward Liam. "You said you were only going on a trip and that you'd be back in a week. I waited. For weeks, I waited. Then years. Finally, after three years, I sent my brother to find you."

"That's . . . not how it was," Liam says, panting. Finding his voice with difficulty. "You and your brother terrified me. I found out . . . found out about the baby. That Sally had her without telling me. I went to the baby."

"Sure, Liam," she purrs. "And Errol, someone even more ruthless than I am when it comes to finding his quarry, was just looking for a good camping spot all the way out here in Oregon. But he never returned home either."

"What does your brother have to do with anything?" I break in. "Doesn't that just prove that more than one person wanted to get away from you?"

Elsie turns to me sharply. "No. It proves that Liam no longer has the moral high ground."

I still, hearing the implication in her words. She knows about the bodies.

"That's right," she says, reading my face. "I came to the house to poke around after I attacked Pearl. Found the fresh mounds of overturned dirt and discovered not one but two corpses, one of which is missing a toe, and the other a finger. An homage, honey?"

Elsie's eyes redden. She sniffs, though she doesn't break eye contact with Liam. "My twin. Errol was buried under that miserable toolshed on the side of the house. He came looking for you, and instead you and Sally killed him. The only person I cared about in the world, after you left."

She spits the words, continuing to train her eyes on him. "Imagine my surprise when I saw a photo of you earlier this year with that woman, your *Sally*, in an announcement for an antique sale. You got a write-up in *Architectural Digest* online, with details about how your lovely Portland, Oregon home is covered in collector's editions of masks. You didn't die somewhere, destitute on the side of the road, out of gas and keening for me. You abandoned me."

She sneers, revealing straight incisors and bright-white teeth. "So I did my own digging and found your address. Learned all I could about your life out West. Started sending you postcards from cities with my favorite murders just to build the anticipation to our anniversary—a kind of collage form of storytelling implying future bodily harm; I thought it was a nice touch. For weeks, I followed your sidepiece, trying to learn where this Sally may have stashed you. I think she knew I was after her toward the end. She was hiding you from me."

Big brown eyes gleam, turning to me, beseeching me for understanding or solidarity. There's a magnetism about this woman, exuding grace and menace like a pitcher plant.

"Is that why you killed Ursula and Finn, because you were searching for Liam?" I ask. "You wanted to find him, to kill him next and get all of Sally and Liam's money as his legal spouse?"

"Why is everyone obsessed with money?" Elsie scoffs. "I killed those two because they were speed bumps."

"What do you mean?"

"They slowed me down. The woman was rude. Stingy with information. When I approached Ursula at her secondhand hovel, asked her a few questions about Sally and the mask that she auctioned, Ursula told me to get lost. Said she wouldn't divulge information about her best friend's family, no matter that Sally was already dead by then. Later, when I surprised her at her house, Ursula told me Sally knew I was watching her and she made plans to stop me from getting *her money*." Elsie rolls her eyes.

The secretive phone calls that Sally made a couple of months before she died begin to make sense. She didn't want me listening to details about the trust. She wanted to write me into the will, just in case Elsie got impatient and did something rash.

"And then there's Finn, the winery owner," she continues. "I nearly dropped my champagne flute when I watched the playback of Sally's auction and saw him standing in the corner, scowling like a child. Recognized him as a Hound that my brother had known years ago. Though I'd already decided to have a chat with him, when I saw Pearl speaking to him at the market, I didn't know that Finn had begun connecting the dots."

"And what dots are those?"

Elsie pauses. Her gaze softens into an empty expression, and new fear unlocks inside me at facing the last image Ursula and Finn held before dying at her hand. Her mouth twitches as she stares.

"Did you figure out my favorite pastime?" Her voice is curious. Quietly threatening.

"Tell me," I say, mirroring her volume.

She grins, pleased with herself. "Say it yourself and I'll let you die *before* I remove a finger."

Sweat lines my collar. I lick my lips to speak, my thoughts frantic. "You—You're—"

"I'm the Turnpike Bloody Brontë. The killer from back east." She pouts, twinkling her fingers at me. "Too bad you didn't say it fast enough."

Understanding circles my neck, gripping my throat. Elsie is the murderer who tortured her victims in psychological games before killing them, relishing the violence, then writing gory fan fiction about her conquests. Not Sally.

I struggle to process her words. The level of danger we're all in. "But why come for Pearl? Purely because she's the daughter Liam went to see?"

"That would make sense, right?"

The time must be past midnight, judging from the silence coming from the main road outside. No sound of the police arriving to investigate Liam's whereabouts. No sign of Twin Pines sending their own search and recovery party.

"Killing Pearl was always my plan," she continues, "after I played with her a bit. Wrote threatening postcards that I left for her beside my Portland victims."

"Played with her, how?" I cut in.

Desperation to keep Elsie focused on the conversation, instead of dismantling our bodies, suddenly drives my thoughts. If she is a serial killer, maybe she likes to talk about her methods. Her triumphs. This is a woman who sent her own creative fiction to the police, for fuck's sake. Hopefully she'll do a deep dive while I try to convince her to leave us alone.

She's average height for a woman, backlit by a streetlamp that bleeds through the front windows. I can't tell how muscular she may or may not be, thanks to the cape that still covers her frame—but whatever. If this woman killed multiple people, she has the strength to handle me and a man with a bullet wound.

Elsie pauses, as if debating which anecdote to share. "Well, before I knew where Liam was, I thought I would use his daughter to lead me to him. Scare her a bit at work and watch as her world imploded. When she ran to her daddy, with whom she seemed tight knit, I would be there to follow."

Realization dawns on me. Pearl was accused of stealing a priceless historic artifact from the museum.

"You took the mask?" I ask. "How did you get access to it?"

Elsie beams, as if she's letting me in on her secret to reducing fine lines. "Corporate hack fact. Those little badges that white-collar peons wear to work can be reprogrammed the way that a car fob can. I found Mr. Kai Weathers's badge, made myself a copy with my RFID scanner, and started poking around, enjoying myself. I've always liked art up close without the crowds."

"So you stole the mask, then planted it in her office to get her fired."

"Then watched the fallout while pretending to be a maintenance worker at the museum, yes."

"All while using Kai's ID, so if anyone looked at the timing of the theft, they would see that Kai was in the building."

"Correct. Though I didn't get what I wanted from Pearl. She didn't go to Liam immediately, the way I thought she might. I had to dig into that wine guy's reports to uncover Liam's current address. Once I had that, I could move on to the final phase of my visit."

"Her death." I shiver, reliving the moment I stepped around the warehouse shelf and saw Pearl's blood on the floor. "But she didn't die."

"Before you skittered up, I paged through her notes. Admired her thoroughness and dedication to figuring out just how bad her mother was."

Elsie tilts her head forward. She smiles, making her vacant stare disturbing. "I realized then, thanks to Sally's recordkeeping in her address book, that Pearl's birth date was incorrect."

"Why does her birth date matter?" *This hinges on poor fact-checking?*

"Because, Zelda," Elsie draws out. "I'm the woman that Pearl was looking for. But you know what?"

Shivers tear down my back. I force the word from my lips, fighting the swirling sense that I know what comes next. "No."

"Zelda, you're the girl I was looking for."

My stomach twists—drops out of my body. A car engine outside accelerates along the road, but it doesn't slow down. "What?"

"Liam told me he was going to seek out his daughter before he left New Jersey. He wouldn't tell me where he was going exactly, because he said he didn't know. He only just learned that she existed, thanks to a nosy aunt who specialized in private investigation. You remember that, darling?"

Liam doesn't answer. His grip has loosened on his wound, allowing more blood to seep onto the carpet. Even in the shadows that douse the living room, he doesn't look good.

"You said you'd be back as soon as you had your little girl. And do you remember what I told you before you took off?"

His head rolls to the side.

"I'll find you," she whispers, never taking her eyes off Liam. "After several years of marriage, by 1999, he suspected what I was. Especially after I brought false charges of domestic abuse against him when he refused to buy a penthouse I found at a steal. And though I always kept my proclivities separate from my basic-bitch lifestyle, I knew he knew about my favorite pastime. So when he said he'd be home in a week, I didn't question it. Didn't think for one second that he would be stupid enough to betray me."

"Pearl is his daughter," I say, quietly. "You were looking for Pearl."

"No, Zelda. His daughter was born in secret and not revealed to him until years after her birth and adoption by another family. His daughter was born shortly after he and I met in 1992."

The blood drains from my face. My tongue feels thick against my teeth as I struggle to reply. "That's . . ."

"Say it, Zelda."

"Sally is my mother. Bert Truman is my father. He's buried in the field behind the—"

"Liam killed Bert, Zelda. Liam was casing the place and weighing how to approach Sally when her partner Bert fell for the trap and hired his contracting business. Before I killed Finn Hoskie, he told me everything that he knew. Swore to it, trying to buy time. That's why he hated Liam and Sally. He feared them."

"No." I shake my head, insistent. Rack my memory of Pearl's notes. "It's not true."

"Liam surprised Sally and her then-partner Bert at the house, when Pearl was three years old. Bert was never seen again after that night, so you do the math."

I turn to Liam. "This isn't—tell her I'm not—"

His mouth twitches; he's visibly pained. "I . . . I can't."

"Zelda," Elsie stage-whispers. "Give it up. Liam Davis is *your* father, and he killed Bert Truman, Pearl's dad. She never knew the truth. Better that way, considering what a scumbag he was, according to the wine guy."

The tension that has held me upright since I came to leaches from my core, shock taking its place. I stare without blinking, without moving, a pitiful sponge absorbing the poison of her words.

If what Elsie says is true, everything—everyone who was hurt or killed—I'm the reason for it all. Ursula, Finn, Pearl. Even Sally, if the heart failure during her car accident was rooted in the stress of being circled by the Turnpike Bloody Brontë. I'm the catalyst for all the violence—the polar opposite of everything I worked for, struggled out of foster care for, to later become a nurse.

Stomach bile lurches into my throat. I reach out a hand to steady myself on the mantel.

"You are Liam's daughter," Elsie continues. "You're why my life imploded in 1999 and the only man that I ever cared for abandoned me, leaving me a disgusting, sniveling, enraged mess."

Her words wash over me in a cold sheet, and I falter backward. Toward the bookshelf that lines the wall and the corner of the room. "You blame me for Liam's betrayal. You blame me more than you do Liam?"

Elsie peers at me. "Once someone catches my interest, I do tend to fixate on people. It's true that after the initial challenges in this town, I didn't know if I'd be able to find you. Once I learned that Pearl was not my girl and that Liam was living it up at the facility, I was planning

The Lie She Wears

to torture him to lure you out, thinking you two must be very close by now. I hadn't realized you had yet to meet as kin."

"Zelda," Liam says, his face twisted. "Zelda, I didn't know. I'm . . . so sorry."

Panic hovers at my edges, threatening to engulf me, and I tune him out. Focus on surviving. On the most emergent need of this crisis—a weapon. Where is a goddamned weapon? The fireplace poker was stored in the garage for summer, and there aren't any obvious choices within reach. But Sally's habit of stashing sharp items, a quirk I figured was part of the degenerating cognition, may have extended to the living room. *Zelda and Pearl, you're each other's best hope out of this now.*

"I do so love reunions," Elsie continues, her eyes drawn wide like a wolf eager for supper. "And now you're going to give me mine with my brother—before I try out Liam's pliers on you."

She points the gun at my feet. "Walk. We're going to visit Errol."

"In the shed?"

"No, the fucking morgue. Of course the shed. I want to see him."

Every muscle in my body recoils from this plan. My mind pulls, wishing for the peace of unconsciousness again after Elsie tranquilized me. But I have no other option. Not with her pistol aimed at my heart.

"No, Zelda, don't—" Liam starts.

Sweat pours down my back and under my arms. I scan the carpet again, the coffee table and the mantel, desperate for a way out of this. *Think, think, think, Zelda.* I know the house better than Pearl does. But, as my gaze passes over Liam, the armchair, the hallway, and the front door, not better than Sally did. I knew her to be deliberate. Cunning even when she was losing her mind. A planner.

I force my feet forward until I'm nearly level with Elsie. Flex my fingers into a fist.

She sneers. "Don't make me laugh."

I swing a punch, grazing her chin, and she knocks me to the floor without even shifting her body weight. A pop issues from my jaw where the joint slams into the tile.

"So impulsive. So reckless," Elsie muses.

Throbbing pain pulses at my ear. I cringe, ignoring the fiery need to cradle my face, and reach for Sally's old slipper by the front door. The pepper shaker is exactly where I last saw it—where Pearl mentioned she saw it too.

"I would have expected better from the eldest chi—"

With a quick twist of the top, I dump half the container into my palm, then turn and blow. A cloud of black pepper engulfs Elsie's face, choking her open mouth. She dissolves into heaving, retching coughs that stifle her words, her fingers clawing at her eyes, while I scramble to my feet.

I pound a path into the hallway as Elsie unleashes a primal roar behind me.

Chapter Forty-Seven

Elsie

My fucking eyeballs are on fire. Literal fire, thanks to that stupid girl. Even the tears stinging my face feel like acid on my skin. That bitch got me good.

I run to the kitchen, feeling my way and moaning blind, shoving countertop trivets and napkin holders to the floor with a crash. I flip the sink faucet on, then splash my face, my eyes, over and over again with water, diluting the pepper gunk now caking my lashes.

Pawing around for a towel, I find one on the oven bar, then blot my skin. When I can see again, I take in the mess I've made in the tiny kitchen. The open oven is deeper than I would have guessed. As good a spot as any to hide Zelda's body when I'm done with her, while I get the hell out of this state.

"Zelda!" I scream. "We're not done, stepdaughter!"

I lurch into the doorframe. A moan rumbles from deep in my chest, matching the rage fighting the pain in my face—in my lungs, when I inhaled the serrated cloud of pepper.

Rubbing my eyes with the heels of my palms, I unlock fresh tears cascading down my cheeks. They're not enough, of course. A fire hose wouldn't be enough right now.

Stumbling forward, I clutch on to the railing that separates the living room from the walkway to the bedrooms. The earth shifts again, and I have half a mind to get the fuck out of here and go recover in the luxury hotel I've been using as home base in Portland. But I'm not leaving without finishing what Errol started.

Lifting my gun to chest level, I blink hard, trying to kick loose the fuzzy halo marring my vision. I can see well enough to aim. Zelda might take a few flesh wounds first, but I'll manage to hit her head. Usually, I dislike guns. Too pedestrian. Too quick. There's nothing quite like torturing someone with the sharpened end of a steel blade across an hour before deliberately nicking a major artery and watching the fallout with a warm bowl of popcorn.

I pull myself forward along the iron railing. Liam is splayed on his back in the living room, his head knocked up against an armchair. A puddle of blood soaks the shag carpet beneath him. Bled out. Good riddance.

"Zelda?" I call in a singsong voice. "Come out, come out, wherever you are."

Silence is my answer, but it doesn't deter me. She's here. I can smell the tension. The fear.

Slinking down the hallway as fast as my body will go, fueled by adrenaline, I rub my eyes again. The glass of a framed photo on the wall reflects my mottled, mascara-crippled face, and I gasp aloud.

My beautiful face. My skin that's serviced by my dermatologist once a month and my Botox technician once every three months. It's going to cost a fortune to fix this shit.

"I knew I should have kept the mask on," I growl.

Pearl's bedroom to my right looks untouched from childhood, posters of One Direction still taped to the walls. Beside it, a window seat alcove contains a dozen photo albums, and a framed certificate recognizing Liam Davis for being "The Best Husband Ever."

"Jesus, Sally." I tsk. "Had you no self-respect?"

The Lie She Wears

The bathroom at the end of the hall is empty, which leaves the primary bedroom. Of course. "How original, Zelda. Returning to the first place we met."

Pulsing continues behind my eyes. A new round of stinging forces them into long blinks. A sliver of moonlight cuts from the primary bedroom into the darkness of the hallway, and I step past the worn threshold and into Sally's room. Despite the thick taste of pepper still coating my throat, the scent of eucalyptus invades my nostrils like I just entered a Chinatown boutique. I inhale deeply. The herbal remedy clears my senses a bit, making it slightly more possible to breathe.

"Better," I murmur.

In the poorly lit room, moonlight cascades from the opened sliding glass door. An inch and no more, as if Zelda skittered outside while I was eye flushing. She should know that I wouldn't be waylaid for too long. Would she really make a run for it, leaving dear old daddy Liam behind?

Pearl, I know pretty well now. I've stalked her long enough, listened to her conversations, and poked around her office and her boss's office enough to learn she's a prize employee and a loyal family member. That sad sack would stay.

Zelda just rolled in, relatively speaking. I'm less confident in my assessment of her. But no one in their right mind would stay behind for a parent they just met, right? Choosing certain death at the hands of a homicidal icon, out of—what? Gratitude for ejaculating thirty-one years ago?

"No one smart, at least." I frown, taking in the bedroom's possible hiding places. Flick on the light switch.

"Zelda . . ." I start again in my singsong voice. My favorite kind while circling. "Not very nice of you to attack me out there. I might even say that was rude."

I stoop beside the quilted comforter, probably decades old at this point. Scan the dust bunnies underneath the dark slats of the bed frame.

No thorn in my side, no female version of Liam's long face and dimpled chin. My head pulses, and I know I'll need to lie down soon—but after.

A drop of blood hits the shag carpet. Mine. I touch my face, then pull my hand away with more red on my fingertips. Son of a bitch, that bitch gave me a nosebleed.

"Zelda," I call out louder, and more aggressively. "The last person to piss me off this much lost their finger while they were alive. Where the fuck are you?"

I check the bathroom, turning on the lights as I go. No one in the shower. No one shoving themselves in the cabinet under the sink. Returning to the bedroom, I check the closet. Reach for the chain above that engages the light bulb overhead—but it's missing. The chain is gone. I pause at the doorframe of the six-foot walk-in closet that's suffocating in clothing, plastic dry cleaning bags, boxes, shoes lined along the perimeter, and trinkets on the floor. Beside a box with wineglasses embossed on the ajar cover, the chain lies in a small heap.

Something catches my eye, and I look up, matching gazes with Sally's gaudy Buddha mask. It stares at me from the back, nearly buried among winter coats. Empty eye sockets shadowed beneath wool return my gaze too long, as if my grandmother herself placed it here. For a moment, my skin hums as I recall the smell of a Sunday at home in the Bronx: uncooked beef, tarragon herbs, soy sauce, and newly splattered entrails covering the wooden cutting board of her kitchen. The feeling of the slippery guts weaving through my fingers as I made a bracelet, then a necklace with them. The sharp sting of Ying Ying's slap as she yelled at me to stop playing with our dinner. The taste of the raw tripe, her punishment for me.

What if the mask is my grandmother's doing? It's not, of course. But as I take in the mask's upturned smile, its blip of a nose and its deep eye sockets casting long shadows down its creamy cheeks, it could be. What if, instead of Sally's pack-rat habit of collecting garbage being responsible for this Dollar Tree reject—as I saw firsthand during the month that I followed her before she very conveniently died—what

The Lie She Wears

if my ying ying is to blame? Her revenge on me for taking her life in her kitchen the last time she beat me. A spiritual incarnation of my ancestors coming to spy on me, to punish me, as Ying Ying always threatened they would.

I hesitate, returning the mask's unrelenting stare. Using my phone's flashlight, I throw light in the corners of the closet. No head of black hair. Wiping a new drop of bloody paste from my upper lip, I turn back to the bedroom, gripping my gun.

The attic next. Zelda could have scrambled up there while I was moaning and groaning on the other side of the house.

"Stop playing, Zelda." I raise my voice to be heard from the rafters above the rickety pull-down ladder. "Come out, come out, and we can settle this thing like adults. With gunfire—"

A scratching sound pulls me up short. No, not quite—a pressing. A pressing?

I turn back to the dark closet, itself a gaping mouth with lined-up high heels for teeth. I still, scanning the corners another time. Hear that pressing sound again. Like the screech of Saran Wrap when you force a thumb through.

A coyote howls outside, obscuring the noise. I cast the light of my phone to the back of the closet again as a plastic bag shifts, moves so slowly, I almost don't see the shiny material straining forward. The mask tightens the plastic, gliding out from the shadows like a headdress possessed. I watch with narrowed eyes as gooseflesh wanders my skin, but I hold my ground. The mask pauses.

The coyote's howl abruptly stops.

Did that really just happen? I shake my head, though I keep the Buddha's face in sight. My grandmother was a Buddhist, culturally, as many Chinese elders are. Not clairvoyant. Sure as shit not powerful enough to command anything from beyond the grave.

But sudden doubt steals my confidence. The house quiets; the animals outside and the street traffic are all quiet. I run my tongue along my lips. "Ying Ying?"

The mask lunges, tearing through the plastic bags, its empty eyes trained on my face. I raise my arm, the gun, but a body lands on mine, throwing me backward. My head hits the bed frame as my eyes focus on the shining knife raised above. The Buddha head breathes heavily—hesitates—and I slam her off me to the side.

"Zelda! I thought I told you to stop"—I kick her stomach, shoving her backward—"playing games!"

She stumbles but stands, yanking off the mask. She jabs a knife at the air in front of her. "You started it!"

She charges and I shoot, landing a bullet in her shoulder. She stumbles backward, this time landing on her ass. Gasping in pain, she writhes, but still paws for the Buddha head beside her.

"For the love of God, leave that annoying mask alone," I say, coolly, wiping more blood from my nose. "It's not helping you."

Zelda moans as I approach her by the open sliding door. The neighbors will have heard the shot, but who cares? I'll be gone before anyone can call—

Pain splits open my knee as Zelda slices across my slacks, the switchblade in hand. I scream, agony ripping through my nerves. She grabs the mask, uses it to knock the gun from my hand.

"It's my *family's* mask," she pants, lunging for the gun. "And I'm doing better than you!"

Knees be damned, I throw myself to the corner of the room where it fell, but she's got the longer stretch, the longer wingspan, and she reaches it first beside the dresser.

"The hell you are—" I grunt, clutching her ankle boot, wrenching her back. She kicks my face, knocking me off-balance, and I fall as she whirls toward me, jabbing the knife aloft, where it slides between my ribs. White-hot horror rushes my senses. Her switchblade cuts the cotton of my shirt, into the flesh of my skin, my muscle and organs—its stiff steel connecting with my heart.

My eyes pull wide, pepper trauma forgotten. I gasp. Open and close my mouth without forming words. My fingers fly to the knife where it juts from my body as my face crumples in pain.

"No, no," Zelda whispers. She releases the knife, pushes the mask aside. "No, I didn't mean to. Don't touch it. Don't pull it out. We can still—"

I tug it free, spilling my own blood as it goes.

Zelda rushes me with both hands. Tears off the bedspread behind me, using it to apply pressure to my wound.

"Get . . . the fuck off," I say, lying down. "Let me enjoy this."

I close my eyes. Inhale a strained breath. Soak in the pain that floods my senses in vibrant colors.

I've never wanted to go, and definitely not at the hands of an amateur.

Fucking amateur.

But there's something poetic about choosing the timing myself, if not the method. I don't want to be some damned vegetable, of course. And I've had a good run. The police never caught up to me. I can die knowing I lived my life the way I wanted to. And never changed for a single soul. I was myself, through and through. Murder and all.

Darkness eats at the edge of my consciousness.

Then, pressure on my eyelids. Zelda staring at me from above, again.

Zelda holding something over my face. My cell phone. She's unlocking my phone.

"You bitch . . ." I whisper as some woman speaks from far away.

"911. What is your emergency?"

Zelda says something. An address. My name, my other name. All while pressing on my chest, until a shrill ringing pounds my head. Closer. Closer, like a rusty, creaking swing set on the playground that you know will give you tetanus.

Chapter Forty-Eight

Pearl

Beep, beep, beep. The vital signs monitor continues its relentless song, the way it has the last three days. Sharp lines spike on the main screen at each of my heartbeats, while my oxygen levels occupy the top right. The nursing staff said that I've made great progress and we can probably silence the annoying noise if I promise to remain in bed. "No more sneaking out to walk across the room. Not yet," I was told.

I grumbled last night, after my gauze was changed, my wound was restitched, and my hospital gown was switched for a clean one free of vomit. But now—after Zelda and Detective Sims came to my room together early this morning to confirm the good news—the beeping sounds like a jubilant chorus instead of a sadcore ballad. Police arrested Elsie after she was stabilized on a lower floor of this same hospital, in the intensive care unit. She's got an officer guarding her room, though after two open-heart surgeries, she's not going anywhere. It's over.

Tears spilled down my cheeks, wetting my clean hospital gown all over again. Zelda and I sat in silence while Detective Sims ran through the details as the police knew them. He received the text I sent before I passed out on the hospital couch, and sent an officer to Zelda's apartment for a welfare check. What they found was her place trashed and ransacked, the dead bolt broken. Elsie had been looking for something while Zelda was in Eugene—maybe proof to confirm her suspicion that Zelda was Liam's child; we don't know. After Detective Sims left, Zelda, too, said she needed to go home to rest and clean up her apartment. Although she only got a grazing bullet wound thanks to Elsie's shitty aim, she was exhausted. Elsie really should've stuck to her usual weapon.

Kai dropped by later in the afternoon. Most everything had been explained by that point, and he just came to check on me. I must have looked as bad as the soiled hospital gown that had been peeled off me, but he didn't seem to mind. Instead, he sat with me for a solid hour, stroking my hand with his index finger until I fell asleep.

I glance at the wall clock, confirming what the setting sun through my window already shows: Another evening is here. The clock's own tick, tick, tick starts to amplify in volume the more accustomed I become to the monitor's beeping. Though I was elated this morning, every minute that marches me toward the future outside this hospital room and learning how to live with the last two weeks' revelations now feels like the gong of a funeral procession, one I'm still not sure how to handle. Liam isn't my biological father; Bert is.

"Staying here forever wouldn't be so bad," I whisper, clutching a scratchy blanket to my chest.

"Who are you talking to?"

Zelda sweeps into the room wearing a lavender cardigan and navy trousers. She looks freshly showered, to add insult to my own sponge-bathed injury.

I clear my throat. Bert is my biological father, and Zelda is my half sister. Although our relationship has changed considerably, I was not prepared to learn I have a sibling. That Zelda, the pushy yet effusive nurse my mother hired, is actually related to me by blood. Staring at her calm confidence and the chipper expression she wears, I have a hard time seeing a resemblance between us.

"The wall clock," I grumble. "It keeps allowing minutes to go by without consulting me."

"That's kind of what they do?"

"Yeah, well . . . The machines in this place are driving me batty."

Zelda smirks, as if primed with a backhanded comment, then purses her lips. She approaches the whiteboard just beside the love seat. Peers up at the plastic timepiece and steps onto the love seat cushion for added height. She lifts the clock from the wall, leaving the nail. Crossing to a small cabinet beside the sink, she pops the clock under a stack of blankets within.

"There." She dusts her hands together. "What's next?"

A smile tugs at the corners of my mouth. "You're gonna get me in trouble again. The nurses already consider me a problem child."

Zelda shrugs, appearing pleased with herself. She takes a seat on the gray chair at the foot of my bed. "Well, you are technically a second child, and the youngest. You're allowed some rebellion. Plus, what's the worst that can happen?"

I take in Zelda's bright expression, the levity she wears like a cozy sweater. "I guess you're right. The worst has already been done."

She nods, tucking her leg underneath her. "Have you seen your dad yet?"

"Not yet. But I think he should be here soon. He was going to try and come while you were visiting."

Although we both now know the truth—that Liam isn't my biological father; he's actually Zelda's—neither one of us has modified the names we use for him.

For my part, it's way too soon. Bert Truman was a violent alcoholic, according to Sally's letters and Finn's recollection, and an indifferent father to me, according to Liam. Recalling all the times that Liam consoled me after a fall when I was a kid, or tutored me in whatever school subject I was having trouble with, he was the best father I could have asked for. I don't want there to be distance between us. I don't want those memories to be repainted with a layer of separation just because he took over raising me when I was three years old. And yet, when he came out of surgery for the gunshot he took to the leg, he asked that Nurse Frances get a message to me: an apology for not telling me about my paternity sooner.

He's doing better than expected, according to his doctors. Better than anyone knew, since he was exaggerating his relapse after he realized that Elsie was sending him the postcards. He knew she was nearby, and feigned additional weakness to lower her guard, knowing she was likely to pop in soon. Not knowing she actually meant to target us both.

"Any word on Elsie's arraignment date? She probably won't be out of here for another week or so, right?"

"At minimum." Zelda bites the corner of her mouth, suddenly lost in thought.

"Hey, you saved her." I lower my voice. "You know that, right? Your quick thinking and your nursing skills allowed her to get to the hospital in time. Don't second-guess that."

Zelda nods, though she doesn't reply.

Elsie will admit to no wrongdoing, but Detective Sims assured me and Zelda that the case is open and shut. All the evidence points to her, either circumstantially or concretely. A neighbor on Ursula's block told the police that she saw a woman with black hair and wearing a mask checking the windows of Ursula's house—though police originally thought I had been lurking with one of the masks stolen from the museum. Security cameras caught the same figure at Pour Water winery wearing a mask as they slipped into a side door left propped open for a delivery truck. Again, the police were suspicious of me, considering I reported both crimes directly after they occurred. And the museum's servers finally downloaded the security footage from the day that the mask was stolen from my exhibit; it was Elsie, barely concealing her face with a hood.

Although Sally was undoubtedly behind the wheel of her SUV the night that she crashed, there's also reason to believe Elsie was in the area, as her cell phone pinged near the crash site the same night.

Zelda sighs. "From what Detective Sims says, there's no arraignment date yet. But considering he just bagged himself the Turnpike Bloody Brontë, he said he's happy to enjoy the limelight as long as necessary. There's already talk of a film deal, apparently. And with over a dozen known victims, the police in New Jersey have been working on a case against Elsie for a long time. He says she's not going anywhere except prison."

"Right. We don't need to worry anymore." I roll my shoulders. Try to diffuse the tightness that locks my muscles each time I think of that woman. "She's never coming after us—after you—again."

When the police discovered Bert Truman and Errol Peng buried on the ranch house property, Zelda says that Liam played dumb, at first. He tried to follow through with his original plan of suggesting that Elsie must have killed them both, then buried them close by to incriminate him, but Detective Sims quickly quashed that theory. Not only had I shared with him the letters that Sally wrote, but he said that a distant cousin to Bert confirmed he lost his toe to frostbite when he was a teenager, swimming in the Columbia River during January. Elsie didn't kill Bert and take his toe as a trophy, nor did she off her twin brother, Errol, and take his finger.

Police forensics also confirmed that it was Bert's blood on the switchblade I found in Sally's closet. Investigators concluded that Sally must have killed both men, without Liam's knowledge, since she confessed as much in the letters. Sally, taking the heat for her husband's freedom as a final gift from beyond.

Zelda pats my foot from where she sits at the end of my bed. "We can move on. We're safe."

I glance at the door, still wary, as if Elsie might walk in any second. "How do you seem . . . okay with all of this? Like, you're in a better mood than I've seen you yet, honestly."

Zelda lifts her eyebrows. "I guess I am. I'm just so happy to finally have the truth, even though it's a complicated, kind of scary one. I spent so many years trying to fit a mold that would make others happy—make them love me—feeling rejected all my life. It's kind of . . . I don't know, freeing, to know my family history now. It makes everything else feel secondary. Smaller than it did before."

"But . . ." I pause, searching for tact. "Our family history is devastating. No one dreams of this."

Zelda smiles without showing any teeth. "You're right. Never in my wildest nightmares did I envision this. And I also feel like I downloaded a new level of resilience in getting here. Understanding what came before me to make me who I am, even while my environment and the people I've met and loved until now have done that too—it's . . . changed me. Knowing what you all look like, how you talk, and recognizing in you, Liam, and Sally the traits that tie us together."

"You do seem different. Less pushy. Like you're more quietly confident that you have a right to be here, versus openly insistent."

She smirks. "Yeah, I guess that was me."

"Knock knock." My dad waves a hand as he is wheeled in by a nurse I don't recognize, who delivers him to the other side of my bed. His leg that just underwent surgery is elevated in a harness, but he wears a smile.

"Aren't you a sight for sore eyes, Pearlie?" He pats my foot, wincing with the effort. "How you feeling?"

"Good. So much better knowing that you're safe."

The nurse warns Dad that he can have ten minutes with us and then he needs to return to his room on the third floor. Once she leaves, he gazes at both Zelda and me, as if marveling at our collective luck.

"I'm grateful to see you girls."

I glance at Zelda's strong chin, the same one my dad has. How awful that they were separated for years, and without his consent. Sally adopted out Zelda all on her own—a fact I'll never understand.

"Dad," I begin, "do you ever think about what life would be like if you and Sally hadn't broken up? If you hadn't then met Elsie?"

"You mean if Zelda, me, and Sally had all . . . stayed together?"

Zelda stiffens, leaning away from the conversation.

"Yeah, sort of. I mean, I think it's great that you and Sally found each other again—obviously. But I guess I don't understand how you could have forgiven her. Weren't you furious?"

He looks at each of us. "I mean, well—it was hard at first. When I came to the house that night and spoke with Sally and Bert directly, I was enraged. Out of my mind that she had given Zelda up without telling me first—offering me the chance to be the father that I always wanted to be."

"I'm sure that was hard," Zelda murmurs, ever the empath.

"Worse, Bert practically offered me Pearl." Dad glowers, nodding to me. "He said she was always into trouble and had an attitude."

"Sounds like most three-year-olds," Zelda says.

"Right." He scoffs. "That set me off. The idea that a father—as drunk and high as he was—could give up his own child to a stranger angered me even further. We got into it—"

Dad pushes a deep breath from his lips. Glances back at the closed door to my hospital room. "He punched me, and I've never known when to quit. Muscle memory took over, and suddenly I was back in Brooklyn, squaring up with a guy in the boxing ring after work. I knocked him into the fireplace at the wrong angle, and he died instantly."

The monitors beep their steady rhythm. Everyone is quiet a moment.

"What was Sally doing during all of this?" I ask, my voice unsteady.

"Protecting you, Pearl. Trying to keep you away from the fighting, then the blood. She locked you in your room while we cleaned up."

"So, what Sally wrote in her letters was true," I say. "It was a confrontation gone badly. What about Elsie's brother?"

"Errol." Dad nods. "Errol came during the summer three years later. When you were away at camp. I, uh, I realized he was hiding inside the house. And I surprised him."

Contrary to Sally's letters, which claimed her responsibility. A younger Liam crosses the threshold of the ranch house in my thoughts, on the prowl with a weapon in hand—a bat? A gun?

"How did Errol lose a finger?"

He purses his lips. "Believe it or not, that was the hardest part about all this. The insurance that I took out."

I nod slowly. "In case the police discovered the bodies, you could point to their missing appendages as confirmation that the Brontë attacked them."

Dad tilts his head to the side. "That was the idea. For Errol, I knew his body would never be found unless Elsie came here herself. And Bert, well, he had already come prepared."

"He sounds terrible," I start. "And I need to—I'm going to have to . . ."

Zelda places a hand on my arm. "It's okay," she murmurs.

I clear my throat. Despite everything that happened, all the bitter thoughts I had for her, Zelda was the one to fill me in on the true identity of the body buried beneath the oak tree. I was grateful I was afforded the space away from my dad to understand. Bert was my biological father. And my adoptive father killed him in self-defense.

"I'm still processing . . . all of that," I resume. "How did you manage to go about your life, knowing two people were buried on the property? How did Sally?"

"Well—"

"No, don't answer that. I know Sally compartmentalized at an Olympic level," I add.

Dad pauses. "Your mom wasn't always there for you, Pearlie. I know that. But she was the best wife I could have asked for, once we got over ourselves and got away from the stress of New York that caused us to break up in the first place. I was a little too flirtatious with other women, as a bartender, and Sally didn't like that. Understandably. Things were better in New Jersey, for a while."

"Sally always seemed so in love with you," I say. "And she covered for you in the letters she left me and Zelda."

Even up to the one hidden in the Wishing Tree. Instead of giving us more detail around Elsie—that Elsie was Dad's first wife—she left only a name, ensuring zero written connection to him.

"I loved her too. Deeply. After Bert was killed, it took a while for us to even look each other in the eye. But once I held her in my arms, I knew I could never give her up again. I also thought Sally was too hard on you. And told her so."

My throat closes as my dad echoes a long-held suspicion of mine. The validation I wanted from them both for so many years. "Why do you think that was?"

"I think . . . part of her subconsciously pushed both you girls away to protect herself." He furrows his brow. "And you took after your dad, Pearlie. After Bert. Although you have Sally's dark hair and features, you have Bert's gray eyes. Sally had a hard time looking at you and not recalling what we did to keep you safe. To keep us all safe."

I nod. Take a moment to listen to the sound of traffic on the main street behind the hospital. The fan kicks on from the vents overhead as Zelda clears her throat.

"Why didn't Sally tell you about me—six months ago, when she figured out that she was my mother? She said that my dad was dead."

Dad folds his hands across his own hospital gown and the green robe he wears. "If I had to guess, I assume she thought the shock would hurt me. Send me into a relapse of some kind, like what my conversation with Pearl did. I think she was shielding me, albeit in a shortsighted way. Probably the same reason she didn't tell me about all the postcards that Elsie was sending to the house."

He lowers his gaze to the beige blanket across my feet. "Sally regretted giving you up, Zelda. She kept a yellow knit sweater for you for years in the attic, I think always hoping to reconnect with you."

"My knit baby sweater?" I ask, lifting both eyebrows. Zelda shifts in her seat.

Dad nods. "She told me that she needed one of her babies to wear it, when I came across a photo of you being held by Bert. But yes, the sweater was meant for Zelda. And repurposed into an item for you."

I sit, dumbfounded. To me, that knit sweater served as proof that Sally cared enough about me, at least in the beginning, to have spent countless hours clacking knitting needles together. But the little outerwear wasn't meant for me. It was a painstaking example of her love for someone else. Conflicting emotions—grief, disappointment, understanding, and resignation—swirl within me.

Typical Sally. I don't know why I still get my hopes up for her.

"Try not to be angry with her," Dad says quietly. "It won't help anything."

Zelda nods. But I press my lips together, internally debate arguing with him. Part of me vehemently disagrees with the idea that we should just let all this go. But rather than promise to forgive Sally of her extensive wrongdoings—the way she treated me and subsequently made me fear that I could never be enough for her, for my career, for anyone; the way that Sally continued to hide the truth of Zelda's existence from my dad, and inadvertently made Zelda feel unwanted from birth on; and the fact that she and Dad kept the deaths of two men a secret for decades—all I want to do in this moment is rest. To defer to the capable nursing staff of this hospital. To the rhythmic beeping of the monitors that dwarfs my worries about the future and regrets about the past and reminds me—despite the heartache and physical pain—I'm alive. There will be time to process everything that was done, from all angles. Thanks to Zelda.

Dad sniffs. He lifts his gaze to her. "There is something I need to say—I should say to you."

"Oh?" she asks.

"I am mad at Sally, to answer the original question. But that doesn't really matter when I've been waiting thirty-one years to meet you."

"I guess not," she replies, meeting his eyes.

In a tentative gesture, he holds out his hand on my bed. She takes it.

"What matters is that I braved the ire of my sociopathic ex-wife to come find you. My first baby girl. That's the headline that needs amplifying here. That's the kind of love I have had for you since I learned about you, even before I knew you as a compassionate and inquisitive adult."

She sucks in a breath, visibly moved. Tears fill my eyes as I watch my dad's warm expression for Zelda—for my sister.

She struggles to speak. "My—my whole life, I've been waiting for a parent to say half of what you just did. Thank you."

Dad smiles. "Thank you, Zelda. You found me after all."

A moment passes, then he clears his throat. "One more thing. Sally had a message for you girls."

My heart clenches. I lean forward, searching his face for a sign to confirm he's joking. "What? Like, another letter?"

His eyebrows steeple together. "No, no, nothing like the ones you found. A few months ago, during one of the last visits I had with Sally, she said something. I thought it was a slip of the tongue, a simple mistake due to the cognitive decline, but it was probably deliberate, in hindsight."

Zelda is still. "What did she say?"

Dad gives a small smile. "She said, 'Tell my girls I love them. Victoria and Pearl. I've always loved them. Even when I can't quite say it to their faces. Even when I'm seeing someone else's face.'"

We sit in silence, quiet tears falling down our respective cheeks. The nurse returns for my dad to wheel him back to the third floor, then Zelda rises to leave. As I wave goodbye to them both, the ache in my chest that moved in when Sally died eases the tiniest bit.

Sally wasn't a perfect mother, far from it. But after the last few weeks, I'm finally beginning to glimpse—to really see—the imperfect love she offered. And that's not nothing.

Chapter Forty-Nine

Pearl

The rest of the weekend spins by, and then I'm discharged into Zelda's care Monday morning. She stays with me in my apartment for the two weeks that follow, exercising her best judgment as a live-in nurse. Sally had the right idea in hiring this professional.

Together, thanks to Zelda's care and my strict regimen of rotting on the couch and bingeing Miyazaki films with her, the day comes when I'm able to return to the museum a full two days ahead of schedule. Kai said he's "thrilled" he won't have to drive into Northwest to see me every day, though he's enjoyed our trio. I only laughed and shared a smile with Zelda. He thinks that's ending.

"You know you don't have to go in today, right?" Zelda clutches her coffee outside the Portland Art Museum. Steam rises from the paper cup.

"I'll be fine. I want to. I miss it." I gaze up at the newly completed pavilion, at the space where so many hard hats and cranes used to block foot traffic. When I turn back to Zelda, she wears a smile, watching me.

"I can see that."

Since she insisted on driving me to work, we agree that she'll pick me up for lunch. We'll find a good spot nearby in the Alphabet District, one of the restaurants I've been meaning to try for months.

We say goodbye, then my feet tap the brick steps in a quiet cadence as I return to the lobby that I last exited on a stretcher.

A crowd of people—my colleagues—faces me with shiny balloons, underneath the red ceramic balloons that warn against climate change. The museum curators and security staff all wear party hats as they take turns greeting me, while Griffin appears in the middle, presenting a sheet cake that bears the words "Welcome Back."

Kai approaches from the rear, dodging patrons searching for their electronic tickets on their phones. He takes his place by my side, wearing a smile.

As Griffin ushers everyone farther into the museum, up to the administrative floor, where he promises me there is enough caffeinated boba to fuel the Bay Area, Kai lingers with me, matching his pace with my own thoughtful speed.

"So, Pearl. What's next for you, now that you've been reinstated with bells on?"

"'Bells on'? I don't know about that."

Kai scoffs. "Are you kidding? Do you know how happy Griffin is that you're not filing a civil suit for wrongful termination and emotional damages? I'd be surprised if you don't get a promotion in the next week."

I smile at the thought. At the memory of the old Pearl who doubted herself, thanks to Sally's volatile parenting style. Who always feared she could never be good enough, never knowing that Sally's rejection was due to her own trauma at her role in taking Bert's life, then concealing his murder.

"I wouldn't decline one. But I also want to earn it. If my next exhibit is as big a success as the microexhibit on masks, then I'll be happy to accept."

"Do you think you'll expand on that? Maybe Griffin will suggest you move the masks into one of the larger halls."

The Lie She Wears

Kai pauses at the turn into the Contemporary Art wing, just before the elevators that will take us up to cake. He gives my elbow a gentle squeeze. "Maybe we could do a photography-and-mask mash-up. You could bring in your family's Buddha mask."

I tilt my head, taking in this man's warm expression. The doting way his eyes linger on my face and the smile that plays across his full lips.

"Actually, I'm planning to sell that to one of Sally's appraisers. Along with the rest of her collection to someone who can fully appreciate them. My next exhibit can focus on . . . correspondence."

A small smile from Kai. "Like handwritten letters."

I nod. He takes my hand in his, his fingers twining perfectly with mine. "Sure. Chinese scrolls, parchment, and the like."

"I can't wait."

As we start down the hallway, passing my favorite canvases, my thoughts go to Sally—and also to Elsie, in a weird way. Of the big dreams Sally had for herself and of the dreams she alluded to for her girls, as she called us to Liam. While the only passion that Elsie and Sally outwardly shared was a love of the same man, they each clung to a facade of wholeness. Where Sally used antiquing to form connections and to counter the chronic depression she felt after taking someone's life, Elsie donned a shield of normalcy like a battering ram to amuse herself at others' expense.

To a lesser extent, I used my work as a buffer to avoid dealing with the pain of my relationship with a neglectful mother. And Zelda threw herself into caring for others, showering them with the care she never received herself. Even Kai told me he took up studying photography at a later age because he appreciated the distance it provided from difficult times in his past. Each of us relied on a crutch of some kind to hide our traumas.

Sometimes the lies we wear and present to the world are the only things that keep us going. The blanket in the cold that fuels us as we stumble headfirst into the rain, the tether of string that ties us to the flimsy, shaking branch in life.

At the elevator, I glance back to the lobby and the red balloon art installation suspended overhead. After Sally died, I heard her most critical words in my ear at all hours. But since I've returned home to my apartment, with Zelda as my pseudoroommate, I haven't imagined hearing them once. Now, without the consistent intrusion, I see her everywhere. In the lobby of this museum, the community vegetable garden in Northwest, the way I cross my own letter *t*'s exactly in the middle. And the idea of seeing Mom in these simple, everyday moments is more comforting than I ever would have guessed.

I smile, then give Kai's hand a squeeze.

"Ready for this?" he asks as he pushes the call button.

"I think so."

We wait for the chrome doors to part, then step inside. As the elevator lifts, I scan my bright expression in the reflective panels. Take in the woman before me, the optimism on her face. She looks good. Not familiar to me—not exactly—but good.

The elevator slows. For a moment, we're suspended in the air, hovering at the third floor. A flash of anticipation and nerves strikes my throat—then a ding sounds from above. The shining silver panels part.

"Armchair detectives first," Kai says with a grin, giving me space.

"Only if their partners follow?"

"Anywhere you go."

Warmth floods my core, returned as I am to my happy place, as a happier person. I give Kai's hand another pulse. Then I take the lead, striding forward, leaving my mask behind.

Acknowledgments

A book is never written in a vacuum, and that is beyond accurate for this story. The list of players who helped bring this one to life must begin with my amazing editor, Megha Parekh, plus the entire team at Thomas & Mercer. We did it! Thank you for your patience, candor, and belief in me throughout this process. I'm thrilled to get another book out into the world together.

To the copyeditors and proofreading teams, including but not limited to Haley and Rachel N.: Thank you for all your deliberate and insightful work. You made these pages sing.

To my developmental editor, Charlotte Herscher: Thank you. Despite several roadblocks, and some serious soul-searching on my part that extended way past our original timelines, you brought this book to the next level (a few times).

Loud and enthusiastic thanks must go to my literary agent, Jenny Bent, for being a sounding board, a friend, and a therapist this last year. I appreciate you and your deep well of patience for my many emails.

To my quippy friend Tricia P., whose dad jokes are always the punniest, and whose expertise I consulted while writing this book; to former New York resident Melissa L., whose knowledge of the city added color to Elsie's chapters; and to Erin H. for being my go-to for medical insights, tips, and tricks. Thank you, my dear friends, for your support.

To the Renos, whose home was partly the inspiration for Pearl's childhood home: Thank you for the many memories.

My aunts Jeannie and Sharon for their insight into dragon dances at weddings. Thank you and I love you.

To a local museum assistant, whose insights and helpful weblinks were the boost certain chapters needed: Thank you.

To my readers: Thank you for joining me for another book! Your support and reviews are the reason I get to do what I love. My heartfelt gratitude goes to you, as deep and long as the Willamette River.

Finally, big thanks to my kids, whose excellent sleeping habits are responsible for yet another story. You three are the very best writing team I could ask for. In particular, big squeezes and thanks go to my youngest. You and me, baby! I hope you read this when you are many, many years removed from infancy.

And to my husband, whose generosity and passion for (my) writing are indisputable reasons I was able to knock out this book, despite the ups and downs of life. Thank you for making my dreams your dreams, and helping them take flight. I love you. PC forever.

About the Author

Photo © 2019 Jana Foo Photography

Elle Marr is the #1 Amazon Charts bestselling author of *Your Dark Secrets*, *The Alone Time*, *The Family Bones*, *Strangers We Know*, *Lies We Bury*, and *The Missing Sister*. Originally from Sacramento, Elle graduated from UC San Diego before moving to France, where she earned a master's degree from Sorbonne University in Paris. She now lives and writes in Oregon with her family. For more information, visit www.ellemarr.com.